XENOCRACY
AND OTHER GALACTIC TALES

Tony Chandler

XENOCRACY
AND OTHER GALACTIC TALES

DOUBLE DRAGON

Dedication

For my daughter, Meghan Elizabeth

TABLE OF CONTENTS

Not Without Paradise

At first there was total darkness, a void that seemed impenetrable.

In an instant, it all changed.

And there was light.

He was standing in a beautiful, green valley, on either side of him a tree covered ridge rose to meet the bright blue sky. Directly above, a few white puffy clouds floated peacefully, trailing dark shadows that slid across the curving hills as the fresh breeze pushed them along. A riotous and colorful array of wildflowers carpeted this pastoral scene between the giant emerald shoulders of the twin hills.

Jon felt the wind caress his face. He breathed deeply his new surroundings. He realized that wild honeysuckle was blooming unseen nearby; the sweet aroma filled his nostrils.

It was so beautiful, so peaceful. It really did feel like the Garden of Eden.

Looking up one end of the dale, he began walking to a small stand of hardwoods at its edge. Singing now came to his ears. Happy trills and chirps filled the air while dozens of birds began to fly around his head. Jon raised his right hand, his forefinger extended.

A tiny, multi-colored bird lighted on his finger perch, cocking its feathered head to one side for a better look him. The bird sang to him a happy greeting. The green, almost iridescent feathers, seemed to glisten off its back. Jon recognized it as

9

a finch native to Australia. It seemed a little out of place here.

But then, so was he.

Jon whistled briefly, trying to imitate the sounds around him. His newfound friend answered sweetly.

Looking up, he realized that more birds were now flying all around him, circling him in a growing flock as their merry songs filled the air. Little chickadees, red cardinals, finches of gold and finches of bright green, thrushes and songbirds of every description flew around and around him in cloud of wings. Jon's heart filled with an appreciative joy.

Jon slowly spread his arms apart. The little finch wobbled and tried to balance itself on the moving perch. But with a quick flapping of wings, he flew and joined the feathered throng.

Closing his eyes in silent concentration, Jon rose effortlessly into the breeze.

He willed himself to fly.

The magical weightlessness filled his senses. He opened his eyes and leaned forward. The grass moved quickly under him as he glided low, just above the top of the carpet of wild flowers. Up ahead, the trees were rapidly approaching. Pulling his head back, he rose quickly into the sky, just missing the topmost branches. A squirrel chattered in excitement somewhere unseen inside the mass of green leaves he had just passed over.

The flock of singing birds followed him in a long undulating cloud, whistling their own comments on the joy of flight.

It was such a wonderful feeling, flying once again. He had missed it so much!

The wind rushed into his face, blowing through his hair like an invisible caress. He wiggled his fingers against the force of the air, much as a child would do with his arms outside a car window while it zoomed along.

Straight up he flew now until he was even above the cloud tops. He stopped suddenly in mid-air, frozen in place with his arms wide apart. Laughing, he pitched forward like he was diving.

And he was.

He dove toward the land below, his momentum increasing with each second. It almost felt like he was riding some immense, invisible runaway roller coaster. The ground rose rapidly towards him. He bent his body backwards and flew upward in a great arc. Twisting and diving, over and around, his aerial acrobatics spoke of many hours in this thrilling pastime. Up and around, faster and faster, he filled the sky with his laughter and shouts of joy.

Out of breath, his heart pounding from the exertion of the exciting maneuvers, he flew steadily toward a nearby cloud. The wide azure sky stretched far, far off in every direction. It felt as though he were floating in the middle of everything, the ground below a distant patchwork carpet of green.

His attention was suddenly drawn to the distant line of the horizon. Something was happening there – something huge and unusual.

Across the wide expanse a change hastened toward him like a tidal wave across the sky. The sheer magnitude of it froze his mind with wonder.

And then it hit him; the sky was changing colors. Now, this was something totally unexpected. A chill of excitement ran up his back.

While he hung in mid-air, he waited. The sheer size of it awed him. The entire sky was changing color in just a matter of seconds. Inexorably, the wave of color rushed by him. And not even a whisper of a breeze hearkened its passing. But in its passing, a pristine purple replaced the formerly blue sky. Even the clouds were a lighter shade of this all-encompassing new color.

Below, the green of the trees and grass seemed to shimmer with a purple glaze.

It felt... different.

Jon liked it. Closing his eyes, he concentrated a moment, and then he whispered a command. He opened his eyes again.

The entire sky now became a multitude of colors, more stunning than the greatest rainbow ever known. The deep colors spread apart and melted together with the colors of their neighbors. Various shades of blue, yellow, green, red, mauve – the sky became every color.

The sky became a rainbow.

Laughing, Jon flew faster and faster, rolling over onto his back while he gazed at this new creation. He flew effortlessly now, the wind gently blowing through his hair. Time passed, how much he did not know.

It didn't matter here.

But... it did back...

Jon suddenly began to fall from the sky, but with a quick shake of his head he ejected the illicit thought. Closing his eyes, he let the wonderful feeling of this world flow throughout his very being. Soon he was floating on the wind again.

Opening his eyes, he looked longingly towards the west. He searched for his old friends.

Bright flashes of light sparkled in the distance.

Sunlight glistened off the distant rolling of ocean waves, its blue green color now seemingly a part of the rainbow sky where it melted with the sea. His heart beat with a new excitement. He turned and flew toward it.

The landscape rolled by quickly underneath. Even his feathered friends could not keep up with the speed he willed now. He flew like a shooting star for the waters.

The trees underneath gave way to sandy dunes, and then to the waves. He stopped his forward momentum far out over the waters and lowered himself until he was just above the never-ending waves. He breathed deeply of the salty aroma and felt the cleanness of the foaming spray where the warm waters splashed and glistened upon his skin. He gently lowered himself into the warm embrace of the water.

He heard them almost immediately.

It was a different kind chattering from the birds he'd left behind on land. Almost instantly, he was surrounded by the rollicking gray forms of dolphins. He dove under the water and peered through the clear pristine waters. Dozens and dozens of the playful creatures swam and frolicked all around him. One suddenly appeared directly from below, and the playful creature rubbed the end of his snout against Jon's cheek.

First one and then another dolphin would swim by him, and each time they would brush their muscular bodies against Jon until he was spinning around like a top under the water.

Jon realized he'd been holding his breath a long time. He kicked his feet and seconds later his face burst above the waves. He looked around at the playful creatures swimming all around him.

He spread his arms apart and shouted a single word.

"Ride!"

Two dolphins took off in a burst of speed, swimming with strong, rapid strokes. Their dorsal fins sliced through the waves while they made a wide arc around Jon. In the next instant, they were swimming toward him. But they slowed as they neared him.

One dolphin swam to Jon's right side and the other to his left side.

Jon grabbed a dorsal fin with each hand and shouted out a laugh.

The two dolphins took off again in a burst of speed, but now they gave Jon a ride to remember. He laughed harder while the salt water splashed against his face and his body skimmed over the waves.

Again and again the dolphins surged forward, jumping over waves while carrying their charge. Suddenly, the two dove under water a few feet and then raced back up to the surface. The water exploded all around them as all three leapt into the air.

Jon couldn't hold on any longer. He fell back into the water while the two dolphins sped away.

He laughed heartily while he sucked in huge gasps of air while more dolphins began jumping over him in pure delight.

All at once, dolphins began jumping over his head in an onslaught of sleek, gray bodies. When they hit the water, explosions of water rained down on him. Within seconds, dolphins were jumping so quickly over him that the constant splashing made it difficult for him to breathe.

"Hold on!" Jon laughed.

Instantly, the dolphins disappeared.

He started laughing again, floating alone in the open sea. He loved swimming with dolphins so much, but they could be a bit rambunctious in their play.

Without warning, Jon felt his body forced upward by some gigantic unseen force below the waves. He rolled over backwards once he was above the waves and slid off of the slick, rubbery surface that had unexpectedly appeared underneath him.

There were whales here!

He watched the huge back disappear back into the waves, the huge, fluked tail disappearing last. He quickly looked around for the whale's brethren. More huge backs appeared above the waves and the geysers from their released breath sprayed high into the air.

Rolling onto his back, Jon floated on the rising and falling bosom of the ocean's waves. His ears were just below the surface of the water. And now there came a haunting chorus as the whales began to sing. Mysterious and eerie sounds rose from the depths around him; melodious and magnificent growls, joyous and happy grunts mixed with a singing deep bass vibrato that only humpback whales can utter. And as he listened to the whale's songs, a soothing feeling of complete peace enveloped him. He relaxed and became one in this watery place and its special denizens.

But there was one more thing he wanted to do, before it was too late.

Righting himself, he gazed around at the seemingly empty ocean around him. He whispered a command and his desire was instantly fulfilled.

A lone whale swam slowly alongside him. Climbing onto the wide curve of its back, he scrambled up until he was on top. He straddled the huge leviathan with his hands pressed against the skin of its thick blubber.

He kicked the great beast for speed, like he was riding a horse.

The huge back of the whale started to slide under the bright green waters. Jon held tightly and took a deep breath. The waters pulled at him, trying to unsaddle him while he and his gigantic mount submerged. He felt the mighty power of the whale as it plowed through the water. Each gigantic motion made him feel like...

Suddenly, the darkness returned.

Jon clenched his eyes shut, trying to block out the inevitable.

"OK, pal. Time's up."

Jon opened his eyes, but the void was still there. His hands now began to shake uncontrollably and he couldn't breathe. Jon choked and gagged violently, but he couldn't remember how to take a breath.

Slowly, Jon put his hands on either side of the oversized goggles and pulled them to his forehead. He knew the rubber skull cap he wore was still connected.

The first attendant quickly removed the wires out of the connectors across Jon's cap. He began pulling out the wires connected to the back of his neck and back until all were disconnected. He stepped back, waiting for Jon to get out of the chair.

"Hey! Stop playing around! I said your time's up. And I already checked your credit on the net. I know you can't buy any more time. *So out!*"

Jon's haunted eyes stared vacantly at them.

The bigger of the two attendants, a burly middle-aged man, grabbed him and threw him onto the floor.

Jon went into violent convulsions, his head slamming against the hard floor again and again until blood streamed down the left side of his face.

"Look at how he's shaking all over! And he's bleeding!" The first man said with disgust.

"Convulsions when they come back to reality, that's a sure sign," the bigger man added, shaking his head.

The first attendant looked down at the digital display and noted the player's name and past games. The list of previous game sessions filled first one screen and then another. And that was just for the last thirty days.

Jon lay on the cold, hard floor, his breathing rapid and shallow. Now he shook as if in a fever. But at least the violent convulsions subsided. Still, he felt awful, like he was in the midst of the worst flu he'd ever had.

But it was like that for him now when he came back to reality.

"Jon? Hey, is that your name, pal? Nod if you can understand me"

Jon wretched all over the floor at the feet of the two men.

"Hey, pal. You've got it bad, don't you." The bigger man stared down emotionlessly at him.

"Ronnie, this kid's an addict, he's got all the symptoms," the first attendant said.

Ronnie, the burly middle-aged man, reached over and grabbed Jon's shoulder.

"You think maybe I ought to call an ambulance here for you. There's a good hospital close by, they have one of the best rehabilitation units in the city for your kind."

"*No!*" Jon shouted vehemently. And then he put his hand to his throat, gasping for breath as his entire body began to shake uncontrollably again.

The two attendants took a few cautious steps back.

"Whoa there pal, don't die on us." He turned to his companion. "Stinking VR addict for sure, eh Ronnie."

Ronnie bent down.

"Jon, you're playing these games way too much. They're not only affecting your mind, but your body now," the other said a serious tone.

Jon's eyes finally began to focus onto the darkened interior of the expansive room filled with hundreds of other people wearing the same oversize goggles that he did along with rubbery skull caps that connected them to the nearby MPSC. They were each inside their own world right now, living in a world – or game – of their own creation.

And Jon desperately wanted to return to his. He felt the old fear begin to overpower him again.

"P...Please...I can pay. I can pay!"

Ronnie shook his head again. "You've had too much already, kid. You know the warnings..."

He put his hands on Jon's shoulder to help guide him to the exit. The big man recoiled when Jon grabbed his arm with more strength than his slight build indicated. Ronnie winced at the painful grip. He stood completely still, now concerned this kid might become violent.

"I haven't had too... too much. These are good games anyway. No violence! No sex!" Jon's voice became shrill and filled with panic. "You...ca...can't get too much of..."

Ronnie's expression hardened. He pried the kid off his arm.

"Listen kid, too much of anything is bad for you."

"No! No! No! No!" Jon's voice took on a panic-stricken tone. He began panting, unable to catch his breath. His hands began to shake now that Ronnie had loosened his grip.

"I'm gonna tell you one last time, kid. *Get outta here now!*" Ronnie's voice grew low and serious. "Or I'll add your name to the expulsion list. You'll never be allowed to play here again. *Understand!*"

Jon rose hesitantly, even awkwardly, almost as if he had to relearn how to walk again. He stumbled to the changing room where several dozen people were already in various stages of dressing or undressing. But he wasn't aware of them; he didn't hear their laughter or any of their friendly banter.

Jon slowly removed the rest of the rubbery patches that had once connected his body and mind to the MPSC.

Finally, he left.

Out in the fuzzy lights of the city, with a half-moon shining its pale light through the wet and ghostly mist, Jon turned up his collar and walked away.

He shivered in the freezing cold, wrapping his arms around his body. He had been forced to sell his winter coat in order to get enough money to play today. Now he regretted it. The temperature had dropped precipitously since nightfall.

He walked down the empty street and it began to snow. In a few minutes it became like a blizzard. In a matter of minutes, the parked cars were covered. And then it began to stick to the road and sidewalks.

Jon stopped at the first intersection and looked back. He looked up at the bright neon lights on the building he had left back at the end of the street.

Paradise Games, it read.

But even as he tried to turn and leave, he knew he didn't have anywhere to go.

He had been fired from his latest job last week, the third time this year. He'd moved in with first one friend and then another until he wore out his welcome again.

Oh, they had tried to help him. His best friend had even taken him to see a doctor once. Jon simply left and moved in with someone else the next day.

He didn't need any stinking doctor. He needed VR!

But none of his friends would let him borrow money anymore. And neither would his parents.

He wandered through the empty streets of the city until he noticed a clock on a bank building that displayed it was almost three o'clock in the morning. The snow had been falling heavy for over two hours now.

Newly fallen snow was so beautiful, even here in the city.

Jon felt so tired, but the only way he could keep warm was to continue walking. He couldn't stop shaking now, but it wasn't from withdrawal. Now his body shook from the bitter cold and the wet snow. In fact, his shirt and pants were drenched.

Jon felt so alone. Nobody understood him, nobody really wanted to help him, at least not the way he wanted.

21

He hated this cold and impersonal world everyone called reality.

He found the darkened alley a short while later. Like a blind man, he stumbled and fell into a huge pile of debris and trash. He couldn't feel the falling snowflakes now. His eyes fluttered and finally closed. And soon he dreamed of a better world.

They found the body two days later.

The news media reported his death in a tiny column in the back of the obituaries. The cause of death was attributed to exposure.

But his family and friends knew the real reason.

Jon couldn't live in this world.

Not without Paradise.

HellFear

The ship of ancient legend had returned once more from the mists of time – a ship cursed to fly among the stars forever. And wherever the ship appeared, death followed close behind.

Thus, it was written in countless alien myths across the galaxy.

Those words echoed eerily in the back of his mind as Commander John Jacobs signaled his team to fan out and take defensive positions as their beam-over completed. With a flash of movement, his team obeyed with practiced military precision.

Chief Scientist Tan stepped calmly beside him, the scientist's fingers danced across his hand-held scanner as he performed the initial survey.

Jacobs kept his attention focused on his two teams as they took their positions along the huge corridor. He knew Tan would alert him if something showed up. As he surveyed his teams, he realized three soldiers were spread too far apart and vulnerable. He glanced at the team leader, the newly promoted Lt. Javier Martinez.

Commander Jacobs tapped the comm link located on the collar of his uniform. "Javy, get your people in tighter positions until Tan's *'all clear'*."

"Aye, Commander." Martinez's voice replied with youthful enthusiasm. Almost immediately three figures leapt up with assault blasters at the ready as they raced and took positions closer to the others.

Jacobs smiled and turned his gaze in time to note Simmon's squad take their own positions and begin their sensor sweeps.

"Interesting." Tan's brow furrowed in thought. "My scanner seems to be malfunctioning."

Jacobs shook his head. "The equipment should have been thoroughly checked prior to the mission."

Tan sighed while his fingers flew over the touchscreen.

Jacobs' body grew taut – ready for battle. Without realizing it, he held his breath – waiting. At the edge of his hearing, almost at the point where reality and imagination meet, there had been a sound. A *strange* sound. Something...

Jacobs felt his heart pounding like a runaway jackhammer.

In that instant, the legends of a thousand alien races rushed back into his mind from the mission overview.

The Intrepid's computer contained an ample supply of this particular myth, which until this strange ship's sudden appearance had been categorized as simply an ancient collection of stories meant to 'frighten alien children into being good.' But with the reality of this ancient, gargantuan ship suddenly showing up, Jacobs remembered with sudden clarity certain ominous and disturbing features that all the legends shared.

The vessel was simply called a *monster* ship in most of the tales. But when it was given a name, the three most common were *The Taker*, *Ship of Death*, and *HellFear*.

Figuring prominently in most of the legends was the ship's immense power, so powerful it could make the bright light of day turn into night across the surface of a planet. It was a mystery ship, coming only once an age.

Nothing could stop it. No one could escape.

The ship took poor, unsuspecting souls as if by magic – snatching them from the surface of planets, taking them even from the supposed safety of their own beds – never to be seen again.

And there was the beast that stalked the ship by darkness and storm.

Jacobs took a deep breath. He realized again that he and his team had just boarded that very ship.

He shook his fear aside.

He was one of the best officers in the Fleet. His teams always performed at a high level and achieved their objectives. *And Jacobs always got the job done*. That was his reputation, and he would do it again – even from the bowels of the 'Ship of Legend.'

"Commander."

"What is it, Tan?" Jacobs asked.

"Most interesting... it appears a welcoming committee is approaching."

"Squads, converge on my position. Keep your weapons ready," Jacobs ordered into his comm.

He turned and whispered so that only Tan heard. "There were no life-signs detected by Intrepid."

Tan's eyes narrowed. As the two squads gathered around them and raised weapons, Tan pointed.

With their footsteps echoing down the mammoth corridor, the robed aliens came forward with a child-like openness. The dozen oddly garbed aliens stopped and assembled themselves in a perfect semi-circle before the raised weapons, ignoring the threat as if it did not even exist.

They stood silent, staring emotionlessly at the soldiers. Without warning, they bowed in unison.

As they rose the gilded hoods that framed their strange faces were drawn aside - each alien face was different from the others. Jacobs felt his stomach knot as he realized that none of them was a known alien race.

Two facts immediately stood out to his trained eye.

All of them wore the same loose, blue robes. And all of them had the same drawn, haunted look in their eyes. It was almost as if they were all drugged...

An alarm went off in the back of his mind.

"We boarded when we received no answers to our hails." Jacobs watched them carefully. "Our ship's sensors could not penetrate your hull with any degree of accuracy, so we were sent to investigate. We apologize if we have offended you."

Jacobs extended his hand to the one he sensed as the leader.

"Ah yes, you greet by soultouch." The apparent leader stepped forward and softly put his scaly hand into Jacob's open palm.

"Welcome Ever-Home. I will lead you; I am High Priest."

Jacobs wondered at the odd greeting.

"We've never encountered a ship of this type before. Especially one this large," Jacobs said, disregarding the strange greeting.

"Yes, it was built for the Draegaxx many ages ago." He smiled sadly. "So long ago we have even forgotten the name of the Builders. *All for the Draegaxx.*"

The blue robed assemblage bowed in silence once again in response to the last, hushed sentence.

Jacobs used his right hand to signal silently for Williams and Tan to scan these strange aliens. Immediately they both stepped back and started taking readings.

Jacobs smiled at their quick efficiency. He had hand-picked them from the best Intrepid offered for this mission.

"Your scanners will not work here."

Jacobs frowned.

Another blue-robed alien moved tentatively beside the High Priest.

"They have brought technology onboard." He whispered urgently. "It is another Sign."

Jacobs focused more on the tone it used than the words – one of hushed astonishment.

"It is standard procedure for us to bring our equipment, so we will understand..." Jacobs began.

"Commander," Tan said.

Jacobs turned to the Chief Scientist.

"The ship we are on seems to have *revised* itself, or perhaps reconfigured its shields. Intrepid is no longer in contact with us. Nor we with them."

"Simmons!" Jacobs ordered sharply. "Raise the Captain."

The thick silence from the comm unit was more than an answer.

"We've lost communications, there's some kind of jamming." She stared at the comm unit in frustration.

"What's going on here?" Jacobs approached the alien High Priest and stared into the green slits of its eyes. "Answer me."

"The Ship takes whom it wants."

Jacobs froze at the words for a long moment. "Why did you welcome us home, when this is the first time we have set foot upon this ship? Why?"

The alien leader smiled.

"That is *The Way*. It has always been so; it will be so forever." Raising his hands, the rest of the blue-robed aliens bowed once again in solemn unison. And rising in unison they began to chant a single word. With both awe and dread they chanted that single word repeatedly.

"Draegaxx."

"This is the ship of 'The Draegaxx' – it journeys on forever." The green slits of the High Priest locked with Jacob's stern glare.

A few blasters began to waver nervously from his team.

"Not before we get off," Jacobs snarled.

The High Priest's high-pitched, maniacal laughter now mixed with the surreal chanting of the others. Moving closer, he whispered to Jacobs with a solemn tone.

"Myriads are they that have come here. And myriads are they that have tried to leave." The green eyes narrowed. "And none ever have..."

***

"I have investigated several decks above and below us. It is most intriguing, there are countless layers of refuse that cover the floor of the corridors and other visible signs of deterioration, all of which indicate this is an extremely ancient ship." Tan looked with frustration at his scanner. "This evidence is corroborated by what little analysis I can accomplish with my scanner before the jamming cuts it out. The scanner's results of the hull are intriguing, this ship may pre-date the rise of the human race." Tan reported this last with his usual emotionless expression.

"It's been on a very long voyage – to where?" Jacobs bit his lower lip.

"That cannot be determined. Our equipment is only able to work intermittently at best. I would think, once again, the internal defensive systems of this ship are interfering with our scanners. One interesting fact we did get - the steel used in the bulkheads, like most everything else, is of a composition unknown to us. But it is three times stronger than Trialthiate steel, the strongest composite we have ever produced." Tan's left eyebrow rose with emotion.

Footsteps suddenly rang out as three familiar figures entered through one of the huge doorways.

"Simmons, what did you find at the ship's bridge? Were you able to hack into the systems?" Jacobs asked.

Lt. Cheryl Simmons stepped forward; her blue eyes serious. With a quick movement, she brushed some of her blonde tresses back behind her ears.

"Very sophisticated, sir. Whoever built this ship meant to keep prying eyes away. We're effectively locked out of most of the ship's systems."

Jacobs frowned.

"Except for the navigation systems." Cheryl's voice registered surprise. "It's almost as if whoever built this ship wanted us to access it and input coordinates. But we are limited even there."

"Good, continue with that. Verify just how much control we have, if we can give it a course and the ship accepts it – that's priority one. The second is bringing the ship's shields down, so we can beam out." The Commander paused. "And find out what is interfering with our communicating with Intrepid, maybe the captain can help us. Learn as much as you can but be careful. I have a feeling we're not the first to try to escape this scow."

"Yes sir. And you're right. The computer has already warned us."

Jacob's eyes narrowed. "What warning?"

"When we tried accessing Engine Controls we were hit with weapons fire set to light stun. It seemed to come out of nowhere, directed by the ship's defensive mechanisms. When we regained consciousness, the computer warned us that next time we would be killed."

"Take every precaution."

Nodding, Lt. Simmons took one step for the ship's bridge when the silence was shattered.

"Commander! Commander!"

Jacobs turned to the oncoming voice.

Martinez ran tiredly toward them, appearing suddenly from one of the doors that lined the gargantuan hallway with his squad panting close behind.

"Did you reach the engine room?" Jacobs asked.

"No sir, but..." Martinez bent over, out of breath. "... we.. we found something else."

"Are you running from something?" Jacobs quickly signaled Tan to use his scanner.

The Chief Scientist quickly enabled his unit, trying to get a reading from it despite the ships interference.

"There is nothing behind them." Tan reported.

Martinez stood, letting out a big breath. "Something was. Believe me."

"What did you find?" Jacobs grabbed Javy's shoulder to steady him.

"It was strange. We found room after room all identical to each other – same dimensions, same layout as this one. They seemed to go on forever, lining each side of this great corridor like... like the great Quasada Prison."

"Why do you say that?"

"Prisoners scribble on the walls and ceilings to pass away the time. In each room we found the walls covered from top to bottom with alien script." Martinez frowned. "I was able to scan some of them, recalibrating my scanner each time the jamming shut it down. I got some of it, but not nearly all."

"Translation?"

"It was like everything else in this strange ship, very few were familiar languages. But there were certain phrases that seemed to be repeated in almost every script. Those repeated phrases we were able to translate."

The muscles in Martinez's face jerked nervously with his rising emotions. Somehow, Jacobs knew what he was going to say before Martinez spoke.

"Beware the Draegaxx." Jacobs said before the officer could speak.

Martinez's eyes opened wide amazement. "Yes, several of them said that exact thing – the first phrase we picked out. But the other words were more disturbing."

"And those words translated as?" Tan's expression grew serious.

"Fiend." Javier Martinez took another deep breath. "Dark-Eater and Dream-Eater were two more. But the last word, or combo-word, I still can't figure." Martinez punched his hand-held scanner, bringing the word up.

Jacobs and Tan stepped closer and read the display.

HellFear.

An icy fear gripped Commander Jacobs' heart.

"What does that mean?" Tan wondered out loud.

"It's from the legends," Jacobs said. "One of the names they gave this ship."

A thick, ominous silence filled the room.

"And what was the other discovery?" Tan asked quickly.

"We had almost figured the whole ship was made up of these identical, empty compartments when we came to this huge door. The most elaborate door I've ever seen on a ship. Carvings, glowing emblems, huge inscriptions all over its surface - like something meant for a temple. And the glowing symbols translated - 'The Gate of the Draegaxx.'"

"A large door?"

Martinez nodded. "About ten meters high, the exact same oversized dimensions..." Martinez suddenly paused as the same thought dawned in all their minds at once.

"That may explain the exceedingly high ceilings and wide corridors throughout the ship. I had thought perhaps this design was for the easy movement of freight. But now..." Tan paused as a feeling of dread thickened the air around them.

Tan put into words what they all were thinking.

"This Draegaxx, whatever it is, must be sizable." Tan looked from Jacobs to Martinez.

"The weirdest part happened after we opened the door." Martinez's eyes widened. "Some kind of large holo-display, a map, activated above the entrance. Gartner walked inside and tried a sweep with his scanner. I saw an icon go live at one end of this display, and then I realized what was beyond the door."

"Please continue," Tan said with interest.

"It's a Three-Dimensional maze, Commander. The pure whiteness from it almost blinded us, but I could just make out that the gate opened to four corridors, each leading a different direction. One left, another right. And one curving up while the last led downward." Javy's eyes widened with memory. "A huge, extraordinary maze with several large rooms located along different routes. I think the icon represented Gartner at one end of the display, it only showed up when he entered. The engine room is at the other end, I could almost make out the outlines of

33

hyper-space drives in the crazy outlines on the display. But..."

"Go on," Jacobs prompted.

"We heard it. We all heard it, something... from the depths of the maze." Martinez looked down in shame. "I've never heard anything like it in my life. Like something from a nightmare... I don't know, we just ran."

"Didn't you even attempt to get a scan of this Draegaxx?" Tan asked with amazement.

Martinez looked up angrily.

"No sir, I'm afraid not. You see, I don't know how I knew, but I knew. We all knew." Martinez's face pleaded. "It was coming."

"I must remind you, Lieutenant, as leader of a reconnaissance squad it is imperative that you keep your presence of mind under any kind of situation." Tan said with a calm, emotionless tone. "That data could have proven most useful. As it is..."

"You weren't there! You didn't hear that noise! You didn't *feel* it!" Martinez shouted. "No entiendes!? Eschuchame! Eschuchame!"

"Javy!" Jacobs spoke the single word as a command.

Martinez looked down in silence.

"Lieutenant, you must learn self-control." Tan nodded. "And remember, I am not familiar with the ancient language of your U.E. State. I barely know the rudiments of my own state's original language, Chinese."

"OK, let's pool our data." Jacobs signaled his team closer. "Tan, you coordinate and compile it all. Martinez, you work on translating some more of the alien writing. Maybe there's..." Jacobs turned toward the echoes of approaching footsteps.

Once again, an iciness gripped him – a feeling of impending doom. Without thinking, Jacobs reached into his belt and initiated the recall signal to the rest of his team.

The alien High Priest approached with methodical steps. He came alone this time, alone with his haunted eyes.

"You must come."

Jacobs shook his head as the others gathered closer.

"We don't like what's going on here. We don't like being held prisoner against our will. And we don't like dealing with anybody without knowing their name."

The green-eyed alien smiled, a sad but knowing smile.

"We do not use names here. Names are... awkward. Come, all is prepared." With flowing robes, the alien turned and began walking.

Jacobs held his ground, unmoving. "We're not going anywhere."

The alien priest stopped. He spoke without turning.

"You must follow. The Draegaxx comes, and you are not ready."

***

Jacobs looked over the roomful of aliens, and then back at the familiar faces of his shipmates as they made their way towards his position. Lieutenant Cheryl Simmons arrived first.

"Have you learned anything?" Jacobs asked in a low voice.

She sighed. "Nothing new, I'm sorry." But her eyes betrayed her feelings.

"Are you alright?" Jacobs asked.

She shook her head. "I'm sorry, Commander. I'm a little scared right now – plain and simple. I know, I'm an officer of the fleet." She averted her eyes with a guilty expression.

Jacobs placed his hand comfortingly on her shoulder. He was fiercely protective of his people, and that personal interest fostered both loyalty and trust in return.

And he didn't plan to fail any of them now.

"It's understandable. I'd be lying if I told you I wasn't scared too. But remember your training, Lieutenant. Control your emotions and focus. We'll get out of this. I've already got something in mind," he added with sincerity.

Cheryl smiled weakly, pursing her lips tightly. "Thanks, Commander. I know you'll get us out."

Suddenly everything went dark – a complete and absolute darkness that choked and pressed in from every direction at once.

Jacobs felt as if he were falling – falling through the blackness of space and into infinity.

He fell hard onto the floor amid the total darkness. As his face pressed against the steel deck, he felt a distant thundering that seemed to vibrate through his very bones.

"What's happening!?" He shouted into the black abyss.

It was over as quickly as it began.

As the lights returned Jacobs found himself watching as Cheryl's fingers danced over her comm unit. She squatted on her knees from where she had fallen.

"I had Intrepid for a second." She gasped.

"That was some kind of huge power fluctuation." Martinez struggled to a sitting position as he checked his own scanner. "Power levels are almost back to normal, as is the jamming." Martinez looked up from his scanner. "Some kind of blackout, it knocked out most of their power grid before it corrected."

Jacobs used his hands to signal for the rest of the squad to come closer.

"I am intrigued," Tan began.

Jacobs turned and looked at Tan who was returning from talking with the green-eyed alien leader.

"About our hosts?" Jacobs asked.

"No, about the Draegaxx. I have had some of their history explained to me, right before the power event, though I am uncertain as to its accuracy. No written or permanent records are maintained here."

"They don't store them in the ship's computers?" Cheryl Simmons asked incredulously.

"No, the ship's systems, even the ship, is regarded as Holy. I find it doubtful that any of the alien races here were the original builders of this huge vessel. None show the technological aptitude."

"Then they were taken, just like us." Jacobs mused.

"I would concur with that assumption," Tan said.

"Well, that leaves us with the Draegaxx. Did its ancestors build this ship and send it among the stars millennia ago?" Martinez rubbed his chin.

"That is the mystery." Tan looked back at the different forms, all of them dressed in the same blue robes. "On the one hand, they speak almost reverently of the Draegaxx. As if they worship it."

"And yet they're all afraid of it. Deathly afraid." Jacobs said.

"You can feel their fear in the air," Simmons added.

"So, is the Draegaxx their god? Or is it their demon?"

"It is neither."

Everyone turned to the newcomer.

"And it is both."

"What?" Martinez asked, thoroughly confused.

The new alien smiled timidly at them.

"I am Commander Jacobs, this is my team - Chief Scientist Tan, Lieutenants Simmons, Williams and Martinez." He nodded. "And the rest of my team over there are Ensign Gartner, Stafford, McMichaels and Thomas."

The alien's blue lips curled into a smile. "I was once known as Gaz." He sighed sadly. "It has been so long since I have used my name."

"Were you captured?" Jacobs asked.

"I think so. One moment I was with my villagers tending the flocks, the next I found myself here. The Draegaxx took us." He sighed again.

"How long have you been here, Gaz?"

Gaz shook his head. "I was not adult when taken. Now I am almost middle-life. But I am one of the lucky. All the others of my kind have now journeyed on to the *better place*, taken by the Draegaxx."

"We're going to get off this prison ship, Gaz. If you can help us, I'll see to it you can too." Jacobs' voice echoed supreme confidence.

Gaz laughed. "So many others have tried. But the ship will not allow it. And if the ship does not kill you, then the Draegaxx will take you. But soon it will not matter."

"Why is that?" Tan asked.

"When the ship's engines engage, you will never see your kind again. We will be taken far, far away."

"Unless we could disable them," Tan added.

"The engines are located beyond the Shining Path. No one can make the journey – not with the Draegaxx's home there."

"The maze?" Javy Martinez gasped.

"Yes. Some have so called it," Gaz agreed.

"Why didn't you try to learn the computer systems? Why didn't you turn the ship back?" Jacobs asked.

"It has all been tried before. Unnumbered souls have died trying. We who remain have resigned ourselves to this new life."

"Why are you so few? This ship could carry many hundreds of thousands," Tan said.

Gaz looked furtively around. "It is said that *'The End'* is near. For a long time, the ship does not take more victims. But the Draegaxx continues his visits among those who remain." He sighed. "And there are the Thunderings and Blackness. They happen more and more often."

"He must mean the power fluctuations," Tan said to Jacobs.

"And what kind of life is this?" Jacobs asked.

"We are fed, we are kept comfortable. The ship attends to our basic needs. No one goes without."

"And what does the Draegaxx do?"

"The Draegaxx takes us to a better world," Gaz repeated automatically.

"Good, you remember your lessons well." The alien High Priest smiled as he stepped beside Gaz. "You too must learn The Way – The Way of Life."

"This is not life, being trapped, held prisoner against our will!" Jacobs growled.

The green-eyed alien smiled. "And yet, we live. It has always been so."

Jacobs felt his anger blossom as other blue-robed aliens gathered around them. They were whispering excitedly, and Jacobs knew that they believed he and his squad would be wearing the same blue robes soon.

"What is HellFear?" Jacobs asked, his voice almost a shout.

The blue-robed figures froze, and then most began to shuffle quickly away, some covering their ears in fright.

"We do not discuss this. We only accept it."

"The Draegaxx will not take us," Cheryl said, her voice shaking with emotion.

The green-eyed alien smiled and nodded.

"The Draegaxx *feels you*, yellow haired female."

Cheryl's blue eyes went wide.

The lights dimmed that same instant, but not the pure darkness they had just experienced. After a few seconds, they found themselves under the glow of an eerie bluish light that seemed to come from nowhere, and everywhere. Everything and everyone in the room became a ghostly blue shadow.

"The Draegaxx comes. We must take our places and sleep," the alien High Priest said simply.

"Sleep!" Martinez shouted.

"You must calm yourselves, the Draegaxx will feel you. The sleep is preferred." The green-eyed alien dropped his voice to a whisper. "Because of the HellFear."

"We will fight it, we still have our weapons," Jacobs said firmly.

Williams, Martinez and Gartner pulled the short assault blasters from off their shoulders while the rest pulled their hand blasters from out of their holsters.

"I must teach you the first Law of the Draegaxx, before you kill the last of us – before the ship replenishes. It must not happen this way." The High Priest nodded and held his scaly fingers up, tracing ghostly figures in the bluish light – strange angles and circles...

"K-Yayah Draegaxx." The High Priest mumbled repeatedly. Finally, his eyes opened and gazed deeply into Jacobs angry glare.

"You cannot kill what cannot die. For the Draegaxx is Undying."

Jacob's eyes narrowed. As his mind raced with the alien's words, he felt a tiny prick where the alien priest touched his arm. He jerked his arm away. "We must try. We... " Jacobs suddenly put his hands out as the room began to spin uncontrollably. He couldn't focus... he couldn't...

A great drowsiness flooded his mind.

"We've been drugged!" Tan shouted, as he too stumbled and fell with a robed alien smiling beside him.

The green-eyed alien priest reached out and grasped Jacobs firmly, to keep him from falling.

"We must all to our places in the Walls. The Draegaxx comes."

***

Jacobs *felt* it. Through the haze of his drugged sleep, through the dense comforting numbness, the Draegaxx reached for him.

Fear – absolute and overwhelming reached into his very soul. It choked him, it suffocated him. And the fear was alive.

Now he could almost see it inside the blue shadows, almost make out its huge, hideous form. But he clearly smelled its wretched stench as the fear filled his mind.

He vaguely felt massive talons grope and prod his body.

He tried to scream.

Iron fangs grinned a death's smile inside his living nightmare.

He coughed and struggled to force even the smallest breath to scream. But he couldn't move.

The burning heat sucked at what breath he could force – his mind exploded into a shower of sparks. The flames grew higher and faster. His skin blistered and blackened, sloughing off in bloody layers, revealing shiny crimson sinews and yellow tendons underneath.

And that too hissed away with sizzling pain.

Jacobs lay naked before the hellish fiend – naked except for his fear.

He wanted only one thing in the entire universe. He needed only one thing – to scream. He *had* to scream.

But he could not.

The distant sound of a woman's shriek struck his drugged senses like a bolt of lightning, causing his body to jerk violently.

The shrieks turned into cries of pure, blind horror.

Somehow, he knew they were the screams of Lt. Cheryl Simmons.

A fog gathered in his mind, it swirled in alternating circles of light and darkness. After a seeming eternity, he felt a quiver of hope overpowering the doom that gripped his soul. And mercifully, mercifully, it all melted away like the morning dew under the hot mid-summer sun. Blissful emptiness filled him as the nightmare faded into nothing.

"We are pure."

Jacobs opened his eyes slowly – cautiously.

His body hung tight against the wall. He looked up.

All around the great room everyone else hung in the same defenseless position against the wall. Some invisible force kept them all attached. As he struggled, he felt the wall grip him tighter. It held

43

him firm, cupping him around his back and shoulders and buttocks.

'We were offerings.' The thought whispered inside his mind.

But a new chant from the strange aliens replaced his dream words.

"We are pure."

His bloodshot eyes found some of his team as his eyes focused. Tan, and then Martinez, everyone attached to the wall like some kind of grisly decoration, like some kind of grotesque ornament.

But there was a single, empty mold in the wall.

The Wall released them all at once.

He slid down in a surreal slow motion. Jacobs found his legs weak and rubbery as he landed. He tried to stand but fell face down instead. He grunted with pain.

And then Cheryl's screams echoed in his battered mind. He forced himself to stand.

The green-eyed alien priest looked down upon him.

"Where is she?" Jacobs said sharply. "Tell me!"

"The Draegaxx has taken her. I told her it would feel her," he said matter-of-factly.

Jacob's hands were around the slender neck of the alien in an angry flash. The alien struggled, but Jacob's hands only tightened.

"Commander!" Tan shouted.

Jacobs growled as reason took hold of his clouded mind. He held on to him a moment longer, savoring it, and then he pushed the whimpering alien away.

The alien priest coughed and sputtered, trying to regain his breath. With shaking hand, he pointed.

"We will not give you the potion next time. When the Walls wake, you will be there, conscious, when the HellFear comes. When the Draegaxx comes."

"Tell me where the Draegaxx has taken her."

"To a better place."

Jacobs shook his head angrily. He looked over and signaled Stafford and Thomas. They moved quickly as each grabbed the alien High Priest by an arm.

"Answer me," Jacobs whispered angrily. "Or I'll send you to a better place."

The alien sneered back at him.

Jacob's measured blow caught the alien squarely in the stomach.

He watched impassively as the alien groaned and bent over with pain. Stepping back, Jacobs look around. And found his team looking back at him.

Each pair of eyes fixed firmly on him as he turned to each one. There was a message in each pair of eyes for him. Pleading and silent, but an obvious message -- *'Lead us out of this, Commander. Get us out - alive.'*

There had to be an answer. He had to find Cheryl. There had to be a way. Those words echoed over and over in his mind as he stared into each face.

The alien raised its head and smiled at him.

Jacobs hit him again, doubling him over completely.

The alien's legs collapsed with the blow, but he did not fall. Hanging limply, his arms held tight by the two men on either side.

"Commander," Tan protested.

"Hold him up," Jacobs said calmly as he drew his fist back again.

"Wait," the alien panted.

He coughed for long seconds as he struggled to speak. But Jacobs allowed his fist to drop with newfound patience.

"To the rooms of the Shining Path." He finally coughed.

Jacobs signaled his men to release him.

"Martinez, take Williams back to the Nav console where he and Simmons worked earlier. Lay in a course for the Tamaz system."

"That is a very populous system, Commander. You may be endangering more lives," Tan said with surprise.

Jacob's face grew rock hard with determination.

"That's the very reason I think the ship will allow it. But we may be able to leverage it to our advantage, I'm very familiar with that system. Give me your scan unit, Martinez." Jacobs took it and began typing. As he finished the message, he handed it to him.

"If there's another power fluctuation, hit the transmit button and send this message – fast. It might get through to Intrepid before the jamming starts again."

Tan raised his eyebrows in thought.

"I would like to add to that message, if I may Commander."

Jacobs nodded. "Keep it brief, even with the power fluctuations; this ship is still very powerful."

"I understand."

Tan typed rapidly and gave it back to Martinez.

"McMichaels and Gartner, you're with Tan and myself. You saw the entrance to the maze, right?"

The two men nodded solemnly.

Jacobs took a deep breath.

"We're going after Cheryl. And the Draegaxx."

***

Everything glowed with a ghostly, pure light. The small team stood before the ornate door of the strange maze. Through the open door four identical corridors stood: One angled to the right, one to the left, a third led directly forward and upwards while the fourth led downward.

"Scan for traces," Jacobs ordered Tan.

As the Chief Scientist worked his scanner, fighting the interference of the ship with each touch, Jacobs approached the wall of the rightmost corridor of the Shining Path.

He placed his hand against the intense white glow and noticed that his hand seemed to melt into it.

But it was only an illusion. Like all mazes, this one was meant to disorient. And the glow, along with the ship's interference of their equipment, combined with the twisting corridors of this three-dimensional maze, made their task almost impossible.

"There," Tan pointed to the path leading upwards.

"A good lock?" Jacobs asked.

Tan breathed deeply as he shook his head. "I got only the briefest of readings. But this time it was enough. The Draegaxx's sign was fresh."

"Let's mark our way back. I'll leave the first ones until mine are used up." Jacobs reached inside his belt for the tiny magnetic beacons they would place at periodic points.

Jacobs felt disoriented even as they took their first steps inside, choosing the corridor going forward and upward into the tunnel of glowing, ethereal whiteness. The huge corridor was sized identically to all the others throughout the ship. The intense glow of the ceiling danced ten meters above their heads.

These passages go on forever, his mind and senses told him. It almost felt as if he was in the passage that led to another dimension – beyond life and death. But he knew it was another trick his mind was playing, this strange place adding to the internal fear he struggled to control.

The white haziness seemed to close together far, far ahead, heralding a dead-end. But even as they reached the glowing end point it suddenly moved farther away as their eyes adjusted – a mirage of the glowing whiteness.

And in the mind-numbing glow it was so easy to walk past the side passages.

It would have been so easy to walk, and turn, and walk and get lost and continue into the seemingly never-ending passages – into the whiteness, into the shining fog.

Forever.

Openings led left and right, and others curled upward or downward at certain points. And everywhere the white glow blinded their senses. In fact, except for their intermittently working equipment, time had no meaning. It seemed hours passed in only a few moments.

"The Draegaxx leaves an obvious trail," Tan punched his scanner again, and for a moment, it functioned once again.

Jacobs nodded. "I'm glad."

"I can almost smell it," McMichaels whispered, his voice edged with fear.

"The Draegaxx seems to affect all the senses. We must analyze this phenomenon; only then might we find a weakness." Tan looked carefully around another blinding turn.

Jacobs looked up near the top of the high, curved ceiling. He saw the marks underneath the glowing fog – scratches in the steel. Among the countless old ones, his eyes noticed a few shiny claw marks – freshly made.

His heart pounded faster as he realized all the claw marks were far above them.

The minutes dragged on to an hour as they stumbled onward into the blinding glow.

"I have found blood."

Jacobs bent down and dipped his finger in the dark crimson spot while Tan fought with his scanner as it failed once again.

Jacob's nose wrinkled at the smell. They looked at each other.

"It's Simmons' blood." Tan announced as he looked up from his scanner.

"Oh, no!"

Jacobs and Tan looked up, and then both ran past a frozen form of Gartner who stared unmoving straight ahead.

It was a large room, a huge room, bigger than any they had encountered so far in any part of the ship. A room surrounded and framed by the ghostly whiteness. Rising mysteriously from the shimmering whiteness, the floor was littered with countless dark mounds scattered in every direction like huge chocolate drops. Countless thousands – hundreds of thousands – rose like a mirage from the milky white glow of the floor.

But there was something obscene about these identical objects, something profane about their strange dark shapes which contrasted against the pure whiteness. Even without their scanners, everyone knew this was a place of the dead.

Tan worked his scanner, trying to obtain a good reading as he and Jacobs approached one of the knee-high objects.

It shivered with motion almost as if alive as they stepped beside it – like a huge mound of brownish-crimson jelly, like some kind of droppings. A strange yellow pattern swirled all through its semi-translucent surface... yellow streaks...

Jacobs felt his stomach tighten into a steel knot.

"It has decapitated her." Tan commented as he punched his scanner harshly. "I cannot determine what kind of material her head is encased inside, though. My scanner..."

"Take's them to a better place!!" Jacobs screamed.

"What!?" McMichaels fell to the floor choking and retching his guts into the glow, causing it to swirl away, but the whiteness returned almost immediately to cover the fresh gore.

In the heavy silence only Tan's fingers working his scanner echoed in their ears.

"Why...?" Jacobs shook his head, his voice barely above a whisper.

"I have further news," Tan said as he pointed his scanner at the other piles. "Each of these strange mounds contains at least one head. Hmm, over fifty thousand before my scanner froze with jamming." Tan looked up from his scanner. "Most interesting. Could this be the Draegaxx's excretions? Or some type of trophies. Or..."

Three sets of eyes stared around the huge room.

"There's hundreds of these rooms according to the maze display," McMichaels said, still coughing and wiping his mouth.

Jacobs closed his eyes and stood. "We can't do anything for her now. We need to push on and find the engine room. I want to know why this maze hides it, and why the Draegaxx guards it." Jacobs walked toward the other end of the room and the corridor beyond.

They lost its trail somewhere in the glowing passages after the second room of death. Now with their intermittent scans and gut instinct alone, they made their way forward. At each juncture of the maze Tan carefully marked their way, Jacobs realizing those markers might be their only indicator leading them back out. The trio passed through five more rooms, each filled with the ghastly brownish piles left from the Draegaxx.

Finally, after what seemed an eternity, they reached another door.

Or the remains of a massive door.

It lay smashed and broken.

"It seems the Draegaxx has gained access to the engine room," Tan said as he put his scanner back on his belt.

"Why?" Gartner asked.

Tan paused in thought a moment and spoke.

"It may have finally realized the ship that keeps it imprisoned gets its power from the engines. Destroy them and it wins its freedom."

Jacobs shuddered at the thought.

"Or it may be simpler. Perhaps it saw a barrier and just wanted to bring it down. My analysis shows it took quite some time to accomplish the task – the door was designed to withstand substantial punishment which was only recently completed. Whichever explanation proves correct, the great monster will certainly damage and finally destroy the engines and escape."

"We can't let that happen," Jacobs said with urgency. "If this thing gets loose on a populated planet, it will be devastating."

They all nodded silent agreement.

They entered and each person gasped.

This unimaginably massive place encompassed the entire width, height and breadth of the gargantuan ship, easily a kilometer wide and almost as high. Its immense size boggled their minds.

Fortunately, the glowing fog did not light this room. Normal ship's lighting revealed the vastness.

They walked out into the vast openness while in the distance immense towers of blinking lights and other signs of electronic activity sparkled in the distance. The team walked among the unchanging landscape for almost half an hour, their steps echoing off the great metal walls that rose all around them.

They now walked in a steel-walled desert where only electronics existed.

In the distance, something rose slowly before them – higher and higher.

They finally arrived at the strange, out-of-focus visage. At last, they gazed upon the engines that powered the ship of death. The massive engines glowed and blurred before their unbelieving eyes.

"They're protected by their own shields," Tan said as he forced his scanner to work against the constant interference from the ship's defenses.

"Why shields inside the ship?"

"Power levels are off the scale," Tan commented again.

"Oh, Great Creator, no!" McMichaels gasped.

The *feeling* came again.

In an instant they recognized the overwhelming sense of loss and foreboding.

HellFear ripped the very breath out of their lungs.

Everyone stood frozen – waiting as they *felt* the dread of the Draegaxx coming for them.

The ship's lights flickered off in the gargantuan engine room housing the mammoth power plants. Lightning bolts of raw energy erupted, sending blinding light alternating with a deep blackness. Each man knew its source was the Draegaxx even without verification from their scanners.

In that gathering maelstrom of light and darkness and bolts of energy that sent jagged streaks of lighting far above them – in the middle of that hellish maelstrom they saw it coming.

53

A huge, deformed head danced above them with elephantine ears tipped with icy black horns. Huge, clawed hands reached out and groped toward the ceiling.

The darkness filled everything again – and the beast was the darkness.

Within that darkness they still made out its massive outline. They felt their hearts stop as the misshapen creature seemed to change, to alter before them – and then melt in the darkness.

It wasn't black in color, yet its body seemed to devour light.

But the beast was there. They could *feel* it there.... close.

Oh, so close.

Jacobs fumbled for his blaster as Tan tried to point his scanner at the monstrous form where he had last seen it before darkness enveloped them.

Lightning flashed again and they saw it with raised arms, drawing pure bolts of lightning from the shimmering shapes of the massive engines. It seemed as if it fed off the massive bolts of pure energy.

The ship's weapons were firing in an attempt to keep the monster at bay.

The darkness retreated for an instant with another flash of bright lightning before another power fluctuation darkened everything again.

The Draegaxx stood before them – somewhere close.

"It's...it's..." Tan started. And then his eyes opened wide as he stared at the scanner's glowing display. He threw it even as sparks shot out of it.

It exploded in mid-air right before his face.

Tan screamed as he covered his eyes with his blistered hands as the explosion revealed the Draegaxx right before him.

Jacobs fired his blaster.

But his heart sank even as he saw his blast hit true, for the beast did not even flinch. As he stared dumbfounded, he saw the claw swinging for him through the returning darkness.

He ducked.

Gartner and McMichaels opened up with their assault blasters, sending a hail of fire into the misshapen beast that towered above them. The darkness enveloped the flurry of tracer bolts after they entered the beast's body.

In the total darkness, the Draegaxx roared. It was a haunting sound that reverberated through every part of their very bodies.

Jacobs felt himself swept away by a great glancing blow that sent him far out onto the steel deck. Struggling against the pain and the visceral assault on his senses by the darkness and tracers, he could only manage to cover his ears as he tried to shut out the otherworldly roars of the Draegaxx.

But that too was futile, like everything else.

Jacobs heard McMichaels scream as darkness enveloped the room again. He heard the clawed feet on the steel deck right beside him.

He looked up.

Bolts of steel blue lightning ripped the air and lit a grotesquely large mouth filled with iron teeth. The rank stench of rotting flesh seared his nose and overwhelmed his senses.

He saw Tan draw his blaster out of his holster as Gartner continued to pummel the beast with his assault blaster with no effect.

Tan aimed for the clawed hand right before him even as the darkness blinded them all again.

The Draegaxx roared its horrendous fury.

Tan methodically aimed and fired again.

More human screams rent the air, mixing with the beast's unearthly roars.

There was movement everywhere in the darkness.

Jacobs tried to rise.

The blow was like a tree falling upon him, and everything suddenly went totally black.

But even partially unconscious, Jacobs felt the Draegaxx grip his soul with fear. And there was nothing he could do to stop it.

Through the numbness, he heard McMichaels scream again. Or was it Gartner? In the fog that filled his mind, Jacobs knew only one thing beyond the grip of the HellFear – he knew his people were dying.

Out from the black fog, his eyes focused.

He lay there a long time staring at the blood smeared floor.

There was a blinding pain in his side, which with even the barest movement sent a new searing fire throughout his body. He lay still. The Draegaxx would probably take him next, anyway. Take him to the better place...

"Commander."

Jacobs tried to focus eyes.

Tan lay sprawled several hundred feet away. A massive cut with flowing blood covered his face from just above his right eye down to his jaw and onto part of his chest. Blood glistened across his uniform.

"We must return to the others," Tan wheezed as blood dripped in long crimson streaks. With a shaking hand he picked a small object up and looked at it closely. Quickly, he pocketed it.

"What...about..." Jacobs whispered with agonizing gasps.

Tan shook his head. "Both dead, Commander."

Laying there crushed by the burning pain throughout his body, Jacobs began to cry silently.

Tan approached and forced him up. Taking out what few medical instruments he had, Tan did his best to ease the pain and prepare them for the return journey. But each moment sent a new strobe of pain through Jacobs.

After Tan finished, they stumbled forward together with Tan assisting Jacobs as best he could. The two wounded men moved like broken robots.

Without the beacons they'd left to mark their way back and Jacob's intermittent scanner, they would have been hopelessly lost.

Somehow, despite their wounds, they managed to drag themselves back through the vast maze. It seemed to take days – even years – to their pain-numbed minds. Only Tan's constant urgings kept Jacobs going as one-by-one they followed the signals from the marker beacons.

Several more times the ship shuddered under more power fluctuations as the power grid failed momentarily. Jacobs could see the beast back in the strange engine room, lightning bolts arching from its clawed hands. He imagined many times that it was coming for them.

But it never did.

Finally, they stumbled through the juncture of the first four corridors and the Gate of the Draegaxx.

Martinez ran to them as they came through the other side.

"We got a message off, sir! And Intrepid acknowledged, briefly!"

Williams squatted beside them as he used his Medi-Unit on their wounds. Under the healing technology of the Medi-Unit, Jacob's mind began to clear from the fog of pain.

"Intrepid must find a way to get us off. It's our only hope now," Jacobs said as Williams finished his ministrations.

"I was able to set a course for the Tamaz system. The ship seemed to pick up speed." Martinez frowned. "But I think a lot of this ship's systems are failing from what I saw."

"That would explain a lot," Tan said.

"Tamaz is a tricky system to navigate – the gravity well of the red giant is treacherous and ships must make a wide arc around it to land on the main planet. I hope this ship can do it." Javy shrugged.

In a flash of inspiration, Jacobs knew the answer.

"What is it, Commander?" Tan asked

"Let's get moving," Jacobs ordered. "I've got an idea."

Jacobs led them back to the room of the Walls. A party of robed aliens greeted them instantly.

"What have you done?" The green eyes of the high priest were wide with fright.

"We found the Draegaxx, we've seen it. It's nothing more than a monster. It's certainly not a god," Jacob's growled.

The alien's maniacal laughter echoed off the steel walls, walls scarred for centuries by clawed hands.

"Then '*The End*' has come at last," he said, his maniacal laughter rising.

"Perhaps the ship's defenses prevented the beast's previous attempts to reach the engine room?" Tan thought out loud. "I do not think the builders ever intended for the Draegaxx to get at the engine room, which powers this great ship and its inner defense systems. That may explain...."

Everyone reached for support as the mammoth ship shuddered and groaned. Once again, the lights dimmed. And momentarily returned.

"Woe for the universe if that which does not die returns. That is the final prophecy." The high priest began chanting in a hushed whisper as he turned to leave.

"Perhaps this ship was primarily designed to keep the Draegaxx imprisoned," Tan mused.

"And to feed it – keep it content." Jacobs grimaced with pain.

"I would suspect the original builders set up the engines in their shielded alignment on purpose." Tan rubbed his chin in thought.

"Wouldn't that create a huge energy drain? And why?" Jacobs stared keenly at the Chief Scientist.

"They must have anticipated the Draegaxx one day breaking into the engine room. That field would provide the final barrier to the Draegaxx destroying the ship, not being able to directly touch the engines that maintained the ship's systems."

Jacobs shook his head with reservation. "But it obviously still causes damage, even as it tries to reach through the barrier."

"This ship has held the Draegaxx for several millennia, that bespeaks the care of the ship's original defenses. But there may be no prison that can hold the Draegaxx forever," Tan said with a dark foreboding.

"Why do you say that?"

"The High Priest is right. The worst is true."

Jacobs watched as Tan pulled a small object from his belt. It was black, about five centimeters long and three centimeters thick.

And it moved.

It was the tip of one of the Draegaxx's fingers, a broken claw.

"That means we can hurt it." Jacobs said with hope.

Tan shook his head as he scanned the severed appendage again with Martinez's scan unit. He handed his scanner to Jacobs.

"It's alive?" Jacobs asked in disbelief.

"Already the buds for arms, head and legs are appearing. Soon, there will be a miniature Draegaxx."

Jacobs eyes widened.

"It is true. This Draegaxx cannot die. By striking it, we only increase our problems." Tan shook his head.

"Unless the Draegaxx finds it." The alien known as Gaz stared at the still moving thing in Tan's hand.

"The Draegaxx comes even now for it. It must be One again."

Jacobs watched in shock as everyone stumbled to the enclaves that began appearing in the Walls. The strange bluish light returned, creating a mysterious ambience as the room darkened.

"Gather our team," Jacobs ordered as he rose painfully.

The gut-wrenching roar erupted like an explosion, echoing from the corridors beyond the room, deafening everyone in the room. The lights dimmed with another power flux.

"These power failures are increasing, even though it sounds like the Draegaxx is nearby and nowhere near the engine room!" Jacobs exclaimed.

"The Draegaxx may have caused irreversible damage with its last attempt at the engines," Tan said.

As soon as the power and bluish lights returned, a longer, more ominous darkness heralded another blackout – two in a row within seconds of each other.

Tan's eyes widened.

A twinkling glow appeared in the air before them. It disappeared, leaving a small pile of equipment behind.

"Intrepid got through!" Martinez shouted with joy.

"Commander Jacobs, please respond!" The familiar voice emanated from Jacobs' comm.

Jacobs grabbed his comm.

"Captain, we're here!"

"What's your status?"

"We've got a monster here; we can't kill it and soon it will escape this ship." Jacobs replied.

"The ship's shields are down, and our scans show they're not coming back up."

"Captain, I've got a plan on how to take care of this monster, but we need to get the rest of aliens off this ship."

"Our scans show 211 life forms besides your team. They're clustered in one section; we'll have them off in 20 minutes."

"We only have 10 minutes, Captain!"

"Then we'll …"

Static replaced the captain's voice.

"Let's move!" Jacobs ordered. "Grab anything that might slow it down!"

Martinez ran over and picked up a large weapon that he had to balance on his hip while gripping it with both hands. "This thing can stop an armored assault shuttle." His voice trailed away as another roar reverberated, closer now.

"The Draegaxx cannot die, our weapons cannot stop it." Tan said with Stoic ease.

Jacob's mind raced. He knew time was quickly running out.

"OK, listen up!"

Desperate faces stared at him for guidance.

Jacob's eyes narrowed. "We've got once chance. And even if that fails, if we go down, we take the Draegaxx with us."

Everyone nodded silent agreement.

Commander Jacobs pointed out two more of the heavy assault blasters like the one Martinez held. They quickly retrieved them. He stared down at the high yield explosives with a questioning look.

"I requested them, before we knew about the nature of the Draegaxx," Tan said.

Another roar shook the room – louder and much closer.

"Let's take some. We might get to see how many pieces we can break the beast into."

"The Ship's hull could be ruptured. We cannot risk setting the Draegaxx loose," Tan said.

"Okay, leave it. We've got to get control of ship's navigation."

"You must throw it away." Gaz pointed frantically at the wriggling piece of the Draegaxx in Tan's hand. "The Draegaxx will be One. It will come for itself."

Tan's eyebrows rose in thought.

"I may have an idea on how to bring the ship's defenses completely down."

"If you can do that, then we can steer…"

The roar exploded in their ears.

Martinez shouted, but his words could no longer be heard, his voice drowned in the aural assault of the fiend's roars.

Javy brought his weapon up and fired.

Gaz screamed as huge claws lifted him into the air.

Jacobs and Stafford swung their own blaster rifles around and fired simultaneously.

The beast shuddered under the heavy blaster fire. But the combined blows from the heavy weapons fire merely forced the misshapen fiend back a step – a single step.

It suddenly came forward with a mighty roar. With a single, mighty stroke Stafford was smashed against the wall, the sound of his crushed bones mixing with the roars as his lifeless body crumpled into a limp heap.

Everyone ran.

Jacobs looked back briefly.

The limp form of Gaz rested in its claw, and the claw drew closer to the cavernous mouth.

"Get out!" Move, move, move! Javy, nail it again!!"

Martinez stopped and turned. He kneeled to better balance the huge weapon and fired as the others ran out the doorway and into the corridor.

Again, the blasts from the heavy weapon caused the misshapen creature to shudder and stumble backwards. But only for a moment.

As it regained its balance, it attacked straight on.

"Tan! I need you in the lead. Move!"

Javy retreated beside Jacobs out in the corridor.

"Where to, Commander?" Javy's eyes were wide with fear.

"To the Command Center, the Bridge," Tan shouted from up ahead.

Jacobs nodded agreement. "It's our only hope now."

"But the ship's defenses," Martinez shouted.

"Tan and I devised a plan for that on our way back through the maze." Jacobs smiled.

And then the great head emerged into the corridor and roared angrily at the retreating figures. With a huge step, the fiend entered the corridor and came after them.

Martinez fired and the blast knocked the creature backwards against the wall in mid-step.

They ran, their hearts gripped once again by the blinding HellFear. Lightning crackled and thunder boomed with each step of the beast. The lights dimmed as the pounding footsteps drew closer with each ominous roar.

The HellFear reached out from the fiend's twisted body and the humans knew despair inside their souls.

They felt despair too at the fact that their weapons only angered it.

With a roar it leaped closer with a single bound.

"Hit it again, keep it off-balance. We've got to gain a few seconds on it!" Jacobs shouted.

First Tan stopped, quickly aiming, and firing his heavy assault weapon and knocking the beast off-balance, and then he ran again. Jacobs nodded at Martinez, and he too dropped back, took aim, and fired. Each man with a heavy blaster took his turn to keep it off-balanced.

But the weapons were only powerful enough to knock it off stride and make it stumble.

Relentlessly, the misshapen beast came on.

The fight-and-run cycle continued.

The HellFear seemed to squeeze their lungs and chests. It made their knees wobble and made them stumble.

Quickly, the beast gained on them.

"Martinez, Williams and Thomas – prepare your weapons." Jacobs waved Tan to keep moving.

Three sets of eyes stared into his.

"You two, against the bulkhead there. Williams, you're with me."

Four weapons pointed down the wide corridor as the beast raised its huge claws and charged forward.

"Hit it's left leg at the knee. On my mark!"

The beast roared as it reached them.

"Now!"

Four tracer lines formed into one and converged on the contorted leg. The beast roared and staggered as it fell over.

Right at the joint of the inverted knee, the left leg severed as thick syrupy fluid erupted in a splashing geyser from both severed ends.

Against the bulkhead the severed foot rested. But something began to happen immediately. In almost surreal rapid motion, it began to ripple and move as the huge appendage morphed into a new shape.

Something began to sprout – arm buds appeared. And more.

It was no longer just a severed appendage.

It was becoming alive before their very eyes.

The beast reached its claws around the moving thing as it tried to wriggle away. With a rush of movement, the iron teeth closed over it. As its head jerked back it ripped the dark flesh away in tattered shreds. The sickening crunch of bones filled their ears.

The Draegaxx ate itself – becoming One again.

"What...?" Williams said with shock.

And then he screamed.

The claw enveloped Williams before he could move.

Jacobs fired again as the other two scrambled and fell back as another claw reached for them.

"Give me cover!" Jacobs yelled as the beast's head lowered toward him.

But it was too late.

Jacobs fired into the hideous maw lined with teeth like stakes around a fortress.

The beast's head jerked back with the blow. The mouth turned and closed on the flailing arms and legs of the screaming man already in its grasp.

Jacobs rolled away.

He *felt* the beast begin to reach for him even as he scrambled away.

Twin blasts from heavy weapons fire blinded him as they knocked the fiend backwards and onto its back.

Jacobs pushed himself up and ran.

He met Thomas and Martinez at the end of the main corridor.

"What's beyond?" Jacobs panted.

Tan appeared from the small door behind them. At last, the oversized corridors narrowed. The door and corridor beyond were designed for human-sized beings.

"It would seem the designers did not intend the Draegaxx to go beyond this section of the ship. Of course, with its food supply housed in the main sections of the mammoth ship, it would have no need to try."

A roar shook the room and Jacobs turned.

The beast hobbled towards them, but with each step it became steadier as the bloody stump grew longer – growing itself a new leg.

"Move!"

The four men closed the reinforced door behind them.

"With the raw strength of this metal, and the hardened door locked, one would almost assume it could hold the Draegaxx back." Tan surveyed the door.

But the first blows showed how wrong that assumption was.

Through six centimeters of solid steel, the outline of the beast's clenched fist slammed the bulkhead inward.

"It won't hold!" Martinez shouted in disbelief.

Jacobs nodded. "OK, Martinez. Where's the Command Center?"

Martinez's eyes continued to stare as the wall grew more deformed with each mighty blow, the thunder of each blow deafening them.

Martinez shouted. "Three more corridors, and then up one more level. But we can't take the weapons."

"Why?" Jacobs shouted back.

With a sickening metallic shriek, the steel door ruptured. A single talon protruded through the gaping hole of the failing barrier.

Everyone turned and ran.

"Why?" Jacobs shouted again as they raced down the second corridor.

"Force field, the defense systems must be programmed to only allow unarmed visitors onto the Bridge. It stopped us before, until we removed our blasters. Then we could walk through."

Jacobs' mind whirled.

The horrendous groan of steel being ripped apart behind them assaulted his ears.

Suddenly, another ear-shattering roar deafened them.

The beast was inside.

"Throw your weapons down!" Jacobs shouted.

As the sounds of destruction came ever closer, the remaining members of Jacobs's team made their way through the force field.

"I sure hope your idea works," Jacobs said through gritted teeth.

"That is my wish as well," Tan agreed.

Together they climbed up the narrow stairs and entered a large room – the Bridge of the cursed ship of death.

And before them stretched a veritable temple of technology.

As far as the eye could see – flicking displays, blinking control panels, lights and diodes flashed forth as though beacons of digital truth. There were enough computer systems to run an entire planet inside the Bridge.

This was indeed the heart of the ship built to imprison the Draegaxx – forever.

Jacobs stood speechless.

But even as this sanctuary hummed with activity, much as it had for millennia, the lights suddenly dimmed with an echoing roar mixed with the sound of thunder.

"The force field must be programmed to defend against the Draegaxx," Tan said.

"That'll give us a few extra minutes." Jacobs stepped toward the nearest data station.

Thomas was punching at the controls at the next station as the power grid fluctuated again. This time the lights did not return to full brightness. The digital temple reeled from the effects of the attacking Draegaxx.

"I wonder if the Draegaxx has ever been here?" Jacobs asked.

Tan paused at his data station.

"I don't think so," Martinez said. "The corridors were not designed for its bulk, nor did we see any signs of bulkheads ripped open from past entries."

Jacobs smiled at Tan. "Good!"

"It is coming for its severed claw." Tan smiled knowingly. "It will come here for the first time ever."

Suddenly a shower of sparks erupted from every direction as the power grid once again took a dive. Everyone scrambled away from the burning embers and rolled face down on the deck to protect themselves from the rain of fire. Electronic sirens echoed around the darkened room as the ship strained to redirect power in its fight to keep the Draegaxx out.

The fountains of sparks increased in number as the lights dimmed and went completely off. In the near distance, the beast roared its fury as small explosions erupted from various places.

With an electronic sigh, some of the lighting and equipment came back on.

But the temple had been violated.

Seconds seemed to last an eternity, but the ship was not dead. It grew obvious that not all the equipment came back to life with the returning power, but the main systems that occupied the center of the room hummed again with activity.

The ship was not finished yet.

A roar reverberated from the steel deck just below them. Seconds later, the sound of steel being ripped and rent apart assaulted their senses – a sound that went right through their bodies.

"It's through," Tan said.

Thomas rose and screamed.

The energy bolt leapt unseen from the ship's defense systems. Thomas' limp body fell dead before them.

"We've got a problem!" Martinez shouted.

"Tell me about it," Jacobs shouted back.

Two more bolts shot out and just missed the two men.

"Find cover! I can't make a fix on where the ship's weapons are hidden."

Bolts of energy streaked around them as the ship's defenses tried to locate them through the thick plumes of smoke and geysers of sparks. The flying debris helped to keep the aim of the weapons inaccurate.

Jacobs found himself underneath the data station he had been trying to use.

The steel floor suddenly rose before his eyes. With a shriek of tortured steel, a single talon ripped upward. A second later, the talon disappeared downward.

Up from the steel deck five talons emerged ominously, piercing the steel. With a single stroke the fiend tore the steel hull as if it were tin foil.

With heart-stopping effect, the misshapen head slowly rose into full view.

As it did, the HellFear rose into each of their throats and noses until they choked with its overwhelming stench and power.

There was nowhere else to run.

The grotesque head and shoulders slowly rose far above them toward the ceiling. The gut-wrenching sound of metal being ripped apart assaulted their ears as the claws forced the opening wider.

Tan screamed.

"Do it!" Jacobs ordered.

From his belt pocket Tan drew out his bloody hand, crimson streaks dripped down his wrist and onto the floor. In his shaking hand he held a tiny Draegaxx exactly five centimeters tall. Its mouth swallowed a bloody hunk of meat eaten from Tan's own hand.

In a single motion, the huge Draegaxx brought himself fully up into the bridge and roared his deafening anger as it caught sight of its miniature self now fully alive.

Tan glanced over at the main computer system that filled the center of the bridge.

He threw the tiny Draegaxx toward it.

They watched as the miniature Draegaxx rose from the floor where it fell and then fled into an opening and inside the center of the equipment array – into the heart of the digital Temple.

The Draegaxx roared as the energy bolts from the ship's defenses suddenly pounded it from every side. Weaving from the multiple blows, a giant claw smashed into the ship's systems lining the left wall.

As the huge monster staggered and slashed with blind rage, sending more showers of sparks and debris into the air, Jacobs watched in horror.

Jacobs flinched.

When he opened his eyes, only fire and destruction remained. The beast suddenly staggered again, until it was right above Tan's place of concealment.

"It's going to destroy everything!" Martinez screamed.

The beast suddenly leapt forward, chasing a tiny form that disappeared again into the bowels of the equipment.

Tan stared with sweat dripping down his face as the huge Draegaxx passed him.

"Martinez, see if you can raise Intrepid on your Comm now." Jacobs rose quickly and reviewed the destruction. Under his feet, he felt the mighty ship shudder and vibrate.

Alarms began to vie with other alarms as they mixed with the deafening roars of the fiend.

Tan managed to drag himself up and began punching the alien control panel.

"Ship's systems are going off-line. The ship will not last long at this rate."

Showers of sparks and explosions blossomed from multiple directions as the humans dodged their burning plumage. The alarms increased dramatically.

Jacobs stood beside Tan.

"We have entered the Tamaz system and its red giant. Twelve billion life-forms live on the surface of the fourth planet." Tan stared at him. "We cannot allow the ship to crash on it and release the Draegaxx." Tan's eyes clenched shut as more sparks fell around him.

In his mind's eye, Jacobs saw the devastating results of the Draegaxx loosed upon a planet's hapless population – unending death and destruction.

73

Terrific explosions from the far end of the huge ship, from far back in the engine room, now shook the entire ship, throwing the men down onto the floor.

The engines were overloading.

Nothing could stop the Draegaxx, Jacobs thought. Not even the immense power of this ship. It had held it prisoner a very long time, but...

"We've got to turn the ship, Tan. Turn it straight for Tamaz's sun."

Tan and Martinez stared at him with disbelief.

"The fires of this great star will not destroy the Draegaxx," Tan shouted back.

"It doesn't have to." Jacobs smiled wryly.

Martinez jumped up and began to access the navigation systems, fighting against the dying ships attempts to stop him. At the same time, Tan fought to keep the engines on-line at the bridge station he worked.

Before their very faces the equipment exploded in sparks forcing them to jump back. But even as the sparks faded, they were back at the blackened control pads.

"I've got the captain!" Martinez yelled

"Jacobs, prepare your team for immediate beam out." Captain Johansen's voice shouted from the comm unit on his shoulder.

"Hang on, Captain. We've got to finish this beast once and for all. Or else we'll have a much bigger problem on our hands." Jacobs wiped the sweat from his eyes.

"Our sensors show you have less than two minutes before those engines blow." The captain replied.

74

"Right. Next time I push the retrieval button on my scanner, get us out." Jacobs stared at the fire and explosions that filled the other end of the large room. The Draegaxx was destroying everything as it searched feverishly for the tiny Draegaxx.

"I have the engines under control, but I don't know how long I can hold them!" Tan shouted through clenched teeth.

Through the smoke, they felt the ship begin to move.

"We're maneuvering," Tan announced.

"It won't hold a course, Commander. We're going to have to stay with it and steer it manually!" Martinez screamed.

"We've got to steer it until the star's gravity well has the ship!" Jacobs checked the coordinates. The red giant drew steadily closer.

The terrible roars and explosions stopped all at once without warning. The deathly silence sent a chill throughout Jacobs' body.

At the far end of the huge Bridge, the solid wall of smoke and fire parted like a curtain.

The Draegaxx stepped towards them.

"Let me guess, the Draegaxx is One again!" Martinez shouted.

"Our time would appear to be limited," Tan shouted back.

"Are we on-track for the star?" Jacobs shouted as he stepped into the middle of the burning room – directly into the beast's track.

"The engines are faltering."

"One more minute, Commander. I need just one more minute before the star's gravity has us!" Martinez looked up as the beast loomed closer.

"You've got it."

Jacobs ran straight toward the beast.

With a roar, it swung a huge claw at the puny creature running at it.

Jacobs fought the fear that blinded him, as well as the fire and smoke. Out of the corner of his eye, he saw the talons reaching coming for him.

Leaping forward, he rolled between the tree-like legs of the Draegaxx.

The beast roared its rage at being fooled so easily.

The other clawed hand suddenly rushed towards Jacobs and struck him from behind. He felt himself flung violently into the air – and back down right at the edge of the hot licking flames.

The scanner flew out from his grasp and slid into the fire.

The fire seared his arms and hands as he frantically searched the flames for it. He screamed as he felt his skin burn with the terrible heat.

A shadow darkened him.

He heard the roar directly above him and he knew it was too late.

"The star's gravity well has us, Commander. Get us out of here!" Tan shouted.

The Draegaxx turned its head back to the voice behind it.

Jacobs felt the smoke and intense heat begin to fog his mind. He smelled the skin on his right arm as it sizzled and burned.

His thoughts grew troubled and confused.

He had failed. He and all his team would die...

With his last thrust into the flames, he touched something hard.

And with his last wisps of consciousness, his searching fingers found the button and pressed it.

The familiar twinkling glow began, taking him and the others back to Intrepid at last. He smiled up at the hideous face as the Draegaxx turned back and reached out for his disappearing form.

But it was too late.

Jacobs shouted at it through his blinding pain as the beam began the transfer. He shouted his victory at the monster of HellFear.

"I've found the perfect prison for you, undying Draegaxx – in the belly of a star!"

What Will Never Be

It was a coastline like many others, on countless other worlds.

There was sand, of course, and the never-ending march of waves.

One after the other the ocean bulged far beyond the breakers and unseen forces molded and fashioned and urged another newly coalesced wave forward. It gathered speed with each moment of its tragically short existence and rose higher until the waters began to curl and break in anticipation of its final rush into oblivion. Each wave quickened the closer it approached the beach until with a sudden rush of power it crashed headlong into the sand with a final eruption of spray.

But within seconds, Mother Ocean called the spent waters back to its bosom again.

And as quickly as one wave crashed, another took its place.

But this coastline was unique in many ways. The beach was the color of pure silver, and under the myriads of twinkling stars it seemed to glow. The waters beyond the breakers also glowed, but they shimmered with a purplish sheen from the billions of microscopic creatures who lived and died just under the ocean's surface.

On this isolated stretch of silver sand, two barefoot figures walked side by side with an easy and familiar gait.

Both Krangok warriors wore faded dress uniforms as if ready for some ancient ship-board inspection – except for their missing footwear. Long they walked, silent and content, each enjoying the cool salty breeze that caressed them amid the calming sound of the breakers.

But time does not stand still, not even for the Krangok.

"I feel a great emptiness inside me, Changra." Rass took a deep breath. He turned to the purple sea, staring out over the dark waters to the distant horizon that melted into the universe. His gray eyes narrowed, causing the deeply etched wrinkles to become more pronounced.

He gazed silently as they walked.

Changra felt his own heart pounding. He remembered the words he had carefully prepared these last weeks; he knew them by heart. And he knew the time had come for him to speak them. But he didn't.

He put off the inevitable event even as Rass did with his silent gaze over the ocean before them.

They continued their silent journey.

On the fresh night wind, the invigorating scent of the salt laden air seemed to infuse them, stirring the life force deep inside their souls. The ocean was always a place for healing.

And they needed its natural healing power, now more than ever.

A wave crashed with a mighty explosion of water and sent its foaming remnants swirling above their ankles. They felt the refreshing waters engulf their feet a moment. But seconds later, they felt the irresistible force of the ocean pulling the waters back from where it came. Standing still in the swirling, foam laced waters, they felt the tingling sensation as the sand under their feet eroded and gave way.

Finally, the wave was gone.

But they remained.

They walked forward again across the silver sand.

"Imagine... my building a house within sight of an ocean." Changra smiled. "And I would walk on the beach every night just like this - and swim in its waters every day." His smile grew wider.

"May your dream come true," Rass added wistfully.

But the pressing matter at hand would not go away.

With a sigh, Rass finally spoke.

"It is a great emptiness that hurts, my friend. It hurts more than a blast from a Hazor rifle, more even than forty strokes by barbed whip," he said with deep feeling. "And you know I have taken both."

Changra chuckled softly at the shared memory. After a moment of contemplation, he answered.

"Yet, recall it was I who nursed you back from that blaster wound all those long weeks, enduring your endless moans and groans – tending you like an old mother Gahen."

Rass raised his hands in mock defense. They smiled at each.

Changra continued. "But I too received the forty strokes... *plus one,* for that botched adventure on Jissus V." Changra shook his head and laughed out loud.

"You'll never let me forget that will you, you old Sargus hound!" Rass laughed.

They laughed together, remembering the adventures they had shared over the years. Their laughter slowly faded until the crashing of the waves again drowned all sounds.

Rass looked up at the wide-open sky filled with stars. "We have known each other more years than there are stars in this sky, my friend."

"True. And *all* of them good!" He added with great sincerity.

It was Rass' turn to burst out with laughter. He slapped his thigh and roared with his unbridled mirth.

He waited while Rass' laughter continued unabated. Changra fought the smile that finally materialized from the contagious sounds of his friend, but he gave in at last.

The two old warriors laughed together until their sides ached. Finally, their laughter subsided.

"Well, most of them were good." Changra admitted.

"The exploration of the Tradian system..." Rass raised a knowing finger. "*That* was an adventure!"

Changra rolled his eyes. "Yes, I had put that misadventure deep away in my memory and buried it." Changra shuddered. "That was the closest brush with death we've ever experienced." He nodded. "That indeed, was a time."

The two life-long friends looked deeply into each other's eyes.

Rass wore, for the first time in recent memory, the uniform in which he had received the Star of

Coronium, highest honor of the Krangok. The blue color had faded with time, but the gold of the emblem still shone brightly under the starlight.

Changra too wore a uniform of the past, from one of the early journeys among the unknown stars – so long ago now. Both reflected silently on the numerous adventures they had shared during their lifetime – a lifetime many ages longer than most sentient races lived – for the Krangok marked each stage of their life by ten thousand years.

An unseen bird above them squawked in its flight.

Changra drew his body up as if on military parade. His face grew harder at the deed ahead. He also felt the great emptiness that burned inside each of their hearts.

"I do not think I can do this thing, Rass."

They waited amid the never-ending sound of the crashing waves.

At this significant juncture in their lives, their friendship, they paused in awkward indecision, afraid to go further... but unable not to.

"We have each been given a great mission, my friend. The highest honor, orders from the Supreme Leader himself!" Changra said at last with chin held high.

"We are too old," Rass answered simply.

Changra's eyes narrowed angrily, he hesitated only a moment before he spoke. *"We are the best!"*

Their eyes locked and each smiled proudly.

But Rass' smile quickly faded. "That's not what I am afraid to do."

Rass' eyes filled with watery emotion as he looked back to the purple seas.

"We shall not say..." Changra, the accomplished speaker, paused in surprise as his voice faltered with emotion. He fought his burning embarrassment, coughing nervously, trying to find his voice to say his practiced words. Finally...

"We shall not say... *good-bye*. We need only wish the other success... and a safe journey."

"We go to the edge of the universe and beyond! Each Captain of our own vessel! And each of us will travel to the opposite ends of known space!" Rass' voice sounded angry even to himself. He stroked his beard, calming himself. He continued; his voice much subdued.

"Even a Krangok dies."

Somewhere deep inside, something happened to both – like a star suddenly going supernova.

Changra reached out and grasped Rass' arms. He held his friend and his eyes moistened with tears.

At first Rass felt puzzlement, Changra's hands dug so hard into his arms that it hurt. He reached out and grasped Changra with the same firmness.

They stood there, grasping each other, trying to hold on. Suddenly, they both felt the overwhelming power that they could not stop. It began to push them forward.

Changra and Rass gripped each other harder – trying to hold on a few more moments.

But they knew the moment had finally arrived.

They each released their grip on the other at the same time. They faced each other in stony silence.

Changra, the man of words, had no words now. The words he had memorized, the words he had practiced especially for this moment, disappeared from his mind.

It was Rass who spoke for them both.

"I will think of you often in the years to come..." He paused a second. "I will always remember you, my friend. I will always remember you..." Rass' voice cracked with his intense feelings. He swallowed painfully.

Now he spoke with an urgency, and he spoke from his heart.

"No matter where this long journey takes me, no matter what forms of life I meet." He smiled. "I will tell them that I have a friend. Though you are untold light years away, I will tell them of you. And we will laugh when I tell them about our many adventures together." A solitary tear streamed down the old warrior's cheek. "And I speak of the battles that we have fought together. And I will speak of the years, the ages that we have shared. Yes, they will hear that you... *Changra... are my friend.*"

Rass and raised his hand, pointing heavenward.

"Of all the things that I have lost in this life, of all the things I will dearly miss." Rass' hand began to shake. "You will be what I miss most."

Changra stood silent. Down into the depths of his soul, he felt Rass' every word. Many of his speeches came to mind – great oratory, moving words. But he had none for this occasion, this great sadness. They had all fled him.

Rass looked from the stars back to his companion.

And Changra gazed at him with tears streaming down his eyes like a steady autumn rain.

Rass smiled, raising his arms wide.

The men hugged each other tightly, pounding each other's back with love.

They held each other long in that warrior's embrace.

And finally, they released their hold and stood apart, rubbing their eyes briskly. Above them the stars twinkled brightly above the turbulence of the crashing surf. Silence marked the passing of their great melancholy.

"We shall see each other again – sooner than we think," Changra said with great sincerity, knowing it was a lie even as he uttered it.

Rass smiled at his friend's words, *knowing that it would never be*.

But it sounded so good.

"What a grand day that will be," Rass added, as if he believed it.

On that twilight beach they walked together one last time – side by side, with an easy familiar gait.

***

Rass and Changra never saw each other again.

Far, far away their separate journeys led. Wild, wonderful things awaited each – worlds of exquisite beauty, adventures among haunting, fantastic sites.

But despite their lasting separation, their friendship never ended. For in each, in their heart and their memory, they carried that friendship with them wherever they traveled.

Kragon's Gold

I know aliens –they're my specialty. I have to be, since humans are such a minority in this great, wide galaxy.

Most important, the expertise I gain by careful observation, detailed analysis and especially strong drink has gotten me out of a lot of jams, and I've been able to keep all my body parts intact – so far.

I pick up on things – little things - from their expressions, body language and especially their eyes – if they have four or fewer. More than four eyes, well, it just becomes confusing.

After a few drinks, a few hands of cards or some other bar game with an alien, I quickly learn his tendencies, his mannerisms. I soon understand what makes them laugh, what makes them angry, and what makes them tick.

It's a gift.

But even the best of us makes mistakes, right?

I was tired too.

We had been flying hard for seventy-two hours straight. Dtang gripped the starship's lone pilot's wheel, his ebony knuckles taut with his iron grasp. We were almost there, which was good, since we'd both missed two sleep periods and the energy pills were beginning to lose their effectiveness.

Kragon had picked his booty planet well.

A large asteroid field completely encircled the solitary planet and the star it orbited. Most of the asteroids showed up on our scans as only a few dozen meters in size – too small for any star charts, but large enough to shatter your shields and your hull if you struck one dead on. Worse, if there were any seeking mines, and knowing Kragon there were plenty, we would need to fly through at top speed to avoid their deadly grasp – and that wasn't the smartest thing to do in the middle of an uncharted asteroid field.

But there was the promise of treasure.

"I'm hungry."

I looked over at the hulking form guiding our fast starship – Dtang was big even for a Hollith. In the dim glow of the lights from the main console, his dark skin became barely discernible from the black of space that showed through the port window. Leaning back, the profile of his head and pointed snout blocked out enough stars so I knew he was still there.

"We'll be in the middle of those asteroids in a few minutes. Can't you wait?!" No doubt, my exasperation carried over into my tone.

The huge Hollith bared his fangs at me.

So, I figured he couldn't wait.

"How about a little specialty from Earth?" I asked tiredly, hoping he would decline.

A low growl rumbled from his muscular mid-section while used a talon tipped hand, one of four he possessed, to scratch the side of his face contemplatively.

"What this specialty?" He snarled questioningly.

"Peanut butter sandwich. Sticks to your ribs. Good source of protein, actually."

"Hmmmmmph! Never heard of this food!" His stomach growled again – a subtle sound like a low level nuclear explosion.

"Yes, Dtang needs something to fill belly." Dtang's large red eyes turned towards me. "Make me this Earth food. And," he pointed a claw directly at me. "Dtang *real* hungry, want it *really* stick to ribs!"

Holliths are not known for their manners, but I needed this big, bad one – especially now.

You see, old Captain Kragon had just kissed this universe good-bye. Dear old Kragon – that Pirate of all pirates, Cutthroat of all cutthroats, that… (well, you get the picture) Yes, Kragon had finally bought the farm – probably a blaster to his back, deservedly so.

Yeah, there wasn't a Trader or Space Pirate in all the twelve Quadrants that he hadn't cheated, swindled, lied to, or robbed. Of course, his killer may have come from the less savory likes of Planetary Governments, Royal Houses or Intergalactic Corporations that Kragon had *angered* in one way or another through his many misadventures – all of whom were certainly celebrating his unexpected demise.

Actually, it was more surprising that he hadn't been killed years ago!

However it happened, during his dying breath Kragon spilled the beans on one of his most closely guarded secrets – the whereabouts of his main treasure horde – and I mean the *big one*.

Such a deal.

But that meant, I knew, that a good number of other starships filled with his former enemies were hurtling to the exact same destination as Dtang and I.

Naturally, I was willing to share.

It's just that I couldn't trust some of these other low-lifes to reciprocate my good nature.

Now, I'm not a pirate, far from it. Besides, this wasn't really stealing – this particular treasure didn't belong to anybody right at the moment.

I'm more like an Independent Trader, though I don't really fall into that nebulous category either. Let's just say I'm a Galactic Opportunist – yeah, I like that one. And goodness knows there are plenty of sweet galactic opportunities out there, waiting for someone who knows what they're doing.

Which I do, *most* of the time.

Anyway, I wouldn't take all of it, just enough to see me through a few years of easy living on some tropical world with countless beaches, never ending glasses of adult beverages and lots of good-looking female-type alien babes.

Problem is, like I said, not everyone is as generous as I am.

So, I hired Dtang. He handles himself pretty well in a fight as long as the odds aren't more than, say, eight to one. And pound for pound, there's nothing meaner in the known galaxy than a Hollith when they're riled.

The tricky part is getting them riled at the right time.

And now wasn't the time.

I stumbled back to the small kitchen and ordered the computer to make a sandwich up the way I like 'em. See, I'm almost addicted to the stuff – I eat peanut butter every day. I crave it. So, I slap the stuff on thick, real thick. And because Dtang is so much bigger than me, well, I instructed the computer to make it about three times the size of a normal sandwich.

Like I said, I was tired. My mistake was that I forgot how Holliths eat – if you can call it eating.

After I sat back down in the darkened forward section next to him, I handed the two pieces of bread stuffed with over an inch of the thick brown specialty to him.

Dtang grabbed it with his lower right hand and stuffed the entire thing into his mouth.

My eyes opened wide while I watched in horrified fascination.

Dtang started chewing with rapid, appreciative motions of his massive jaws. But seconds later, the muscles in his cheeks began to bulge as he chewed in slower and slower motions and I knew that the peanut butter was adhering to his mouth's interior. Strange gurgling noises soon mixed with groans began to emanate from him – that's when I first realized something was wrong.

Suddenly, I remembered Hollith physiology – the stupid aliens don't have noses! Or nostrils… anywhere! They *have* to breathe through their mouths.

I stared in shocked realization – Dtang was going to have to breathe again and real soon!

And wouldn't you know it, right then, the ship's main alarm went off.

Our starship was on a collision course.

I looked out the forward viewscreen and noticed the first asteroids flying by.

91

Dtang steered calmly around the first few. But his chewing motions grew slower and slower and his eyes grew wider and wider.

I didn't get nervous until Dtang stood up in his chair – still grasping the pilot's wheel.

His ebony face grew a little paler as he tried to chew and breathe at the same time. The strangled noises mixed with groans increased. The glazed look in his eyes now froze my blood. But still those four muscular arms gripped that wheel while he calmly guided us around a few more asteroids.

With the alarm now blaring non-stop in my ears, I decided it was time to take over the wheel. But I couldn't even pry one of his fingers off.

He held it with a death-grip.

I looked into his dilated eyes – Dtang was going to suffocate before he swallowed that sandwich, or else we were going to be smashed into a million pieces by an asteroid.

Then and there, I realized that peanut butter is not good for a Hollith.

***

"Sensors show a ship approaching!"

Vicki Bronde walked over and peered down at the small sensor screen in front of the alien officer who sounded the alert.

"They're traveling at a very high rate of speed. They will easily beat us to the treasure," the junior officer added matter-of-factly.

"Put them on main viewscreen," Vicki ordered.

The main viewscreen came alive – in the center of the star field a small starship became visible. The ship was sleek, its hull obviously designed for speed. As they watched, something amazing began to happen.

The starship veered drastically around a large asteroid, barely missing it. Suddenly, the ship began to roll non-stop, first clockwise a few moments, and then after it righted its flight with a jerk, it began to roll counterclockwise. All the while the ship sailed in and around the growing number of asteroids with an obvious expertise for this kind of dangerous flying.

"They have inadvertently entered a thick portion of the asteroid field." The large reptilian captain stepped next to Vicki and the junior officer, all of them now watching the high-speed aerobatics with intense interest.

The three of them gasped as the starship – rolling clockwise once again – sailed right through a huge cluster of asteroids, barely missing a dozen by less than a meter. Still, just as the ship exited the first cluster and entered another, they noticed the ship's shields brighten under a glancing blow.

"They're flying a little hot to be in the middle of an asteroid field." Captain Tarec shook his head in disbelief.

While they peered at the viewscreen, the ship suddenly veered straight up.

It rolled counterclockwise again. The ship flew around one asteroid, suddenly changed direction and breezed under a second, and then flew straight toward a third, turning only at the last instant to avoid a head-

93

on collision – each time flying precariously closer and closer, barely avoiding total destruction.

All during the ship's full speed aerobatics, continually swerving and rolling and diving and the sudden changes of direction, the three on-lookers grew dizzy.

"They are very courageous," the junior office said with unabashed awe.

"I have never seen such magnificent flying in all my years as a raider." The captain smiled with admiration.

"Looks like he's flying drunk to me," Dran Rork said candidly.

The First Officer was the same alien species as Captain Tarec. He glanced at the newest crewmember of the Impaler. "Vicki, have you ID'ed that starship yet? It's obviously trying to beat us to Kragon's planet."

Eyeing the alien pirate carefully, Vicki paused a moment before she spoke. When she did, it wasn't to the First Officer but to the junior officer.

"Hrazz, run a check."

First one name and then a second, and in quick succession three more identified the same ship which appeared on their console. Vicki looked back at the viewscreen with a look of contempt mixed with a subtle hatred.

"How many names has that ship sailed under?" Dran asked.

The ship on the view-screen suddenly righted its flight and headed straight for the Impaler.

"Helm!" Captain Tarec screamed. "Hard over!"

Grabbing the corner of the console to keep from being thrown bodily across the bridge, Vicki stared at Tarec with shock.

"They can't possibly know we're here. We are still cloaked, right?" Vicki looked from Dran back to Tarec questioningly.

As the Impaler finished its turn, the ship on the view-screen rolled completely upside down and then veered off in the opposite direction from its original course.

"We are still cloaked," Tarec said with relief. "I think their turning for us was nothing more than coincidence."

"Shall we go to Battle Alert and destroy them ship to ship?" Dran asked with obvious enthusiasm.

All eyes returned to the viewscreen where the starship grew smaller with each passing second – still flying upside down.

"We outgun them, though they definitely can outrun us," Captain Tarec thought out loud.

"I suggest we let them pass us, let them get into orbit first. If they get through Kragon's defenses on the planet, they've done us a favor. We just follow their tracks and then attack them there. We'll have surprise on our side and will take them *easily,*" Vicki said with emphasis.

"Yes, yes. I don't relish fighting a ship with such a spectacular pilot at its helm. If they can shoot half as well as they fly... they could be more of a match than we want," Captain Tarec said with a nod.

Dran growled angrily and walked away.

The ship on the view-screen finally pulled into a tight turn, righted itself, and returned to its original course.   Now only a slight rocking of the ship indicated it was not on automatic pilot.

Vicki half-smiled/half-snarled with remembrance while the ship grew smaller and smaller – sailing straight for Kragon's gold.

She knew the captain of that ship, and she had a personal score to settle with him.

***

Dtang was wheezing horribly – brown peanut butter clung in gobs everywhere inside his wide-open, cavernous mouth.

I could tell, my own face was bare inches away. And mine were one pair out of three pairs of hands clutching the ship's wheel as we tried to right the ship one more time and evade collision.

I had decided it best to help Dtang steer just in case he suffocated in the middle of one of his desperate maneuvers.

But now we were through the worst of the asteroids, and even better, Dtang had almost chewed his way through the remnants of the brown mortar.

He was breathing again too, almost regularly, smacking those big lips with each successful intake of oxygen.

Life was getting better.

However, let me assure you that Hollith breath mixed with peanut butter will never be bottled. In fact, it would probably be banned on most civilized systems.

I swallowed queasily as I released my grip on the wheel.

After Dtang managed a final, mighty, gargantuan swallow – his gasping breaths returned to a semblance of normalcy. I fell back into my co-pilot's chair. It was right then that I realized how badly my stomach cramped. I needed the toilet – desperately. But I decided it prudent to wait for Dtang's reaction before I made a move.

After all, that sandwich had almost killed him – well, had almost killed both of us.

Dtang remained silent for only a moment after he took his first, unimpeded breath. He turned to me, red eyes glaring.

"Water!

I jumped out of my chair like it was on fire. But before I grabbed him some water, I did duck into the bathroom... just for a moment.

"Dtang need water! Now!!!"

There's nothing worse than an angry Hollith. I finished my business and grabbed a big glass of cool, refreshing H-two-O.

Dtang slugged the entire glass down in a single gulp, swishing the final ounces around his mouth to loosen the last clumps of the Earth delicacy. With a big sigh, he handed the empty glass back.

A *very* healthy belch vibrated the entire cockpit. And a strange smile spread over his face, a smile like only a Hollith can smile. He stared at me a moment before he spoke.

"One more peanut butter specialty and Dtang will be right."

I stared at him dumbfounded.

"Make it!"

I jumped up again – I was well practiced now – and headed toward the kitchen. From somewhere in the darkened confines of the cockpit, Dtang kept muttering to himself the same words over and over again.

"*Good* Earth food. *Strong* Earth food."

Believe me, I ordered the computer to make this next one with a little less peanut butter on it.

An hour later, we neared the small planet orbiting its orange star, both well inside the surrounding shield of asteroids. A quick scan revealed we were the only ship.

I never doubted it.

My starship, the White Lightning, is fast – a modified Hariette Fast Recon class. She's tachyon injected with turbolight-powered hyper-space engines – twin powerhouses encased in solid titanium blocks. Yeah, I personally installed those sweet Thunderbolts – the fastest engines known in this part of the galaxy.

She's even outran a few Szellian Corvettes, and not too many starships can lay claim to that kind of speed.

We continued scanning, for good reason. Ship's scanners soon found a faint trace of electronic equipment, no doubt the first line of defense protecting Kragon's treasure horde while he was away – which he was, permanently.

Dtang landed us on a plain just outside the jungle that ringed our target inside its leafy confines – a partially hidden cave entrance. We figured the odds were more in our favor going on foot – at least with the first line of defense.

Still, we had only gone a few hundred feet when my hand-held scanner started blinking continuously. I signaled Dtang to slow down with a wave of my hand – this would be the most dangerous part.

Successful space-pirates like Kragon usually had several caches hidden away. There was no need to put all your gold bars in one basket, so to speak. But each one would be guarded with the most sophisticated weapon systems. And Kragon, with all that money, would keep them upgraded with the latest military grade electronics available.

It's common knowledge that most who try to take gold from an Azarian pirate's treasure horde never live to tell the tale. But I'm better than most, and I planned to do more than live after we left this planet with the gold.

We continued forward and almost made it to the overgrown path that led through the jungle when I held my hand up for a stop.

I pointed to some bones scattered among the tall weeds about two hundred feet away in the middle of the little-used path.

"Weapons?" Dtang whisper-growled.

"Booby traps," I whispered back.

A look of total confusion spread over Dtang's features – an almost natural expression for Holliths.

"What this Booby trap?"

"Devices that trap boobies. Or anyone else stupid enough to get caught by them."

Dtang grunted acknowledgement.

I adjusted my scanner and frowned. There were mines, of course, but they would be easy enough to walk around once I tagged the signatures for each individual type Kragon and his crew had planted.

But there was something else. The wide dispersal of some of the bones...

I tuned my scanner farther out and found them.

My scanner pinpointed two hidden gun emplacements on either side of the path located just inside jungle – Azarian Model RX-5s. Nasty things – rapid fire with bio-locks – anyone or anything living and breathing and foolish enough to come within range so the guns could obtain a lock – and poof!

Using my hand-held, I started hacking my way into their system. I probably couldn't disable them; they held subroutines to detect that blatant kind of a hack. No, I was just going to add a few lines of code that would confuse the bio-locks and make it possible for us to pass right by. I'd have to repeat it on the way out, but first things first.

"Got it." I smiled victoriously at Dtang. "Let's go. But follow my every move; we've got to go around these mines real careful."

"Dtang understand."

We moved quickly, Dtang following my circuitous route among the minefield as we side-stepped some and hopped over others. We picked up our pace a little more as we started passing by several of the grisly remains right in the midst of the gun's range.

We both heard the RX-5s swivel toward us, but they never fired, not being able to obtain a firm bio-lock.

I smiled to myself.

We almost made it through the minefield... when I heard it.

A high-pitched sound pierced the air and sent chills up my spine – the long whistling sound-of-death that meant an Azarian mortar was priming itself and getting ready to fire its projectile toward its target.

That meant us.

Just as the foreboding whistling stopped, I flinched. The resulting explosion knocked both Dtang and myself to the ground. As I lay there, I realized it had gone off way too soon.

In a flash, I resync'ed my scanner and found it expertly hidden off to one side of the RX-5s. I should've figured – Kragon had three layers of defense. I also found out why it exploded too early – with the passing months some of the forest had grown over its emplacement, the mortar had taken out the top of a nearby tree.

My scanner blared out a warning tone – the Azarian mortar was locked on us again and rearming.

"Move!"

With its firing path clear now, we were sitting ducks.

If we were moving fast before, we flew now. Holding my scanner out before me to avoid the mines, we danced and hopped past the last dozen or so like a couple of caffeine injected aliens.

The whistling roar of the incoming mortar suddenly grew deafening.

We jumped the last mines in a single, mighty bound, rolled into the tall grass, leapt back to our feet and threw ourselves behind the trunk of an ancient, fallen forest giant.

As we landed, the air filled with shrapnel along with the roar of the mortar detonating – too close for comfort.

But we'd made it.

We paused a few seconds until we remembered how to breathe on our own again. Finally, I looked over at Dtang with a semblance of renewed confidence.

"Well, we made it past the first line of Kragon's defenses. Things should be easy until we get inside the cave."

Dtang glared at me with growing distrust.

"Hey, c'mon now. We're still alive, right?"

Yeah, he had to agree with that, our hearts were trying to leap out of our chests – at least mine was.

Still, I did a very thorough scan before we moved. But there was nothing – no weapons, no power signatures, nothing except the normal flora and fauna.

"Stay alert, Dtang," I said as we got up to make our final sprint to the cave and the treasure within. "I figure Kragon's got at least one attack droid at the entrance and maybe one or two other toys beyond. But I can't read anything through solid rock. We'll have to take it real slow when we reach the entrance."

Dtang grunted approval.

"I'll need to check the cave ceiling for hidden charges too, Azarian's have a bad habit of wanting to entomb any would-be robbers. We'll want to disable those first." I winked confidently.

"And then treasure!" Dtang smiled.

"We'll cross that little item when we get to it, and I'm sure Kragon will have something special waiting there too." I grimaced with the thought of all the nasty things that Kragon probably had in place.

But I had a few tricks of my own.

I felt around inside my utility belt, mentally checking off some of my own special toys. My fingers came to a pocket that held one of my favorite devices.

"Ever see one of these?" I held up the small, round metallic device.

"What this?" Dtang admired it with a nod.

Smiling, I rolled it in my hand like a well-used baseball.

"These little toys are hard to find, Dtang. They call it a DENG – short for de-energizer grenade. Quite illegal, you know. You've heard their motto I'm sure – 'Deng'em with a DENG, before they DING you.'"

Dtang nodded with fuzzy remembrance.

"Anyway, I picked this one up at the edge of the quadrant, part of my payment from my last little job." I smiled knowingly.

Putting it back, I noticed Dtang's look of doubt. "I've used it a few times when fire-fights get a little too intense for my taste. It has the remarkable ability to drain off the charges from any type of blaster within a range of fifty meters – rendering them useless. It even sucks out any spare charges an alien might be carrying – bringing the fight down to a more *personal* level." I chuckled, noticing the look of eagerness cross Dtang's face as he bared his fangs.

"Dtang like this DENG!"

"Yeah, a DENG can be a handy deng… thing."

We came around a bend in the jungle path and there before us was the cave entrance. The jungle growth almost hid it from view, and I might have missed it except my scanner showed it plainly despite the tangle of overhanging vines and brush. But my scanner revealed more of Kragon's own toys – two more automated guns even now seeking a lock on us. And two others located deeper in the growth came active.

I pushed Dtang back behind some brush on the side of the path. Silently, I reached into my belt and pulled out my Scrambler. I needed to completely disable these bad-boys, I figured when we came back out, we might be in a bit of a hurry and would not want to fiddle with them again.

Quickly, my fingers tapped in the instructions as I hacked into the gun's controls. Kragon was falling down on the job here; these were older type Azarian military issue, their programming fairly well known. I'd hacked these models before.

In a few short seconds, my scrambler did its work. One by one the lights on my scanner showed each gun going silent as they powered down – and they wouldn't power up any time soon, either.

I took one more careful scan, just to make sure there was nothing else guarding the entrance. Satisfied, we started for the cave and Kragon's treasure.

"There is one problem with a DENG, though," I said as we drew near the tangle of vines.

"What that?"

"Once it's used, it takes almost two hours before its ready for another go. So, use it wisely."

I chuckled as we passed the first silent gun – well pleased with myself once again. We stopped short when we came to the tangle of vines that now completely covered the ground under our feet. Prudently, I scanned for anything I might have missed now that we were up close and personal.

I found the expected charges above the cave's entrance, but to my surprise they were already disarmed. That seemed odd.

Oh well, don't look a gift Ansy in the mouth, as they say.

"All clear?" Dtang asked.

"All clear," I whispered with confidence. "No sign of weapons, electronic surveillance, or any technical signatures at all, except for the natural growth around us."

We stepped forward, pushing aside some of the vines hanging across the cave entrance.

Suddenly, the entire universe went upside down.

Dtang howled and I let out a startled yell of my own. It felt like my left leg almost jerked out of my hip socket. I bent upward trying to relieve the pain – but to no avail.

We hung upside down a moment in silence.

I vaguely noticed Dtang staring daggers at me. I tried to ignore him as my embarrassment grew.

I was none too happy either – we'd been caught by the oldest trap in the book, a hidden rope snare. And worse, it was all so low-tech!

Dtang growled menacingly at me as he swung in slow arcs from the rope attached to an unseen limb above us.

"Dtang think we must be boobies now. Trapped like harr-rats in a trap."

"It's all right, don't worry." I started fishing in my utility belt for a blade. "Nothing major, Dtang," I said with growing irritation as I tried to find my knife and couldn't – I hardly used the thing anymore. "We'll cut our way out of this and continue on in just a bit."

But the surprises just kept coming.

From out of the darkness of the cave two surly-looking Azarians appeared with blasters set to kill – not a good sign. In a flash, one of them pulled out his short sword and cut us down while the other kept a steady blaster aimed on us.

"Who are they?" An unseen Azarian asked from the darkness.

My stomach knotted up as I recognized the all-too familiar voice. I turned my disbelieving eyes toward the cave.

Kragon.

He looked a lot bigger in real life.

And it hit me – life! Kragon was alive!

Kragon, like all Azarians, are fierce aliens with muscular bodies covered by short, gray fur except for a shock of shoulder length, jet-black mane that grew in the middle their head and down their neck. Kragon stood head and shoulders above the other two warriors as he stepped closer, eyeing us warily – I figured he was easily the equal of Dtang in stature and build.

"So, what have we here, Razon?"

"I don't recognize either of them, sir," Razon snarled with contempt. "They are not *known* enemies, at any rate."

Kragon stepped right before me with black eyes glaring. "Who are you human? And why did you come here to die?"

Oh great, I thought. That's not why I came here. I grimaced as my mind raced for a good answer.

"Wrong turn?" (Hey, it was partly true.)

Kragon pulled his blaster out and slammed the butt hard into my ribs, causing me to grunt with pain. He turned it around and pushed the business end of the blaster into my ribs while he smiled at me – which I didn't like either.

"A petty thief, eh? Perhaps wanting some of Kragon's treasure after hearing about my most unfortunate demise?" Kragon twisted the blaster a bit for emphasis, sending another bolt of pain through me.

I looked over at Dtang. He rolled his red eyes with disgust.

"Well, we figured you didn't have a need for it anymore…" I groaned as Kragon sent his fist into the ribs on my other side, so now everything hurt with equal pain across my body.

Kragon seemed to enjoy my responses, so he hammered me a second time. I bent over as I tried – very hard mind you – to breathe through all the pain.

"Well, puny human. I have staged this little party to rid myself of a few of my enemies. I counted on their blind greed to bring them here fast after I leaked out this location, along with my death." He laughed out loud, obviously enjoying himself. "And if the mined asteroid field didn't get them, or my hidden guns among them or some of my other devices here on the surface, they would find me and my crew waiting patiently to greet them with our blasters."

I remained bent over, still learning how to breathe through bruised (and probably broken) ribs. I felt an iron grip on my shoulder and suddenly I was standing straight up and staring into Kragon's eyes.

Kragon stared mercilessly at me.

"But I was most impressed by your skills as pilot – or the Hollith. You flew so fast through the asteroid field and executed your maneuvers so skillfully, well, my hidden guns could never get a lock on you." Kragon's iron gripped tightened. "What is the secret to your skills?"

"Peanut… butter!" I wheezed painfully.

"Take note of that, Razon!" Kragon ordered a nearby office. "Look it up under skills peculiar to humans."

He turned back and firmly patted the side of my face.

"You have ruined only some of my fun – for which you will pay dearly."

"Kragon!" Razon pointed at another Azarian emerging from the cave. Kragon turned to the newcomer.

The new Azarian raised his clenched fist before his bowed face as he stopped under Kragon's glare. He held the salute a moment before he spoke. "Long-range sensors report two ships destroyed by mines on the star side. Another ship on the moon side has been destroyed by our guns. Just now, six ships have ended a battle in orbit right above us – with five ships destroyed."

"Eight less of my enemies," Kragon growled with pleasure.

"The surviving ship has just landed. We've identified it as the Impaler. Its occupants are now coming this way. We expect them here in eight minutes."

"Even better," Kragon added. "Any others?"

"Yes, two more ships have just entered the asteroid field from opposite sides. We expect them and one other very soon."

Kragon returned his blaster to his holster. "Take these two away and chain them. They are small game. I'll deal with them later."

The two Azarian pirates quickly removed my blaster as well as the assault blaster strapped in its holster across my back. I held my breath, but they took my utility belt anyway. I could've spit as they placed all my stuff in a large bag and one of them threw it over his shoulder.

They took Dtang's weapons just as efficiently.

They led us deep inside the dark cave. Finally, the two Azarians stopped near a pile of chains and shackles – they looked well-used.

Holding out his four burly arms in response to their urgings, the guards wisely chained Dtang first.

I stood there in the dim light, my mind working overtime to come up with some way out of this little predicament. But for once, I thought of nothing.

The distant sound of blaster fire came to our ears. It lasted only a few short minutes. I didn't know if I should mentally hope for the newcomers or not, they might dispose of us just as quickly as Kragon would. But Kragon is Kragon, so I decided to pull for the newcomers anyway – for the little it was worth.

Dtang and I stood silent before the two Azarians. I knew Dtang was waiting for an opening and I hoped I could make one.

But timing is everything in an escape, so I bided my time a little longer.

The sound of footsteps grew louder, footsteps coming toward us from the cave's entrance and the brief fire fight that ended too quickly.

The surprises kept coming.

They led the beautiful blonde right up to me – probably because she was human too.

I tried to keep a straight face, but I guess my mouth falling open gave it all away. Humans are still rare in this part of the galaxy, but still, I never expected to see *her* again.

"You do know her then," the Azarian escorting her barked.

"Uh, yes," I groaned.

"No!" Vicki shouted simultaneously.

She put her hands on her hips and stared angrily at me – if looks could kill I'd have been a goner then and there. She certainly hadn't gotten any friendlier since the last time we saw each other.

"Who is she?" Her guard asked angrily.

"My ex-wife."

She looked me up and down with those big, blue eyes as if I were O'landa garbage.

Nightmares do come true.

"His name is Chase Broughton. But he's no pirate – not smart enough." Vicki glanced at Dtang, mild surprise showing on her face.

Her eyes narrowed with thought.

"Thanks," I replied sarcastically.

She gave me that special look that I had tried so hard to forget all this time – an expression of absolute contempt.

Of all the worlds in this great, wide galaxy and I had to land on the one with my ex-wife. Where was the justice in it all? The only thing left now was for Kragon to walk in and put me out of my misery.

At least Kragon would be quick about it.

"He's not worth the effort to kill. Just throw him out with the trash!"

The three guards fixed their gaze on her in anticipation of a fight brewing between us.

She moved closer, until her face was inches from mine. She glanced quickly at Dtang and then winked at me.

She turned back to the guards.

"But his starship, now that is something worth taking. One of the fastest in all the known quadrants." She smiled as the three Azarian guards looked at each other.

"You never did know when to keep your mouth shut!" I sneered, putting some extra vehemence in my tone for good measure

"Yeah, I should've figured you were somewhere around, what with everything going wrong almost from the start of this little jaunt. A deal to-good-to-be-true, that was always your style, wasn't it Chase?" Vicki stepped closer until we were only inches apart.

111

She smiled dangerously. "When I recognized your ship, I should've recommended we pull out then. But we all know how strong the power of gold is, don't we?"

Her tone became downright icy.

"I couldn't decide back there if I was hoping you'd miss those asteroids... or slam into one and go out in a million pieces." She glared at me a moment to let her words stab a little deeper.

She was really going to make me mad.

"You make for good entertainment, though you always manage to screw it up in the end!"

A man can only take so much. I've faced pirates, assassins, automated attack droids and the like, but even if Vicki had a plan, this was getting to be too much.

The three Azarians began laughing out loud.

"Ah yes, those long, agonizing months being married to you are coming back to me. You've only been here for five minutes, and I remember *exactly* why I left you!"

I don't believe I've ever been slapped that hard my entire life.

Two of the Azarian's bellowed with laughter so hard that their eyes teared up. The one that brought Vicki bent over he was laughing so hard.

Even Dtang began to chuckle.

"Shut up, Hollith!" One of the guards shouted.

The guard covering her turned to watch the other two as they approached Dtang to put a gag on him.

With a flash of movement, Vicki reminded me how good she was in a tight spot.

With a twist of her body, she sent her foot hard into the guard's chest. The Azarian bent over double and then Vicki brought her fists down on the back of his neck, sending him down onto the ground.

I turned, just in time to see Dtang swing into action. The guards had gotten too close, even with his four arms chained. Dtang grabbed one each with his lower right and left hand and began working them over with his fists using his upper arms. He managed to knock one of the blasters away, but the other Azarian began firing wildly while Dtang held onto him.

I thought about helping him, but instead found myself diving out of harm's way.

Behind me, Vicki put the finishing touches on her Azarian while I simply tried to keep from getting shot.

Dtang's blows came quick and fast as he kept his grasp on both Azarians.

Finally, after getting the right angle, I jumped on the back of the Azarian firing his weapon and grabbed the arm that held the blaster.

Dtang sent one of his fists right into his face and we both went down. The Azarian went limp for just a moment, but it was enough.

I rolled away from him with his blaster in my hands. Keeping the barrel aimed at him while he glared back, I took a quick look to see how Dtang was faring with the last guard.

Dtang delivered three quick blows and that was it.

I could tell right away that an extra set of arms are a good thing in a fight.

Setting the blaster to stun, I put the last Azarian's lights out. Grabbing the keys off his belt, I quickly unchained myself and Dtang while Vicki retrieved the other two blasters laying on the ground. I retrieved our confiscated weapons, including my utility belt with its goodies.

I stunned the other two guards lying on the ground just for good measure, we didn't need them waking up too soon.

"Now we leave?" Dtang asked.

I started to answer, but...

"It's a good thing you're still so sensitive." Vicki said with a smile. "Or my little plan wouldn't have worked quite so well."

"Did you have to slap me *that* hard." I rubbed the side of my face tenderly.

"I had to make it real."

"I think you enjoyed it a little too much."

"Chase Broughton, why in the world would I ever want to hurt you?" She smiled innocently but her blue eyes sparkled with mischief.

The sound of dozens of blasters firing continuously diverted our attention – they came from the direction of the cave entrance. It sounded like Kragon was entertaining more of his friends, and from the sound of it he was getting more than he bargained for – it sounded like a small army was dueling it out.

That was fine with me.

But I had something to do before we cut and run. Actually, two things now that I had my toys back.

"No, we go this way, deeper into the mountain. I'm thinking Kragon's treasure is really here."

"You think so?" Vicki asked doubtfully.

"I believe Kragon turned one of his treasure hordes into an ambush, using the concealed traps and weapons already in place and adding a few more. If you study the sensors, you'll notice that some of them have been here a long time, long enough for the jungle to grow so thick that it even got in the way of some."

Dtang smiled.

"And we are well past Kragon and the cave's defenses now," I added.

"Okay," Vicki said with a hint of hope. "Let's go see if we can find some gold – enough to make this thing worth-while."

I love it when I'm right.

"But let me use my scanner and check, just in case. Knowing Kragon, we can't be too careful." They both nodded. "And keep your blasters on stun – we're not pirates, remember? At least Dtang and I aren't," I added for good measure.

Vicki glared at me.

A short time later, we found the treasure.

Naturally, there were two attack droids guarding it. Good thing I had spotted them.

I destroyed one with my assault blaster while Dtang took out the other with his, and the treasure was ours for the taking.

Unfortunately, we could only take as much as we could carry. Although Kragon's treasure was deep inside the cave, there was only one way in and one way out – the way we had come. And that meant we had to get through Kragon's party in one piece.

We hurried back down the tunnel toward the sound of blaster fire, which seemed to grow more intense the closer we got. I was panting under the weight of the two bags if gold I had slung across my left shoulder while I kept my eyes glued to my hand-held scanner. Dtang carried four bags across his left shoulder, holding the rope with his two left hands while he wielded a blaster in each of his two right hands. Vicki carried four small sacks inside a backpack. She carried her assault blaster at the ready.

Finally, we came to the cavernous room just inside the entrance. The rapid fire of blasters echoed eerily off the high cavern walls all around us as we crept to the edge.

This was it.

We were one level above the all-out melee below. I made out the tunnel that led to the cave entrance on the far side. Not only would we have to get down to the main level below, but we also had to get through Kragon and every other space-pirate scum known in this sector – all crowded together and firing at anything that moved.

It wasn't going to be easy, especially lugging all this treasure.

A sudden hailstorm of blasters lit up the cavern room like fireworks on 'Galactic Day.'

I felt my heart beating faster – this was actually going to be fairly dangerous.

Unless…

I smiled confidently, feeling like my old self again. Turning to Dtang, who gazed longingly at the fight below. I could see he was sad at being left out of all the fun. I motioned for him to come closer.

Quickly, I whispered to him. He growled disbelief only once as I revealed my ad-hoc plan. Then the big, ugly Hollith began to chuckle with pleasure while he flexed his muscles with growing anticipation. I saw by the gleam in his beady red eyes that he loved it – a plan perfect for any fun loving Hollith.

"Vicki," I whispered. "Give Dtang your weapons."

She gave me one of those *are-you-out-of-your-mind* looks – just like old times.

"We're going to DENG'em."

"What?" she asked.

But she complied, with a gentle hint from Dtang, who simply grabbed the blaster right out of her hand.

Dtang hurried back toward the treasure-end of the cave with our blasters and an ammo belt of spare charges. I counted three minutes to give him time to get out of range.

Yeah, things were about to get interesting down below.

I was going to play the great equalizer – and make things less dangerous at the same time.

I calculated the total area with my scanner and determined the best spot that would affect everyone and everything in the cavern below.

Pockets of alien fighters were spread out everywhere below – aliens of almost every size and shape and none of them very friendly looking either – firing back at the Azarians and sometimes at each other when the mood hit them. Shooting from behind boulders and crags, it was a complete free-for-all. I also noticed the numerous forms of those who had fallen.

Kragon had placed his Azarians around three main points of the cavern, giving them a deadly crossfire. I looked along the edge of the upper level I was on. It encircled the entire room and I noticed at various points that a few of Kragon's Azarians fired down with deadly accuracy. He had them pinned down below, confused and trapped, and the Azarians were picking them off one by one.

The poor aliens didn't stand a chance.

I pulled the DENG out of my belt and set the timer.

My movement caught the eye of an Azarian warrior directly across from me on the same level, but on the far side.

He pointed his blaster my way. Rock exploded all around me and I ducked behind some cover and heaved the DENG. Time seemed to slow as I watched the silver orb as it rose in an arc through the air.

The Azarian's blaster fire made rocks explode all around me again. It suddenly stopped.

Foolishly, I wondered why.

I glanced up over the edge of the boulder for a look-see and realized with a sickening rush he had the business end of his assault blaster pointing right between my eyes – not a good feeling even from fifty meters away.

The Azarian smiled and I watched his finger tighten on the firing contact.

The entire room exploded with a blinding flash of light as the DENG went off like a miniature star gone nova.

My face and skin grew hot as if I were inside some huge cosmic oven.

There must have been a lot of blasters in that cavern!

A DENG is awesome enough when it sucks the energy out of every weapon in range. I had used them only a handful of times – only when I had to, of course. Like I said, they're very rare and once you use one, it's hard to get them back in all the resulting chaos.

I shielded my eyes from the blinding glow, trying to find the white-hot center that would indicate the location of the DENG as it fell to the ground.

"Look!" Vicki shouted, pointing below.

Aliens everywhere were dropping their blasters or pulling them out of holsters as if they were on fire – which in essence they were, as my neat little DENG sucked their power into its complex circuitry.

I closed my eyes as the intensity became unbearable. With a sigh, I knew I would just have to take a good guess on where it landed and try to get close enough to turn on retrieval mode.

It took about three whole seconds for everyone down below to realize what happened – all their blasters were useless now.

Now, the real fun started.

I figured there were portions of about seven alien crews trapped by Kragon down there. They rushed the Azarians with their fists held high. Kragon found himself suddenly outnumbered. Still, the fierce Azarians rose as one to meet this frontal assault.

I could tell by the size of the Azarians that this was going to be one humdinger of a fight.

Oh well, Kragon seemed to have a thing for low-tech traps; an old-fashioned brawl with bare knuckles would be right up his alley.

I heard footsteps behind me.

Dtang threw my blasters at me, which I caught with a smile.

"Remember, keep 'em set to stun. Charges last longer."

Dtang groaned and rolled his eyes, but he complied.

I strapped on my holsters and Vicki did the same. I noticed a certain *eagerness* in Dtang's face as he watched the hand-to-hand fighting below. And this was the exact reason why I had hired him for this trip.

"Dtang," I leaned closer to him. "I need to retrieve my little toy somewhere over there in that pocket of fighting." I pointed to the largest group of aliens battling it out. "I need you to clear a path for me."

Dtang smiled wolfishly.

Vicki gasped, pointing right behind me.

That same Azarian who had targeted me earlier was approaching, his useless weapon in hand as he popped out one empty charge and slapped in another – useless but unknown to him.

I pulled out my assault blaster from my shoulder holster and stunned him down.

Vicki smiled approvingly.

"Well, you have some talent left after all."

I smiled.

She stared down at the growing melee below. It seemed fists and bodies flew in every direction.

"By the way, I like that little DENG of yours."

"Handy, isn't it."

We both ducked as a rock flew over our heads from below.

"It sure gets a party hopping."

"I'll say."

I handed her a blaster as she tightened her backpack.

"Ready to go to the party, dear?" I asked in mock politeness.

She smiled and raised her assault blaster.

"Dtang and I are going to pay our respects to Kragon before we blow this party. My starship is primed to go." I looked at her questioningly. "Want to fly out with us?"

She took a deep breath. "My crew got shot to pieces and are scattered down there. Maybe I will join you – for a while."

"Don't let me force you."

She rolled her eyes.

Fierce shouting turned our attention to the raging fisticuffs below. A group of Kragon's personal warriors gathered close around him while angry alien fighters pressed in from all sides.

I looked over at Dtang. "Time to crash this party."

Raising his two upper arms above his head, Dtang stood, roaring out the legendary Hollith battle challenge. The fighting below slowed as many of the combatants looked around fearfully for the source of that ear-splitting roar.

Dtang laid the bags of gold on the ground. Clenching three hands into fists while he clenched a blaster in the fourth, Dtang leapt out into the air.

My mouth dropped open.

I watched in awe as Dtang landed on top of three aliens below. Pounding them unconscious with a few quick blows, he jumped among the next four and lit into them with his fists flying and his blaster stunning the rest.

He left a path of fallen aliens behind him as he moved on to the next group.

I love to watch a Hollith enjoying himself.

I quickly tied one of Dtang's bags of gold to her backpack and then I grabbed one and attached it to the rope hanging over my shoulder. We'd have to leave the other two because I was going to have a hard time walking straight carrying what I had.

"Here, this way is a bit safer." Vicki pointed behind me.

She pointed out a rope ladder and we scurried down it after we carefully dropped our loads first. I fired a few times as we made our way down each time I noticed a someone running toward our bags of gold. And then I simply started stunning folks to help keep the confusion at a high level, especially if I noticed any particular group starting to get the upper hand in the pockets of fighting all around us.

We jumped down the last rungs, grabbed our gold and took off in the wake of Dtang's path.

Dtang was a one-Hollith wrecking crew – he'd gone through half a dozen small battles and either laid everyone low with his fists or stunned them. A line of unconscious aliens showed us the way to Dtang.

A few minutes later, we drew close to the main pocket of fighting clustered around the flowing mane of Kragon. Kragon was holding his own, pummeling anyone who got near him while fists and groans filled the air all around him.

Kragon seemed to be the most popular alien here.

We finally drew close to Dtang as he punched it out with a couple of tough Azarians at the edge of all the fighting near Kragon.

I suddenly realized that very few people had ever gotten this close to Kragon and ever lived. An idea hit me just as I ducked a fist sent in my direction. I quickly stunned its owner. Grabbing my scanner, I did a quick scan up and down Kragon's muscular frame. I had no idea what to scan for in particular, but you never know.

Kragon picked up a stout, reptilian alien pirate over his head and started to smash him upon the floor, when he spotted me with my scanner pointed right at him.

I could feel his anger.

Still holding the struggling warrior over his head with only one hand, he pointed an angry, finger at me.

I worked my scanner quickly – something about the rings on his fingers, the ancient runes carved on them – and the strange tattoo on his bared bicep from where his uniform had been torn got my attention. I scanned him thoroughly, better than anyone before me, I was sure.

Suddenly, I remembered.

A dark rumor whispered in the pubs and taverns where Traders and Pirates frequent far from Azarian space – the right hand of Kragon holds the secret of all his treasure worlds. I didn't know if it was true. But even though there was a sizeable cache of treasure here (which would probably be gone by daybreak), it was obviously not Kragon's fabled treasure trove.

Kragon flung the alien down with a thud. Roaring his rage, he headed straight for me, his eyes filled with death.

I stunned two Azarians right next to him, which allowed two more of the reptilian pirates to pounce on Kragon while more Azarians and others to rushed in.

"Let's go!" I skirted past Vicki. She followed, keeping a keen eye behind us. I punched my sensor again and again until I finally got results – from among a pile of weapons and unconscious aliens my DENG came flying toward my outstretched hand – I love that retrieval mode. After putting it safely away in my utility belt, I made for the exit.

Ahead of us, Dtang fought his way toward two Azarians that guarded the tunnel entrance. After a sudden flurry of fists, he made it to them.

Dtang grabbed one of them and flung him aside like a toy while he stunned down the other. Two more rushed him. Grabbing each in a mighty grasp, he punched first one and then the other with unusually great enthusiasm, even for a Hollith. He stunned a couple of other aliens who stumbled too close to his fun.

Dtang pummeled them a few moments more until both Azarians went limp.

They were all down for the count when Vicki and I stepped beside Dtang.

"Well, it's been fun Dtang. But we mustn't overstay our welcome."

Dtang looked positively sad.

We rushed down the tunnel together, leaving the melee behind us still going in full swing. Fortunately, we didn't run into any stragglers late for Kragon's party – none still alive, that is. Kragon had been very efficient – even deadly. The sound of the fighting behind us began to die down right as we burst into sunlight.

***

Kragon stood resolutely among the fallen, his great chest rising and falling from his exertions. Only five of his remaining warriors joined him as he surveyed the carnage all around.

Shaking his black mane, Kragon spoke. "Razon! Signal my ship to prepare and lift. We will do battle with any fools still in orbit." Kragon's eyes narrowed dangerously.

Razon bowed his head to his clenched right fist in salute as he stepped away to relay Kragon's orders.

"Hraag! Get weapons and kill all those left alive."

"I'll have to retrieve them from our ship."

"Do it!"

Hraag looked around with a furtive glance. "What about our wounded?"

"Only the strong fly with Kragon. Kill all that cannot stand!"

Among the Azarians, crumpled forms began to rise hurriedly.

Suddenly, everyone crouched in fear as a sonic boom rumbled and shook the cavern, sending loose rocks falling like rain from the ceiling high above. Kragon alone stood tall, staring upward, almost as if he could see straight through the solid rock of the mountain above.

Kragon raised his fist heavenward, clenching his teeth and growling each word with bitter rage.

"I have defeated my enemies today in spite of you, human!"

Kragon's ferocious growls mixed with the rumblings of the fading sonic boom. "And know this," he whispered savagely to himself in solemn oath. "Chase Broughton, today you are an enemy of Kragon! I vow to hunt you down and deal with you personally."

**

I jumped into the pilot's chair and rammed the power full. It was time to redline those tachyon-injected engines, and they roared nicely as we climbed into the air.

The G forces smashed me back into my seat while I gripped the wheel. Sensors showed three ships in orbit above us, so I quickly banked the White Lightning in the opposite direction after we cleared the upper atmosphere. I heard all kinds of loose equipment falling in the back as those big engines screamed.

I didn't pull back on the power until we cleared the last of the asteroids and the mines.

As I dove around the last one, I banked the ship over. I even impressed myself as we left those three starships in our dust.

Dtang laughed the entire time, begging to take the wheel. But I only handed it over after we had made our jump to hyperspace.

I was totally exhausted now. All I wanted was my soft bunk and a well-earned snooze. And to gaze proudly at the small, but choice amount of gold we had managed to carry off.

Yeah, life was good.

"The Impaler was one of the ships giving chase back there." Vicki gave me one of her old looks. "You can drop me off at the first registered planet in this sector."

I sighed a moment, rolling my eyes. "I want to get some distance between us and Kragon. We'll figure it out tomorrow."

She glared at me.

"Dtang, disarm her."

I heard Dtang move a little too enthusiastically.

"Let me reword that order – take her weapons."

I turned around, to make sure he understood me.

She gritted her teeth and handed her blaster over to him. "I have to admit, you did one thing today that *really* impressed me."

I turned.

"I've never seen anyone fly through an asteroid field faster than your ship today. It was amazing." Vicki paused. "How'd you learn to do that?"

I paused a moment, took a breath, and smiled innocently.

"Peanut butter."

Her dumbfounded expression was priceless.

"Dtang hungry! Make another peanut butter specialty!"

I chuckled under my breath while I ordered the food processor to make one up. I tried not to think about all the rest of the treasure we had left behind – after all, one must learn how to be content – right? I also didn't think too much about how close to death we had come – again.

I hate to dwell on negative things.

I handed him the sandwich and he gulped it down with a smile.

"Strong earth food. Dtang like!"

Now, it was nap time. I headed back to my bunk, feeling pretty good again.

After all, tomorrow would be another day in the great, wide galaxy.

And another adventure awaited...

By the Numbers

Armies of the heaven, the stars ge`o'vud!
The ethereal ocean, golden nebulae of Sirese.
All these wonders I knew and loved.

The floating Castles Dranymeirre;
Noble borne in mokron skies
Soft silver laces, great web of life.
Amaranthine breezes – a lover's gentle sighs.
O planet- not a planet. O Dranymeirre!
You, yes you, were most wondrous to my eyes.
--- excerpt from *Travels of Onsymyiees*

The sunlight of the small twin suns warmed the fur across Xax's arms. Closing the well-worn pages of his black book of poetry, Xax closed his eyes so that he too could look on the magnificence of the sky castles with his mind.

He smiled and repeated his favorite calculation of Numbers, the formulae which explained the star drive. Xax so loved the Numbers, for they were pure and they were truth.

From the park around him came the happy cries and laughter of the children of Chillith at play, this added to the serenity he felt throughout his being. However, their youthful vigor was often too much for him, and so he would bring out his favorite book of poetry to read and relax. And after reading about the wonders of the universe from the eyes of

Onsymyiees, he would pause and meditate longingly about his Life Goal.

He sat in this peaceful park as was his custom in his free time, relaxing on a bench with the gentle breeze ruffling his fur, his long tail swishing contentedly. Xax was the perfect picture of contentedness.

But the spell was abruptly broken.

He felt the intrusive eyes first; he knew he was being watched again even though his eyes were shut. He opened his eyes and glanced quickly. He noticed two females staring with critical expressions at him. He closed his eyes as quickly as he had opened them. His heart grew sad and now his sweet resting was disturbed beyond repair.

And then the wind brought snatches of their conversation to his pointed ears.

"...not *quite* right.... ...clean, but doesn't..." Xax squirmed with growing uneasiness. More critical words became audible. "...something wrong, maybe... *disease*..."

Xax sat bolt upright at the last word. He turned to the source of the voices with his tail flicking with anger. The two females showed sudden shock at being caught so openly. They looked away in embarrassment, continuing their conversation now in unheard whispers.

Xax took a deep breath and reached self-consciously to adjust the scarf around his neck. To his horror, he found that it had shifted. Now he knew why they had stared at him – the blackened scars that would never heal had been exposed.

That is what had drawn their unwanted attention to him.

He winced with pain while he adjusted the soft folds of his scarf to cover his secret shame. But even the slightest touch of his fingertips brushing the blackened and deformed skin caused him intense pain. The deformed skin was most pronounced across his neck, where his golden fur only grew in sparse patches, unlike the rest of his fur-covered body. And though the rest of his body was covered in fur, the scars of his disease affected even that.

His hands shook like an ancient while he gently tightened the scarf. Yes, even after all these years there was still pain, and especially deep inside his heart. Xax knew it would never go away completely.

Once again, the nights of raging fever and the burning ache that consumed his body haunted his mind, nights when he had wished that someone could have pulled his skin completely off, taking that blinding, searing agony with it.

But he had been fortunate – at least he had survived.

The Black Rot normally killed its victims when it ravaged a planet – indeed over four billion had died when it struck his home world, killing six out of every ten who contracted it. And now over twenty years later, it took a keen eye to see the aftereffects of that tragedy upon Xax, unless his loosened scarf openly exposed him as it had now.

His mood changed, Xax now watched the innocent play and gleeful laughter of the children with a hint of melancholy. He still returned their smiles when they

131

called to him, but he shook his head and feigned tiredness if they asked him to join their play.

As usual, Xax suffered in silence. He did not want to burden any other creature with his own problems.

"May I sit here?"

Xax looked up, startled. It was Mirim, the Karresh female and the Headmistress assigned to the local Chillithian orphanage. It was she and Xax who had brought this group of children to the park today.

"Yes, please." Xax motioned for her to sit.

She smiled at the orphans playing. "You are most kind to spend your free time with the children. They enjoy it so much."

Xax followed her gaze to their carefree play. But once again the tragedy that brought the last of the Chillithian to his world troubled his heart, multiplying his sadness.

"We have much in common," Xax said somberly. Mirim peered at him closely, and he realized what he had said. Under his fur his embarrassment grew. "Of course, I get much enjoyment being with them. It makes me feel young again." He forced a weak smile.

Mirim continued to look deeply at him. But she did it with kindness. Flashing a smile, she nodded with understanding.

"It is sad about the Chillithian orphans." She said aloud, as if directing her words to the air.

"Who could have imagined an entire adult population committing suicide like that. It's unthinkable. I don't think anyone has come across such a desperate act ever before!" Xax shuddered in the warm sunshine.

"And they were so close to joining our Galactic society, so close to completing First Contact," she added.

The rumors came flooding back to Xax's mind – dark and terrible. He knew he should purge them from his mind, repeating the sacred formulas if needed. But strangely, he did not.

"I want to ask a favor of you, Xax," Mirim softly touched his forearm. "You are one of the few of your people to take an active interest in the Chillithian children. I have read reports from the other orphan complexes around your world, and most of your people avoid contact with the remnant of Chillith as if they carried the Black Rot!"

Xax sat up straight and coughed nervously, wondering if she too had seen his exposed scars. But when he searched her clear, silver eyes, he could see she had used the expression innocently enough.

"You would ask a favor." Xax smiled.

"Yes," she looked back and smiled at the children's laughter. "Would you aid the children if they were in danger?" She waited for his reaction.

Xax raised his eyebrows in disbelief. "I know not what danger you imagine." He shrugged and looked down. "But I am not strong. I could not do much to help physically."

"One never knows what one can do, until one tries." She answered him with the ancient proverb.

"I... I am not in the best of health." Xax admitted sadly.

"We just need to know if we could depend on you. Even... even if it were *your* people that endangered them."

Xax felt his anger rise. "My people are unjustly accused by these rumors. I am sure the Galactic Investigation will prove our innocence in the Chillithian tragedy. We are an honorable people. We are righteous; we live 'By the Numbers!'" Xax said defiantly.

Mirim's gaze became far off. "The single home world of Chillith had mineral riches equal to a thousand other worlds combined. Even a righteous race might be tempted to take it... if they could. And it is written in the protocols of First Contact that if a planet is uninhabited, or the native sentients have become extinct, all planetary rights revert to the race that discovered..."

Xax stood up angrily. He glared with righteous indignation at Mirim. When he spoke, there was an angry edge in his tone. "We had nothing to do with the mass suicide of Chillith. Nothing!"

Mirim looked deeply into Xax's gray eyes.

"I believe you had nothing to do with it." She sighed. "But what a terrible weakness they possess – a gland whose secretions would kill its owner in times of extreme stress or danger. The Chillithian's fail-safe gland – it would save them from impending doom and provide a painless alternative to help them die quickly, blissfully, before a worse fate took them." Mirim looked knowingly at Xax. "Like lower animals who kill themselves before they are taken by a predator. The adult population of Chillith could have been easily led to such a state – emotionally and psychologically – First Contact is most stressful for all sentients."

"And now only the children are left, because this fail-safe gland was not fully developed in their immature bodies."

"*The rumors slander me and my people*! I order you to stop! Silence!" Xax shouted down at her. All around them, Chillithian children stopped and stared in shock at him. They knew it was out of character for him.

Xax quickly restrained himself, his lips trembled while he repeated a sacred formula silently. Only his lips moved while he repeated it in his mind. He grew calm and their play resumed.

"I feel you are overreacting," Xax said calmly. "But be assured, I would help the children against any danger. And so would any of my people." Xax quickly added, sitting back down beside her.

Mirim smiled. "You are most kind."

But now they sat together in silence while the afternoon waned. Soon, it was time for the children to return to the orphanage. Xax helped her round up the children, but it was the Headmistress alone who walked them back, leaving Xax alone with his thoughts – and his doubts.

He was not aware when the Master silently approached, his face half-hidden by the black cowl. He stood in silence over Xax for several minutes. Xax only realized he was not alone when he heard the tense swishing of the Master's tail as he waited for recognition.

Xax jumped to his feet.

"May the Numbers favor you," Xax said with bowed head.

"May your Numbers always be positive," the Master answered with the traditional greeting.

Xax waited pensively.

"Let us sit, dear Xax. It is such a beautiful day." But Xax was uncomfortable sitting with the Master because he *felt* something wrong in the Wise One's greeting.

"Why do you spend so much time with the poor Chillithian orphans? Do you not realize that the Numbers are not positive with them?" The Master asked severely.

Xax looked down, avoiding his piercing gaze.

"We are kindred of a sort, Master, though I am not Chillithian. I understand their pain, their loneliness." Xax cleared his throat. "The Numbers do not favor me either, I am... diseased. The Numbers will never favor my union with a Life Partner. Never." Xax swallowed nervously. "And because of that stigma, friends from among our people are few for me. And thus, I seek friendship among the otherworlders, such as these poor children." Xax kept his eyes averted from the Master.

The Master ignored his words and coldly changed the subject.

"The otherworlders say *we* are to blame for the Chillithian tragedy." The Master sighed. He pulled back his flowing sleeves revealing gnarled hands and then pulled the black cowl off his head, revealing his old, wrinkled visage. The aged eyes stared at Xax. "This most intolerable Galactic Investigation invades our computers even now. How can anyone lay the blame for *their own insanity* with us?!" He leaned closer to Xax. "Surely you support your *own kind* in this matter."

Xax felt a growing discomfort and he leaned away, continuing to avoid eye contact.

The Master continued. "The Chillithian are a jumpy, sensitive people. Ever since we made First Contact with them, that fact has always been highlighted in our reports to the Galactic Council." The Master paused. "We gave them technology. We began Rebirth for them, welcoming them into the universal community. We followed the protocols exactly!" A large, wavering smile grew on his face. But the Master's eyes remained cold and hard.

"But a terrible tragedy occurred." Xax sighed deeply.

"Before our First Contact with the Chillithian, they had no idea any other intelligent life existed outside their single world. It is well documented how stressful First Contact is upon such primitive societies – to suddenly realize their entire way of life, their philosophy and religion is suddenly outdated, perhaps nullified. Everything they thought they knew about life and the universe – changed in one day. The Chillithian mass psyche was – overwhelmed!" The Master closed his eyes with a contemplative sigh.

"It is said *we* changed the Numbers. We quickened the Rebirth too rapidly..." Xax's voice was full of sadness. He immediately wished he could take back the words when he saw the anger on the Master's face.

"Blasphemy!" The Master rose with indignation. "We always follow the Numbers." His gnarled fingers sketched invisible symbols in the air as he

137

chanted. "They explain all, they are all. Kaydah. Everything that is done is done just so – 'By the Numbers.'"

Xax repeated the sacred phrase with quivering lips.

The Master's eyes stared far away now, as if Xax were no longer there.

"But let us speak of you now. I have read your Life Tale in the database. Your Life Goal is to go to the stars, is it not?" The Master did not wait for a reply. "Remember, Xax, the ancient saying of our people; 'The stars call to many, but few are chosen.'" He shook his head and smiled. "The odds are against you traveling to the stars, no matter how hard you try."

Xax felt the rage explode inside him. He rose suddenly. He looked straight into the Master's burning eyes. But the Master's eyes were twinkling strangely.

"To practice Kaydah, to live *By the Numbers*, that is what leads to the stars. I will attain that. My dream will be achieved!" Xax said angrily through clenched teeth.

The Master's lips curled into a half-smile/half-snarl.

Xax felt the pain in his heart explode. "Will I not receive my due reward for all my years of effort and study? I will have satisfied the requirements... I will have completed..."

The Master held his right hand up for Xax to stop speaking.

Xax's heart burned, but he obeyed and held back.

"Does everyone attain their dreams?" The Master asked caustically.

"Does everyone try?!" Xax replied instantly.

The half-smile/half-snarl grew wider. "Not everyone gets what they deserve. And sometimes in this great, unjust universe, even a Life Goal that is duly earned... is *not* granted."

Xax felt the hot tears welling up in his eyes, but he fought against them. He would not allow himself to cry, not in public so others would see his pain.

"But..." The Master's expression instantly changed to one of soft cunning. He leaned closer and whispered into Xax's ear. "...if certain of the Masters *want* something good for a disciple of Kaydah – then it can be assured."

Xax felt shocked at this perverseness, at this misuse of power. Yet he couldn't help but to listen more.

The stars were the only dream he had left.

"Leave the Chillithian children. Do not associate with them from this time onward. And I will see that your Life Goal is made known in high places," the Master crooned.

"But why? Why can I not help with the poor Chillith? They are but children!"

"Do you realize what Numbers go into the care and feeding of them? Why, until this accursed investigation is finished, our people alone bear the burden for them, although otherworlders are assigned direct oversight. Here on our planet we maintain twenty-four huge complexes filled with children, and on their home world dozens more. It is a great

139

burden for our people!" The Master's voice rose to a shout.

Xax remained frozen and much intimidated. But his gnawing doubt returned. He nervously cleared his throat before he spoke.

"*We* would never tamper with the Numbers, for any reason, would we? I mean, all things should be done – 'By the Numbers.'" Xax looked down at the ground, unsure if he really wanted to know the answer now.

"You must trust your Leaders, Xax. The Numbers must always be in our favor."

Instantly the oldest proverb came to Xax's mind.

"Only the foolish and the stupid dare change the Num..." Xax began.

"Silence!" The Master commanded. With a rush he gathered his robes close around him while he covered his face with his dark hood. He stood without a sound and left.

There were no more words... that day.

The next few weeks were hard on Xax in his lonely existence. He did not go back to the Chillithian children, but his heart burned inside him – accusing him. He wanted to see his little friends so much – but he also wanted to travel to the stars more than anything in this life.

So Xax put off any decision.

He concentrated on the Numbers instead, filling his waking hours with them. They alone were true and pure. They did not hurt him; they did not want anything from him.

But his studies did not help his desperate loneliness. He found his thoughts constantly turning to the children.

He missed them more each day, especially the young Chillithian boy named Nanon. Nanon had become like a son to him – a son he would never have due to his disgrace.

The turmoil in his twin hearts grew with each long, empty day. It was like a storm that inexorably builds to a climax on the hot, summer breeze.

And finally, he could hold it in no longer. He missed the children so much. Most of all, he missed little Nanon.

Xax drover his hovercar to the orphanage.

When he neared the huge orphanage complex, he saw dozens of children playing near the wire fence. One of them called to him eagerly. It was Nanon.

Xax smiled as he approached, but Nanon, at first beaming, seemed almost afraid the closer he approached. Xax ignored the boy's fearful attitude and walked right up to him. He patted him tenderly on the shoulder.

"How are you, my little friend."

The boy shuffled his feet nervously.

"Come now, aren't you happy to see me again."

The small boy looked up tentatively.

"I thought the father-friend did not like me anymore." Nanon choked back a sob. "Or maybe… maybe you had died, like our parents. And I would *never* see you again." Nanon spoke in a hushed whisper.

Xax's hearts burned inside him.

"No, no, that's not it at all." He tugged at his scarf nervously. "I was busy, I couldn't get away, that's all. But now I'm back!" Xax's words sounded hollow even to him. But the smile that lit the boy's features revealed that he was eager to believe Xax's lie.

"We were going to start a game of Hoffl ball soon! You want to play?" Nanon tossed the round ball to Xax.

"Yes, I would. But let me speak to Mirim first." Xax tossed it back and made his way inside.

Xax found Mirim sitting in her office. She looked up in obvious surprise, but her expression changed quickly.

"So, you did come back," she said with disbelief.

He looked away. "I have had my own problems and conflicts; I could not come."

She rose from her desk. "I had *thought* you really cared! Why, as large as this complex is, the word about your kindness had spread to all the children – one of the few of the Rajjan people that cared." Mirim's eyes hardened. "You were so unlike the rest of your people who go out of their way to avoid these poor, pitiful creatures." She pointed an accusing finger at him. "The Galactic Council has placed these children under the direct protection of *your* people! Yours is an old and trusted race. Yet children need much more than food and shelter, they need love. They need attention! You are a strange, cold race!"

Xax felt his anger grow. "My people, the noble Rajjan, are a decent people, we are good. We would never do anything that would harm others; we would never change the Numbers!" His voice had risen to a shout.

Mirim walked around the desk and right up to Xax. "And yet, there is an official investigation into how your people handled First Contact with the Chillithian."

Xax looked away.

"If this last generation dies, your race will inherit the vast riches of their planet."

"There are hundreds of thousands of children who will grow up and…" Xax began.

"You're wrong."

Xax stared at her wide-eyed.

Mirim cleared her throat as she tried to compose herself. Nodding her head, she continued. "Only a select few know what I'm about to tell you. And you must swear not to reveal this knowledge."

"I swear!" Xax peered at her with concern.

"You can imagine the grief these children carry in their hearts every day – not only knowing their own parents are dead – a terrible burden for a child to bear, but also knowing that everyone's parents, uncles, aunts – are dead." Mirim paused. "Since that planet-wide suicide, every Chillithian child that comes of age has died in its sleep, its own fail-safe gland killing them."

"It cannot be!" Xax exclaimed with shock.

"It is. We who have direct oversight have done extensive studies into their emotional make-up. We hope that with a few months of peace, this will stop."

"That is good news!"

"But the converse is also true."

143

"There are still tens of thousands of children left in many different complexes." Xax said.

"Our emotional studies indicate that these Chillithian who survive live on a dangerous psychological edge – fear dominates their every thought. We believe that if there is even one more tragedy involving them – then everyone left will die when he reaches maturity."

Xax choked back a sob.

"And we fear that next tragedy is coming."

Xax looked at her. "My people have nothing to do with this. We live 'By the Numbers.' We respect life."

"And what if you are wrong, what if there are some who have done the unthinkable?" Her voice grew rock hard. "Would you go along with them; would you look away and focus only upon your *precious* Numbers?"

Her words were like a hammer-blow on his fragile hearts.

Once again, he felt that no matter what he did, it always came out wrong – he couldn't do anything right. His anger dissolved, to be replaced again by the cloak of his well-worn sadness. Xax turned away from her, blinking back his hot tears.

Mirim bit her lip, realizing how much she had just hurt him. "Listen, I didn't mean it like that. And... I don't mean your entire people are to blame – only a few greedy ones. Xax, I truly fear for the children. I fear for our children. And the children are so scared deep inside; their life is tainted by fear."

"Fear..." Xax repeated that one word while he regained control of his emotions. "Fear is the most terrible thing of all. Fear of the unknown, fear of the future or the fear that your dreams will never come true." For the first time in his life, Xax wanted to share his hearts – to share his pain – with another.

"I too have fears." In Xax's mind those pent-up fears screamed to get out. He turned away, tears running down the soft fur of his golden face.

Mirim felt uncomfortable, she saw the sadness on Xax's features, and now she felt his loneliness. Her heart went out to him as she witnessed his terrible pain expressed. "What is it that you fear, Xax? Tell me, you can trust me."

Xax answered her like a child needing comfort.

"I fear that, when I die... no one will care that I was."

Mirim felt his sadness clearly; it gripped her tight in its dark folds. She touched his shoulder lightly. "The children would care. Nanon would care." She whispered softly.

Xax wiped his eyes several times with the sleeve of shirt before he turned back to her.

"I will try to come here, but it is difficult for me. But know this, I promise; if there is trouble, I will help."

"I believe you," she answered. "I know the news reports say the explosion was just an accident, but..." Mirim shook her head as she walked back to her desk. "Many times, the maintenance workers, your people, check the building systems here. Too many times they check. It frightens me."

"I will log into the network here every day. I will watch." Xax said firmly.

"Xax, it is so important that you do. This complex is the largest on your planet. It is reputed to the safest of its kind and the children know it. If something was to happen here and children died, like they did last night back on their home world, then those that survive would not feel safe anywhere. That constant dread, on top of all the other tragedy this race has endured the past months, would haunt them to their maturity and their fail-safe gland would kill each one."

"I will help. I promise." Xax smiled sadly.

That afternoon was the happiest Xax could remember in a long time. It was a bright spring day full of singing birds and the laughter of the children. Everything heightened Xax's feeling of joy. He laughed with them, he played with them. And Mirim looked on smiling.

The hours passed quickly and too soon it was time to close the sprawling complex for the evening. Xax drove home slowly, cherishing the happy feeling still inside him. It left suddenly, as he took down the paper attached to his door.

Numbers, complex calculations covered the sheet with an ice-cold precision – most were of him, some of his Life Goal. And the rest explained the Chillithian children. The Numbers totaled easily – Xax would never go to the stars, not if the Chillithian children were a part of his life.

He balled the paper angrily, and this time he sobbed out loud as an intense bitterness overwhelmed him. He could scarcely believe it. And yet the Numbers did not lie.

Still, something seemed wrong.

He thought long and hard as he lay restless in his bed that night – about the Numbers, about the children – about himself. Everything came down to one, final decision. A decision that rose like some mountainous crag he was afraid to climb – for the decision was about his very way of life, and his future.

Would he obey the Numbers? Or would he do what he felt was right?

And if he acted on the latter, he would forfeit his Life Goal.

Xax hid within himself again, unable to decide. But he did keep part of his word from the privacy of his home. He did access the network of the Chillithian complex. But though it did seem that too many times there were checks and changes made on the systems that controlled and protected the building, Xax could find no overt harm.

Day after day he kept check until he had become thoroughly familiar both with the system itself as well as the physical layout of the complex. He soon had it so memorized he could see it when he shut his eyes. The days turned into a week, and then a second week passed.

He kept in touch with Mirim and Nanon by remote communication only, he was too busy with his studies to visit in person.

His next day off arrived and with it renewed courage to go back to the children, no matter what. But just he was ready to leave there was a visitor at his door. It was the same Master he had met at the park.

He entered, his face again covered by his cowl and cloak. Xax again waited for his words.

"I have good news, Xax. One of our starships waits in orbit – for you."

Xax felt his hearts miss a beat. He could not believe this!

"I...I have not finished Kaydah, Master. I thought..."

The Master waved his hand.

"You will finish on-board. But..."

Xax held his breath.

"...you must leave tonight. Or else the Ancient Ones and I may not be so generous tomorrow." The Master smiled/snarled again.

He turned and left as suddenly as he had arrived with Xax still frozen in shock.

His life's dream had come true.

As soon as the door shut, Xax was up and packing at a feverish pace. His voice chanted with song his favorite Numbers as he went from room to room happily gathering his most precious possessions which he would take on his journey to the stars.

The stars – *the stars* – he would go to them and see their beauty now with his own eyes, no longer through the words of his books. He stopped packing. Xax felt a sudden overwhelming panic as he began to search feverishly – afraid he had mislaid his most prized possession. But no, there it was on the table, his book of poetry.

Xax reached for it and held it tenderly. And then he saw the drawing on the table where he had just taken the book. Putting the book down, he picked up the single sheet of paper.

It was such a simple drawing, crude uneven lines of crayon across the sheet – green strokes at the bottom stood for grass, and blue strokes at the top were sky. Two barely recognizable figures stood in the center – one tall and furry with a tail and wearing a brightly colored scarf at his neck, and a little figure without a tail beside him. There were names below each smiling figure.

Xax and Nanon. The figures were holding hands.

A terrible thought came to Xax. He rushed over to his terminal and began punching up the network for the orphan complex. He stared in total disbelief when the screen remained blank – for some reason the local network was not responding.

Seconds lasted forever and a terrible fear began to grow inside his pounding hearts. Grabbing his portable terminal, he rushed for his hovercar. But Xax stopped suddenly. He turned and looked around at the jumble of suitcases and things packed and ready to go to the stars with him.

Everything was ready, and somewhere above a starship waited for him.

All he had to do was go.

But he didn't.

Rushing out the door he jumped into his vehicle and roared out onto the empty streets. Surprisingly, the closer he got to the complex the emptier the streets seemed to be.

This was very odd. Usually there was traffic, people walking, anything. His fear increased as he accelerated way beyond the speed limit.

The night seemed darker than normal, and then Xax realized the streetlights were not working. He pushed his vehicle to its maximum speed, careening wildly around curves.

There was a light ahead as he neared the complex. But it was like no light that Xax had ever seen before. He stared in amazement and disbelief. What could make a light do that? It shifted and moved. And there was thick darkness above it.

A distant memory clicked.

Fire.

How could there be fire? Fire was the most feared disaster of his people, the Rajjan. And because of their thick, soft fur, fire was almost always fatal. With that in mind, every precaution was taken against it, including complex safety mechanisms built into each building and its network that would prevent and...

The network was off-line! And a fire had started so conveniently?

Xax's headlights flashed upon the security guard's post as he jammed the brakes so hard that everything inside his vehicle slammed forward into the dash – everything except his portable terminal which he grabbed with one hand before it launched forward.

He jumped out the door and ran to the guard who was just standing there watching the flames rising higher and higher into the night sky filled with billowing clouds of black smoke.

"Call for emergency help!" Shouted Xax.

The guard grabbed Xax.

"You can't go in there; all the safety systems are off-line. It's too dangerous." He stared at Xax with panic etched on his face.

Xax couldn't believe his ears. "That is a huge complex – tens of thousands of children are in there! With no power, no emergency lighting indicating the escape routes... they will all die!" Xax shouted angrily.

"Here are the Numbers. I must obey them." The guard indicated the terminal on his desk filled with columns of computations.

They totaled for no action. They totaled to let the children die. Xax growled under his breath as he read them.

"We can't help them – the Numbers dictate it." The guard shook his head sadly as he looked back to the spreading flames.

"*Krag* the Numbers!" Xax cursed angrily.

The guard put himself between Xax and the gate.

With a swift blow, Xax felled the guard and ran past. The flames were on each end of the massive complex, blocking both main entrances. The flickering death was starting to grow inward to where the living quarters were all located.

He stopped, suddenly feeling the primeval fear of his people. He wondered if he could help or was it already too late. And how could he get inside with no power?

But Xax knew this building. He had seen its outlines many times from his daily surveillance. He ran toward a group of darkened windows where he knew a small maintenance entrance existed.

The flames roared and grew higher as he approached, urged on by some force that Xax knew not. But pushing his rising fear aside, he rushed closer to the terrifying maelstrom in order save the children.

His hands grabbed at the small door, but it did not respond. Xax could not believe it, not only was main power out, but even the emergency power? That meant no emergency lighting could guide the children to the emergency exits and even the exits themselves would be shut! Straining his body with all his might, Xax pulled at the door and opened it manually – it took every ounce of strength he had. He was on the ground instantly, coughing and choking because his lungs filled with the acrid smoke that billowed out the open door.

Somehow, he crawled inside and into the main hallway where he stopped to get his bearings. Inside this darkened corridor, darker now as smoke filled its upper reaches, screams and cries came to ears – the heartrending cries of terror from the thousands of trapped children.

Xax realized he could not physically help them all. But what could he do now that he was here? He had to think! The children were going to die, and he could not think what to do to help them.

And then his hours on the network paid off. There was a backup system that should have come on-line. Xax was near where that batch of equipment was roomed. Blind, he crawled forward, silently repeating the Numbers of the Formula of Life – the most sacred Numbers of his people.

It calmed him, and he now imagined he was back on the network looking at the outline of the complex. He suddenly knew where he was. Within minutes, he arrived at the closed door.

He shoved it open again with his bare strength, but the room full of terminals and equipment was eerily silent. Using his portable terminal, he found the main link and connected it. Xax typed feverishly.

Seconds later, a few lights appeared on some of shadowy equipment in the room.

Typing even faster, Xax searched and powered on the only thing that mattered now – the emergency power and lighting. In each hallway, located down the center of each floor, lines of lights were installed that would pulsate and direct the children to the nearest exits now. And those very exits would begin to open with the renewed power Xax had enabled.

But had he done it correctly?

Sweat dripped down the fur on Xax's cheeks as he looked back out into the main corridor. To his relief, red lights glowed on the ceiling, and on the floor a sequence of pulsing lights directed the way to safety.

Xax shouted out loud at his triumph. They would live! But looking back at the map of the complex on his terminal, one sector remained dark.

Xax's twin hearts skipped a beat. It was the sector where Nanon lived.

Making sure his terminal was securely in place, Xax ran into the dimly lit halls toward that one section – into the heart of the disaster. And he did not need the Numbers to realize that the odds were against him.

All around him children suddenly appeared. They were still crying and whimpering, but now they followed the lights that beckoned them onward to safety. Xax encouraged them as he continued to run in the opposite direction the lights indicated.

He alone ran toward the flames.

Finally, there was only darkness before him. He was coughing again as the smoke grew thicker. He couldn't see anything, but they had to be somewhere nearby. He charged on into the darkness – running and coughing as the smoke stung his lungs and as the heat from the unseen flames drenched him in sweat as if he had plunged into the ocean. Suddenly, the flames seemed to be everywhere.

"Nanon!" Xax shouted in panic. "Mirim!"

He heard something! And just as he made out their answering shouts, the wall next to him exploded into flames and everything went dark for Xax.

Something happened, and there was pain, terrible pain. Xax's skin burned with the Black Rot again. Everything was confusion. He felt a great desire to run, but he knew he couldn't run away from the Black Rot.

He wished his skin... wait, he heard someone crying. And there was a smell. Something awful. He felt his stomach cramp, felt the bile juices suddenly erupt out of his mouth and nostrils, searing his sinuses as he threw up violently.

He had to run....

"Xax, Xax, get the fire off. Get the fire off!!"

Xax finally regained consciousness, thrashing his arms around wildly as the flaming pieces of debris came off his body. The hallway seemed to be filled with fire everywhere he looked, and where the wall to his right had been there was now a wall of deadly flames.

Xax realized that the rank smell had been his own burning fur and skin, which now mixed with the sickening smell of his bile.

"Xax, help us!"

It was Nanon's voice. In the wild dancing light of the flames, Xax could see the crowded faces down the darkened hall from him. But there were no flames on them, yet.

"This way, come this way quick! Before the flames cut you off!" Xax shouted to them.

"There are no lights? We have been running in circles!" Mirim shouted back.

"There are lights ahead of you, about three corridors this way. Hurry!"

The children, with a few otherworlder adults helping them, began stepping gingerly around the burning debris as they passed Xax.

Xax started to rise, but he couldn't. He could not feel his body below his waist.

"You must hurry on, I will follow in a minute," Xax panted.

Mirim and Nanon stared down at Xax with fear.

"No Xax, I won't leave without you!" It was little Nanon. He ran out of Mirim's grasp and up to Xax. Tenderly he began removing small, smoldering pieces that were still burning on Xax's bared flesh. Mirim stepped up beside the boy.

"Can you move, Xax?" Mirim asked.

"I will be fine in a moment; you must go on. Please!"

"No," Mirim said forcefully. "You came back for us. We will not leave you."

Xax was surprised at her strength when she reached under his arm and half raised him up. Nanon placed himself under Xax's other armpit. And then they both began to drag and carry him into the darkness and away from the raging flames.

But Xax felt more pain. Some of his ribs were crushed, and he felt so strange – so dizzy, it was an almost surreal feeling. He knew he was hurt badly.

But despite his pleas to leave him, Mirim just pulled all the harder. And soon they were to the lights that pointed to safety.

Fresh air never tasted as sweet after they fell out the opened exit door. Xax blacked out again as he felt other hands pull him farther out.

When he awoke, two familiar faces were watching him tenderly.

"Please be still, some of your people are here rendering Medical aid." It was Mirim speaking.

"Did the children get out?" Xax whispered hoarsely.

"Yes, almost all of them did. Thanks to you." Mirim smiled down at him.

And then she stood aside as two robed forms appeared. Of the robed figures had a black cowl covering his wrinkled face.

It was the Master, and with a savage motion he grabbed Xax as he lay helpless.

"You disobeyed the Numbers." He sneered, full of hate.

Xax groaned with more pain as Mirim stared in shock.

"By the Numbers, you will die!"

"Get away from him." Mirim began beating the Master who pushed Xax harshly back down onto the ground. The other Rajjan held her back while the Master stood over his helpless form.

"You turned your back on your own kind... you are dirt to us." He spit on the ground near Xax's fallen form. "You are banished forever! Exiled! There will be no help Medical aid for *you*." They turned and left, motioning the Medicals to follow.

"You can't do that!" Mirim shouted as she grabbed the old one. "He's hurt badly! He can't wait!"

They jerked her hand away and walked mercilessly away.

Xax groaned and Mirim bent back down to him.

"You must be strong; I will find help. I will!" Mirim said soothingly.

But Xax shook his head. He turned and coughed until blood came out of his mouth. After a moment, he whispered weakly to her. "Please, bring me to where I can see the stars. Please."

She obeyed, though Xax groaned with pain while she tried to move him as gently as she could. She pulled him to where the smoke did not hide the star filled sky.

Myriads of stars twinkled, and Xax smiled. Nanon began crying with Mirim as Xax began coughing up more blood.

Xax reached over and touched the little boy's tear-stained face. And then he looked up to his beloved stars – his dream. And he spoke his hearts again.

"I wish I could have gone to the stars..."

He slowly let out his final breath, and Xax did not move again.

***

The members of the Galactic Investigation Team found Xax's terminal where he had left it – still keeping the Emergency systems online. And it became the final piece of evidence they needed to bring the Chillithian ordeal to its end. The corrupt Rajjan leaders were soon rounded up along with the fanatical faction who had dared change the Numbers and had instigated the macabre domino effect in the hopes of owning the empty, but priceless world of Chillith.

Justice was duly meted out.

Mirim made sure the Galactic Council knew of Xax's love and courage. She made sure they knew of his courageous sacrifice on behalf of the Chillithian orphans. She also made sure that all the children were told as well, every single one of them. Xax had saved them, and most important, Xax was their friend.

Several of the major sentient races took the Chillithian children under their direct care. The remaining orphan complexes were quickly transferred to ships for the ride back to the Chillithian home world where this precarious generation would be nurtured and protected, and hopefully the Chillithian race would rise again.

There was one other that left with them.

They held Xax's funeral at the midpoint of their journey. Mirim dressed him in the finest clothes, and she placed a special scarf of exquisite colors around his neck.

They cast his body into space – to the stars he loved. And there were many... many who cared that he had been. And there were many who cried for him.

***

The Chillithian race did not die.

That generation matured – and because of the love and kindness they were now given, the fail-safe gland did not take them when each matured. Other generations soon followed. The Chillithian were soon welcomed as a full-fledged member of the Galactic community.

And most surprisingly, these gentle beings soon became the foremost of the star faring races. The Chillithian race grew to become some of the greatest explorers of the stars of their age.

Any expedition headed toward the unknown quadrants of space hired at least one Chillithian officer – they knew the stars; they loved the stars.

One Chillithian went on to become one of the greatest explorers – Nanon. Everywhere he went, it was said, he carried a small black book of poetry.

A Chillithian tradition began, a tradition they performed whenever they set foot upon a new world for the first time. And they always uttered the same words.

"I discover this world in honor of Xax. We will never forget you..."

The Dream Plague

The Dream Plague came without warning...

Across planet Earth – in every home and in every mind – the bizarre nightmares began in a single night. People experienced more than simply waking up in sweat-drenched fear from these nightmares. You came out of this surreal-world thrashing and screaming with mind-numbing terror, desperately relieved to be awake once more.

But as the horrific nightmares continued, the final outcome became obvious...

The Dream Plague made you insane.

***

Jim fell breathless into the garbage strewn road, struggling against the invisible tentacles that were numbing and squeezing his sleep deprived mind. He had endured five long days without sleep and there were no more drugs left to keep him awake. The stores had long ago been ransacked and their shelves emptied in the massive riots. The streets he walked were still littered with the rampage of that fear.

The *fear* of going to sleep.

But sleep must come, eventually. Jim's glazed, blood-shot eyes began to turn upward, and he *felt* the images coming – images so familiar, so fear inspiring – nightmare images from the beginning of his life, from the very edge of his personal existence.

These new nightmares were many times more powerful than they had been inside the young, impressionable mind of the child he had once been. Throughout his childhood these vivid, recurring nightmares had haunted him, so pervasive that even when he was awake their intense images vied with reality itself.

Jim's tired, conscious mind flickered. He felt himself suddenly falling.

And there were giants...

He recognized the place immediately and knew he had to run – to hide. But his body remained frozen, paralyzed – crushed by fear. He knew inside his soul that nothing can stop the one-eyed giants.

Strangely, a part of his mind told him this was a dream. He realized he had dreamed this very dream many times before.

In that same instant, he knew would die – *horribly*.

The powerful upper body of the giant became visible above the line of trees. The giant was relentlessly stalking him, his all-seeing eye ever searching for him. Every movement of the giant was performed with a cold, calculating precision. He was a towering predator that *felt* for its prey.

No matter where Jim hid, it always found him.

It stood there watching above the treetops, and Jim could *feel* its irresistible power, its inescapable pursuit – for there were always more than one giant.

And every time the giant would find him.

Jim watched with growing fear, still frozen in place, while the huge form turned slowly toward him.

Unimaginable fear gripped him when the eye fixed upon him. Jim knew he could not escape. But he had to try.

In the darkness, he tried to escape one more time.

Jim ran and ran but he didn't move, he couldn't move. It was if he were in a broken movie.

But somehow – despite his overwhelming fear – he willed his body to move.

In blind panic, he bolted out into the open – through the streets and between the houses of his childhood neighborhood.

He ran.

It was a useless gesture. Even without turning, he could *feel* the one-eyed giant gaining on him.

It came closer, ever closer. And then it had him.

Jim was now suffocating, unable even to breathe, his body encased in a steel vise of its huge hand.

He wanted to scream, *had* to scream, but he couldn't. With his whole might he tried, but the scream would not come – it died stillborn.

With a sudden, heart-pounding shudder, his entire body jerked.

Jim's mind suddenly switched back to reality. At least he hoped that it had. The room around him certainly looked like reality.

Jim gazed numbly at the others who were waiting like him. He didn't even know how he had gotten here.

Where was this place? Who were these people all around him? What were they waiting for?

He recognized the all-too-familiar signs on their faces, the dark circles under their eyes from extreme exhaustion – just like him. Others twitched and jerked while underneath their closed eyelids he could see the rapid, darting movements of their eyes while they dreamed.

It was hard for him to watch those who were dreaming. He cringed and had to fight down the panic to run. But he watched unwillingly, watched their moving eyes and listened to their horrible moans.

He knew they were trapped inside the Dreaming.

He closed his eyes to keep from watching, but immediately his dread grew. He might fall asleep if he kept his eyes shut! He would go back!

But it felt so good, his eyes closed so nicely. It couldn't hurt for just a little...

"Off! Get them off me! Help me!"

Jim's eyes jerked open. He gazed tiredly while one of the dreamers across from him continued to cry out through his living nightmare.

The man sitting next to the dreamer, himself paralyzed with fear, cast quick sidewise glances around the room as if seeking help. But he was obviously too tired or afraid to move away on his own. And then the dreamer beside him began to thrash about violently.

Jim, like most every other person there, watched with an exhausted and knowing dread. A few in the room began to whimper and cry. The crazed man next to the dreamer, his lips now trembling, began to rock his haggard body back and forth with painful moans.

Jim wished he were somewhere else.

Suddenly, it was over. The dreaming man, now awake, looked around with outright shock, and then relief. He began to laugh in a strange, high-pitched cackling.

Men and women began to sob.

Jim looked away, fighting his own overwhelming sadness and the heavy despair that threatened to smother him.

But for a while they were all in the safe confines of consciousness again. And that was something.

For a while...

***

The mammoth ship sucked at the fires of the rich star. For several revolutions they had worked their way around its shining surface harvesting the abundant chemicals from the mature star.

THEY were being filled. But something else had come to their attention – something quite exciting.

THEY had noticed the puny creatures on the third planet that orbited this ripe star, a glowing blue-white planet. THEY had communicated their *Need* toward the creatures. And THEY had received the answering images coming from the billions of tiny minds.

But in all the images received, there was still no definite acceptance. THEY were confused and frustrated. And so, they had sent their probes to communicate more effectively with the puny sentients. The probes had orbited around the blue and white planet communicating their *Need* in greater clarity for seven rotations of the planet.

Seven more revolutions of the planet, and still the puny creatures sent back their mixed feelings – their clear but confusing images – but had they reciprocated? Had they truly answered?

Another meeting was convened inside the blackness of the great ship. Shadows writhed and twisted and heated arguments buffeted the bizarre creatures.

Cooler heads did not prevail.

The great black ship itself would go to the blue-white planet and once there in close orbit it would send the *Need* directly into their minds seeking a definite reply.

It had to be known – were the puny creatures really calling out to them?

Hours later, the harvesting of the rich star was complete. THEY only took what they needed, as usual – no more, no less. But still, the *Need* summoned them.

THEY had to know.

The circle ship, bristling with black spires hundreds of meters tall all over its shiny dark surface, began its three-day journey. It was a huge ship, gargantuan in size – bigger even than the moon that orbited the blue and white planet. As it crossed the scorched planet closest to the star THEY had just harvested, a great black shadow cut across and entirely enveloped it, an event visible to even the most modest telescopes on the blue-white planet.

But no one was watching there – no one was sane enough anymore.

The *Need* began to grow – reaching, searching, groping inside the tiny minds that lived upon the surface of the blue and white planet.

THEY were irresistible.

And THEY were coming.

***

Jim turned away; his eyes still tightly shut. A whirling feeling filled his mind and suddenly he was falling... falling. Underneath the smooth skin of his eyelids, his eyes began to dart rapidly back and forth. His body strained and shuddered under the cumulative effects of stress and fatigue, and he fell into another dream.

Jim became deathly still. The images came alive, filling his senses – his entire being. He was lying in the desert again. He recognized it immediately, the harsh bright light of the sun beaming down onto the hot, baked ground. He felt the cold sweat begin to drench his clothes.

Deep cracks suddenly spread outward from where he lay, getting wider and deeper until it formed a dry patchwork puzzle all around his frozen body.

Jim knew the ground was alive here.

He looked hurriedly around for them and realized with relief that he was alone.

But in that same instant of relief, he heard it – a noise. Or was it the wind? Or was it the fearful whispering of some nightmarish machine? He shut his eyes in his dream, but instantly knew that was the worst thing he could do.

He groaned at his fatal mistake. And then he *felt* them all around him.

Everywhere – crawling and slithering closer and closer while the wet sucking noises grew steadily louder. The *bizarre whispering* grew louder.

He started to shake with fear and he knew instantly he had erred again. It would just make them mad, and now they would *feel* his fear. But he couldn't help it any longer – his fear crushed him like a giant vise.

Inside his nightmare, Jim opened his eyes.

The snakes were everywhere!

Slowly, irresistibly, the mass of slithering bodies moved all over his body, crawling inside his shirt, up inside his pants legs, all around his arms and all across his neck and face. His body shuddered and stiffened with repulsion, his entire being cringed against their cold, wet touch as they slid over him again and again and again...

He watched in petrified horror as his body disappeared under the mass of wet, slithering snakes. There were thousands on him now!

He groaned when he noticed the shiny, slimy goo left behind on his exposed skin and clothes while they crawled over every inch of his being.

His clothes loosened with the growing wetness, and he felt their burning stench sting his nostrils as he tried to breathe against the wet bodies crawling slowly over his nose and face. Jim fought the urge to vomit. His body and clothes now dripped with the wetness and the crawling sensations intensified

167

along with the burning sun blazing above him in the desert sky.

And still the snakes crawled over him – thousands of wet coils tingling and burning and dripping over his entire body.

Jim tried to scream. But he couldn't even breathe.

Laying there, shaking and moaning while the snakes crawled and crawled over every part of his body, an overwhelming urge came over him – he *had* to move, he *had* to get up, he *had* to get the slimy things off.

Something out of the corner of his mind beckoned him. Slowly he turned to look, even though he knew he would regret it.

A single, vicious snake had raised its head and stared back at him with bared fangs.

It was one of thousands, but this one was different. This snake had horns all over its pointed snout. While he watched helplessly, the horny snout opened, and the head grew larger and closer.

In breathless horror, Jim stared into the smooth white interior of the mouth as it came closer – the extended fangs poised over his stiffened body. And all he could do was wait for the teeth pierce his skin.

He knew it would happen, that same snake had bitten him many times before in this same nightmare.

In a slow, surreal motion, the horned head and fangs fell upon his bared arm, piercing him with its burning fire.

Suddenly every snake began to bite him!

His body now jerked uncontrollably. He felt every bite. It was like a thousand needles piercing his brain, the pricking of their tiny fangs shooting exotic pains all throughout his being.

They needed it.

Jim knew they needed it.

His dreaming eyes focused on the slithering, coiled mass that totally engulfed him.

He watched in horrified fascination as their scaly mouths gnawed feverishly, forcing the fire deeper and deeper into his body.

His mind exploded.

Jim opened his eyes and screamed. He screamed and thrashed his arms and legs to get the terrible things off.

But he couldn't. He couldn't... He couldn't...

Jim's open and unfocused eyes didn't recognize the man bending over him – a real man.

"Oh please, I don't want to sleep. I don't want to. Please, please, please." Jim sobbed uncontrollably.

The Doctor pulled out a hypodermic needle while the male nurse held Jim's thrashing arms.

Jim's eyes widened. "Pleeeeese! I don't want to sleep. I'm afraid ...I'm so afraid..."

But sleep came, a deep dark blanket without dreams, a numbing blackness that rose and blocked the nightmares – for a while.

"See that he's taken to one of the shelters." The Doctor sighed out loud. "I just hope we have enough volunteers left to watch over them all."

The uniformed nurse gently closed Jim's still open eyes.

He too, had been awake for over a week now by artificial means – that was the only way to fight the plague.

"Doc, we've all got to sleep soon. I'm so tired I'm not even sure I'm really awake anymore," the nurse said tiredly.

"We're running out of time," the doctor replied. "Soon even our strongest sedatives won't be enough to block out the nightmares."

***

Jim slept over twenty-four hours before he awoke from the dreamless, drug induced sleep. He found himself somewhere in the heart of a darkened high school gym, surrounded by a sea of blankets and sleeping bags filled with frightened, confused people.

Moans and whimpers permeated the large, darkened room. Out from the darkness a single voice of total panic filled the silence.

"Get them off me! Get them off! Get them off!!"

Several white coated men raced over to the shouting dreamer. Quickly a shot was given, and the shouts became a murmur and then silence. Only the moans and whimpers of those still awake continued unabated, softly echoing in the darkened gymnasium.

Jim shuddered uncontrollably. Because even though he wasn't alone, he still felt the fear.

***

"They want it."

Inside the mountainous ship, now in close orbit around the blue and white planet, THEY debated among themselves. THEY were again trying to decipher the answering images from the puny sentients below.

Already the planet below them suffered, pummeled by the ship's immense gravity well, disturbing the mighty oceans and sending the storm-tossed waves far inland over the darkened cities. Throughout the vast, dark interior of the circle ship, voices whispered with ear shattering explosions.

"We have finished the harvesting of their star. We are gone," a myriad of whispers shouted.

"They do want it! They call us!" Others whisper-crooned.

"They are not intelligent enough to know what they want. They are not answering. They are not answering!"

"We allow the star to shine on. We take only what we need."

The whispers now shouted in unison. "And we N*eed*!"

Whispers joined whispers until all were one.

"Those called humans have answered. We shall give."

THEY came to fulfill their *need*.

***

171

Jim had made friends among the others huddling inside the old gymnasium. If misery loved company, then fear absolutely craved it.

One complete day had passed since he had last awakened.

Jim sat under the diesel-generated fluorescent lights of the gym talking to the Simmons family sitting around him – Frank and his wife Edie along with their nine year old son Bill.

They all looked sick and haggard; their faces drawn up as if drained by some terrible disease. The son alone smiled – an odd, mesmerized smile as if he were telling himself about some humorous joke inside his mind.

People all around them broke out in laughter as they talked and whispered, but their smiles and laughter betrayed the fear that weighed upon them all. The fear was thick and oppressive. One could almost taste it in the stale, musky air. Their smiles too were strange, like young Bill's, and their laughter forced.

"Funny, I can't remember why there's no TV anymore. I turn it on but there's just static – every single station. I can't even get the news," Frank said absent-mindedly.

"Maybe they're all sick, like us? Yes, yes, they're all sick. All sick." His wife's voice was both half laughing and half crying with hysteria.

"I wanted to see more about the UFO sightings. Last week, before we came here, there had been hundreds of sightings," Frank said with a sad voice.

"Probably hallucinations. Or, or dreams!" A man nearby began laughing with wide-eyed fear. In the wink of an eye, he began to cry – sobbing as if his heart was breaking.

Others around him joined, tears flowing down their cheeks as if something terrible had just happened to all of them simultaneously. Their utter despair became contagious – like a virus in the air.

"They must have been dreaming... to have seen the UFOs."

Jim stared at young Bill Simmons as the boy's impish smile broadened after he uttered those words.

"What do you mean, they must have been dreaming?"

Bill closed his eyes and then he answered. "The ships. *THEM*." And then he too began to laugh.

Jim felt like laughing too, even though he felt the panic rising inside his chest. He almost felt like he was dreaming, but he was wide awake. He grabbed the kid by the shoulders, forcing him to open his eyes.

"Do you know!?" Jim shouted down at him as he slapped the laughing child savagely, knocking the boy to the ground. He struck him again when the child's mindless laughter grew louder.

And he slapped him again.

Both parents changed from sobs and began to laugh hysterically as they watched Jim hitting their son.

"We must go to them." Bill whispered as blood ran down his chin.

"And then what?" Jim's body began to shake.

Bill closed his eyes as the answer came so softly that he thought he might have imagined it.

"Dream with them!"

"I see them!" Someone shouted from across the room.

People began to scream as they shut their eyes. Jim looked around in horror as everyone began to shut their eyes. Many screamed, and then suddenly fell over. Each person went still, almost as if they were dead.

Edie's scream deafened him. In the next instant, she collapsed, still and unmoving. He couldn't even see her breathing.

He scrambled over the sleeping bags to her while her husband and son began to moan and shake, their eyes still closed. Jim became suddenly still as he stood next to her.

Edie was dead.

Others screamed and fell over, and Jim knew with a certain horror that they too had just died.

As he looked slowly around, everyone moaned in eerie unison with eyes tightly shut, but underneath their eyelids he could make out the rapid movements of their dreaming eyes. From the huddled crowd a kind of chant began – eerie and off key. It sounded like a wail as of a billion lost souls crying out from the depths of the deepest prison and blackest pain.

Jim began to shake uncontrollably. But he kept his eyes wide open, desperately afraid to close them.

The lights flickered and went out – everything was darkness now.

If he could have watched from space, he would have seen the small islands of lights on the surface

174

of the planet going out one by one, the darkness racing, engulfing the entire planet.

But it would not have mattered. It only mattered that he was in darkness right here – right now.

While he sat there in the total darkness with his eyes wide open, the dreaming began for him too. Yet he was awake, he wasn't asleep.

Had he closed his eyes? No, his mind answered. No! He hadn't closed them!

Perhaps he could control the nightmares? Direct the dreams?

He felt the familiar fear begin to grow in his stomach. People shouted around him, he heard and felt movement. One part of his mind told him that he was still in the high school gym, with people all around him beginning to run in their growing madness. Running and running. But there was nowhere to run.

He still couldn't tell if his eyes were open or closed.

Jim looked harder.

There was a bright light all around him – day – and he was in the desert again. He choked on the overwhelming familiarity of it all. The dried-out ground covered by sand was warm under his feet, but it did not burn. And best of all, there were no cracks.

He remained deathly still as he waited for the sound that he knew would come.

And yet he knew was dreaming.

Was he still awake? Or was he asleep and *aware* he was asleep? *Or had he gone mad like the others?*

175

Jim kept very still. Even when the sound came out of the sky – from the very air – a strange and horrible hissing/whispering sound, he kept rock-still.

THEY were coming.

The snakes were coming to cover him, writhe over him… bite him over and over and…

He steeled himself, forcing his body still and keeping his eyes wide open. He *willed it – controlling the dream* with all his strength so that his fear remained distant.

Yes, his fear was so small and far away.

Time… time… forever… and forever.

Soon, seconds or eternity, how long he could not tell, Jim knew he was safe. He knew that the danger of the snakes was past. Relief lifted him bodily upward…

…ever so gently he was lifted. He was floating – up and down, slowly rising upon a huge, gentle ocean wave.

He realized with a sickening dread that he had closed his eyes.

Now he crushed his eyes closed, as tight as he could. He had been here too. And died here, many times. So many horrible deaths he had died here.

The turquoise water would be beautiful – so clear, so inviting. Jim tensed as he felt the first huge body brush against him, the harsh touch of sandpaper burning against his wet skin.

The ocean would be full of the sharks.

All around him, everywhere in the water while he floated helplessly, the monsters would swim closer to him with each heartbeat. Swimming death was toying with him until the overwhelming fear would seize him and force his fatal scream. Then, only then, would they take him with their razor teeth and gnawing mouths.

Suddenly, he felt the massive jaws close around his body, the razor-sharp teeth burning his skin like fire as he fought to control his rising panic. He knew that if he screamed that the huge mouth would only close tighter.

Jim remained frozen while the shark held him in its mouth.

Slowly, the huge mouth tightened around him, but the teeth did not cut through his skin. He felt the pain embrace him and toy with him.

But Jim refused to scream.

Jim waited this eternity out as well, willing it, controlling it. He would not give in to his fear. He would not die.

And like the snakes, the sharks faded away – melted away.

The sound of crashing surf filled him as he *felt* the sharks leave the dream. Finally, all at once, Jim opened his tired eyes.

Inside his dream.

He was still in the water, but he saw the white frothing foam crash onto the beach before him. Just past the glistening sand he saw the dense green jungle, while above the tops of the trees, far into the distance, he saw the rolling sand dunes of the desert. His mind told him that the horned snakes were there, in that desert beyond the thick jungle trees. He did not want to go there again, but he also knew that the one-eyed giants roamed this jungle that bordered the pristine beach.

He had been here many times before.

The next wave lifted him abruptly, and then he was tumbling head over heels in the water until suddenly solid land reached up and pummeled him. Realizing he was on the shore, he picked himself up as quickly as he could and ran madly for the safety of the trees.

He was drained of energy and out of breath as he hid behind the trunk of a palm. He stared down the long empty beach looking for it, but nothing was there but the never-ending waves.

And then something caught his eye.

It was a solitary tower constructed of latticed steel that rose high above the treetops at the edge of the beach.

It was a one-armed tower, a steel track stretching from the very top of the surreal visage like some mighty arm pointing the way into the midst of the jungle. The track with twin rails stretched away from the tower out above the leafy tops of the jungle canopy. At regular intervals another tower of steel lattice protruded up through the trees to support the phantom rail as it extended on and on and on…

It went on forever. It went nowhere.

Jim closed his eyes inside his dream.

And he opened them inside a car atop the tower. The twin rails stretched endlessly before him to the edge of the horizon.

The open-air car jerked forward ominously, and he quickly began to look for a way out. But it was

178

too late; already he was far out on the level track above the ocean of treetops.

Rolling inexorably along, he felt completely naked and exposed inside the open car that rode the twin rails to nowhere. He felt his heart pounding and leaping inside his chest like a jackhammer, a rhythmic force rocking him so hard he couldn't take a breath between the hammer blows.

Suddenly, his heart stopped.

The one-eyed giant rose so familiar above the treetops before him. Jim already knew what was going to happen – right before his eyes.

And there was nothing he could do to stop it.

The one-eyed giant waited for him while the car carried him relentlessly closer. The monster waited for him, the huge face just level with the track as Jim approached at a steady, gut-wrenching speed.

The monster was going to get him, and all Jim could do was wait for it to happen. It would be so easy for the giant to reach in and get him.

As the huge face came ever nearer, his old childhood fear gripped his heart and his throat. But again, although his *entire being screamed* with the total panic that seized him in an iron grasp, he couldn't scream.

The giant's face came right up to him – its hand raised to take him and crush him.

Jim stared in total numbness at the monster waiting for him. But through this mental fog, he willed his fear to be silent – controlling the dream again.

The rolling car passed the giant as it watched him with its all-seeing eye.

179

Somehow the straight, steel track began to curve to the left. In complete surprise, he noticed a mountain he had never seen before in any of his previous dreams. It was so near, how could he have missed it? The curved track led there, and the open car carried him toward it.

A dark cave entrance swallowed the track. And as he steadily moved inside the dark mountain and inside the vast cavern, he suddenly realized that he could wake up.

He opened his eyes.

There were trees around him, oak and pine and poplar trees that he instantly recognized. Peering through the dense darkness, he saw the forms of hundreds of people lying in the grass. Some were still moaning, their bodies jerking with the Dreaming.

Others were too still. Jim knew they were dead.

Rising from his sitting position, he began looking around with a growing fear.

Something was wrong, and it was worse than those dead and dreaming around him. He stood and began running. But he stumbled, falling heavily to the ground. As he fought to get up, he looked up at the sky and saw it.

The black orb of the sun had horns! And the sun was darkness. And the day was night.

He shook his head in denial of this living nightmare. He had almost shut his eyes when he heard it.

Sitting there among the dead and dreaming, *he heard his nightmare coming to get him.*

And he wasn't even asleep.

Whispers, shouting whispers called to him. He looked apprehensively toward the dark shadows of the forest.

There was movement among the trees – darkness writhed and coiled in the darkness. It beckoned to him.

Rising, he knew what they wanted.

They wanted to crawl his body.

As he stumbled closer, he began to make out individual black shapes. They were huge and snake-like. And they crawled through the very air.

Slithering with the wind, they came straight for him.

He felt his fear explode and his breath failed him. Panting, he tried to take a breath. No, he didn't want to breathe; he wanted to scream – to scream so badly. But he couldn't scream.

Clenching his eyes shut against the horrific sight of this living nightmare, a terribly bright light flashed inside of his mind, blinding him.

He felt the hot burning at their first wet, slithering touch upon his skin.

THEY took him.

He felt them everywhere, even inside his clothes. Their movements became faster, their coiling tighter – the whispering louder.

He forced his eyes open.

They were everywhere, coming to him, writhing through the air. As he looked down upon the clinging, slithering black bodies coiled so thickly that they blocked the view of his own body; he knew they would take him completely. And for an instant he almost knew why.

THEY took him more.

And the unspeakable horror of THEIR touch made the Dream Plague seem like pleasant sunshine.

There were giants, there were man-eating sharks, and there were horned snakes that flew. The phantom rail did go on forever; relentlessly on and on and on...

It was different. It was the same.

He did not know whether he entered the vast cavernous ship inside a dream or awake. He didn't know whether he saw the moving monstrosities or felt them, for everywhere was pitch darkness – darkness so deep, so intense, that its weight seemed to press in on him from every direction, suffocating him.

But he fought his desire to scream. Somehow, he knew that would bring disaster. And so, he endured it.

Like a nightmare inside a nightmare, images were conveyed in horrifying sequences directly to his mind, while he as a human tried to use his normal senses of sight, hearing, and touch to comprehend. He realized they were communicating, but he did not understand the language. As his mind attempted to translate, probably in error, the images of intense, utter horror crushed his sanity.

THEY were power incarnate compared to his own feeble consciousness that was now full of the darkness of the ship. THEY probed his consciousness.

Darkness... Power... The *Need*...

The *Need*, it danced inside his mind. And why had he never felt this need his entire life. Shouldn't every living thing have *Need*?

And why, *why... why did the Need hurt so badly*?

Somewhere his mind snapped, like a dried-out twig.

For the blinding pain – intense and powerful in the Dreaming – *was so much worse here inside the darkness of the alien ship*.

***

THEY were disappointed.

Arguments resounded like antique silent movies in the puny creature's mind as the dwellers of the great ship tried to decide what to do next.

Jim was just one of the puny creatures.

THEY had been wrong.

But the *Need* was great.

In the end, cooler heads prevailed. Jim and the others who had answered suffered the same fate and floated inside the dark ship in silent numbness.

Although THEY tried to heal the puny creatures, trying in vain to undo the damage, it was only partly successful. There was nothing else that could be done. So those that answered, those that were taken, were sent back to the planet's surface.

And the alien ship left.

***

He felt the caressing warmth of the sun on his face before he awoke. Sounds came so clearly to his mind that it startled him.

He heard not only the cheerful sounds of songbirds, but he also heard the beat of their wings as they flew through the air, even from miles away. He even realized he could hear them breathing!

He didn't need to open his eyes. But somehow, he knew that sense would be amplified as well.

He felt wonderful.

Almost.

And at the edge of his mind's eye, he remembered – darkness and movement, and horror that threatened to overwhelm him again.

His mind caressed the mental barrier that prevented the nightmare from overwhelming his mind again, and his thoughts made the barrier higher, and more distant.

The horror lessened.

When he opened his eyes, he noticed how his skin had already changed... transformed, morphing from the thousands of tiny puncture wounds all over his body.

He was forming a new body.

The REBIRTH had begun.

He was becoming something not-human, not-THEM. He felt the power inside his body, he felt himself becoming... different. He was being born a second time. He was becoming a new life-form like all the others awakening around him.

He who had once been Jim had to run, hide. He was vulnerable now, but soon, very soon, he would be mature. And this blue and white planet would be his, along with the others like him.

THEY might even condescend to share it with the puny humans that remained human.

Maybe.

And a distant part of his mind realized just how insane he really was.

***

Out in the vastness of black space the gargantuan ship continued its endless journey. Vast shapes danced and whispered in the sweet darkness, renewed again from the harvesting of the rich star and its nutrients.

Others whispered/roared back that it had not been a union after all. No, not a union, not a normal reproduction between two consenting species as was THEIR Way.

Yes, there was conception, the *Need* joined. But it had not been a union.

In fact, it had been *rape*.

Love Is Not Relative

Captain Chris Hunter had a black hole inside his chest.

And it hurt...

Once again, he felt that numbing emptiness welling up inside, sucking all emotion from his being – slowly killing him. His breathing grew shallow and strained, he placed his hand lightly across his chest – the deep darkness inside seemed to have finally taken his heart, though somehow it continued to beat.

In fact, the black hole of loneliness now numbed Captain Chris Hunter to such an extent that he imagined he might actually disappear into its overpowering embrace before his next breath.

He didn't, though a part of him wished it so.

Long minutes passed before he roused himself from his despondent stupor – duty called. And as captain of this starship and leader of its valiant crew, he could not allow himself the luxury of becoming wrapped up in the strangely comforting folds of his melancholy.

After all, his crew depended on him.

But in his privacy, alone with his memories of her, he allowed himself *the right* to feel that painful loss once again.

He took a deep breath as he wrestled with the overpowering urge to see her again, to hold her again – to love her again. Clenching his eyes shut, he tried once again to fight his irresistible need. But he knew it was hopeless even though he tried – and the black hole took a little more of his soul.

And then he smiled. *There was something he could do*

He chuckled to himself as the rules and regulations opting against this course flashed in his mind. And there were the published findings of the Fleet's psychiatrists which prohibited what he now planned. They were all against him.

He silently cursed all their rules, regulations, and recommendations. They would not stand between him and his true love.

This time, he would follow his heart.

He had given Fleet everything these last seven years. He owed this one, important thing to himself – *to spend just one minute more with her*.

Another pain, this time from a real part of his body, suddenly bent him over as he struggled against its burning, consuming fire. His vision blurred and it felt like he was falling. Quickly grabbing the edge of his desk, he fought the blinding pain.

It was the old wound, the one he'd taken at the Battle of Branalf where he had almost died. The Cobra had taken a direct hit amidships with her shields down. Many had died in the flames and explosions that engulfed the mangled bridge from that terrible blow.

And not for the first time, he wondered why he had survived. And he again imagined that maybe it would have been better for him to have died then and there.

He reached for the pills, spilling several as his shaking hands tried to grasp just one. At last he succeeded, swallowing it as a man would in the grips of a raging fever, coughing and spilling water down

187

the front of his shirt in the process. He felt the soothing effects immediately. And once more, he felt the pain slowly diminishing.

He considered the two wounds objectively – the one inside his heart and the other that physically scarred it. Captain Hunter noted again that the unseen wounds, the emotional ones, were indeed the hardest to bear – the most painful of all – the ones that sucked away your very life.

A few more minutes passed before he felt well enough to stand again. He steadied himself a moment and then reached inside the drawer of his desk, searching for the case that held his most precious possession. His fingers gently touched the edges, caressing it longingly, while he steeled himself for the effect it would have on him.

Slowly, he drew it out.

He held the holo-picture tenderly, reverently, almost as if it were alive. The young woman smiled back at him once more – so beautiful and so in love with him – that unforgettable smile for him alone. Her brown eyes glowed with happiness that still reached out to him across all the empty years.

Chris Hunter's hand began to shake.

His door chimed without warning, announcing a visitor outside.

Clearing his throat, he put the treasured object away and turned.

"Come in." He announced tersely, his voice sure and steady once again. Captain Hunter pushed aside the burning emotions that were his private self to take on his duties. A young junior officer named Griffiths stepped through the opened door.

"Excuse me, Captain. I have word from Earth Control. Lt. Crandell said you would want to know immediately." The young officer stood rigidly at attention holding his salute.

"At ease mister," Captain Hunter replied, running his fingers through his jet black hair now tinged with gray. "What name are we orbiting under Griffiths?"

"The Mako, sir."

Captain Hunter nodded approval, remembering the proud ship that once carried that name.

"We lost her at Trandallos two weeks ago," the young man said, though Hunter knew it well enough. "In fact, her loss will only be reported to Fleet HQ when we download our data – after we leave Earth. Per fleet protocol, her loss will be reported two weeks from now."

"Fine, fine," Hunter sat farther back into his chair to relax. He knew this covert act was meant to confuse the enemy in addition to honoring that proud ship and crew one last time. "And how long will it take us to restock the Cobra?"

"About eight hours, sir."

Hunter nodded. "Dismissed."

But as Griffiths started to leave, Hunter spoke again. "Tell Crandell I want to talk to him. Here in the privacy of my cabin."

"Yes sir."

Captain Hunter started to get up after the youthful figure disappeared. But he knew he couldn't do it, not now. It would be hard enough doing it face to face. He closed his eyes and went back in time.

It was ten years ago. He was a whole man again standing on a sugar white beach near the rolling waves of the Gulf of Mexico with the salt air filling his senses. Seagulls squawked overhead while small terns skittered across the sand.

He always loved the ocean.

Suddenly she was there, walking slowly towards him up the sandy beach. She was so beautiful – in his mind he watched as she pushed back her long, locks of blonde hair that the wind whipped around her face.

After she noticed him watching her, she laughed.

She always laughed at him when she caught him looking at her. Maybe it made her nervous, he never knew.

His mind whirled further back in time.

She came up and stood close before him. He slowly drank in her beauty with his eyes. Her smile changed as she studied his face in return, trying to catch his eye.

And finally she would.

Their eyes locked in a deep gaze filled with love.

He reached out and held her – one more time.

As that wonderful memory filled his being, he realized he could hold her like that forever and never want to do anything else.

The door chimed again.

"Come." Hunter took a deep breath, steadying himself.

A middle-aged man with dark red hair streaked with gray at the temples stepped inside. He walked in with a calm familiarity; his warm smile directed at Chris Hunter spoke of their time together in space.

"Captain, the Earth looks as blue as ever." He raised his head and closed his eyes with the fresh memory. "Ah, good ol' Earth. There's not another planet like her in a thousand quadrants."

Hunter smiled. "So, we fly in as the Mako, eh. Have we determined if the Haugons have broken our latest code yet? They'll be puzzled about out how they destroyed the Mako, and yet she makes planet-fall here on Earth today, if they have broken it!"

Lt. Crandell nodded. "No word from Central on it yet. But no need to take chances either, which is why we orbit as the Mako." He sighed. "A good ship and crew they were. I thought we would honor their memory with one more port of call under her gallant name."

They looked at each other in silence. Crandell's smile slowly faded as he rubbed the red stubble on his chin.

"I know why we're here, Captain. I know you too well." The smile now disappeared while he leaned over the desk. He looked earnestly into Hunter's eyes. "You shouldn't do it."

"But I am."

Crandell shook his head. "Captain, I know it seems so simple, so easy. But there are reasons this kind of thing is frowned upon." He leaned over the desk. "Forget the disciplinary actions they'll slap you with, think about what the psychological studies warn about. How it could affect both you and her."

"There have been contacts without ..."

"Only a handful!" Crandell said forcefully, cutting him off.

Chris Hunter shook his head as he ignored the other officer's impropriety. "Captain's prerogative, mister. It's a done deal as far as I'm concerned."

"You can't go back, Captain. None of us can. You can't ever go back home," Crandell said with conviction.

Captain Hunter's expression grew hard, but he knew the facts as well as Commander Crandell.

"Not after you've gone to the stars," Crandell added somberly.

Captain Hunter rose to his full height to face his First Officer.

"You can do one thing for me. Go with me, Ken."

Commander Ken Crandell started chuckling and his familiar smile returned. He shook his head in disbelief.

Hunter laughed with him.

"We've been through a lot together Captain, haven't we?" Crandell finally said.

Hunter nodded as his own laugher subsided into a thoughtful smile. But he didn't reply.

"We've been to many planets, my friend. We've seen a lot of good times together." Crandell paused, studying him a moment longer before continuing.

"And we've seen too many good men and women die – too many good ships butchered and destroyed."

Hunter's gaze dropped to the floor.

The smile faded from both their faces with the hard memories they shared.

Crandell's eyes narrowed. "This will be harder, Captain."

The silence grew thick. But the look in Chris Hunter's eyes didn't waver. Finally, he spoke.

"As hard as Branalf?"

Crandell started to laugh, but in the next instant his face reflected somber recollection. Several emotions washed quickly over the First Officer's face. When he spoke, his voice was edged with sadness.

"We were outnumbered three to one – outgunned and almost surrounded." He scratched at the red stubble on his chin as the memories came flooding back. His movements stopped all at once and he nodded almost imperceptibly. "I thought we were all dead that day."

Captain Hunter remained silent.

"But it was brilliant, the way you sent us into them in four squadrons. I don't think they expected us to attack," Crandell added.

"The Haugons didn't know humans as well as they thought they did," Hunter retorted. "They didn't realize how crazy we can get when facing certain death."

"Yeah, our new torpedoes gave them quite a surprise as well!"

Both men laughed, but only briefly.

"I thought we were dead that day, too," Hunter confessed.

Crandell's eyebrows rose in surprise.

"But I wasn't afraid to die," Hunter continued. "We were protecting Earth from certain defeat." A sigh escaped his lips. "And I figured even if we died that day, we needed to buy Earth some time. We had to hit them hard." He slapped his fist into his hand. "And I hoped somebody, maybe even the Sicians, would come to Earth's aid after hearing about our supreme sacrifice there – if it came to that."

For a moment, the decisive battle replayed in their minds.

The two great fleets closed once again in a deadly dance of death. And before the Haugon ships came into their weapon's range, hundreds of torpedoes leapt from the smaller Earth ships. The deadly new torpedoes streaked forth, tearing holes in the enemy shields with single hammer blows. The exploding, dying hulks of the cruisers careened wildly while the two fleets continued to close.

Haugon torpedoes finally launched, and now Earth ships shuddered and exploded. But many of the small Earth ships danced around the oncoming missiles.

And then the two fleets joined.

In the silence of space, laser broadsides erupted in deadly streaks – beams of red and green crossed paths as massive broadsides fired from every ship. But the starships from Earth, half the size of the enemy ships, engaged with unexpected tenacity.

The smaller, more maneuverable starships swarmed around the larger and slower enemy ships. As they whipped among the larger ships, thick laser fire lanced through the darkness of space. But the blasts of the enemy lasers proved just as deadly when they found their mark on the fast Earth ships.

Twisting... turning... the battle quickly rose to a fever pitch. Orders roared over the Comm channels. Counterattacks launched amid a hail of lasers. And ships battled nose to nose as shields buckled and failed. Warships exploded and their twisted hulks glowed with death in the stygian darkness – in that moment there was nothing in the universe but war and death.

"And we wound up cutting their ranks to pieces," Crandell said with a smile.

"Yes, Commander, the enemy retreated in confusion. But we did lose half of our fleet in that single action."

"As did they with their greater numbers. But ours was the victory."

"And I was left in pieces myself – badly wounded," Hunter said.

Crandell now took a deep breath and let it out slowly. "You're going to go through with it anyway. No matter what I say, aren't you?"

"Yes. I want to get in, see her, and leave as quickly and quietly as I can. That's it."

"That's it..." Crandell repeated with somberness.

The First Officer rubbed his chin. "You know you'll have to wear a disguise if you want to get through customs quietly."

"Why?" Hunter's face filled with surprise.

Crandell reached into his pocket and pulled an object out. He unwrapped the folded bills of money until he found the one he wanted. He smoothed it out and handed it over.

"I was going to surprise you. The patrol ship that rendezvoused with us after our last jump passed this on to me. Recognize anyone you know?"

A familiar, though slightly younger, visage stared back at Hunter. He stood and walked over to the mirror. He placed a hand over his beard, trying to imagine his face clean shaven again. Then he looked back at money.

Hunter's clean-shaven face stared back.

"And you're not even dead yet, buddy! What an honor!" Crandell stood beside him. "Of course, they had to doctor the picture up a bit, just so people wouldn't know how ugly you really are." He laughed.

But the Captain continued staring in silent contemplation at the face on the paper money, ignoring him.

"Small denomination bill, too. You probably ought to complain."

"We hero types just take what we can get," Hunter countered with a wry grin.

"You know," Kenneth Crandell said, still joking. "You probably ought to color out that gray. Make you look younger for all your fans."

He looked at the tinge of gray that recently sprouted throughout his trim beard.

"It reminds me of my mortality," Hunter said simply, feeling every one of his thirty seven years of life.

"Huh? Don't you get reminded about that all the time in this old universe?"

"It reminds me that I'm not invulnerable," Hunter replied. "It keeps me from taking careless chances."

"Okay, I'll buy that."

Captain Hunter reached out and put his arm on his friend's shoulder and squeezed. "Crandell, you know me better than anyone. And we both know the old saying is true, that being a leader, Captain of a ship, can be a lonely vocation." Hunter shook his head. "I bet less than a dozen crewmembers have even heard me talk about Sandra." Hunter looked deeply into Crandell's eyes. "But you know."

The red headed man held his breath.

"Just go with me tonight, please. I need to tell her good-bye..." Hunter took a deep breath as he waited for an answer.

"I'm with you Captain, no matter where you lead me," Crandell replied with a nod.

The warship dropped into Earth orbit, announcing herself under the assumed name – the Mako. The ground crew was happy to be of assistance to any ship which had left for the deeps of space to fight for the safety of humanity.

But, strangely, the Mako asked for little – simply to be restocked with food and arms while in orbit. And only two crew members would go ashore on Earth via a shuttle to deliver a private – and secure – report in person.

All was easily arranged. The two men received a hero's welcome as they went through standard Security and the routine of customs at the base. Minutes later, they found themselves alone in a ground car.

The night was bright and starry. Commander Crandell smiled as Hunter peeled off his face.

"OPS did a pretty good job back on Cobra. I think you ought to leave it on – better than the original, you know." Crandell grinned.

"Shut up and drive." Hunter's words were strained, in contrast to Ken's jab to lighten the tenseness.

Hunter was already disoriented. The courageous Captain stared at the twinkling skyline of the city he had grown up in.

And he could tell it was not the same.

Yet this had once been his home. It said so on his birth records.

He had expected things to be different, that's progress. But everything seemed to be so different – everything so changed. And as the car proceeded via its auto-nav controls and guided them toward the street he specified, the differences only increased.

Hunter began to feel light-headed.

The very road he traveled was different beyond recognition. Trees were in different places, street names changed, and parks existed where none existed before. Everywhere buildings and even most houses were different; it was like he had never been here before.

Hunter felt his heart pounding like an assault blaster as his breathing grew shallow and rapid. He felt a paralyzing fear, even though he was a seasoned warrior. A throbbing, dizzying panic suddenly gripped his entire being.

"You okay?"

Hunter stared at the unfamiliar surroundings. "Y-yeah, I'm alright. Just a little nervous," he lied.

Crandell nodded, and then shook his head in the darkness.

Finally, something familiar fixed in Hunter's haunted eyes.

"Take over manual control and slow down. Yes, yes. There, over there, take that street." Hunter pointed. The rising excitement in his voice could not be mistaken. "What time is it? I mean what time is it local?"

Crandell glanced at his wrist. "Just after ten p.m."

"It's getting late. She might be sleeping. Or..." Hunter's words trailed off. "Wait, pull off here."

Crandell pulled off the road – nothing but woods stretched into the darkness to their left. Hunter literally jumped from the car with Crandell close behind.

"There's a trail somewhere...here!" Hunter flicked on the small flashlight and the beam of light found the leaf covered path.

The two men stumbled through the darkened forest as leaves and branches crunched under their feet.

"You're sure this is right? I mean, after all..." Crandell began.

Hunter stopped suddenly, raising his hand. The trees came to an end and just ahead a house came into view – a large house. Between them and the house they could make out the manicured bushes and flowers of a well-kept garden. The silvery light of the full moon revealed the beauty of its manicured pathways. In the center an unseen fountain gurgled forth its crystal-clear contents.

"It is the same," Hunter whispered in relief. And then his heart missed a beat.

There, coming from between two trees, he saw a ghostly figure. A flowing white gown seemed to drape the feminine form that walked slowly along the dimly lit garden path.

Hunter's breath became rapid and uneven, his pounding heart felt as though it would leap right out of his chest.

This was how he had last seen her, here in this very moonlit garden.

199

Chris Hunter stepped out and began to walk toward her.

The figure in the long, flowing dress froze as he appeared out of the woods. It was obvious that she was startled. She raised her hand to her mouth and turned to leave.

"Sandra! It's me!" Hunter cried out to her.

She stopped, as still and silent as the scenery etched with moonlight around her.

Hunter burst from between two flowering azaleas and quickly drew close to her.

But he stopped short.

It wasn't her! It was some... old woman!

The hammering of his heart almost bent him double as a tidal wave of intense disappointment pushed the tears into his eyes.

"No..." he whispered weakly.

The old woman stared at his sobbing form. Her pure silver-white hair, bound tightly in a bun, framed a thin and deeply wrinkled face. Tears streamed down her cheeks onto a scarf that covered her aged neck.

And for the first time in his life, Captain Chris Hunter turned and ran. He wasn't sure why; he just knew he had to leave this terribly wrong place and this ancient woman.

"Chris, don't! Don't leave me! Not again..." The woman choked back a sob as she raised a shaking hand. She felt his rejection, his disappointment, and his fear. But she felt something else too, and it caused her to speak even though a part of her knew she should just let him go.

He stopped in shock.

The old woman had called to him with Sandra's voice.

The voice was changed somewhat, but it was still...

He turned and wiped the tears from his eyes, but his vision remained blurred. And now the soft moonlight seemed to glow around the woman – Chris strained his eyes.

She raised her hands to her hair and took out the hair pins one at a time, and her silvery hair suddenly seemed blonde to Chris as it fell softly around her shoulders – just like she used to wear it for him.

He approached again, putting out his hands and gently grasping her shoulders. Still, his tears blurred his vision. But now he smiled through them.

Two familiar eyes gazed back at him. He fixed on them, and with the moonlight and his own tears, the wrinkles smoothed away until he could finally see her.

It was Sandra – those sparkling brown eyes were still the same.

She smiled back.

He knew that smile.

His arms reached around her and ever so gently, he held her once again.

His mind ignored how much smaller she was. The firmness, the curves of her body, had also melted away with her youth.

But it was still her.

"Chris," she said through her tears. "Chris, I've thought of you all these long, long years. I've never stopped loving you." She buried her face in his chest while he gently held her.

The voice was just as he remembered. He held her tighter. She tried to pull back, but he held her firm within his warm embrace.

Looking up, she studied his face. "You don't look much older than the day you left," she said with amazement.

He looked back into her brown eyes.

Oh, how he loved those eyes. He started to brush his fingers through her silver hair, but she stopped him.

"I wish you could have remembered me as I was. When we were young... together." She strained against his embrace, and then she stopped.

His lips slowly drew closer to hers.

There in the soft moonlight, among the sweet fragrance of flowers growing throughout the well-kept garden, he kissed her as softly as the morning dew washes the grass.

She started crying as his lips pressed against hers.

He held her a long time and felt her tender embrace once more. The moonlight slid away, and he looked down on her again.

And this time he saw her clearly.

She was old now. He could see the countless wrinkles and his mind now informed him how fragile she really was as he felt her body against his.

"I loved you then, Sandra. I love you now, just as you are." He suddenly choked on his powerful emotions while he fought back more tears. And after he partially composed himself, he hurriedly whispered.

"I will always love you."

His heart cringed at the lost years they had missed. He choked back his tears as he kissed her forehead.

And in their final embrace, Chris Hunter repeated the words he had prepared for that first bittersweet farewell a few years ago – a few years for him, but decades for her.

"My love is as true and bright as the fires of the sun itself. My love..."

She put a finger to his lips to silence him.

"You told me that once before." She smiled.

He smiled back at her. "I think we made love that last time right over there in the grass, in the darkness by the fountain."

Her hand slapped against his chest in mock attack.

"You always did remember things like that."

He drew her near and embraced her gain. The warmth of their bodies mingled. They started to sway, ever so slightly. The seconds seemed eternal, one more time.

"Why... why did you come back?" She whispered through her tears.

Tears streamed down his own face.

"To hold you one last time…"

He held her long in the stillness of the night. A gentle breeze caressed them in the moonlight. Finally, it was time to go.

And for the second time in his life, Chris Hunter left his true love behind.

As he entered the dark recesses of the forest, Crandell didn't notice the moistness on his friend's cheeks. But he guessed the tears were there.

They walked in silence. As they got into the ground car, he was careful to look away as the car's lights came on. They were almost to the starship port when Hunter spoke.

"I guess there's really no such thing as 'happily ever after', is there? For me or for anyone?" Chris said sadly.

A heavy silence settled between them as they drove on through the night.

But they both knew that there had been no other choice. The Haugons had put a stranglehold on Earth. Without free trade via the space lanes, mass starvation faced Earth's inhabitants. Earth mustered their small fleet and sent them away to war. And every man and woman had known that even if victory was theirs, the Law of Relativity still meant that they were leaving everyone they loved behind – never to return – for those left behind would age at the normal rate while those that flew beyond the speed of light would not.

"Life is a funny thing." Ken sighed. "It's a mixture of good and bad. Sometimes we face it alone, sometimes with the support of family – but we all live it. And sometimes these storms of life are so strong that the best we can do is simply hang on and keep from being swept completely away." Ken stared straight ahead while he drove on. Taking a deep breath, he continued.

"And yes, there are the good times that are even better because we share them with our friends or family. But no, there really is no such thing as 'happily ever after' in this universe, for anyone"

Silence filled the darkness; the only sound was the rushing air outside the ground-car. The buildings began to look familiar as they drew near the base where the Cobra's shuttle waited.

"I loved her, Ken," Chris whispered. "I'll never love anyone like I loved Sandra."

Ken took a deep breath and thought a moment. "Many people never experience love like you knew. But you did, treasure that."

Chris Hunter stared ahead silently.

Ken continued. "There have been many times that I've had to scratch and claw to find the least bit of happiness. And I cherished that small sliver of bliss amid the cold reality of life." He paused. "But sometimes people allow these bad things to color them for the rest of their lives, becoming bitter... angry... or sad and depressed. And even though these tragic events shape us as surely as our triumphs, some sink so far into their dark emotions that they become unrecognizable from their former selves – changed forever."

Ken turned to him in the darkness. "We must rise above tragedy. Life is always a mixture of good and bad. But beyond it all, life goes on. And so must we."

Hunter clenched his eyes shut.

"And even if you could have spent the rest of your life with her, there still would have been hard times. You might've been happier – sharing it with her, but it still wouldn't have been any 'happily ever after' deal."

Chris smiled momentarily. "Yeah, I guess that's true."

"Better put your face back on, space dock coming up," Ken reminded his captain as the shuttle space

205

port came into view. Within an hour, the small shuttle returned them to space and the orbiting warship they called home.

They entered the ship with no further words between them. Crandell noticed the slump in his captain's shoulders, as if he carried some invisible weight. He put his hand out and grasped his friend's arm.

"I've got some good news I've been saving. I think now is as good a time as ever."

Hunter turned to him.

"I received a personal message from that patrol ship the other day," Ken began. "From a young kid fresh out of Fleet Training. He had just joined the Fearless and knew the Cobra would be joining their squadron. He wanted to surprise someone – to meet them for the first time."

Hunter waited. But he wasn't in the mood for...

"His name is Robert J. Hunter."

Chris Hunter looked bewildered for a few milliseconds. Crandell's smile widened as Hunter's face changed to surprise and then expectation.

"Yeah, your grandson has joined up and sailed to the stars with us."

Hunter chuckled. "My grandson!"

"I told him that I hoped there wouldn't be too many more battles to fight, not with the treaty nearing completion. But I did tell him that there were a lot of planets to discover. And a good captain to meet and get to know."

Hunter slapped his First Officer on the back.

"That's the best news I've had in a long time, Mr. Crandell"

Their shared laughter echoed down the hall.

"How about I buy you an ale before you sack out. We can talk about *our* days back at Fleet Training. And our first assignment together," Ken said with a twinkle in his eye.

"Lead on, mister. I've got a big taste and all night to quench it."

For the first time in a long time, the black hole of loneliness seemed to recede in Chris Hunter's chest as he thought about meeting his grandson and getting to know him. Captain Hunter and Commander Crandell entered the ship's pub amid joyous greetings from their fellow shipmates. Pints of good ale were drunk, and the evening's conversations lasted well into the wee hours of the night.

That night the Cobra sailed back to the stars, leaving the Earth far, far behind. She jumped past the speed of light just outside the orbit of Neptune a few days later.

An entire galaxy stretched before her, perhaps a more peaceful one soon. And even though everyone who sailed away knew they would never see their loved ones on Earth again, yet they soared with a growing excitement and formed a strong bond with their shipmates who flew with them to the stars.

And they looked forward to meeting new friends, alien and otherwise, under a thousand different skies.

Enon

It is written: 'We, humans, are made in the image of God.'"

Enon's body tensed with fear after he finished speaking. He kept his eyes averted from the twenty-foot-tall guard. And although he could not see his reaction, he heard the huge alien's breathing grow more rapid.

The horny mandibles of the huge Qarzaak slowly opened and closed. Dancing reflections from the lights of the cavern ceiling played across the ridged scales of the Qarzaak's abdomen as it tensed. The giant alien slowly bent over until its arm touched the cavern floor. The misshapen head now swiveled lower until Enon felt the hot breath of the alien sweep his face.

"You have an ugly god," The Qarzaak hissed.

Enon's brown eyes grew hard, and his heart burned with anger. He wanted to raise his ebony face toward the lumbering hulk above him and look the alien in its multi-faceted eyes, but he continued to gaze at the ground in deference, realizing such an action meant instant death. Slaves were not allowed to look a Qarzaak in the eyes for any reason. Enon sighed and fought against the anger burning in his heart.

The huge alien continued to laugh and click its giant mandibles in mirth.

Enon breathed deeply to regain his composure. He focused on a single thought, something he could hold onto even in the face of humanity's never-ending injustice. He knew that he was more than a nothing-slave. He was more than Enon, surnamed Hallaway.

He was a *human being*.

"You want a breeding license – that's it. That's why you told me this bizarre thing." The Qarzaak's mighty laughter echoed throughout the large cavern.

Now Enon's anger vectored in a single heartbeat – to white-hot lust. But the images in his mind were unclear because Enon, like every man on this god-forsaken planet, had never actually seen a woman.

The Qarzaak controlled their human slaves better that way.

But there were the hushed rumors, whispered around the fires before sheer exhaustion forced their aching bodies to sleep. This was the only time that they could think, with a few precious moments to themselves. And before their exhaustion forced them to sleep, they thought of things that were not, but wished them to be.

Dreams.

Enon remembered the oft told tales that the Qarzaak actually kept women on mythical mother Earth.

But his dreams of Earth had long since died in the pain of this terrible place.

"What I have said is true. It is written in our most sacred book." Enon clenched his eyes tightly shut and pushed away the unattainable dreams of women and Earth with a single mental blow.

The Qarzaak's laughter echoed louder.

"You are a self-centered race, puny human. To think the Giver would fashion himself into the

209

image of a single race. And that of a pitiable *sub-species*." The Qarzaak emphasized the last word as the basest of obscenities.

Enon held his anger at bay in frustrated silence. He dared not clarify the words of the ancient book – humans were not literally created in God's image. Humans were created with God's qualities - especially love and mercy.

"You are nothing but savages." The Qarzaak stood to its full height, over three times that of the ebony-skinned man before it.

The huge mandibles opened wide.

"I should take your head for that gross lie. But I don't since you are a native Healer. Still..."

The blue spit shot from between the Qarzaak's mandibles like a superheated geyser.

Enon clenched his eyes shut with the wet impact that enveloped his body. He shook with blind revulsion as his skin crawled and screamed under the slime that covered him in its filthy, dripping embrace. His nostrils burned with the acidic stench, and he dared not open his eyes under the thick, burning syrup.

"The CairE wants you."

Enon barely made out the words because the Qarzaak's spit filled his ears.

"Do not forget that. He wants you to come immediately. That is the only reason I have wasted my breath with you."

And there was silence.

Enon wiped with urgent, rapid motions across his mouth and nose – like a man drowning. And he was.

Finally, mercifully, one nostril cleared enough to fill his aching lungs with air. Still, it was mixed with the gut-wrenching stench of the blue saliva. Enon choked and gagged while he bent over with pain as the blue spit slowly burned his skin.

He wiped faster.

With each pass, more of the syrupy saliva clung to his hands, and not his face. But the heavy stench would irritate his nose for days to come, and his black hair would glow with a blue glaze for days.

But like all humans, he would wear this dishonor with pride. All humans knew that if you had been subjected to the blue spit, you had done something to anger them.

He removed his clothes carefully, rag by tattered rag. They were ruined. As was his sense of smell temporarily. But at least that would come back with time. But his clothes would fall apart in a few days.

Now completely naked, his hair shining with a bluish glaze from the overhead lights, he walked among the laborers with his head held high.

But not even one of the hundreds of men once noticed him amid their overwhelming tiredness. And not one cared, because it was near the end of another twelve-hour working shift in the mines.

Enon found a pile of clothes. They were in the usual place. The Qarzaak always stripped the dead humans and put the clothes here before they threw the nude bodies away.

After they had popped their heads off.

He smiled broadly while he dressed himself in his handpicked rags. Enon knew he was one of the few humans any Qarzaak would condescend to speak with one to one.

And though his stomach screamed for the one decent meal that would be served by the Qarzaak soon, and what precious free time he might have for himself would also be wasted – he obeyed.

To disobey was a far, far worse thing.

Picking his way back through the dimly lit caverns, Enon found his store of bags filled with dried plants – roots and leaves. Enon chose carefully, remembering the words of his mentor, Joktan, and partly guessing from the few symptoms the Qarzaak had given him about the sickness.

Placing the leather straps of the bags that held the chosen herbs over his shoulders, he began his journey to the surface.

He forced his drained body to move among the sweaty bodies of his fellow laborers. Through the narrow confines of their dimly lit underworld, he weaved his way until he finally passed the twin Qarzaak warriors who guarded the Outer Gate with swords and claw.

But once past them, he paused a few minutes while his eyes slowly adjusted to real light. He sat down on the ground cross-legged. He rested a moment; his exhausted and numbed mind needed it – sweet rest...

"Over here."

Enon turned to the whispered words. A grimy, dirt-streaked face emerged out of the shadows. But Enon recognized the man's yellow complexion and his slanted eyes framed by greasy jet-black hair.

"Have you been called by the CairE?" He asked.

Enon nodded wearily – it was only Merk.

"Then I must come with you." Merk's nose wrinkled in disgust. "You have been dishonored. Good. Your heart will be with us as I strike a blow for humanity."

Enon shook his head. "Leave me alone."

Merk's dirty smile widened. "I have made myself a *living bomb*."

Enon grew very still.

Merk opened his shirt and revealed the cloth belts strapped tight around his body – each belt had many small pockets filled with different minerals. "Separated, they're harmless. But if I crush two and quickly mix their contents against a third it will ignite and then they all explode. The haughty Qarzaak will never suspect anything this primitive."

"Man, you're crazy." Enon whispered in disbelief.

"Aren't we all?" Merk pulled his shirt closed. "Aren't we all," he repeated with a smile.

Enon watched as Merk's eyes looked off into the distance. He felt his heart pounding faster when he realized how Merk's countenance transfixed as if in a vision. Enon stepped away until Merk grabbed him roughly and pulled him close.

Enon struggled vainly.

"We strike a blow for humanity. Together."

"And we both die – together." Enon added.

Merk's transfixed expression broke into wild-eyed smile mirth. "That is the plan."

The lumbering form of a Qarzaak guard came into view.

"Let's go, before they suspect." Pushing Enon before him, the two young men moved forward.

The fresh breeze swept his face and body with cool refreshment. Enon breathed deeply, appreciatively. And wondered how many more breaths he had left.

"What will I tell the CairE?" Enon looked intensely at Merk. "About you."

"Tell him that I too am a Healer. Hey, I carry my own bags." Merk laughed again.

Enon pulled at the straps that hung over his shoulders as they walked into the false night under the smaller third sun.

"They even picked a planet that doesn't have a true night – to torment us," Merk said with bitterness.

"And far away from any kind of civilization – even Qarzaak civilization," Enon said.

"How do you know that?"

Enon glanced at his old friend. "Because they have not replaced Joktan, the Qarzaak Healer, after all these long months after his death. There is much sickness with this new outbreak of the virus, even among them."

"That is good. That is good," Merk repeated.

"No, it isn't." Enon stopped. "Joktan was the only Qarzaak Healer. The only one who could treat the virus native to this world." Enon gazed far off. "He was the only one of them that *ever* talked to me."

Merk waved his hands. "It's wrong. You shouldn't talk to any of them. They're the enemy."

Enon sighed.

Merk shook his head in thought. "And you even learned some of their language, I can't believe that. And he even allowed you to use his Med-Tools?"

"More. He taught me how to use them, and how to make medicines using the native plants here. Joktan wasn't allowed to treat any humans, so he taught me. He even taught me how he used his Med-Tools on his own kind when they became sick. And he would have taught me more, until you killed him."

Merk laughed again. "I didn't kill him."

"No, not you personally. But your stupid resistance did." Enon turned and marched away.

Merk matched Enon's rapid strides.

"Men were born to be free, not slaves. And we're not a sub-species." Merk stared straight ahead, his face hard and sure. "We have to fight until we are free again."

"Or we're all dead." Enon whispered.

They walked in silence, each deep in their own thoughts – troubled thoughts filled with the curse of being born human.

"Are you a coward, Enon? Is that why you do not join us?"

Enon looked at him with narrowed eyes. "No."

Merk nodded. "Perhaps you're too good for us. Is that it?"

Enon looked away as he kept up his quick pace. "No."

"Then why?" Merk stopped as Enon continued forward. "You owe me at least this explanation."

Enon stopped. He placed his hands on his hips as he turned, pushing aside the bags that hung over each shoulder.

"Humanity lost the Great War, Merk. We've lost every rebellion since then – even the petty uprisings the resistance launches from time to time on this god-forsaken world." Enon looked up at the auburn sky. "We lose every time, Merk. Can't you boys figure that out. We can't defeat the Qarzaak."

Merk shook his head and laughed. Suddenly, his entire countenance changed, replaced by a deep sadness etched across his face.

"No one is our friend in this universe, Enon. Nobody cares about humans." Merk's voice grew low, full of emotion. "We must look after ourselves. Nobody else will."

Enon waited for more.

"Ever since they drove us from our home-world." Merk looked up into the twilight sky. "Not a single alien race spoke up for us. Not a single one of them, all Qarzaak controlled, cared enough to question our treatment." He shook his head sadly. "They drove us away like animals."

"The *Exodus of Tears*," Enon said with his voice full of emotion.

Every human knew that story by heart now. A tale seared and scarred into every human memory. Enon heard the cries once again, the screams, as the entire population of Earth was herded into the Qarzaak ships. Men separated from the women, packed like so much disposable freight and shipped out to distant, unknown worlds among the stars.

In his mind, he again heard the cries of the hundreds of millions as they died from new, alien diseases. They died in dirty, unsanitary cargo holds packed like cattle. The Qarzaak didn't care - humans were only a sub-species, after all. The Qarzaak let humans die like unwanted pests.

Tears burned in Enon's eyes.

Merk placed his hand on his friend's shoulder and squeezed it in mutual recognition of their sad plight.

"There has been so much suffering," Enon whispered.

"And still, nobody cares for us. Nobody loves a human. We work our short lives away in these holes." Merk bit his lip. "And if the diseases or the work don't kill us, we get our heads popped off because we angered some high and mighty Qarzaak."

Enon nodded.

"All the different races of aliens who call themselves Qarzaak." Merk gritted his teeth. "All the Qarzaak despise us. They..."

"...call us sub-species," Enon finished.

"Yes." Merk groaned.

They trudged through the shallow valley a long time in silence. In their minds, they relived that epic, tragic time once again. They died once again along with that single, cursed generation.

"Even if we are in the right. We can't defeat them in war," Enon said.

"We kill them. We kill a few more every time." Merk turned and stared at him.

Enon's eyes met his.

217

"They kill more of us. And then make our miserable existence that much more intolerable for the rest." Enon looked at the sky and shook his head. "You're fools."

"Are we? At least we're willing to die for what we believe in. What about you? Do you like what they've done to us? Do you?"

"No. I don't like it. But there must be another answer. There must be better way," Enon said.

"OK, tell me. Should we just give up and live out our pitiful existence under their terms? That's it; we'll bow to them and make them our gods. We'll just go right along..."

"Shutup!" Enon shouted.

Enon's breathing grew rapid and he realized how his anger had erupted all at once. He must control it, he reminded himself. They would soon be in the Qarzaak city. Anything even remotely resembling rebellion would be punished with their heads removed.

Enon closed his eyes until he felt the calmness returning.

"Perhaps it bothers you that you will kill along with me tonight? I had forgotten what you are, dear Enon. A healer." Merk smiled. "Or perhaps it bothers you that we die together as heroes."

"Dead heroes." Enon repeated. Enon's thoughts swirled in a turmoil of emotions. He knew what would happen if the CairE, the Qarzaak leader of this planet, was assassinated. It would mean the death of tens of thousands of those back at the work camp in retaliation.

And many more would be killed on other planets. And women? Would they kill some of the women too? Enon's heart burned. But dare he fight his own kind? His own friend? Surely, if Enon revealed Merk's intention to the Qarzaak, Merk's head would be taken without a second thought.

Could Enon choose between his friend and the CairE? And if he chose Merk, he chose the death of untold thousands.

Enon continued with his shoulders bowed under a greater weight than his herb bags. He breathed deeply, chasing the thoughts away. His eyes turned upward at the burnt-orange sky, the only sky he had ever known.

And for the thousandth time, Enon tried to image a blue sky instead.

He smiled. Sometimes at night during the mild winter, when the Qarzaak allowed them to camp above ground in the cool, crisp air, people would point to a small yellow star. It was said that star was the Sun around which fabled Earth orbited.

Then the old stories would be told of long ago, when men were free to travel among the stars. And even more astounding, humans had been masters of technology, both designers and builders – like the Qarzaak.

Enon shook his head. He found it difficult to imagine such things. He emptied his mind and he and Merk trudged on through the forest.

The groans of pain came to their ears long before they saw him.

The man was dying.

The rattling, labored breathing told Enon of the fluid slowly filling his lungs. That is what would kill him in the end. That is how 'The Death Virus' killed in its most lethal form. You drowned a slow suffocating death, unless the Qarzaak found him hiding here first. For a sick slave, one that could not work, was useless to them.

Enon knelt beside the shaking form. The man's eyes fluttered and he began to struggle violently.

"Hold still. I am a friend. I am human."

Dilated pupils tried to focus but could not.

Enon fumbled with his right hand in his bag while he pulled the sick man upright.

Merk watched from a distance, knowing Enon's efforts were in vain.

Enon's fingers felt first one object, and then another, searching for the right container. "What's your name?"

The man coughed, trying to answer. Drool mixed with crimson and yellow phlegm flowed down over his chin. Enon realized the man had blood in his lungs, the end wasn't far off for him.

"Jaa... Jaxxes."

"I'm going to give you something, Jaxxes. It will ease your pain."

The dying man's labored coughing was his only answer.

Enon found the all too familiar pouch near the bottom.

The man struggled again while Enon leaned his head back and opened his mouth.

"I... was dreamin'... I seen it..." The dying man suddenly went into spasms, his body racked by coughing fits. Finally, painfully, it passed. "I was there. Really there. I was on Earth."

Enon felt the callused hands grip him; he gazed into the worn and haggard face. A face wrinkled and scarred from a lifetime of hard labor. He guessed the man's age to be thirty-five.

Enon rolled the brittle leaves into a ball and inserted it into the man's mouth.

"Remember the stories again, Jaxxes – dream again. You will go to Earth; your dream will come true."

The man chewed instinctively, and his unfocused eyes peered with a sudden intensity.

Enon laid him down gently, trying to make him as comfortable as possible. The herb would ease the man's pain and cause him sleep deeply in his final hours before he succumbed.

And he would dream he was back on Earth.

The death of this one man did not dampen Enon's spirits, he saw death every day. He began his trek again, as if nothing had happened.

And then something crystallized in his mind, something that had been lurking in his thoughts a long time now.

Enon no longer believed.

His heart and soul wrenched with this most intimate revelation of his being. A secret he dared not share.

He was a Believer who did not believe.

No, he would never see the fabled home-world of humanity. Not because he would never travel there, but because there was never such a planet.

Earth was simply a myth. Earth was a Fable of a long-enslaved race who yearned for a home-world of their own, who yearned to be free to walk the under the sapphire skies of their own planet.

It was supposed to be a garden planet, a paradise full of life – so the stories told. The whispered stories told of animals of every shape and description which dwelled there, unlike this barren planet. There were animals that crawled and swam and walked. There were animals with fur and scales and skin. There were trees, bushes and flowers of untold varieties.

And there was something called birds...small animals that could actually fly. Why, the stories said there were birds of every color. It was even said they could sing. But Enon had always doubted that last fact.

How could an animal sing? He shook his head.

When had he stopped believing? When had the pressures of this crushing reality buried the one dream man had left to believe in? Enon felt so old – old for a man of twenty-three.

"Do you believe in Earth?" Enon asked Merk, breaking the silence and trying to get away from his own troubled thoughts.

"Of course," Merk grunted.

Enon bit his lip. "But no one we know has ever been there."

Merk held his head up, his mind turning these words over. The silence stretched.

"Perhaps the stories about a home-planet. About Earth... are..." Enon's words trailed off.

"No one we know, has ever seen a woman either, have they?" Merk said at last. "But you believe they exist, don't you?"

Enon had no memory of his mother. Male children were taken away immediately after birth. But somehow, he knew he had a mother, and she had been a woman. So...

But Merk was right; no man on this god-forsaken planet had ever seen a woman. Not even a holo-image of one. Over the years, a precious few had left this world, each given the longed-for breeding licenses. But none had ever returned to tell their tales about seeing women and living with them.

And yet, Enon did believe women existed.

"Do you really think that women are soft and sweet and pretty? And... and kissing a woman is better than candy?"

Merk did not even hesitate.

"Absolutely."

***

The bright lights of the Qarzaak city appeared between the slopes of the two small hills. Enon drew a deep breath and thought again about the futility of life – and his life. And about the pitiable existence he had known and that his race had known.

And this day, life would end for him.

"Come," Merk said. "We will die as heroes – for our kind."

Enon sighed. "I think I would rather live. And let someone else die a hero."

Merk laughed out loud. "Don't worry, my old friend. It will be quick. Just get us close to the 'High One' of the Qarzaak."

Enon did not answer. He was tired of war. He was tired of death. He was even tired of living.

The city streets were surprisingly empty, which was stranger for the fact that the Qarzaak preferred the low light of this world's false night. But except for a solitary Qarzaak gliding above the surface in one of their hover vehicles, the two men were alone.

Enon and Merk walked with bowed heads on the main road. They kept their heads bowed with good reason – the Law was clear, no human dare look upon the face of a superior species under penalty of death.

The great black pyramid rose before them as they continued walking. It drew them forward with its foreboding blackness, as if it the dark structure sucked up the light from the very sky just as the Qarzaak sucked up the lifeblood of the human race.

Casting quick, furtive glances upward at it, Enon saw the famed lights that periodically raced up the pyramid's edges to the dark pinnacle far above.

Slowly the huge, black gate became discernible. Just before they reached it, two Qarzaak warriors approached. The bone-spurs of their feet appeared to Enon's lowered gaze.

"Why are there two?" The warrior's legs moved closer.

Enon glanced over at Merk. "He is helping me to carry all I need to heal." Enon said in a low tone.

The familiar sounds of a Qarzaak scanner became discernible. "What is in the other's bags. It is a mineral, not leaves and plants like you carry."

The two men looked at each other, heads still bowed.

"Minerals may be needed." Enon said.

"It is used to heal." Merk lied with confidence.

The warrior's voice echoed unseen above them. "Only you were requested, slave. You could carry them all. Who decided to bring a second slave?"

Enon shut his eyes, hiding under his bowed head.

"Answer me!"

Enon's heart skipped a beat at the shouted words.

Merk stared accusingly at him.

"I asked him to join me." Enon took a deep breath.

"Slaves do as they are told!" The Qarzaak shouted back.

Merk growled under his breath in frustration.

Enon closed his eyes and tensed for the explosion.

Still staring at the Qarzaak's feet, he heard the sounds of struggling, and grunts mixed with the sounds of cursing. The sounds rose into the air.

Merk screamed somewhere above.

Enon glanced up for the briefest moment and saw the mandibles near Merk's neck.

'Please God, no. No.' He shouted those words in his mind while he clenched his eyes shut.

They're going to pop Merk's head off! He thought.

Enon jumped at the ripping sound – but he realized the guards had only ripped the bags off Merk's body.

Enon heard the familiar sound of the blue spit splattering all over Merk.

Enon tensed and waited his turn.

"You, Healer. You alone were ordered by the CairE. Carry these bags from the other slave and go inside."

Shocked and numb, yet somehow still alive, Enon walked as though in a daze inside the black pyramid.

"Humans are liars and imbeciles, every last one of them." The well-known insult echoed down the black corridor from the Qarzaak warriors holding Merk behind him.

Tears stung Enon's eyes.

"And now they try to make decisions on their own! Stupid sub-species!" The second Qarzaak guard added.

In a mental fog, he followed the beckoning lights through the black maze.

'Nothing ever changed. Another life wasted if the Qarzaak to kill Merk. But since he had been dishonored by the blue spit, perhaps that would suffice this time.' Enon thought.

Enon bowed again under the injustice heaped upon his entire race. He burned with the Qarzaak's prejudice for his species, felt the rage of their smug self-righteousness for all humans. Worse, he felt his spirit die again under their relentless burdens, their unjust condemnation – all humans condemned as an incorrigible species, not capable of achieving Qarzaak.

Not capable.

But never allowed the opportunity.

Enon screamed in his mind.

'The Qarzaak were always right. They always won. They were far too advanced in their technology for humanity to ever have a chance to defeat them' Enon brushed those hideous thoughts back. But more thoughts raced in to replace them. 'Even if Merk had succeeded, it would only have meant three more lives wasted. Violence would never solve anything.'

He glanced at the belts containing the minerals for the weapon. Merk hadn't instructed him how to set it off. But he wouldn't have used it anyway.

He was a Healer, he tried to save lives, not take them.

Enon paused, tears falling from his eyes.

Nothing ever changed.

He continued forward. Somehow, through the confusion of his mind, Enon walked into the antechamber.

The huge Qarzaak bent over a bed upon which a smaller version of itself lay. It was immense, bigger than any Enon had ever seen.

The CairE's misshapen head turned to him.

"Come, sub-species. Come. It is my offspring."

Enon approached and heard the all too familiar wheezing.

"The virus has mutated again. It attacks Qarzaak now. It is almost always fatal to humans," Enon said absently, staring at the Qarzaak child.

227

The bulbous eyes of the CairE regarded him carefully.

"But maybe the Qarzaak's immune system can fight it more effectively," Enon added quickly.

The CairE nodded solemnly.

"No, human. It also kills most Qarzaak. Our population has been decimated the last few weeks. Without Joktan the Healer, my staff has been unsuccessful in finding a cure for this new strain," the CairE said solemnly. "Perhaps in a few days." The mandibles snapped together, and a segmented arm reached for the figure lying so still. "But it would be too late for my only offspring."

"I will need your Med-tools." Enon said.

The CairE nodded.

"I will reward you for this, if you can save him."

Enon took the Med-scanner, trying to remember what Joktan had taught him both in its usage and what little Joktan had shared with him about the Qarzaak immune system.

Surprisingly, he did not acknowledge the CairE's promise.

He didn't want the CairE's reward. Bitterness welled inside his heart again – rage and frustration. Enon wanted nothing from him or his kind.

"I am the CairE of this world, though it is distant and insignificant – name your desire." The mighty Qarzaak commanded.

The Med-scanner came active and Enon scanned the life-signs of the young Qarzaak.

"I will let you breed. Yes. A breeding license. That is what humans desire most of all." The CairE's huge head nodded. "Food and drink, a buffet that will never end. I will give you more than you have ever known or dreamed."

"He is very weak," Enon said, still ignoring the High One's words. "His body is losing its battle with the virus. It may already be too late."

In his mind, Enon knew how easy it would be just to let this young Qarzaak die. It struggled to breathe even now. It wouldn't be his fault if it died. Many hundreds of humans and Qarzaak had died today on this pitiful planet. What was one more death?

The bulbous eyes and the huge insect-like face lowered right before him.

Enon felt his heart pounding. He was looking a Qarzaak right in the face – eye to eye! And it was the great CairE himself!

"What will it take to save him? I will give anything to save my son."

Enon caught his breath a moment. Now he gazed at the huge Qarzaak face impassively, and then watched as it moved and hovered over the smaller form of its child.

He watched in surprise as the Qarzaak father took its horny arm and softly stroked the small face.

And there was a sound.

Enon's eyes narrowed at the strange sound. The two faces were so near each other; he couldn't make out where the sound had emanated.

He nodded with sudden realization.

The father and son were humming to each other. It was a calming sound, an intimate singing one to the other.

'How strange.' Enon thought with surprise. 'The CairE *loves* his offspring!'

Enon became transfixed by this sight. He felt his heart pounding and his anger beginning to fade.

"Nothing," Enon said simply.

"You will let him die," The CairE said sadly. The huge head swung back to him, mandibles open.

"No, I will try to save him." Enon raised the Med-scanner. *"For no reward..."*

The mandibles worked nervously. "But what must I give you?"

Enon pulled the bags from his shoulders and laid them on the table next to the CairE's dying offspring.

"For what reward will you save him?" The CairE urged again.

And Enon replied with a single word – a Qarzaak word.

"SzoGapee." Enon carefully enunciated the alien word.

The bulbous eyes blinked in astonishment. "You speak Qarzaak?"

Enon nodded. "Joktan taught me more than your medical instruments."

"It is hard for me to imagine that a sub-species can..." The huge head shook slowly.

"Speak a Qarzaak word." Enon finished. "Or learn your tools? Or your mathematics." Enon's voice almost rose to a shout without his realizing it. He quickly took a deep breath to control that rash emotion while he searched among his bags for the plants and herbs he needed.

It was a long shot, but it was the only thing he could offer the CairE's sick offspring.

After he found the correct combination and began mixing them, the CairE spoke again.

"Perhaps you are *just* a mimic." The mandibles came near. "What does the word you uttered mean, human?"

Enon took his crude knife and began to chop the leaves to make the paste. As his hands worked quickly, he answered.

"Love... or undeserved-love." Enon paused. *"Love without expectation of any reward.* That's the closest human translation." Enon smiled as he added water to the liquid paste.

The mammoth Qarzaak snorted loudly. "How is it that a sub-species such as your violent race can understand this concept? I do not believe you."

"We know. We understand love. We can express love... even to an alien."

"You are a sub-species —we have analyzed and judged your species – little more than animals with a primitive mind."

Enon almost lost his temper. Why was he trying to save this Qarzaak, anyway? The Qarzaak would let him die if it was him lying there instead. After all, humans were only sub-species.

Enon smiled. Without thinking, he looked upon the face of the up-right Qarzaak again. And he spoke to him as an equal.

"I will do for you, what I would want done for me."

The CairE's mandibles froze in shocked surprise.

"SzoGapee." Enon repeated.

Placing one hand behind the young Qarzaak's head, Enon carefully placed the preparation between his small mandibles. Weakly, it sucked.

Without looking, Enon felt the CairE kneel beside them.

"The Qarzaak know your kind. Your greatest desires are to breed, to fight and to destroy." The huge mandibles clicked. "It has always been said that humans can never become Qarzaak, that you are savages. A *sub-species*."

Enon continued his gentle ministrations.

The CairE watched. And saw the first signs of relief on the offspring's tiny face.

Enon looked up again and began using the Med-Tool, remembering the instructions of Joktan. With the combination of natural medicines from this cold world in concert with the Medical technology of the Qarzaak, Enon fought the deadly virus.

The CairE's mandibles clicked softly. The father leaned close to his son, and both hummed to each other.

Hours passed, and the irregular breathing softened and finally returned to a semblance of normalcy in the young Qarzaak. In those hours, the two beings talked, the mighty CairE and a mere human. They talked of knowledge and music and art. They talked on many subjects.

It was like the times he had conversed with Joktan.

They discussed life and death. They conversed in detail about many things. But most of all, they talked about love.

Enon used the Med-Tool for the third time to stimulate the young Qarzaak's immune system and help it fight the retreating effects of the killer virus.

Enon felt the CairE's face near his.

"You are different." The mandibles clicked rapidly three times. "You do understand..." The great body rose. "I have decided your reward. I shall bestow upon you the greatest of privileges. You will become my personal slave.

Enon stared incredulously at the CairE.

"You will be taught Qarzaak. I will teach you personally and I will bring in Teachers. You will learn science and math and the arts. And more, you will travel with me when I attend the next Great Council. Together we shall plead the case of humans in the Qarzaak language. And there will I tell them that humans are more than we realize, more than..."

"More than a sub-species," Enon finished for him.

The CairE nodded.

"What is your name," the CairE asked.

"Enon."

"You helped us purely out of love. I will never forget your act loving-kindness for me and my offspring, *Enon*."

Enon was astounded at hearing his name uttered for the first time by a Qarzaak. He felt the room spin momentarily.

"You will live here with me and my family. You will be taught Qarzaak. One must know Qarzaak before one is considered Qarzaak."

Suddenly, he remembered Merk's stricken face as he was dishonored and taken prisoner.

"I would ask something of you, High CairE, but not for myself. I ask you this request in the true spirit of SzoGapee."

"Speak!" The CairE gazed at him thoughtfully.

"My friend, Merk, was arrested when I first arrived. Please release him," Enon said with bowed head.

"I was informed he accompanied you without my permission. Perhaps he came here to kill me?"

Enon's mind worked furiously. "He was confused. Please, I ask that you forgive his ignorance. He can learn SzoGappe too, by your expressing it for him this time."

The CairE gazed a moment, carefully considering Enon's request. "Because you have saved my son's life, I will believe you. But if any other human comes near our city without permission, he will be exterminated on the spot."

"I will teach Merk so that he will not make that mistake again."

"Teach him well, human. Teach him thoroughly, as you will be taught the ways of Qarzaak."

Enon nodded silently. He was drained, physically, and emotionally. There had been too much death, too much pain, this day.

Later, after the CairE's offspring awakened with signs of definite improvement, Enon curled up in a corner of the room deep inside the black pyramid – ready to sleep at last.

He had just finished eating – the best meal he had ever eaten his entire life. He relished the wonderful flavors and felt renewed strength from its nourishment.

A wild array of thoughts flashed through his weary mind. He would become a house-hold slave, a position at the bottom of the rung in the order of Qarzaak society.

Enon shook his head. He would always be a human deep inside. But now he wondered, could he be both human and Qarzaak?

It was better than nothing. And that's what he was now.

And there was something more he realized. Even the lowliest Qarzaak could travel wherever they wanted, once they achieved Qarzaak, once he was taught and qualified he would rise in status above a house-hold slave.

Enon would be free.

He would find a place and live in their galactic society.

And that first small step had been taken today by Enon's unselfish gesture. He hoped it was the first step for freedom for all humanity after the Great Council was addressed.

In the next second, a flash of ominous understanding struck him. Enon realized how alone he would become. After humans learned about his new status, he would be despised as a traitor. He would also be scorned by those now called Qarzaak because he *dared* to join them.

He would be very alone in the universe, the first human Qarzaak.

Tiredness overwhelmed him and his muscles ached with a fiery pain. His eyes fluttered and exhaustion pushed his worrisome thoughts away. Fatigue enveloped Enon, and he fell into a deep slumber almost before his eyes fully closed.

He slept.

And for the first time in many years, Enon dreamed of Earth.

The *New Adventure*

Now he'd lost everything...

Derrick retreated deeper into his hiding place while he watched in utter disbelief the terrible event unfolding right before him. He swallowed hard, fighting back his tears. But still, the tears rolled down his cheeks.

It wasn't fair.

He watched as the alien dressed in the black suit leaned closer to Faban.

Faban, that good-for-nothing Tescy drunk. Yes, he could pilot a starship. And he was pretty good with running a crew. Unfortunately, he had no business sense at all. And worse, when he was drunk, he did stupid things. Derrick was sure Faban was the reason he was losing the last vestige of his childhood, the last connection to his parents.

The reason he was losing his home.

Derrick wiped his eyes dry. This was no time to cry like a baby.

He looked frantically around the tiny compartment in which he sat hidden within the network of maintenance tubes that lined the interior of the starship. He finally found what he was looking for amid a jumble of food packets and other items he'd quickly thrown together and hidden here when he realized all was lost.

He knew the banker would order a complete scan to make sure the ship was empty before they put it up for auction. Derrick took the straps of the vest-like covering and pulled them tight around his body.

His fingers danced over the control panel sewn over a section of the chest. He felt the low hum when the device went active.

Derrick managed a low chuckle. As long as he kept the IDS on, no sensor scan would pick him up. The IDS would make him invisible to almost any kind of scanning. He could hide here forever if he stole enough food and water.

And no one would ever know it.

The thirteen-year-old boy now began rummaging through another pile of food packets and miscellaneous tools and mementoes he'd grabbed from his quarters. He found the hand-held scanner and quickly crawled back to the grate that looked out over the main cargo bay. He tuned the device until the faces came into focus on the tiny screen.

Derrick watched intently.

"Faban, please don't take this personal," the alien said without any pretense of emotion. "You realize this is all strictly business." The alien financier attempted a smile, but he only managed a grimace.

"Yeah, right," Faban said angrily. "You take everything we have and say it ain't personal. What else is it?" The green faced Tescy snarled to punctuate his feelings.

"Come, come. Is that any way to behave? Surely you don't want me to call in the authorities and have you incarcerated as well?"

Faban's green complexion deepened and he looked away with disgust. "No, I don't need any more time in a cell."

"Are you the last of the crew onboard?"

Fabian looked around the cargo bay, his red eyes avoiding the other alien. "Yeah, I'm it. Sure."

The alien gazed at Faban with a doubtful expression.

"I sent the Engineer packing yesterday. When I told him there were no credits, nothing even to pay his last month's wages, he left in a hurry." Faban rubbed his swollen left eye. It was a distinctly darker shade of green due to the bruise.

"I see you two didn't part on good terms either." The alien finally managed a smile.

"Yeah, we had a fight. But believe me; he's hurting worse than I am."

"Any other crew?"

"No, times have been hard. I couldn't afford to pay anyone else."

"I understood there was a boy – a juvenile human."

Faban suddenly looked up at the grate and straight at Derrick via the data pad – almost as if he knew.

Derrick held his breath.

"Naw, he's long gone. He was an orphan. He struck out on his own back on Zerra VII."

"Then, I'll have to ask you to remove your personal belongings while my bank completes the repossession process. We need to prepare this starship for immediate sale so we can try to recoup some of our losses."

Faban shook his head. "Sure, I'll get my stuff and leave right away." He turned to go but the alien in the dark suit reached out and grabbed him by the shoulder.

"Mister Faban, if you had used sound business practices and taken care of your bottom line, we wouldn't have been forced to take this distasteful action."

Faban stared into the alien's eyes a moment. "I take too many chances. I had a couple of good deals coming my way, some really profitable cargo. If I could've had a little more time..."

"Mister Faban, our records also indicate your perchance for gambling. We know about your mounting debts – quite substantial debts in fact."

Faban brushed the alien's hand off his shoulder. "Yeah, well, I guess it's time to move on."

The two turned and left the cargo bay heading toward the forward section and the exit ramp.

Derrick turned off the data pad and crawled over to a corner. He shrugged and shook his head. He hated Faban for lousing up everything and losing the ship. But at least he'd covered for him. No one would suspect he was hiding inside an empty starship now.

But still, he should have never trusted Faban. Lesson learned.

Derrick decided right then and there that he could never trust anyone else ever again. He just couldn't. It seemed everyone he ever trusted always let him down, sooner or later.

He rubbed his tired eyes. He had not slept in almost twenty-four hours, not since the ship had been put into lock-down after they landed on this planet.

And even as he promised himself he could never trust anyone again, his father's words echoed in his mind.

'Surround yourself with people you trust.'

But how could he tell who to trust?

His father had run a tight ship as an Independent Trader. Derrick remembered his father telling him many times how he'd bought this old starship and refitted it. His father had taken his mother and a small crew and flown to the outer edge of the galaxy and back again, seeking his niche, his part in the galactic scheme of things.

And he'd found it.

Derrick smiled at the memory.

But his dad was dead. And his mom had died years before that. And now, the only home he'd ever known was being sold.

Derrick's father had left the title to the starship in his name in his will. Derrick had only been eleven years old at the time – he knew he could never run it by himself much less get a license as a Trader.

Faban had talked him into it.

He'd told him he would take care of it all. If Derrick put the starship in his name, gave him the title, he would take care of the business and make some nice profits for them. Faban would get his Trader's license using the last of dad's money. He would run the business and take care of Derrick too.

And when Derrick was old enough, he'd sign the deed to the starship back over to him.

Yeah, right.

Derrick was older now, he knew more. He could see the bad traits in Faban now, the long nights

241

away drinking and carousing and then coming back to lay up in his room for a couple days at a time until he sobered up.

He'd realized things were getting bad when Faban began lifting off from planet after planet, leaving first one crew member and then another behind because he couldn't afford to pay them.

He looked over the jumble of things and noticed his mother's hand mirror. It was the only personal item he owned of hers now. He lifted it up and looked at himself.

He had red hair, but not just red hair. Derrick's hair was the color of burnished copper. He had his mother's small nose, but his father's deep brown eyes. He was tall for his age, lean and lanky. His mother had always worried about how thin he was – but he rarely got sick, and he always had an abundance of energy.

Derrick stared at the impish face in the mirror.

He crinkled his nose while he stared at his freckles. Reddish-brown freckles were sprinkled across his nose and cheeks like the stars in the sky.

The impish face did not smile back.

Derrick carefully put the mirror down among some of his strewn clothes. He looked around his hiding place.

He had enough food to last a few days. He knew from what he'd overheard that a thorough cleaning and scan of the ship was due and then the starship would be auctioned for sale.

And they hoped for a quick sale.

Derrick wondered if he should sneak off and try to find someplace to live on this planet.

But he didn't even know the name of this planet, much less if he could find a place to live here.

In a flash of insight, he knew his only choice was to stay. He knew this ship inside and out. His father had trained him on every system, and he'd even piloted it a few times – with his father watching closely over his shoulder.

Derrick went over to the control panel just inside of the grate of this maintenance tube and started punching commands. He soon realized the ship was empty and the outer doors were all shut and locked – from the outside. He wasn't going anywhere anyway.

He unlocked the grate and prepared to go out. He needed to get more food and water.

But even as he leaned out and jumped to the floor with his heart thumping, he wondered out loud.

What would the new owners do when they eventually found him?

***

Derrick woke from a deep sleep. He looked around disoriented. For a panic-stricken moment, he didn't know where he was.

But the sad memories of yesterday flooded back into his mind.

He stared at the jumble of food packets and various tools and personal possessions he'd added last night to his original stash after everyone left.

It was a real mess and completely blocked this section of the maintenance tube. He sat up.

He had slept on top of a thick blanket and used both pillows he'd taken from his cabin.

Derrick yawned and started to lie back down. After all, there was no one...

The sound of voices came to his ears.

Derrick froze – he realized that was what had awakened him in the first place.

He searched frantically until he found the IDS jacket. He threw the straps around his body and fastened them tight. He switched the unit on and grabbed his hand-held unit. He tuned it until he found the intruders.

"I've started the system diagnostics, they'll run a while. I'll perform a scan of the ship while you check out the maintenance tubes – start at main cargo."

Derrick looked around frantically at the jumble of things all around him as he realized the alien would enter the tube seven meters from where he sat.

He jumped into action.

His heart pounded at light-speed as he hurriedly grabbed everything within reach and threw it on the blanket. He'd only collected about half the stuff when he heard the hatch being opened.

He stared in that direction in horror.

"Ratcka, I'm taking the hatch off and entering the maintenance tube now."

"Okay, Pek."

Derrick heard the voice plain without need of his hand-held. His heart felt like it was going to leap right out of chest. He knew for certain he was going to get caught right off.

Suddenly, an idea hit him. He smiled mischievously. He watched the hatch closely as the alien unlocked each latch one at a time.

With a flash of movement, he scurried silently to the control panel right beside it. His father had installed it so anyone working inside the maintenance tubes could access the ship's systems without leaving, so he or anyone else could quickly test repairs.

He arrived just as the door to the hatch opened and disappeared. At any second, the alien would step inside.

Derrick looked up at the buttons on the control panel.

Suddenly, two hands came into sight as the alien prepared to enter.

He quickly keyed a command.

The collision alarm roared to life throughout the docked starship.

"Ratcka, what in the great galaxy are you doing up there? That's the collision alarm!"

"I dunno, Pek. I don't understand how that got triggered!"

The red lights strobed on and off while the claxon roared with ear-splitting volume. Derrick had initiated a test of the collision system, including the alarm.

It worked quite well.

"Can't you disable it, Ratcka?"

The alarm continued to deafen them all.

The hands disappeared back outside. "Hang on; let me see if I can help. We don't want the Dock Authorities upset with us."

He heard the footsteps disappearing in the distance toward the command deck. Derrick slumped down with relief.

Derrick punched another button and the collision alarm subsided. Still, he needed a few more minutes.

He noticed the progress bar of the system diagnostics that Ratcka had started from the main computer on the command deck.

Derrick smiled again.

He entered a command to pause the diagnostic. And with a few more quick strokes, he initiated sub-light engine start-up.

Derrick listened a moment.

"Hey, that's the engines firing up! Ratcka, what in the blue blazes you doing up there? Shut'em down fast!"

That should keep them busy for a few minutes while they powered down the engines and then pondered the frozen diagnostic routine.

He scurried back down the tube and his jumbled mess. He knew he needed to hide everything, those two were about to do a complete scan and a physical survey of his starship.

Suddenly it hit him, he knew just where to hide everything. He should have done it last night.

His father had built three secret compartments, one each behind hidden panels in the main and secondary cargo bays – for items he didn't want the authorities to document or question. Or added to any cargo manifest.

He was going to use the smallest compartment – the one located in a maintenance tube near the engines. Like the other two, it was shielded against external scans and its entrance was well-hidden. And because it wasn't part of the network of maintenance tubes, it would allow him to stay hidden better.

After he grabbed the rest of his things and wrapped the blanket around them to carry them, a smile slowly grew on his face. He realized that prospective buyers would be visiting his ship next.

And Derrick was going to have some fun...

***

The alien in the black suit was back. And he had customers.

They were big, hairy aliens – long black fur protruded from everywhere – the sleeves of their shirts as well as their pant legs and any other place their clothing revealed.

Derrick didn't like the looks of them, but that was probably because he knew they were here to buy his home, his starship.

He tuned his hand-held so he could hear them while he watched from the nearest grate inside a maintenance tube.

"...the previous owners maintained all the ship's systems in optimum condition. You'll find the engines tuned and in excellent condition for a ship of this age."

The two big, hairy aliens nodded approval.

"And I'm prepared to offer excellent terms."

"We are interested in a small, fast starship like this one. Still, it is an older model and has no doubt seen a lot of hard travel. We were really hoping for a newer model."

The alien banker smiled broadly. "Let's go to the command deck and check out the systems so you can see their prime condition. I'm sure you'll be convinced that this ship is a fantastic buy. And I'm positive you'll be impressed with the power of the engines. They have been specially upgraded."

The three walked through a door and out of sight.

Derrick scrambled in the opposite direction, heading toward his control panel. He got there just as they entered the bridge area and pilot station. He could see them on his small monitor.

Derrick chuckled while he watched the alien banker enter commands to display the starship's system status – all main systems.

On the monitor, he saw them flash green one by one.

In the next moment, they all changed to red.

"What? Something must be wrong." The banker nervously moved to another station and typed the same commands requesting system status.

Suddenly, every monitor on the bridge went blank. In the next moment, the overhead lights turned off, leaving the three aliens in total darkness except for the light coming through the windows from the docking bay outside.

"It seems this ship is not in as good as shape as you would have us think," the biggest hairy alien said with disgust.

The two aliens turned to leave.

At that moment, a thick white vapor erupted from several points in the ceiling. The fire suppression system had initiated.

All three aliens coughed and shouted as the darkness mixed with white vapor.

Derrick heard first one and then a second loud thud followed by muffled growls and shouts.

The lights came back on, and Derrick saw both aliens lying flat on the ground. He laughed while they gathered themselves up and hurried away with the vapor swirling around their heads.

The banker simply stared in horror.

He laughed off and on for hours with the memory of it.

A few days passed before the banker brought more prospective buyers. And this time Derrick got *really creative*.

"I prefer to enter the commands myself." The multi-armed, multi-legged alien stepped up to the console and typed a command. Ten flexible arms waved constantly while it used the other two to type.

But as the alien typed, Derrick read its command on his monitor back in the maintenance tube and typed a different command with a priority override.

Instead of displaying logs for engine utilization, the console displayed a famous recipe for grilling Laryduk roast pies.

"What the?"

"Uh, we seem to be having some trouble retrieving those logs." The alien banker tugged nervously on his collar. "Why don't you bring up the Navigation system and check it out."

The alien's twelve arms waved in an impatient manner. "All right, let's see a star chart for the Messidian System." Two arms reached over to the next console and entered the commands.

The console remained blank while soft and serene music began to play from the speakers.

"I think this ship has a mind of its own!"

And another prospective buyer stormed away.

Within two hours Ratcka and Pek returned and ran a lengthy and detailed diagnostic on the entire ship. And instead of leaving, they brought two bags of personal items and each took an empty cabin.

Derrick couldn't stay for a long period in the secret cargo with them on board – he needed to get at the control panel to see what they were doing. He stayed inside the network of maintenance tubes now. His movements were limited. But still, he adapted.

Ratcka and Pek brought in a bunch of new food supplies the next day. They stocked themselves up for a long stay until the ship sold. But on the very first night, they discovered a few items missing. And on the second night, even more items disappeared.

Each began to accuse the other when some of their personal items came up missing next.

However, Derrick soon found his control panel disabled. He studied it and even took it apart to trouble-shoot the problem. He quickly realized it had been disconnected from some other junction inside the ship – perhaps at the command deck or somewhere in between.

He sighed. In their haste to ensure everything worked properly, they'd probably disabled everything except necessary ship's systems.

And so, Derrick hid in the secret cargo hold and simply watched as more and more aliens came onboard and inspected his starship. For a while, it seemed the alien bankers would never find a buyer.

But the fateful day finally arrived.

***

Derrick awoke suddenly.

He felt the familiar throbbing of the sub-light engines and knew instantly the ship was readying to depart. In the next moment, he felt the ship lift right after the docking bolts were released.

He threw his clothes on and enabled the IDS. Next, he removed the secret panel to his hideaway. He crawled rapidly to the nearest maintenance tube and to the nearest grate and looked out.

The main cargo bay was empty.

He removed the grate, stepped out and replaced it. He sneaked toward the command deck by way of the secondary cargo bay and on through the outer hallway on the starboard side of the ship. Derrick kept a sharp lookout. But he seemed to be alone. If this was a trial run as he hoped, all the aliens would be on the command deck directing the ship up into orbit.

Derrick found the small utility room and ducked inside. This room held all the backup systems for the command deck – Nav systems, Environmental controls – everything vital.

He found another control panel and enabled it. With a few quick commands, the screen resolved, and he found himself looking at the command deck and the four occupants flying the starship.

The first alien was big. He wore what looked like an old uniform, but Derrick didn't recognize any specific fleet insignias from the two faded markings on his broad shoulders.

The alien's skin was smooth and black as space itself across his exposed forearms and face. Contrasted by the deep black complexion of his smooth skin, Derrick realized that a single line of bony ridges extended from his nose and back over his hairless head and down the back of his neck. The hard ridges of cartilage-like flesh were a startling, pure white color.

Derrick knew this alien was the leader. He could tell by the way he stood behind the alien in the pilot's chair and how the other two glanced back at him while they stood before their own consoles toward the rear of the deck.

He looked down at the short, muscular alien in the pilot's chair.

This alien's exposed arms and head were covered by layers of overlapping greenish-brown scales. And not just scales, these were thick, armored scales. His face was covered by scales, his nose barely perceptible as well as his mouth. Two rows of smaller scales curved completely around his eyes and created the most striking feature on his face.

A female alien stood before the Nav console. Her electric blue hair seemed to glow through some natural iridescent power and contrasted beautifully with her smooth skin – a beautiful orange complexion.

But the weirdest alien sat on top of the Engineering Console.

He was small and only stood about one meter tall. He was a bird-like alien with two large, folded wings covering his feathered body. Some kind of clothing, Derrick guessed they were pants, covered his loins and reached down his spindly legs to his feet. The rest of this alien was covered by beautiful red and black feathers. At the main joint located in the middle of each folded wing, Derrick noticed its fingers. The alien peered with black eyes at the console, the tip of his large beak hovering just over it. And then he extended his wings forward and worked the controls with his fingers.

"What do you think, Vintar? How does she handle?" The black-skinned alien rubbed his hand over his head-ridges

"She's very responsive, captain. And she's fast. I can't wait to put her through her paces." The armor-skinned alien smiled, revealing a mouthful of pointed teeth.

The captain turned. "Katt, enter the coordinates. I want to get out beyond the gravitational reach of this star and see what the sub-light engines can do."

"Aye, Captain." The lithe female's orange fingers danced over the console.

"Doctor Awk, give me status."

The bird-alien peered at the controls. "All systems normal. We're not even close to pushing her yet."

253

"Let's try." The captain smiled wryly.

Derrick heard the sub-light engines revving higher. They were pushing them to the max. He smiled, waiting for what he knew would come next.

The ship lurched and suddenly the engines stalled.

"What happened?!" The captain peered at the engine console along with Katt and the bird-alien.

"They've modified the injectors."

All four nodded appreciatively.

"It means we can really get some speed out of these engines, once we figure out how to configure them correctly." The captain turned.

"I'll make it a priority." Doctor Awk clicked his beak for emphasis.

"OK, keep checking. Let's see if there are other modifications or problems before we buy her." The captain ran his hand over the console as if he were caressing a pet.

Derrick watched in silent awe as the foursome worked as a team. They put the starship through its paces alright. Derrick had not heard the engines roar like that for a long time. He held on while the ship leapt forward with sudden bursts of power and then turned in tight maneuvers. His dad had never pushed the engines this hard. But every time they pushed the sub-light engines toward maximum, they stalled.

He watched in silence. And for the first time, he didn't interfere.

They stayed out almost an hour before they returned and landed in the same docking bay.

The foursome headed toward the main cargo bay by way of the main corridor and through the kitchen. Derrick scurried back the way he had come. He reached the cargo bay first and ran across to the grate and quickly opened it, jumped inside, and closed it just as the four entered.

He listened closely.

"I don't trust that banker. He never makes eye contact when he speaks to you," Vintar said.

"At least he finally coughed up the real story on this starship and its previous owner," Katt said.

"Yeah, he coughed it up like a hair ball." Vintar laughed with pure mirth.

They all chuckled in reply.

"Seems the previous owners were called humans – both licensed as Independent Traders."

"One of them kept this ship in prime condition," Awk said with appreciation. "I checked the maintenance logs and confirmed with diagnostics. The last couple of years, the ship hasn't been maintained quite as well. But it's nothing we can't get back into shape."

"Katt, what about the engines. Did you notice that unique injector system upgrade."

"Yeah, very unique. It has four stages instead of the normal two or three. It's sophisticated, although home-made."

"She's an old Carvarian Recon ship. They were built for speed, not to engage the enemy. They carried a small contingent of troops, dropped them off, and got out fast – real fast," Vintar added with a smile.

The captain smiled approvingly.

"The engines were totally rebuilt five years ago per the logs. I've confirmed that with my checks. They're probably as powerful as any starship in this class. Those quad-tachyon injectors will likely double the acceleration when engaged correctly," Awk said with muted awe.

Home-grown tachyon injectors can be tricky." Katt nodded knowingly. "You remember that triple stage unit on Jaratt's ship we used to fly?"

The alien captain smiled. "Sensitive, weren't they. It always gave us trouble."

"Well, this ship fits our needs – small enough to enter atmosphere and land on a planet. And fast enough to outrun almost any other ship in sub-light or hyperspace."

"Someone took out the troop quarters and created this main cargo bay, which should be large enough for any trading we might do." Vintar looked around approvingly.

"Awk, we'll convert the smaller cargo bay. We'll install your scientific equipment and use that as our main science center."

Awk spread his wings and flapped them with enthusiasm.

"It looks like we could do a decent business carrying small quantities of high valued cargo. And any scientific missions we may bid and win, we have enough room to rent extra equipment and run it. Or anything else that brings us a profit…"

Katt's blue eyes twinkled in rhythm with her electric blue hair. "I'd imagine there are at least two hidden cargo areas. I'd guess one here and one in the smaller bay. I'll make finding them my first task if we buy her. We may want to keep them to handle cargo we don't want on any public manifest."

"Good. Vintar and Awk, I want you to perform one more diagnostic – a thorough one. I want to make sure there are no hidden costs."

"There's always a price to pay," Katt said matter of fact.

"Yes, I just want to make sure the price is acceptable."

Derrick watched as the four turned and went their separate ways.

But Derrick didn't care any longer. It seemed certain these aliens were going to buy his starship and take his home away.

And there was nothing he could do about it.

***

The sale proceeded quickly.

Derrick awoke the next day and watched as the aliens brought in crate after crate until the main cargo bay was filled from one end to the other. And shortly after that, the starship launched for the stars.

The thirteen-year-old boy lay huddled in his hiding place and wondered a long time about what the future held. He wondered most of all what would happen when the aliens discovered they had a passenger.

Derrick didn't have to wonder long. In fact, they discovered him before the second day in space ended.

Derrick's food rations had almost run out. Donning his IDS, he had been caught red-handed. A few minutes later, Derrick found himself on the command deck with the four aliens.

The captain stood next to Katt as she piloted the starship. He turned as they entered the command deck.

Derrick's heart was beating so hard it felt like it would leap out of his chest. He wanted to run so badly, but the alien called Vintar had a death-grip on his shoulder. He knew if he made one false move, Vintar could snap him in two.

"What's this?" The captain's voice boomed.

Derrick felt like disappearing under his piercing gaze.

"I found him sneaking into the food locker. I think it's a human – a juvenile."

"A kid?"

"He was wearing this." Vintar held up his IDS vest.

"That's military issue, isn't it?" The captain took the IDS from Vintar and examined it closely.

"It sure is. And quite illegal for civilians." Vintar chuckled appreciatively.

"Where'd you get this kid? Who's is it?" The captain walked closer until he towered directly over the small boy.

Derrick wasn't intimated by the big alien. He held his head up and spoke without hesitation.

"It's mine. And I want it back." Derrick crossed his arms defiantly.

"I like this kid already." Vintar smiled.

"Well, this explains why he escaped our sensor scans – and everyone else's too." The captain turned to Katt. "Where do you think he was hiding?"

Katt punched the autopilot and stood. She eyed the young boy carefully a moment. She walked closer and bent down on her knees and examined Derrick's pant legs.

"He's been crawling a lot. I'd guess somewhere inside the Maintenance tubes."

"Makes sense." The black-skinned captain walked slowly around Derrick, looking him over with keen eye. Vintar released his grip and stood next to Katt.

Derrick swallowed hard, trying to get his heart to slow down.

"Who are you kid? And why are you on my ship?"

"It's *my* ship." Derrick replied angrily.

Derrick felt the captain's hot breath on his forehead after he bent over and put his face right up against his face.

Derrick closed his eyes.

"I didn't see your name on the bill of sale, juvenile human."

"Fabin drank and gambled too much – he lost it all!" Derrick shouted.

Katt walked over and stood between the captain and Derrick. She nodded at the captain, raising one blue eyebrow.

He nodded.

Katt placed her hand gently on Derrick's shoulder.

"What's your name?"

"Derrick."

"Well, Derrick. Why do you think this starship is yours?"

"My dad owned it. He upgraded all its systems from scratch after he bought it. It's... it's my home."

Katt's blue eyes softened. "Where is your dad?"

"Dead."

"Well, it's my ship now, kid." The captain said, stepping beside Katt. "And we don't need a kid on it."

Derrick felt his heart drop. He looked down at his feet, fighting his tears.

"We'll drop him at Mirada after we dock," the captain said.

"We can't just drop him." Katt pointed at Derrick. "He's just a kid."

"He can't sail on my ship. I mean, sometimes things get... *dangerous*."

"I was born in space. I ain't never lived on any stinkin' planet," Derrick shot back. "And I never will."

"The kid has spirit," Vintar said with appreciation.

The captain turned to Katt and Vintar. "Our first job has a high level of danger. Most of our commercial jobs always will – else the money won't be good enough. And I suspect if we bid and win any science mission for Awk, they won't be any safer. By the great central core, they'll probably be more dangerous." He turned back to Derrick. "And we can't afford to baby-sit any kid."

"I've been on dangerous missions." Derrick's eyes locked with the captain's eyes.

Vintar laughed again. "We need someone with courage, kid – someone who can handle themselves when things get rough."

"I've got courage," Derrick growled.

"Tell me the most courageous thing you've ever done, kid."

Derrick thought a moment.

"I held my father's hand when he died."

The room went silent.

"That's…that's not what I meant," Vintar stammered. "I mean, courage like if you've got to fight a bunch Qantaran warriors – hand to hand even. Or you're flying in the face of a gigantic ion storm. Or…"

"Courage enough." The captain's eyes narrowed while he peered intently down at Derrick.

Vintar crossed his arms. The muscles in his huge biceps caused his armored scales to ripple. He looked at Derrick with puzzlement.

"What are we going to do, captain?" Katt asked.

But before he could answer, Derrick played his last card.

"I bet you haven't figured out dad's Quad Injected System yet, have you?"

The three aliens stared down at Derrick in surprise.

"I can work it. I know how to sequence it. Dad taught me how to keep it configured too. And best of all, I can tell when it's almost out of alignment and tweak it back before the engines cut out."

261

Katt, Vintar and the captain looked at each other a moment.

"What else can you do?" Katt asked with a challenging tone.

"I can pilot her and land her too. I can use the Nav system and plot a course to any star you like. And I can fix any system onboard this ship. Dad taught me everything. He showed me everything. I know her inside and out because I've lived on this starship my entire life."

"He's pretty confident for a kid." Vintar laughed.

But Katt and the captain remained silent. Suddenly, Katt whispered in his ear. He smiled and nodded. He turned and faced Derrick.

"Tell you what, kid. We'll see if you know half the things you say. And if you can..."

Derrick felt hope blossom inside his chest.

"First, you show us how the injector system works. And, how to configure and maintain it. If you'll be straight with us, we'll do likewise. Then we'll decide if you can stay."

Derrick felt his heart leap. "I will. I'll show you!"

Katt bit her lip. "Okay, let's get you back in a real cabin. First thing tomorrow, show us your hiding places."

"Okay," Derrick said. For the first time, he felt like things were going to be better.

"Vintar, you go with him." The captain motioned with his hand.

Derrick led the strong alien toward the crew quarters.

Katt waited until they were out of ear shot.

"I don't know how long we can let him stay with us. This mission is dangerous enough. And then there are those who will kill us on sight if we land on the wrong planet at the wrong time. The odds are against us. It's going to end badly for us one day, Zeg." Katt looked straight into his red eyes. "You know it too."

"Our past might catch up with us one day. But not today. And I don't intend that it will any time soon."

"We don't want a kid getting hurt, or worse, and having that on our conscience." Katt walked back to the pilot's chair and sat down. "And yet, we don't want to abandon him and leave him vulnerable to any wolves who wander the stars either."

"We'll find out what he really knows about this ship first. We'll transfer his knowledge to us. This ship is special; I felt it the first time we powered it up. If what the kid says is true, he can help us learn what makes her tick. This starship might turn out to be the best I've ever flown." He smiled. "And then I'll find a place for him."

Katt's eyes narrowed dangerously.

"I'll find a good place for him – I will." Zeg smiled sincerely.

***

The next few days passed quickly. And for the first time since his father died, Derrick felt happy.

First, he showed them the hidden area behind the double panel in the main cargo bay. It was located just inside the main exterior door and almost undetectable. Katt had even made him stop a moment while she used her hand-held scanner to try and find it before he opened it. Of course, she couldn't.

He smiled as he watched their faces – they were impressed.

Katt and Vintar tried for a while to locate the hidden cargo area in the secondary bay after he told them another was located there. They gave up after half an hour.

Derrick proudly showed them the access panel in the ceiling. The lighting array helped conceal it from their sensors.

He showed Awk the main computer room. Together, both climbed through the maintenance tubes toward the secondary cargo bay where Awk had already moved some of his scientific instruments. Derrick learned from the small, bird-like alien that some of the equipment was state-of-the-art long-range sensors as well as ground-penetrating sensors of the highest sensitivity.

He knew it was costly and wondered how this small band of aliens could afford such expensive equipment.

He wondered even more how they'd obtained the funds to buy this starship outright. He remembered the alien in the suit mentioning that they were paying it off in one lump sum. And even he had been impressed.

Derrick watched Katt and Awk analyze the Quad Stage Tachyon injector system. Derrick remembered his father telling him that most starships had a Dual stage system. And it was only the high-end ships that installed a Tri-stage injector.

Derrick's dad had found a way to add a fourth stage and give the sub-light engines another twenty percent power. Still, it was delicate. Or, as dad used to say – downright finicky.

Derrick decided to have a little fun with them – he explained enough so they could get the system working – but not exactly at one hundred percent efficiency.

The secret was to tune them in two stages so you wouldn't mess up the balance of the engines. To begin with, you needed to adjust the tachyon flow in all four injectors between forty-seven point two percent and forty-seven point nine percent of full flow. After two minutes at this rate, the sub-light engines would balance themselves. Once they were settled, then you could push the flow up to eighty percent up, wait a bit for the engines to settle in again, then set the injectors to a full flow. Derrick could tell by the sound of the engines when they were ready for each stage.

But if you pushed the flow too fast, the engines would never equalize and eventually they'd stall. If you increased it too slow, the injectors would freeze and then it would take almost half an hour to get them back on-line.

But with those settings the Quad injectors made his starship almost uncatchable in a sub-light chase.

Derrick's father had told him that no ship had ever caught them when they were configured right.

He watched silently while they completed another test. He covered his hand and snickered when the ship shuddered and the injectors flooded out once again and caused the sub-light engines stall.

Awk and Katt both shot him dirty looks.

Derrick simply shrugged and feigned a bad memory, promising to search his father's computer system for the correct settings.

He had decided to hold back on this item in the hope they'd feel like they still needed him. He was afraid to tell them everything right away. And there was another reason he held back.

Deep inside, he was still afraid to trust somebody again.

***

They were twelve hours out from their first planet.

Derrick sat alone at the Nav console on the command deck. The ship was on autopilot with the lights dimmed low. Amid the soft lighting, the starship hummed with life while various lights flashed across the boards and messages raced across various consoles.

But Derrick focused his attention on the main console.

He loved to watch the stars as they slowly drew closer and then passed by the starship one by one.

Here, alone in the darkness on his starship at full speed, he really felt at home.

"What have we here?" Captain Zeg strolled through the door.

Derrick turned and nodded his head.

"Shouldn't you be asleep? You have breakfast detail tomorrow, you know."

The boy stretched and groaned. "Yes, I'm going to bed in a minute. I just wanted to watch the stars slip by."

Zeg glanced at the star field. "Yes, it is amazing – sitting here watching the light years passing us by."

Derrick watched the captain's face grow thoughtful.

"Why do you keep Vintar? He's grouchy and complains all the time."

Zeg chuckled. "Too true. But you know, he's the most loyal crewman I've ever known. He'd defend me or any of us to the death against all odds and not blink an eye."

"Loyalty is good." Derrick paused in thought. "It means you trust him, and he trusts you, right?"

"Exactly."

"The crew trusts the captain. And the captain trusts his crew. Sort of like... family..." Derrick paused. His choice of words even surprised him.

Zeg gazed deeply at the boy. "Something like that, I guess." He coughed, as if clearing something from his throat.

"Am I crew now?"

Zeg's expression changed from surprise to embarrassment. "Well... are you part of my crew... Let me think..."

But his non-answer sent a chill into the darkness around them.

Derrick felt his heart grow heavy. He should have known better than to trust this alien captain or any of his crew. Everyone he'd ever trusted had only let him down in one way or another.

Or maybe he didn't deserve anyone's trust.

Derrick rose from the chair and started for his cabin.

"Boy, wait a moment," Zeg said.

Derrick paused, but he didn't turn around.

"See here, many jobs we take are dangerous. There's real danger – the kind might kill any one of us. I don't want to see you get hurt. This job we're taking now – flying a load of Meds. Our drop off is a war zone. I can't..."

"My dad traded with aliens at war. He even flew Meds to plague planets. He calculated the cost in every way, and we did well." Derrick kept his back to Zeg because he didn't want him to see the tears streaming down his face.

"And how did your mother die, kid? In which of those situations did your father..."

"No!" Derrick shouted with raw anger. "Dad didn't cause her to die. It was an accident."

He ran away down the corridor without another word.

Zeg sat in the darkness a long time. He shook his head from time to time lost in deep thought.

Finally, he turned and stared at the stars as they slowly drifted past one by one.

He smiled.

***

Derrick walked among the night-time crowds in complete awe. The city stretched around him with electrified delight under the glowing beams of thousands of neon lights.

Katt, Awk, Vintar and the captain walked abreast in front of him. He hurried to catch up so he could hear what they were saying. And find out where they were going. He clutched his hand-held unit close under his clothes. He wanted to capture some of this planet for his collection. He always scanned something unique from every planet he visited.

"Awk, you and the kid find a nice quiet table away from us," The Captain said.

"Why are we bringing the kid to this space bar anyway?" Katt asked.

"I need Awk here, and you – to watch our back. We can't take any weapons inside and I didn't want to leave the kid alone back at the ship."

"Afraid he'd fly off without us, captain?" Vintar chuckled.

"The kid knows his stuff, except for the injection system. He just might fly off and leave us." Zeg chuckled.

Derrick smiled mischievously.

"I'm beginning to like you, kid." Vintar winked at Derrick.

269

"Vintar, I need you to hang back and enter about ten minutes after us," Zeg said.

"Aw, Captain. Can't I go in first? I mean, I hate to say this, but *I've got to go.*"

"I thought you were walking kind of funny," Katt said with a laugh.

"Hey, I can't help it if we Vraxians have small bladders. Our toes curl up when we've got to go bad. And it's hard to walk like that."

"Okay, you go in first and use the bathroom. Then, find a table where you can watch Weerdan's table."

"Yes sir, captain." Vintar hurried ahead, hobbling along with awkward steps.

Everyone noticed his toes curled up over the top of his sandals.

Katt laughed out loud and Awk joined her mirth.

Zeg looked down at Derrick.

"Okay, kid. You stay close to Awk. Do exactly what he says and do it fast. I'm not expecting trouble, but I've dealt with Weerdan before. And you never know with that alien."

The captain rose to his full height and stared down at Derrick ominously.

Derrick nodded sheepishly.

They waited ten minutes and then Zeg and Katt walked up to the door of a brightly lighted building and strolled inside. Awk and Derrick waited another five minutes and entered.

Katt had dressed Derrick in a leather outfit so he would resemble an Avad. They were a diminutive race who did somewhat resemble humans – except

270

they were completely hairless and had large, flexible ears.

She had completed his transformation quite convincingly.

From the huge amount of exotic clothing Katt possessed added to her clever technique with cosmetics and prosthetics, Derrick was now convinced she had done this kind of thing many times. He imagined she could completely change the appearance of almost anyone.

Derrick and Awk walked inside the bar.

The noise was deafening. They crossed a crowded room filled with aliens of every description.

Awk led Derrick to a table up against the far wall.

Derrick spotted the captain and Katt over at a table in the middle of the room conversing with four surly looking aliens.

They sat down and Derrick looked around excitedly. He'd never been in a bar before, much less seen such an array of different aliens in one place. He slipped his hand inside his leather shirt and pulled out his hand-held unit. He wanted to scan some of them, especially the ones he'd never seen before.

Awk was looking over at Katt and Zeg who were now in deep conversation with the four aliens. Derrick surmised one of them was Weerdan.

He decided to scan them first. They were big and muscular and were covered by tiny scales that shimmered in the artificial light. Although the scales that shone on their arms and faces and heads

271

looked black at times, when they moved and the light hit them from a different angle, sparkles of color flashed.

Derrick triggered the sensor to get a good scan of them.

Suddenly, the lights in the entire bar turned red and an alarm beacon drowned out every other noise in the bar.

Awk looked around fearfully a moment, and then his eyes caught Derrick's scanner.

"Oh, kid. You never use one of those in a place like this. See, you've set off the alarm."

From out of nowhere, three black-scaled aliens like the one's seated with Zeg and Katt walked up.

Derrick hurriedly replaced the hand-held back inside his shirt.

But it was too late.

"Okay, who's got the sensor here?"

Derrick and Awk looked up innocently.

"What do you mean..." Awk started to say.

But the big alien jerked him up by both wings and held him right up to his face.

"I mean, which of you two idiots is trying to scan this place. Don't you know our patrons expect privacy here?"

The alien standing over Derrick reached down and pulled him out of his chair. He searched him roughly.

"Ow," Derrick complained.

The alien pulled out his sensor with a grin. He turned it on and pointed it at Awk and then at Derrick.

His grin disappeared.

"What's this?" He reached down and ripped the false ears off Derrick's head. A second later, they peeled off the rubber skin across his skull.

"What is it?" The three aliens stared at Derrick in puzzlement.

"I think it's a human – one with hair like burnished copper."

"Let's take them to Weerdan; he wants to know what set off the alarm."

The captain eyed him with stern disapproval as they approached. Derrick looked down with embarrassment.

"It was a hand-held sensor unit, sir." They handed Derrick's unit to the alien sitting directly across from Captain Zeg.

"What are you?" He snarled.

"I'm a human," Derrick answered with pride.

"You're kinda small for a human." He looked closer. "I've never seen one with hair the color of fire. And never one with spots on his face."

"I'm a kid. And those spots are freckles."

Weerdan shook his head condescendingly.

"Young human, we don't allow sensors in my establishment. What goes on here is the private business of my patrons." The alien's green eyes peered harshly at him.

"He's young, Weerdan. He probably didn't know. Give him a warning and let him go." Zeg picked up a glass of beer and drank it down in a single gulp.

"Sir, he was disguised as an Avid. He was sitting with this bird alien here. I think it's a Birran." He pointed at Awk.

273

Weerdan's vertical pupils widened. "Why were you scanning my premises, human? And why are you here in disguise?"

"I'm underage," Derrick said convincingly. "And... I always wanted to go into a space bar and... and..." Derrick's mind clouded what he tried to think up an explanation.

"And what, scan the exotic aliens here?" Weerdan finished for him.

"Yeah, that's it," Derrick agreed.

Weerdan nodded.

Suddenly, Derrick felt his face smashed down against the table. He fought to breathe as Weerdan's hands tightened around his throat.

Weerdan bent over until his scaly face was next to Derrick's.

"I don't buy that, human. Not with a disguise as professional as I see in Jeerax's hands. I guess my boys will have to provide you with some *gentle* persuasion."

Derrick heard movement and the sound of chairs falling to the floor. He forced his head to the side.

Katt and the captain faced six of Weerdan's thugs.

"Let the kid go Weerdan, he simply made a mistake."

"You seem to be quite protective of this scrawny human, Zeg. Why is that?" Weerdan sneered.

Captain Zeg growled under his breath as he looked down at Derrick.

"He's part of my crew. He made a mistake; he just wanted to come here with us while..."

"Enough!" Weerdan shouted.

Weerdan looked down at Derrick and then back up at Zeg. "I think you had these two here on purpose – to record our pending deal."

"No, I didn't, Weerdan. It's all a mistake. Let it go."

Weerdan and Zeg stared at each other in silence a few moments.

Weerdan sent his fist into Derrick's ribs. Derrick cried out in pain. And the alien's grip around his throat tightened. He coughed, trying to breathe.

"Final warning, Weerdan. Let the kid go, and nobody gets hurt."

"Ah, you threaten me now, you old alien?"

Derrick saw the captain's fists clench as Katt took a step away to face the aliens nearest her.

Weerdan suddenly began laughing out loud. Derrick then realized that the entire bar was silent while everyone watched the scene around them unfold.

Weerdan's laughter finally subsided. He leaned over the table, his fist pressing painfully into Derrick's back.

Derrick groaned.

"I mean, you see my amusement here, right? One *has-been* warrior. One *female*," he said with contempt, glancing over at Katt. He turned. "And one small Birran and this little boy with spots all over his face. I'm pretty sure that my six trained warriors are trembling just about now."

He laughed again and his warriors joined him this time.

The alien next to Zeg placed his hand on Zeg's shoulder. He looked at Zeg and laughed harder.

Zeg reached nonchalantly and seemed to scratch the back of his neck a moment. In the next moment, the alien leaning against him tensed and his eyes grew wide.

In the next instant, he lay unconscious on the floor.

All the laughter stopped.

"A *has-been*, eh. I think our odds just got a little better."

"What did you just do, Zeg?" Weerdan peered at Zeg with shock a moment. He shook his head. "Little good it does you when I can replace him." Weerdan snapped his fingers.

Derrick noticed four more aliens approaching them from among the crowds.

"Why do you want me to hurt you, Zeg?"

"I take care of my own."

"Then, my troops and I will be forced teach all of you a lesson."

Zeg looked slowly around a moment as if contemplating the odds. He smiled.

And then everyone moved all at once.

While Zeg and Katt battled, Awk flapped his wings furiously into the face of the alien holding him. The warrior stared at the blur of wings, and then Awk slashed with his talons and the alien cried out in pain. He released Awk, holding his bleeding hands.

Awk quickly flew up toward the ceiling.

Derrick felt Weerdan's grip grow tighter, but he saw the rest of the action out of the corner of his eye.

Three of the aliens descended on Zeg while the other three closed with Katt.

Katt twisted her lithe body and sent her foot into one alien's midriff while she punched another. But the third one sent his fist into her and she stumbled backward.

Zeg punched one of them, but the other two came from each side and grabbed his arms.

Zeg grabbed one and shook him a moment. The warrior's eyes widened momentarily and he slumped to the floor unconscious.

But the other sent a blow into Zeg which doubled him over. Another alien appeared and then grabbed him from behind.

Katt defended herself against two more, but she was cornered between them.

The fight seemed to be over.

Suddenly, a blood curdling scream filled the room.

Derrick twisted his head to get a look at the newcomer.

Vintar lowered his shoulder and slammed into one of the aliens holding Zeg and sent him flying. Another alien punched Vintar. But the blow bounced harmlessly off his armored scales.

Vintar smiled with a twinkle in his eyes.

He bent the alien over with a single blow.

After that, everything was a blur of movement and flying debris while tables and chairs crashed under the weight of aliens begin dashed against them. Vintar was like a miniature Hercules – grabbing first one alien and smashing him into a table and then punching another and sending him flying backward onto the ground with that single blow.

Two warriors appeared out of nowhere and each grabbed Vintar by an arm. A third slowly rose from the floor, weaving in a daze a moment before smiling. He pulled his fist back and struck.

Vintar pulled the two aliens holding him right into the path of their friend's fist. The three crashed together and then stumbled around a moment.

Vintar made quick work of them, three blows and three warriors fell unconscious.

Weerdan shoved Derrick and now his face was mashed into the top of the table. Derrick heard chairs and aliens crashing in every direction mixed with the sounds of grunts, groans and shouts.

The hand gripping his neck suddenly disappeared.

"Let's go, kid." Captain Zeg had one arm tight around Weerdan's neck. And Weerdan's eyes glazed over while his body slumped.

Derrick looked around and saw a wide swath of destruction all around them – unconscious aliens and broken chairs and tables. Vintar and Katt stood on either side as they all began backing toward the main entrance. Awk circled overhead, flying just below the ceiling.

Another group of black-scaled aliens waited at a distance. But they dared not get too close with Weerdan in Zeg's grasp.

When they got outside, they flagged down a taxi. Zeg pushed Weerdan away as he stepped into the cab last.

But Weerdan wasn't completely unconscious like the others. He rolled over with a groan and pointed at them.

"You'll never do business with me again, Zeg. And more, the next time I see you, I'll make you pay for this!" Weerdan shouted.

"You'll have to stand in line first," Zeg shouted out the window while the taxi took off. The taxi flew up into the night sky with a burst of power.

"Kid, don't bring anything I don't tell you to bring next time." Zeg's voice was deep and commanding.

Derrick hung his head with shame.

"Ask next time, okay." Zeg looked out the window.

"I will."

Silence filled the taxi a moment.

"What did you use on those aliens," Derrick asked inquisitively.

"A tiny stun device, I wear it around my wrist. It takes a few moments to recharge. But it comes in handy sometimes." Zeg laughed. "It's really a Medical heart stimulator, but I've had Awk modify it so it has enough power stun even the biggest alien. But being a Medical device, it makes it through a weapon's scan every time."

The rest of the trip went by quickly. The taxi dove down onto the docking bay where their starship sat at the ready.

Zeg and Katt rushed inside shouting orders while Vintar ran forward to the pilot's chair.

Derrick ran back to the engine room with Awk.

"We may need those injectors when we hit space, kid. And if I say I need'em that means somebody is chasing us." Zeg shouted over his shoulder.

Awk's talons clicked on the deck as he ran behind Derrick.

"Can you really work them?" Awk asked.

Derrick flashed him a confident smile. "I'll show you this time."

As they entered the engine room, the sub-light engines roared to life. Seconds later, they felt the ship lift off.

Derrick sat at the control panel and began priming all four stages. He paid close attention to the tachyon flow in all four. Once it got to forty-seven percent of full flow, he throttled it back and held it steady.

"Ah," Awk said with keen interest.

"We're above atmosphere now." Zeg said over the intercom.

"I've got a Government Patrol ship changing direction and coming toward us," Katt said with a hint of concern.

"We didn't have time to file our departure flight plan – they probably have orders to detain us."

"I see another ship, a fast one, bearing down on us at one point seven three," Vintar growled. "And it looks like it means business."

"One of Weerdan's ships, no doubt," Katt said.

"Get us out of the gravity well, Vintar," Zeg ordered. "We'll need to jump to hyperspace sooner rather than later.

"That will be in four minutes on my mark... Mark." Vintar hit a button.

"Kid, we'll need to put some distance between us and those two ships. We can't go to hyperspace until we're out of the star's gravity well."

Derrick glanced at the readouts for the engines and then turned his right ear to listen. Right at that moment, the engines balanced under the flow. Derrick quickly hit the controls and increased the flow to eighty-five percent.

"Ah!" Awk repeated, looking at the readouts along with Derrick.

"I'm ready, captain." Derrick replied confidently.

Zeg paused while he glanced at Vintar's control panel.

"That other ship is closing fast. And they're powering weapons, captain," Katt said. "They'll be in range in... twenty-two seconds."

"Kid, engage those injectors!"

Derrick verified and hit maximum button. The starship surged forward.

"Wooooo-weee!" Vintar shouted.

"How about those ships?" Zeg asked.

"Dropping back by the second, captain," Katt answered.

"Vintar?"

"I'm maneuvering us away from both ships and toward open space. Give me a few moments, captain."

The ship continued accelerating. Derrick looked at the display – two minutes passed with only the mighty roar of the engines breaking the silence.

"Vintar." Zeg prompted.

"Recalculating with current acceleration."

Derrick heard a surprised gasp came over the intercom.

"We're past the gravity well *already*, captain." Vintar said with surprise.

"Okay, kid. Keep the injectors flowing for thirty more seconds. Katt is calculating our jump. Shut down on my command," Zeg said with authority.

Derrick waited with his hand above the control button. The engines roared louder with each passing second as the ship continued to accelerate.

"Shut down injectors."

Derrick mashed the control and the sub-engines started powering back.

"I've got the calculations entered and ready for the jump, captain," Katt said.

A few seconds passed in silence.

"Jump!" Zeg ordered.

***

Three days passed with no sign of pursuit. Later that afternoon, Awk called everyone into the eating area for a conference.

"This better be good, Awk. I was taking a nap," Vintar said grumpily.

Katt walked in from the command deck. "I've got the ship on autopilot."

Last, the imposing presence of Captain Zeg entered.

"What do you have, Awk? Have you found us a paying job?"

"Indeed," Awk crooned. "The mining colony of Sarik Minor. They've just hit it big and their newfound riches are burning holes in their pockets."

"Good. What cargo?" Zeg asked.

"Lots of expensive delicacies. I've lined up a couple of planets where we can load up. Several of the items are quite perishable. We'll need to keep the main cargo bay in a deep freeze in addition to making top speed on the return trip."

"How much?" Zeg eyed Awk carefully.

"Enough for a small profit."

Zeg's smile turned into a frown.

"But I've negotiated another job from them."

"Go on."

"I told them about our ground penetrating sensors – the latest technology. They want us to scan five to nine planets in nearby systems. We're to provide detailed geological reports. If we detect signs of mineral wealth, they want to purchase the rights. Or, with their newfound wealth, probably the entire planet outright."

"Why don't they send their own ships?" Vintar asked.

"They haven't had time to get one yet. Besides, they don't want to attract attention. It might drive the price up before anything is known. We're simply a small independent Trader traversing those uninhabited systems looking for business. That's our story if we run into anyone."

"Good." Zeg smiled. "And how much for that?"

"Ten thousand Galactic Credits – for each planet scanned. More if we find anything solid." Awk flapped his wings triumphantly.

"Wait." Katt looked intently at Zeg.

"What, Katt?" Zeg crossed his burly arms.

"That's a wild region of space. Habad Raiders prowl that Sector, especially in the outer systems away from established worlds. And it's not smart to cross their path."

Zeg rubbed his chin in thought.

"They can't catch us! There ain't a starship in this galaxy that can catch my ship!" Derrick shouted with pride.

"You mean, my ship," Zeg interjected.

"How about, our ship?" Derrick asked.

Zeg grunted and continued rubbing his chin in thought.

The others turned to Derrick. His smile beamed back at them.

"Those injectors pack some power for sure, captain. I've never piloted a ship with that much acceleration in the sub-light engines my entire life." Vintar nodded approvingly.

"Which brings us back to the kid." Katt walked over beside Zeg. "What are we going to do with him? We're talking about traveling quite a distance now."

"He knows this ship. And, he mostly stays out of trouble," Awk squawked.

"Sort of like us," Vintar laughed.

Captain Zeg eyed the boy a moment. He cast a long and appraising glance before he finally spoke. "The kid knows this ship inside and out. I think there's a lot more he can show us too. Besides, who would take care of him? Didn't we just defend the lad from Weerdan's thugs?"

"That's right," Vintar added quickly. "And the kid sure knows how to configure those tachyon injectors! I bet there is more he can show us about this ship."

"Zeg…" Katt began.

"He's crew." Zeg paused. "As long as he pulls his load, he can be a part of my crew. And, if the kid finds a better deal, he's welcome to leave – just like any of you."

Zeg held his head up and looked around at everyone. Finally, his eyes met Derrick's eyes.

Zeg winked at him.

Derrick's heart raced with excitement. For the first time in a long while, he felt like he was a part of something again. But even more important, Derrick finally felt like he could trust someone again.

Derrick smiled widely and looked from Zeg to Vintar and over to Awk. Each of them smiled back at him. Only Katt continued frowning even when Derrick caught her eye. But for an instant, it seemed she almost smiled too.

"What say you? Shall Derrick be a part of our crew?" Zeg asked to them all. He crossed his arms and waited.

"I'm for it," Vintar shouted.

"I agree," Awk added.

Katt looked around at all of them. She shook her head slowly. "I don't want to see the kid hurt. But we're all the friends he has right now. I agree."

Vintar slapped Derrick's shoulder with joy.

"Captain, I just realized it!" Vintar shouted out loud.

285

"What?" Zeg asked with puzzlement.

"We haven't named our new ship."

"We need a name – a good name for a good ship." Zeg looked at the others.

"It has a name," Derrick said simply.

"What is it? Vintar asked.

"*The New Adventure*." Derrick crossed his arms.

"The New Adventure?" Sounds like a weenie name to me?" Vintar retorted.

"Who named it? You?" Katt asked.

"No, my mom named her."

"Why did your mom pick that name?" Katt asked softly.

"Mom told me that every time we sailed into space it would be a *new adventure*. Every planet we orbited, every system we visited, every time we jumped into hyperspace."

"I don't like it," Vintar growled. "It just doesn't have a ring to it. It…"

Katt slapped the side of his scaly head.

"Ow!" Vintar rubbed his head.

They all turned to Zeg with silent expectation.

"I like it." The captain smiled and walked over to Derrick. He put his arm around the boy's shoulders.

"Now the four of us sail '*The New Adventure*.'"

Reality Check

The main alarm on the ship's console began to flash red, indicating a breach in the matter/anti-matter chamber. In a few more seconds the Blue Comet, pride of the fleet based at Mars, would be no more.

Captain Tom Majors sat stiff in his Commander's chair, staring with disgust at the pulsing omen. A low vibrating humming began, a sound so low that Tom thought he might be imagining it. His stomach tightened when it increased in volume, causing the entire ship to begin shuddering. Gripping both arms of his commander's chair to keep from being thrown down, Tom Majors spoke through clenched teeth.

"Come on, blow up already."

And conveniently, the ship did just that.

Closing his eyes against the blinding light, Tom counted to five, and then he opened them.

Seconds later Captain Majors began to tap his fingers impatiently, waiting for the Techs to disconnect his body and mind from the VR. He turned after a door miraculously appeared.

"You guys are making this a little too realistic these days, John. I've got a bruise the size of a golf ball here on the side of my head – at least that's what it feels like." Tom tenderly ran his fingers over his left temple.

"Not really, sir. It's a VR wound."

Tom shook his head in disbelief.

"It's a dirty job training you hotshot pilots, but somebody has to do it," John replied with a big grin. "Besides, it's our job to make it just like the real thing."

"Captain Majors," an invisible voice boomed, "we are disappointed with your performance today. The computer had given you an even chance of resolving this situation today without loss of life. Instead, everyone on board perished."

Tom shrugged. "You win a few, you lose a few."

A loud click sounded in the air, followed shortly by another.

The ghostly voice returned.

"We're also concerned with the lack of enthusiasm the Pilot's Corp has developed in participating in these VR Simulations. You don't seem to be taking it seriously any longer. We've gone to a lot of time and effort in the programming of these sessions. And they are designed to ensure the utmost safety of our passengers and crew." The voice paused. "Is it too much to ask for your full support?"

Tom took a deep breath and let it out slowly. He nodded. "I guess after you've died a few dozen times and blown up the ship a few dozen more... well, it's hard to get into it. It doesn't have the same... *urgency*. Not like the first times." He shook his head.

There was another short pause from the hidden voice.

The VR Techs smiled at each other while they stood on either side of him.

"We have been asking," the voice resonated, "for suggestions from the other pilots, Captain Majors. What do you think would make VR more... meaningful? So that you'll take it as seriously as if it were the real thing."

Tom shook his head with a disinterested air. "I don't know, you can't really make it any more realistic than it is."

There was a pause.

"Let me rephrase the question. Once you're connected to the VR and the barrier between mind and muscles is enabled, is there anything – *anything* – that gives it away that this is not the real thing? That you're really in VR?"

Tom didn't hesitate.

"Once I'm inside, it's exactly like reality. And believe me, when things get hot, I'm glad it's *just* VR. I don't know, when I see the Techs attach the connectors to my skin, I realize it's only VR then, so...." Tom held up his hands questioningly.

There was another click, and the silence returned. Finally, the voice spoke again.

"Thank you, Captain. Your insights agree with our other findings. We will be making some programming enhancements for the next VR Simulation. Now, I believe you have a real mission to fly. Have a safe trip back to Earth."

The last words echoed eerily in Tom's mind – almost as if in a dream.

The two VR Techs hesitated a moment. They each pressed a forefinger to their ears and listened to their Comm device.

Tom glanced at them – no doubt they were being provided some last-minute instructions about something, perhaps even the next VR SIM.

Satisfied, they approached him.

Standing up, Tom raised both of his arms while he looked around the *ship* again. VR was exactly like the real thing – the controls, readouts, everything. And the main VR computers recreated every sensation he would feel in actual spaceflight.

He stiffened after the VR Tech's hands begin pulling off the pads with the connectors and wires that were placed strategically over his head, shoulders, torso, and legs.

Tom again marveled at Virtual Reality and the computers that ran it.

Of course, Tom couldn't even tell he had any of the connectors attached to his skin. Once the computer set up the barrier between his mind and the rest of his body, effectively disabling him physically by blocking out any signals from his brain to his nerves and on to his muscles, he could only feel and use his VR body. After he was connected, his VR body was indistinguishable from his real body.

Tom reached up and scratched the tip of his nose.

In reality, he never touched his actual nose. But, it felt like he had just satisfied a real itch on his VR nose using his VR fingers.

The two Techs talked about sports while they disconnected the wires and pulled off the sticky pads one by one.

Tom prepared his mind.

It seemed as if he were starting to come out of himself, like he was part of one universe and part of another at the same time.

He became disoriented, but that was normal at this point. His vision was fine, but all of his nerves, his senses, started to send him stimuli first from reality, and a fraction of a second later from virtual reality, as the signals from the powerful computers lying unseen a few feet away were disabled.

And he always shuddered, even against his will, when he felt the real air brush his exposed face and back for the first time.

But the most uncomfortable part was when they removed the connections around his face and head.

The two VR Techs stood over him. They knew this was the most difficult part of the process back to reality. Both waited for the signal when the computer would kill all the final connections at one time.

Captain Majors had watched impassively while they eased him back into reality the last few moments.

Tom saw both men nod at each other – they had received the signal that the computer was cutting the last of the connectors off now.

But Tom's eyes were now shut tight.

Slowly, very slowly, Tom opened one eye. And instantly shut it again.

His face registered surprise and shock. A moment later, after a tentative pause, he opened both his eyes simultaneously. The sense of sight was the most powerful and when his real eyes sent back signals to his brain for the first time after VR, it could be painful.

"Hey, it didn't hurt so bad this time."

"You're just an old VR pro," John laughed.

"Does it hurt your eyes?" The younger VR Tech named Rick looked at Tom with puzzled concern.

"Usually does. But not much today. Hey, I'm not complaining," Tom sighed with obvious relief. Suddenly, an odd feeling tugged at his mind.

"You see, the past three hours the computer has been sending him sight sensations," John explained quickly, "light, darkness, this ship, the whole nine yards. The VR replaces all his senses. He sees a ship, but not with his real eyes. He feels the ship take off, but in reality his body is motionless on this chair. The VR computers recreate an entire world inside his mind. And it's as real as reality."

"But when he comes out, it hurts his eyes?"

"The other senses adjust pretty readily, but when real light first hits the eyes after VR..." John shrugged and stepped back.

"Better get your *real* Flight suit on, Captain. The shuttle will be leaving as soon as you're ready," the familiar voice boomed over the room speaker.

"I hate doing these VR check-flights right before a real flight." Tom Majors rolled his eyes when the Flight suit was held before him by same two VR techs. Tom placed his right leg into it as the voice echoed from the speaker.

"Administration feels it's a good practice, gets the pilot into the right frame-of-mind."

Tom stared at the speaker stoically. He shook his head in disagreement as he finished putting on the Flight suit.

Ten minutes later, Tom sat with John in the back of the RS-9 Hovercraft while they crossed the red, surreal landscape of Mars. It wasn't much to look at, dirt and rocks stretching as far as the eye could see, and everything some shade of burnt orange or some variation thereof – there wouldn't be much else to see until they got closer to the city.

Tom continued to look contemplatively out of his window as the ground slipped by a few feet below.

"Look over there," John pointed.

Looking up to the horizon, Tom saw the remaining wisps of vapor that had shot skyward for thousands of feet before they evaporated.

"That's one of the biggest Terra-Forming plants in operation now," John said with a knowing nod.

But Captain Tom Majors was occupied with the flight ahead and he only grunted his acknowledgment. Or was there something more?

"We'll breathe from a real atmosphere one day," John continued.

"I hope to see that day," Tom mused as he rubbed his tired eyes. Clearing his mind, he began to think of the mission ahead of him. But he couldn't relax. Somewhere deep in the recesses of Tom's consciousness, something was beginning to gnaw at him – something out of place.

Something wasn't right... He was sure of it.

Opening his eyes, he began looking around the small interior, searching for something, but not quite knowing what.

"What's the matter? Lose something?" John stared at him through narrowed eyes.

"No..." Tom began, and then shaking his head suddenly, as if clearing it, he chuckled, "I guess I just don't like crashing a ship... and then getting right back into another one."

"Must be pre-flight nerves Captain, why don't you close your eyes – relax a little."

But even though Tom took the advice, he couldn't quite shake the uncomfortable feeling.

The rest of the journey was spent in relative silence while they approached New London. At the space port, they boarded the orbital shuttle and were soon off the ground. After thirty minutes of flight, the oval shape of the orbital station, Olympus 3, began to fill their viewports. Shortly afterward, a barely perceptible shudder caused Tom to look out the window to his right. They were docked. Now it would be his turn to take the Commander's seat on a real star ship.

Because of the pre-flight VR simulator run, Tom didn't visit any of his friends aboard the station but went straight to the tunnel that led to his ship, the M.S. Blue Comet.

A haunting sense of Deja-vu returned in a flood of sensation, stopping him just inside the ship.

Something seemed wrong. But he couldn't put his finger on it.

"Hello Captain, all the systems have been checked and the ship is ready for launch." The dark-haired junior officer smiled at him, jerking Tom back to reality. "I'm running a check on the redundant systems now. Should be completed by the time you strap in."

"Good, Hank. I guess I didn't really miss anything, eh?" Tom said with a half grin.

"Not at all, sir. Routine stuff as usual. The only excitement happens in VR." Hank's eyes twinkled.

Tom stared at him a moment, searching the other man's face as if he were looking for something – but unable to find it.

"And that's where it should be." Tom finally said. He made his way to the flight deck.

Located at the extreme forward section of the ship, he would sit there alone; his only company would be the main computer. The rest of the crew would be either in Engineering or with the passengers. Naturally, the redundant systems were located mid-ship, away from the main systems that surrounded him forward.

Engineering, the duplicate of Command Control, could take over his duties if needed. And CC could do their job if needed. Fully redundant.

Well, it was really the computers that did the work. Humans were only there for emergencies. There had been many times that Tom had done nothing but monitor the systems while the computer took him to Earth and back to Mars again.

Oh well, he thought, it's not like the old days.

As he entered his station at the front of the ship, Captain Tom Majors stopped short of sitting down in his chair. Straightening up, he slowly glanced around, looking at the myriad of dials, digital readouts and small monitors filled with data that seemed to flow in a never-ending stream down the length of the screens.

He felt it again, but stronger now, like a wave filling his mind and his body – a dark and foreboding Deja-vu. A feeling that *nothing* was real…

Tom shook the feeling off – this time with a low groan. Going over to the main console, he studied the ever-flowing stream of commands as well as the main readouts.

"Computer, print log of preliminary engine startup starting at sequence three on console A-12."

Instantly the console to his right blanked out to be replaced by a screen full of data. He studied it with a well-trained eye.

"Next sequence!"

Stepping closer, he quickly paged through the log as he vocalized his commands to the computer. He had reached the current entries in the log when the computer spoke to him.

"Final redundant system checks completed. All systems operating at one hundred percent. Engines One and Two are at full readiness for startup sequence." The raspy electronic voice faded away with the last word.

Well, Tom thought, everything *seems* normal. As he turned and sat down in his chair and began to strap in, he quickly reached down on the right arm of the chair to key on the comm device.

"This is the M.S. Blue Comet, our main computer reports all systems are nominal and our engines are ready for launch. Requesting permission to disembark from Olympus 3."

"Roger that, Blue Comet. Our readouts verify your status. Permission granted." The human voice over the intercom paused before he next spoke.

"Safe journeys, captain."

"Thanks, Olympus base. See you in two months." Tom quickly thumbed another button that would allow him to be heard over the entire ship.

"This is Captain Tom Majors welcoming you aboard for our trip to Earth. Flight Attendants, prepare for undocking and main engine startup." He paused a moment. "Once in flight, I will notify you when it is safe to leave your seats. And again, welcome aboard."

Tom left his hand resting on the arm of the chair as he again studied the readouts on the consoles directly before him. Everything showed normal. The Engineering and Passenger sections showed the same status.

Tom scratched the back of his head. Somewhere in the back of his mind, an odd idea was beginning to form. Of course, the flight deck was the same as back in VR, it was supposed to be. It felt the same. Scratching the material on the cover of the chair's arm, Tom listened to the sound, feeling the material as his fingernail pulled at it.

But it would feel the same back in VR.

Rubbing his chin, he turned as the data continued rolling down the consoles. The ship's computers had undocked the ship and were now using the maneuvering engines to get them away from the station in preparation for main engine ignition.

What a jerk! Of course, this was the real thing. He had watched John disconnect him from the VR. He had felt himself coming back into reality just like every other time.

Just like...

And VR had never developed a program that had him traveling to New London for a VR flight. The SIMS had always started with either him onboard the Blue Comet or inside Olympus station. But just because they had always done it that way, didn't mean they couldn't add some programming and fake out a whole mission.

Fake out a whole mission...

Tom felt his heart pounding like a jackhammer inside his chest.

They could do it – with the right programming. And during the ride to New London, something had felt wrong.

Tom shook his head – this was getting ridiculous – was this reality, or was it VR?

He smiled to himself as he remembered hearing about VR addicts back on Earth needing professional help after having too much of the stuff – some of them even got to the point where they preferred VR over reality. And not only had it affected them mentally, but after spending so much time in VR their muscles had begun to atrophy, they lost weight and even their skin grew pale.

And even worse, they got to the point where they could no longer distinguish reality from VR.

His smile faded away.

Tom's stomach became agitated and queasy.

Pulling up the sleeve of his Flight Suit, Tom pinched himself. He winced from the sharp pain. But wouldn't he feel the same sensations inside VR? He had even sustained injuries in VR, injuries when he felt certain he had broken an arm. But...

"Commander, is everything all right up there?"

Hank's voice startled him out of his dilemma.

"Fine, everything's fine Hank. Why do you ask?"

"The computer has just reported that you have an unusually high heart rate." He paused. "You sure everything's okay?"

"Yes, it's just been a long day, Hank. Thanks anyway." With a kind of finality in his voice, Tom switched the intercom off.

Tom's mind instantly returned to his first trips in VR.

They had been so real. Realistic enough to scare the piss out of him at times, though lately they had become routine. He had crashed or saved the ship so many times that it didn't get to him the way it had at first.

"Main engine startup – all systems report fully operational."

Tom was again startled out of his musings, this time by the computer's raspy voice.

Well, the other way he knew this was reality was that everything was so blasted boring. Sitting up straight, he thumbed the Comm switch.

"This is Captain Majors again. In a few moments you'll be feeling the effects of the most powerful engines that mankind has ever built. It is these same engines that has put the solar system

299

within our grasp. As you know, it only takes five months to journey from Earth to the remote colonies on Jupiter's moons." He paused here, letting his words sink in as he turned on the monitor which displayed everyone in the main passenger area. It showed almost a hundred faces peering intently while they watched their own viewscreen which displayed an external view of the ship's massive twin engines.

Both engines were silent in their pre-ignition phase.

"These mighty engines carefully mix matter with anti/matter. In a few moments, you'll hear, or rather feel, why they are the most powerful engines ever developed. Now sit back, relax, and enjoy the rest of your flight."

Tom Majors smiled to himself; his obligatory speech completed once again. He ran a quick eye over another console and noted safety restraints engaged properly for all crew and passengers.

He keyed another channel and took a deep breath, his voice now taking on a serious tone.

"Flight Engineers, all systems are GO for matter/anti-matter release. We are approaching the point of no return."

This was the most dangerous part of the whole journey. The next ten minutes would signal whether their journey would be routine or would become one of almost certain death for all on-board.

There had only been three accidents over the last two decades since these mighty engines had become operational.

But all three had been completely catastrophic.

These massive engines had put the solar system in mankind's grasp, but they were a terrible force to keep tamed. It would take every ounce of processing power by the ship's computers to keep the reaction within safe limits. But once stabilized, the powerful computers would keep the engines on-line until they were shut down after orbital reentry at Earth.

"Computer, current status of main engines." Tom stared at the speaker next to the main console.

"Engines One and Two are in ignition phase. All processes are within tolerance. Anti-matter release and mixture are ten seconds away and counting," the mechanical voice droned.

Suddenly, dozens of lights began to flash in front of him. The lights flickered across the huge panel in a familiar pattern.

Too familiar.

Tom wanted to question the computer again, but he couldn't speak. The wave of *Deja-vu* that had been gnawing at him all day suddenly paralyzed him within its titanic grip, chilling his very soul. With a sickening dread, he realized he couldn't even breathe.

"Matter/anti-matter processes started. Ennnnnnnn........" Ominously, the computer voice did not finish the last word.

Tom heard the thunderclap, he felt the rumbling from the two long engines that spread out from the main body of the ship on either side. The stars on the viewscreen began to move. But Tom's wide-open eyes remained fixed on the main console as the data suddenly became a blur.

An overwhelming fear gripped him like a real, living thing. The horrific force made him jump within the confines of the straps holding him tight in his seat.

"Computer!" He screamed. "Main engine status!"

But the computer voice remained silent.

The data continued to roll off the screen at an unimaginable speed. Tom gritted his teeth. And then an irregular rumbling began shaking the ship violently. He realized that this earthquake-like shaking was totally different from what a normal engine startup felt like with its strong, rhythmic throbbing.

He fought against the confusing array of emotions and mental images that blocked his ability to concentrate.

The computer was having trouble – that much was certain. And if the main computer was having trouble controlling the engines, the fail-safe system should have automatically come on-line.

He keyed a Comm switch.

"Hank! Manually switch over to the redundant computer system! And give me a status. Now!" Tom's voice cracked with emotion.

Suddenly, the entire ship lurched with such an incredible force that it slammed him back into his chair and forced all the air out of his lungs. He couldn't even grunt against the pain that pressed against his chest like a ton of lead. The gut-wrenching screech of the steel hull against this titanic force deafened him. In the next instant, his vision blurred and failed, replaced by a static filled grayness.

An explosion roared inside his ears and inside his mind and it seemed that the entire universe was shaking from these unbelievable forces.

And as quickly as it started, it was gone.

That explosion had been the loudest thing he had ever heard in his entire life. He still couldn't hear anything except an incredible ringing in his ears. It seemed to fill his ears like cotton. But the excruciating pain across his chest had all his attention now. The straps had held him in the chair, but it felt like some of his ribs were broken. His breathing became labored as a blinding pain shot throughout his body with each shallow intake of air.

As he struggled to breath, a single thought ran in his mind.

He wasn't really in space; he was in the VR. He had to be!

He turned his head and concentrated. Something was there... What was it?

And then realized he was hearing something through the ringing in his ears that was now fading away. He concentrated harder and finally heard it.

"Oooooutttt...ooooffffffff...tooooooooleerance...e nnnnnginnnne...twoooo..." The slurred electronic voice brought him back to reality. And once again it failed to finish the sentence.

It was eerie; he had never heard the computer speak so slowly. In VR or anywhere...

Tom shook his head violently. What was going on here? And then the answer hit him all at once, all the computer's resources were max'ed out! The

303

computer had to be at one hundred percent utilization – or more. Its speech programs were failing because there was no processing left for them.

Tom hesitated a moment longer while tried to determine one thing.

Was this real, or...

A large, red light began to pulse from the steel ceiling.

"Code Select!...Alpha...Omega...Nine...Six...Foxtrot!" Tom shouted, carefully enunciating each word to manually bring the redundant systems on-line himself.

While he studied another console which displayed the environmental systems, an ice-cold dread swept throughout his entire body. The engineering section had lost atmosphere. Everyone in there was dead now.

Hank was dead.

If this was reality.

He quickly checked the console for the passenger section.

Good. They had atmosphere to breathe. If they could manage to do that after the horrendous G forces they had just experienced.

He felt his stomach tighten as a strange, ominous sound groaned from the speakers – it was a ghostly moaning which steadily grew in volume.

Tom gripped the chair so tight that his fingernails began to tear through the material. His body began to shake as the haunting sound roared through him, shaking his guts. He clenched his eyes shut.

It was like a voice from his worst nightmare come to haunt him – heralding his impending death.

No, it wasn't!

This had to be real, he suddenly realized. That horrendous groaning was the computer's voice trying to utter a single syllable. They had never done this in VR!

"Emergency shutdown, all...engine...systems! Tom shouted.

Nothing happened.

Painfully, he unhooked himself. After the third buckle released, he collapsed onto the floor with a thud. He panted as he tried to control the pain that flooded his mind.

Somewhere, an alarm began to sound.

Grunting with each movement, he pulled himself forward. Slowly, with each pained movement, he pulled himself up to a keyboard. With his forefinger he began to carefully type his last vocal command. After he hit the enter key, he fell back and closed his eyes as the pain threatened to push him into unconsciousness.

"Shhhhuuuuuuuutdoooooooowwwwwwwwwwnnn nnnnnnnnnnnnnn....."

Tom opened his eyes, staring at the main console again. The data stream had slowed, he could almost make out the shape of the paragraphs as they flooded down the screen.

But would the matter anti/matter processes be stopped in time or were they now uncontrollable. A hundred lives depended on him.

"Started!" The electronic voice returned to normal.

Tom opened his mouth to shout with joy, but instead grimaced with pain. It sure felt like this was real.

As he relaxed against the steel deck, he again realized that pain didn't mean this was not VR. Pain could be programmed.

"Engine One processes are now in shutdown. Engine Two processes are out of tolerance... Redundant computer is..." Tom held his breath as the computer again did not finish a sentence.

"...working. Please wait." The electronic voice finished.

Tom ran his fingers gingerly across his chest, across the zippers of his suit. Suit! That was it! If this was VR, he could just take off the wires. He could rip them off.

No! If this was VR, this wasn't a real flight suit; it just felt like it was. And yet, he had heard that if you focused hard enough, you could break the barrier and force your real arms to move.

With a great effort he sat up and paused as a wave of nausea almost overcame him. Choking back the feeling, he forced all his mind to focus on moving his hands – moving them across his chest and ripping off any wires...

"Uncontrolled anti-matter release is imminent. Repeat, uncontrolled anti-matter release is imminent, evacuate the ship now."

But Tom could not do that. Like the old days, the captain went down with his ship. The only evacuation systems built into these passenger ships were for the passengers.

It was time for Captain Tom Majors to make the most important decision of his life.

"Well, if this is real or not..." Tom said out loud, hoping against hope that someone was listening to him.

With pained gasps, he dragged himself back up to his chair. All he could manage to do was half-sit, half-lay across it because of the excruciating pain.

"Code...Seven...Baker...Nine...Nine...Delta...Release!" Tom groaned with renewed pain.

"Passenger section will be separated in seven seconds... Mark," the electronic voice replied in a normal tone.

"Computer, status on engine Two," Tom requested with a groan.

"Working...," was the mute response.

Sitting in silence, he glanced around. Everywhere readouts were streaming with data while on dozens of other consoles data rolled frantically down the screens. And red lights pulsed everywhere.

The shipped lurched again.

"Passenger section ejected, distress beacon enabled," the computer droned.

Distress beacon!

With painful movements, Tom shifted himself in his chair while he used his thumb to search for the Comm switch. He clicked it on.

"Olympus station, this is... Blue Comet. Emergency, repeat, we have... an emergency," Tom gasped out the last phrase as the pain became more than he could handle.

Only silence answered.

"Computer, status on Comm systems."

"Communication systems are not functioning," came the emotionless reply.

That could be. The explosion would explain that. But Olympus would know something was wrong even from the lack of communication.

And then Tom's dilemma came back to the forefront.

Many, many times in VR they had cut off the Comm systems. Of course, he could still communicate with his own engineering crew in resolving... but they were dead!

Or were they?

Was this real, or not? If it was real, he was going to die soon. If not, well, he was going to need a long, long vacation...

"Eight minutes, twenty-seven seconds to uncontrolled anti-matter reaction."

The words were uttered emotionlessly, but they were full of meaning for Tom.

"Computer, give me the radius of the impending uncontrolled reaction."

The computer replied instantly. "Destructive radius will extend outward from ship approximately eighty thousand kilometers."

The passengers would die with him then, just like they had in the other three accidents.

Or would they?

"Computer, status of engine One."

"All systems functioning within normal tolerance."

Stupid computer, that wasn't what he wanted to know. "Can we start it?"

The computer hesitated. Tom immediately realized he had not used the proper command phrase.

"Computer, can engine One complete startup cycle and ignition phase?" Tom grimaced with pain. "And how long to ignition once started? He hurriedly added.

"Engine One is operating at one hundred percent capability, ignition sequence will finish four minutes seventeen seconds after..."

"Computer!" Tom cut it off. "Begin engine One startup and ignition on my command. Begin startup sequence... Mark!"

"Engine number One started, matter/anti-matter process begun." The computer paused. "Uncontrolled reaction in engine Two will occur in seven minutes, forty-four seconds."

It was going to be close. But he might get far enough away to save the passengers.

If this was reality.

And then he started to laugh. Except that hurt too. Clutching his chest, he looked at the speaker above him.

"Okay guys, this is getting really strange." Tom Majors laughed again, a hopeless, crazy kind of sound. He looked over at the blank wall to his right. "Have I passed the test?"

But only silence answered.

Tom coughed, and blood spilled down his chin. "Hey guys, I think I'm really hurt here. Let's cut this VR off... please."

The heavy silence became ominous.

Long seconds continued to pass – eternal seconds. Captain Tom Majors began to laugh uncontrollably. Of course, if this was VR, they wouldn't answer him until the drill was over. It was fleet policy – you always completed the VR.

"Please use proper command syntax," the electronic voice chastised.

"Stupid computer," Tom laughed through his clenched teeth.

He tried to stand again, but instead fell in a heap on the floor.

"I'm hurt guys. Please," he pleaded. And then his expression changed. He began groaning as the intense pain started to push him into unconsciousness.

The stubborn silence began to scream in his ears.

While he choked back his hot tears, the computer again addressed him. But he ignored it. If it was real, well, he had done all he could do. That was that.

"Ignition phase complete, engine number One engaged. Speed increasing."

Tom heard that clearly. And inside his heart, he knew the passengers would survive. But everything else was only a growing confusion. He couldn't stand and he wasn't sure what he should do now.

But Tom didn't care now, one way or the other. It just didn't matter.

Eternal seconds slowly ticked by, but his mind revolved around two simple questions – *When this was over, would he open his eyes in VR? Or would he die as a hero, giving his life so that others would live?*

The main alarm on the ship's console began to flash red, indicating a breach in the matter/anti-matter chamber. In a few more seconds the Blue Comet, pride of the fleet based at Mars, would be no more.

Tom Majors lay sprawled across the deck where he had fallen. Suddenly, a low vibrating sound began. It was a sound so low that he thought he might be imagining it. His stomach cramped as it increased in volume, causing the entire ship to begin shuddering violently.

Captain Tom Majors smiled.

"Come on," he whispered defiantly. "Blow up already."

And conveniently, the ship did just that.

311

Friends of the Flower

"I am afraid," Wey whispered and then paused. "I am afraid that I will fail in the end."

He felt the all-too-familiar sadness grip his soul again. A sense of impending disappointment filled his being. It was replaced with such powerful remorse it seemed there was no hope for him.

Wey noticed Bez's puzzled expression, but his mate remained silent as she glanced at the others to see if they might have heard. But everyone seemed intent within their own private conversations.

She gently squeezed his arm with reassurance.

A large crowd waited with hushed expectation all around Bez and Wey. Aliens of every shape, form, and color; aliens from hundreds of different worlds all stood in silent unity waiting for the main door to open out onto the planet's surface.

But although they were all different, they all possessed one thing in common – each alien held a flower from which grew a solitary bloom of various colors.

Many held their delicate flower with both hands wrapped tightly around an ornamental base. The exotic base itself indicated they possessed a precious Life-Flower. Others held it firmly with one appendage while in the other they carried a book with a well-worn cover indicative of contemplative and frequent reading.

Indeed, the majority carried both a Life-Flower and 'The Sayings of Life' – the most ancient book of wisdom in the known universe.

Bez stood close beside Wey, the petals of their Life-Flowers bright with color and reflecting their deep love for each other and their flowers.

But a look of sadness replaced Bez's normally joyful countenance.

"Why are you sad as we approach Assembly, husband? We should be happy. You do not need to fear failure at this joyous event." Bez smiled at him.

Wey looked over at his mate. "KOR wants everything. It offers everything." Wey groaned; his heart torn. "It seems so good to me at times."

Bez slowly shook her head, pausing in thought before she spoke. "KOR is necessary. They are the System right now. They not only rule, but they also control all trade and business. They oversee every facet of society and provide everyone on every planet with food, shelter, and oversight."

"But they want more," Wey whispered. "They want our hearts. They want our minds. They want our souls."

"Everything inside a being is sacred and personal." Bez repeated the sacred proverb without hesitation, its memory ingrained even prior to her birth.

Wey shook his head. "But I am confused. KOR states that they embrace the same values and the same goals that we do – peace and happiness for all."

"KOR tries to achieve their goal with power and laws." Bez smiled knowingly.

313

"Order and law can be legislated. Happiness and love cannot. These come only from inside." Bez touched her chest just above her three hearts.

Around the main room of the shuttle, the display screens flickered to life.

"See, KOR will tempt us again." Wey pointed to the displays.

A crowd of smiling alien faces appeared, each as varied and ethnically diverse as those waiting happily within the shuttle. Their smiles beamed just as joyfully.

But unlike those preparing for Assembly, none of the aliens on the display carried a Life-Flower.

"Friends of the Flower, you have journeyed long and far. You now arrive at one of the pre-selected planets for Assembly. And for what reason?" The unseen announcer's carefully enunciated words and manner were familiar to everyone – his voice was heard each day during the KOR Official News.

The unseen voice continued after the calculated pause.

"It is not necessary. Your time could be better served for the betterment of the entire galactic civilization. If you utilize your time and energy and focus on the goals of KOR, you will be duly rewarded. We will reward you even now if you forego this ancient tradition of Assembly and return to your planets and your work assignments. We will provide you with a *scheduled* vacation according to our plan. And better, KOR will fully fund it if you return now."

Bez and Wey looked around at the other alien faces.

Some seemed lost in thought while others maintained their simple, yet joyful countenance.

And all held their individual Life-Flowers a little tighter.

"We leave you with this thought while you contemplate our offer." The rich voice of the Announcer paused appropriately for optimum effect.

"Unlike what the ancient proverb states, scientific research proves that if *your* Life-Flower dies, it does not mean your imminent death. And more important, it does not mean you are unworthy."

The eyebrows over Bez's three eyes rose with surprise. "Well, they take another proverb out of context."

"True," Wey agreed. "A Life-Flower may die due to unforeseen circumstances – disease, tragedy or accident."

"The ancient Word states if the owner of a Life-Flower *allows* one to die, then that one is unworthy of life."

Bez lovingly stroked the long, slender leaves and gazed at the deep blue petals sprinkled with orange and yellow laces of color.

Wey blew his warm breath up and down his own flower with tender affection.

"Unlike simple plants, a Life-Flower requires more than soil, water and nutrients." Wey held his flower close to his fur-covered chest.

"It especially needs love." Bez kissed the petals of her Life-Flower. The plant swayed back and forth at her familiar touch. Bez felt the Life-Flower reach out with its invisible power and touch her heart and her emotions deep inside. She shivered with delight.

"And it gives love in return." She smiled at Wey.

"I can't imagine life without my flower." Wey kissed his flower too.

"In most cases, Life-Flowers outlive their sentient partners. Even the youngest Friend knows that fact," Bez said.

"And a child given such a Life-Flower, loved and tended thousands of years by its previous partners – is doubly Blessed." Wey smiled with a spiritual glow.

"But a child given a newly seeded Life-Flower, both starting their lives together, is also Blessed," Bez reminded him lovingly.

"The Blessings of sharing life with a Life-Flower are many. It is the most special of all symbiotic relationships known."

Bez and Wey turned to the alien standing next to them that had just spoken. The alien smiled.

"You speak true, Friend of the Flower," he said in greeting.

Bez and Wey repeated the homage simultaneously back to their unnamed friend.

"And one should never neglect a Life-Flower in any way. Or else both the flower and partner will soon die." A female alien said as she held her own flower up, the bright burgundy and purple petals almost iridescent.

The main doors of the shuttle opened.

Outside, a green forest of trees swayed in the wind. Above them, a ruby sun shone down from a cloudless sky of the most delicate shade of purple.

"We must go to our assigned Assembly City and find our courtyard," A voice said through the speakers to everyone inside the shuttle.

Everyone moved forward with harmony and a gentle politeness despite the fact they were crowded together in the confines of the shuttle.

"As always, we will place our Life-Flowers side-by-side in our Courtyard while we attend Assembly." Bez moved her flower until its petals gently touched Wey's petals.

The petals of both flowers shimmered at the familiar touch.

"And then, you must tell me why you have such a dark foreboding of failure." Bez whispered to her husband with concern.

"I will…

***

The huge courtyard of the city quickly filled from end to end with a riotous array of Life-Flowers placed carefully in each assigned spot. From the roofs of near-by houses and buildings the residents gazed in awe. From a distance, patterns and shapes became discernible as individual flowers became lost in the sea of colors.

But up close, the courtyard seemed to be a huge garden of Life-Flowers.

When the Life-Flowers reached tens of thousands in numbers, the slender green stems holding the colorful petals began to sway and move – although no breeze touched the living plants. The Life-Flowers danced, heralding Assembly.

Wey placed the green and blue bloom of his Life-Flower beside Bez's.

They both stepped away as more aliens moved forward to place their own Life-Flowers in their assigned positions.

Bez and Wey walked down a side street toward a small café where they had booked reservations. They sat at an outdoor table and admired the ancient city square of Astram.

"I understand that one of the 'Million' is here with us." Bez noted Wey's surprised expression with delight.

"Really! That will be a treat indeed, to be in the presence of someone a million years old and hear him expound on the ancient texts." Wey smiled.

"He is named Adrent. Or so I've been told. And it's said he's almost two million years old."

Wey whistled.

A waiter approached their table, greeted them, and waited while Bez and Wey looked over the menu. They ordered some wine and two of the planet's vegetarian delicacies. The reptilian waiter bowed and left.

Bez studied Wey's fur-covered face a moment. "I have another secret to share with you."

"It couldn't be anything better than the first one. I can't wait to meet Adrent."

Bez leaned closer and spoke in a hushed voice. "Urud and Elyn are attending this Assembly."

"You're kidding! They came all the way across the galaxy to this particular Assembly? There are dozens of other planets holding Assemblies far closer to them."

"Urud and Elyn gave up their positions in KOR. They now travel from world to world with the seeds of Life-Flowers. They seek those who *Yearn*."

"That took a lot of commitment!"

They paused as their reptilian waiter brought two glasses of wine and set them on the table along with their appetizers. After he left, Bez looked deeply into Wey's three eyes.

"What is troubling you, husband? Why do you fear failure?"

Wey looked down at his fur-covered hands and his carefully manicured talons. Without raising his eyes, he spoke.

"I fear KOR will swallow me up. They offer so much – pleasures, riches, and power. They offer this to all who pledge their complete loyalty to them. And now, they control every aspect of life on every single planet."

"Not every aspect." Bez smiled reassuringly. She reached out and caressed his hand lovingly.

"But what they claim is true; they have made the universe a better place, a place of safety and peace. They produce for the 'betterment of all.'"

"No one – no society, no business, and no government can provide all that."

"But KOR has." Wey placed his hands together to calm his emotions.

"It *seems* they have. Do not be fooled by their propaganda." Bez smiled innocently.

"And now, their scientists have proven they can nurture a Life-Flower *without* a partner." Wey nodded at her.

"But only in a lab and only for a short time." Bez's joyful smile grew brighter. "But we already knew Life-Flowers could grow on any planet by themselves."

"It just seems, well, it seems so right."

"Remember the Teachings, husband. Remember the First Proverb."

"I only want us to be happy, to know peace and joy." Wey slowly shook his head amid his troubled thoughts.

Bez and Wey sat back in their chairs. Long moments passed in silence as they sipped their red wine, each contemplating the other.

"I read yesterday that another one of those 'isolated planets' was discovered."

"Really? It's been several hundred years since the last one was discovered. I was a child then."

"Surprisingly, this 'isolated world' is a technology-based society, though still pre-stardrive."

Wey raised all three of his bushy eyebrows in surprise. "If they have technology, why have they not detected us yet?"

"KOR has enveloped their solar system inside a Filter Field. The isolated sentients have only recently developed instruments with the ability to peer out into the universe. The Filter Field screens out all the signs of life that exist throughout the galaxy. KOR wants to study the beings in their natural, pristine state of isolation a bit longer before First Contact."

"Where was this planet and its young sentients discovered?"

"At the edge of the galaxy, out near the end of one of the spiral arms"

"Astounding!"

Bez leaned closer, a humorous glint in her eyes. "And you won't believe it, but they believe they are the only sentient race in the entire universe! I mean in the *entire universe*!"

Bez and Wey laughed with genuine mirth.

"That's so egotistical, in a warped kind of way," Wey chuckled.

"I know, unbelievable. I mean, these sentient beings are isolated in every definition of the term."

"It's amazing such a planet still exists in this day and age." Wey shook his head in disbelief.

"Well, I'm going shopping before Assembly begins tomorrow. Our evenings will soon be filled with warm association and meditation on the wisdom expounded during Assembly."

Wey finished his dessert alone at the table after Bez left.

All the tables around him seemed to be filled with Friends of the Flower. He heard bits and snatches of everyone conversing excitingly about the upcoming Assembly. He sat quietly, enjoying the intense feelings emanating from all around. He closed his eyes and thought of the wonderful peace and harmony he would experience at Assembly in the coming days.

Time slowed down for Wey while he relaxed. The minutes turned into an hour.

After paying his waiter, he left.

Wey entered his room, but discovered he was not alone. An alien in dark flowing robes stood before him, waiting patiently in the darkness.

"Who are you?"

"I am KOR."

Wey looked at him puzzlement. "No single being is KOR."

"KOR is One and All is KOR. We are each KOR. Or we can be."

"KOR wants too much."

"We work for the betterment of KOR and thus the betterment of all beings – that includes each race and each individual. And we are succeeding."

"I can remember before there was even any mention of KOR. KOR has been in existence for less than a thousand years." Wey said firmly. "How old are you?"

"I was born after KOR, after it bound the universe with its laws and power." The robed alien smiled.

"KOR was originally a business. It grew across planets and the galaxy like none before it. Soon, it even replaced the governments. And it grew richer than any organization in recorded history." They young alien paused.

Wey knew the story, he had witnessed its rise. He waited for him to continue.

"KOR has finally brought peace and harmony to all. Every empire which preceded it failed in that respect, although they carved out their own niches in history for a time. But KOR has succeeded because we combine our power with our *values*." The young alien smiled. "We bring harmony and happiness. We bring order and joy. All who come to KOR increase that harmony and happiness."

Wey stared unflinching at the alien.

"We desire the Friends of the Flower to join us – join us *fully*. Yours is the oldest Order in the known universe. Your ways are practiced on almost every world. And yours is the only organization that has not fully embraced KOR."

"I work for KOR, as does everyone else in the galaxy," Wey countered.

"And the Friends of the Flower understand the tenets of KOR, probably better than most. We understand that fact."

"The Friends of the Flower live those same values – and to a greater degree. We have done so for millennia, long before KOR made its first profit."

"Ah yes, for many millennia. But the Friends never founded an empire; they never even controlled a single planet in all those epochs of time."

"We live in harmony with all. We do not seek…" Wey paused, his nose dark with embarrassment.

"Power or control." Wey finally added.

"Why?"

Wey walked over to the balcony door and opened it. He stepped out onto the balcony overlooking the city courtyard.

A sea of flowers waved gently without the need of any breeze.

"I *feel* my Life-Flower even from this distance." Among the tens of thousands of flowers that filled the courtyard, Wey pointed confidently to a single flower.

"We are bound." Wey placed his hands together and closed his eyes, concentrating on that special symbiotic relationship. Deep inside, he felt a warmth begin to grow. Even more, he felt an inner joy fill him with ecstasy.

Wey turned back to the alien and smiled.

"I want you to join KOR – *unreservedly*." The alien stepped closer and took Wey by his hands. "In reward, KOR will provide you with riches beyond your wildest imaginings. You never need to work again."

Wey felt his hearts all skip a beat in unison. His breathing grew rapid and shallow while he contemplated this unexpected offer. He slowly turned away and stepped back to the balcony. Wey gazed out on the sea of flowers.

He closed his eyes while his hearts quivered with both fear and excitement.

"KOR can make all your dreams come true, Wey. We've done it for billions of other sentient beings." The alien in the dark robes walked out onto the balcony and placed his scaly hand on Wey's shoulder. "We need you to help us persuade others from among the Friends. You can do that; you are part of the leader body. There are already others among you who have accepted our offer in secret – some even attending this very Assembly."

Wey started to reply that he did not believe others had joined KOR. But he held back. He wanted to hear more...

"KOR can make *your* dreams come true," he repeated earnestly.

He opened his eyes, but he could not bring himself to look at the rainbow of colors which formed the patterns of Assembly among the Life-Flowers. His vision wavered out of focus.

"I... I" Wey stammered.

"KOR wants what the Friends want."

Wey looked up at a lone bird sailing on the wind far above. And from far above, the white bird called out joyfully, singing its happiness of flight.

"KOR's basic tenets include – do not lie, do not deceive, do not harm. These are also tenets of 'The Sayings.'" Wey said in a low tone. He looked back down at the courtyard and spotted the precious petals of his own Life-Flower as it waved gently at him.

"Correct." The robed alien replied.

"And yet, I know KOR has lied, both to individuals and entire planets. KOR has deceived," Wey said with disapproval.

"Only when..." The alien paused poignantly. *"Only when it is necessary.* And only for the greater good."

"The Friends of the Flower never lie. Never! We may believe in the same core tenets, but only one of us truly practice them."

"Would you like an entire world?" The alien smiled shrewdly. "An entire planet, yours to rule. Under your rule and backed by KOR, you can make

325

it into a world filled with happiness for all who dwell under you."

Wey felt his hearts beat rapidly. He knew he could be a good ruler, a truly benevolent one. And he would only use such power for good. Deep inside, he felt a powerful urge to accept this offer.

He had secretly desired such a wondrous life of power and riches. It had been whispered KOR rewarded selected ones like this.

And at the same time, he knew it was wrong because it would mean his fall and permanent separation from his Life-Flower.

In fact, it would probably die...

"But you must fully embrace KOR. Together, KOR and the Friends can do so much. Think about it! KOR will give you an entire planet, and you will rule it under your beloved tenets."

"I like... I mean, it is a noble idea. But power is dangerous. The ancient proverbs warn of its corrupting influence." Wey felt his hearts pounding rapidly.

"Yes, the Friends of the Flower do not seek leadership. Nor do you wield weapons – you have no armies, no fleets. How has your Order survived the eons – the rise and fall of countless empires and dictators? It seems it should be so easy to destroy you..." The robed alien smiled strangely.

Wey raised his head. "Deep inside each of us, there is something so powerful that even the mightiest fleets cannot conquer it – nothing can conquer it. Like flowers, the Friends grow and bloom on every world – even amid adversity and trial."

The alien shook his head in puzzlement. After a moment, he pushed back his black robe and extended a hand with seven fingers to initiate his offer. Wey held back, but the alien suddenly reached out and took Wey's manicured talons into his grasp.

"Think it over carefully. Think of the good you could do if you ruled your own world. You could take many wives, as is the right of the ruler. You can make the planet a natural paradise." The alien's eyes sparkled as he leaned closer and whispered into Wey's ear. *"You could re-create a new home-world for the Life-Flowers and grow them for the entire universe, as it was in the beginning."*

Wey felt his body shake with intense emotion. Deep inside, he knew what KOR offered was amazing. And "The Sayings" did state there was an original home world where Life-Flowers grew and spread to all other worlds. He could...

But at the same time, he knew he would be betraying the ancient words. Power would corrupt him in the end. He would fail, no matter what excuses he contrived.

"I will wait for you as you leave Assembly. You will commit to KOR with a simple handshake. Then I will provide you more instructions then. In the meantime, you must encourage the Friends to turn to KOR – *to trust in KOR*."

Wey nodded, almost against his will.

***

An hour later, Bez returned from shopping. She told Wey of her purchases and especially of meeting new Friends recently arrived for Assembly.

Later that night, Bez and Wey slept.

But Wey's peaceful dreams turned into dark visions of fear and dread. Deep inside his mind, he felt the overwhelming power of death. Death came relentlessly. The death was merciless, and unstoppable, filled with pain and fury and mindless violence.

Wey awoke screaming.

He noticed Bez sitting up in bed already awake.

He put a hand over his mouth in embarrassment. Wey started to apologize to Bez for startling her, but he stopped after he noticed the tears streaming down the fur of her cheeks.

At that moment, he heard the distant screams from the balcony window.

Wey jumped out of bed and ran onto the balcony.

In the vast courtyard below, he sensed rather than saw the heart-rending tragedy.

"They've killed all the flowers!"

Wey cried, huge sobs shaking his entire body. He cried for his Life-Flower. He cried for Bez. He cried for everyone.

The flames rose higher, dancing in the breeze. The heat almost singed the fur on his face. But Wey would not leave the balcony. He cried for his flower. He cried for all the flowers.

And deep inside, he knew this tragedy was being repeated in every city on this planet. And worse... on every designated planet, in every assigned city and in every courtyard where Assembly was being held.

Across the entire inhabited galaxy, inside billions of broken hearts, the 'Chant of Mourning' was heard once again.

***

"Terrorists enacted a heartless atrocity against the Friends of the Flower this day. On all planets where Assembly is set to begin, in every courtyard where their precious Life-Flowers were placed in symbolic display of their love for all beings – every flower has been killed."

The newscaster from KOR paused.

"The virus was engineered to target only Life-Flowers. The virus mutated within seconds and destroyed itself by bursting into flames. There was no way scientists could attempt to trace the genetic design back to any of the known Terrorist groups who've used this same tactic before."

"KOR has promised a swift and thorough investigation. KOR will bring the terrorists to judgment and punish them severely. In return, KOR simply requests the trust and cooperation of the Friends while they aid them in their darkest hour…"

***

Wey stumbled as he entered the vast auditorium of Assembly.

An overwhelming dread seized him. He fought for control while Bez grabbed his arm to prevent him falling.

Wey groaned.

"Careful, husband," Bez said with concern.

He closed his eyes when a new wave of despair filled his being. He felt his hands shaking again, as if he were freezing. Suddenly, a wave of nausea bent him over.

"Sit down, Wey." Bez guided Wey to the nearest empty chair and helped him fall into one. She leaned over him while he started to moan again.

"You are suffering from *the parting*." Bez gently patted his shoulder.

Wey looked up with a pained expression.

A small alien sitting in a chair on the other side touched Wey's arm.

"We all suffer the *'Great Emptiness'*, Friend." The small alien smiled sadly. "We all suffer."

"It..." Wey stuttered, forcing himself to speak. "It is so hard. I am so... *hollow* inside."

"We must support each other," Bez whispered urgently. "I feel it too. It hurts so much."

Wey's entire body shuddered uncontrollably. "You are doing so-so much better than me, Bez."

Bez sat down. An expression of intense pain filled her face. "There's a hole in each of my hearts." Bez clutched her blouse and groaned out loud.

"I don't want to be here. I want to be alone." Wey's eyes pleaded with Bez.

"Assembly will help us."

"I need something..." Wey whispered.

"What?"

"I don't know…" Wey cried softly, hiding his face behind his hands.

"I've heard rumors that all the Seed Houses were poisoned," the small alien beside him said.

A female alien in the row behind them covered her own face with fear.

"Who can help us?" Wey said with sadness. "Who cares?"

"The authorities will get them – KOR will get them!" The small alien nodded his head up and down rapidly.

Wey wrapped his arms around his body and rocked back and forth. "KOR is… good. KOR is good." Wey forced the words out.

"KOR wants to help us. Perhaps we should embrace them into our hearts." The small alien nodded more rapidly.

"We can trust them…" Wey added.

"We are not here to discuss to KOR," Bez said angrily. Suddenly, she pushed Wey back into his chair to stop his rocking motions.

Wey rubbed his eyes, fighting the dark despair of the 'Great Emptiness.' "I just want…"

Bez nodded toward the stage. "Assembly begins, husband. We will find the answers to our inner anguish here. KOR does not have the answers. And besides, what does KOR want in return for your trust? There is always a price to pay for KOR. – a very high price. But here at Assembly the words of wisdom are given without cost, and the comfort of the truths shared here is free. Please, listen to the healing words."

Bez sat down beside Wey and together they faced the stage.

The stage was carefully prepared and adorned with plants and artwork. The gentle murmuring throughout the crowd quickly faded when a single alien walked slowly into view.

Adrent of the 'Million' walked slowly across the stage with his legs and body bowed with age. Even at a distance, one could see he was ancient.

The crowd grew silent with respect.

All the other planets of Assembly viewed Adrent on huge display screens while they awaited the first words of Assembly.

Adrent looked out upon the alien faces with a great sadness.

"A great tragedy has befallen us – a tragedy as terrible as the destruction of the original world on which Life-Flowers first grew. But out of that great tragedy, we learned that Life-Flower seeds would grow on other worlds – in the right environment."

Adrent slowly wiped a solitary tear from his cheek of gray, cobbled skin.

"We must not suffer alone or else the 'Great Emptiness' will destroy us. We need to heal in fellowship." Adrent cleared his throat. "Let us reflect on the Life-Flower – and that precious symbiotic relationship."

Adrent stroked his chin in deep thought.

"Those who know us realize we do not worship a mere flower. However, the flower is much more than a pet that we feed, nourish and love. A Life-Flower lives for ages untold. One of the oldest..." Adrent choked on the last word. Suddenly, tears flowed freely from each of his nine eyes. He paused in sadness for long seconds.

Finally, he spoke.

"My own Life-Flower was given me when I was but a child, and it had already been tended by two previous partners. Yes, my Life-Flower was older even than I – and I am over a million years old."

A collective sigh filled the auditorium.

Wey reached over and took Bez's hand into his own.

"We share our *entire* existence with a Life-Flower. The flower's inner essence feeds on its partner's emotions, its partner's care, and its partner's love. It is a symbiotic relationship, a physiological symbiosis that links our inner emotions and which feeds a self-reciprocating cycle between partner and flower until there develops a great *need* for each other."

"The Life-Flower also serves as a barometer of our inner selves and our love. The more we love – *in everything* – the stronger our symbiotic bonds grow with the flower."

Adrent smiled sadly at the audience.

"It is so written – 'With love and tender care, a Life-Flower can live forever.'" Adrent choked back a sob.

"But we live in a universe where tragedy can befall anyone at any time and even destroy that which is so very carefully tended." Adrent's eyes grew hard.

"Some think we want revenge. KOR offers to help us seek out and destroy the Terrorists." Adrent smiled for the first time. "KOR does not yet understand what makes us different from all others. Each of us comes from all the alien races and civilizations, but we left them – deep inside – when we became a partner with a Life-Flower."

Throughout the crowd, heads nodded in silent agreement.

"We are sad. And we grieve. But, true happiness does not come from a symbiosis with Life-Flowers – as nice at that is." The wrinkled old alien nodded silently a moment, deep in thought.

"Happiness does not come from things, it does not come from money, or power, or even pleasures. Real happiness emanates from inside – from inner contentment and from our precious relationships with other sentient beings."

Adrent spread his arms apart as if to embrace the entire crowd. "Everyone, reach out to the Friend sitting on either side of you and hold hands."

Inside the vast auditorium, over one hundred thousand aliens reached out to each other in their pain and sorrow and held hands. And across the galaxy, at all the other worlds where others attended Assembly and listened to Adrent via the communication network, billions of others held hands in comfort.

Adrent broke into a wide smile, gazing benevolently out into the crowd. "Life will continue. And happiness will return. Anger and violence is never the answer – nothing good ever comes from anger. We will support each other. We will answer hate with love." The old alien laughed out loud. "And we will plant new seeds!"

The crowd shouted its agreement in sustained and joyous applause. Wey and Bez stood up along with everyone else in a standing ovation.

And with the gentle drumming of the applause filling the air, Wey and Bez hugged each other.

The Assembly completed its weeklong agenda amid sadness and joy.

***

Bez and Wey made their way slowly through the crowd to the shuttle which would take them to the starship in orbit that would carry them back to their home planet.

"Oh look, isn't that a Friend from the aquatic alien race Vrcanth?" Bez pointed to a large alien bidding farewell to other Friends as they boarded the shuttle. In fact, they noticed other aliens of various races gathered around bidding farewell while most walked toward the waiting shuttles.

"Yes, I think so. I guess he must be wearing some kind of re-breather over the gills on its neck?" Wey shivered. "Their skin is so rubbery to the touch; I almost dread his farewell."

"Don't be like that," Bez chided.

Suddenly, Wey saw the robed alien from KOR. The alien noticed him at the same time and immediately walked forward.

"Who is that?" Bez asked suspiciously.

"My dear friend let me extend my sincere condolences." The alien in the black robe offered his hand.

335

Wey looked down at the alien's hand, knowing what was really offered him.

"Thank you." But Wey did not take the alien's hand within his own grasp.

The alien stared at him dumbfounded.

Wey started to walk past.

"What is it with you aliens?" He grabbed Wey roughly by his arm.

Bez and Wey stared at him in shock.

"KOR wants to help you. We can bring the Terrorists to justice." He leaned closer and whispered. "We have created a special drug that will ease your 'Great Emptiness.'"

Wey shuddered, and the dark despair filled him again.

"That is quite a coincidence – KOR having prepared a drug to ease the pain of our separation from Life-Flowers before it even happened." Bez frowned with suspicion at the robed alien.

His eyes narrowed with anger, but he continued. "KOR has kept it out of the news – to protect you – but all your Seed Houses were poisoned." The alien's eyes narrowed. "There are no seeds to plant. You will never again have a Life-Flower."

Wey blinked back his tears.

Bez looked fearfully at her husband. "It can't be true!"

Wey put his arm around his wife. "We don't need your drugs. We don't need revenge."

Wey and Bez turned to walk away.

"I just don't get it. What's wrong with you aliens?" He shouted angrily. "We offer you KOR!"

Wey felt his hearts quiver with delight. He turned and spoke. "I don't need to rule a world to be happy. I don't need a drug to make me happy. We don't need KOR to make us happy." Wey shook his head sadly. "True, we may never again know the joy of bonding with a Life-Flower. And I will sorely miss that."

Wey gently squeezed Bez's shoulder.

"Love will fill the 'Great Emptiness.' Love is all we really need."

In that instant, Wey realized he had not failed. Somehow, he had resisted even his deepest desires and defeated them – with the help of his wife and the words of Assembly – the wisdom of 'The Sayings.' And inside his hearts, he knew what the most important things in life were – and most surprising, he had known it all along.

But he had allowed the glitter and the gold of KOR to blind him momentarily.

They turned and walked away. As they neared the shuttle, they approached the Vrcanth who now appeared to be part of a group of Friends bidding farewell to all.

"A safe and pleasant journey home, Friends." The large Vrcanth touched the fur first on the shoulder of Bez and then on Wey with a flipper-appendage.

Against his will, Wey cringed.

But the soft, rubbery touch felt good against his shoulder – except for a tiny prick.

The Vrcanth winked knowingly at both Bez and Wey, and then he turned to greet more Friends leaving Assembly.

Wey reached into his fur and touched the small round object. He caressed it only a moment, realizing with a surge of joy what the Vrcanth had placed on his fur.

He knew the seed would soon need soil and nourishment to mature.

But he already sensed the seed of the Life-Flower forming the bonds of a new symbiotic relationship with him.

He looked at his wife. Bez's eyes brimmed with tears. He noticed her caress the tiny seed held in the folds of her fur.

KOR had lied again.

Wey walked away triumphant, gently holding Bez's hand.

The Final Rite

Adek marched impatiently down the shuttle ramp onto the soil of Rath while the soldiers of his father's Home Guard saluted. The eldest son of Randurn returned their salutes and quickly stepped past them to the waiting form of his brother, the third-born son.

"Kagart, why the urgent summons?" Adek snarled. He raised his head and waited for his brother to answer.

Kagart's eyes narrowed, and he snarled in reply.

Adek was taller than his brother, but both their bodies rippled with the great strength of their race, and both wore the uniform of the Fleet – each captain of his own warship. The red hair of their shared lineage fell across their wide shoulders, but it was the ring of short horns protruding around their necks which signified to the universe that they were Anka of the Krangok.

Adek noted his brother's disapproval, but his impatience was warranted – the Krangok were on high alert. The Xanaxians were flexing their muscles again and now was not the time to be visiting with family.

"Speak, why this call of urgency that has pulled me from my honored duty?" Adek stood face-to-face with his brother, staring into his unflinching eyes.

"There's been an accident," Kagart whispered solemnly. "It's father…"

339

Adek grunted, a picture of his mighty father fixed in his memory. "We must go and assist him back to health then. What do the Healers say, how long will his recovery take?"

Kagart stepped beside his eldest brother and they marched together toward the great house. Long seconds went by in silence.

Finally, Kagart spoke. "I too was instructed to come quickly. And to let nothing stop me."

The muscles in Adek's jaw began to flex with each step. They soon arrived at the white marble stairs that led to the front entrance. Each warrior took them two at a time.

Adek noted the look of concern in Kagart's eyes.

"Father is only in his seventh century of life, just entering his middle epoch. Do not worry brother, he is strong. He is Randurn of the Anka." Adek smiled knowingly.

But as they reached the top of the marble stairs two female forms waited to greet them instead of Rajel, the second-born son which they had expected.

Adek's face tightened, and his twin hearts pounded from his exertions. Without warning, a strange tightness gripped his soul, a coldness that pressed against his lungs.

"Mother, what of father," Kagart asked breathlessly.

Both women wore long black dresses that hung to the floor like heavy curtains. One was a younger version of the other, each graced with soft, beautiful faces and flowing tresses of auburn hair. But the fine wrinkles on his mother's face and at the edges of her mouth and eyes betrayed her age.

Both gazed at the newcomers with expressions of deadly seriousness.

"Father is dying."

Adek froze with disbelief at his sister's words.

"That cannot be!" He turned to his mother. "Why does Cylles speak such stupidity? Father is strong, he cannot be dying."

But his mother seemed to choke as two tears silently streamed down her cheeks. Cylles put her arm gently around her mother's shoulder.

Adek and Kagart looked on in shocked silence. The sounds of their mother sobbing tore at their hearts like daggers dulled from too much use.

"Where is Rajel?" Adek focused his thoughts. He stepped forward to grasp his mother's arm.

"Leave her alone!" Cylles shoved Adek's hand away from their mother. "Can't you see she mourns for her husband? You act as one of the stupid ones, little brother."

Adek's eyes narrowed dangerously.

She was the first-born of his parents. But he was the first-born son.

"Rajel is by our father's side." She stared defiantly at Adek. "He has not left him since…" Her voice faded and her eyes grew moist. She turned away.

"I will talk with my father's Healers. They will tell me what must be done." Adek marched past as his mother choked back a sob.

Cylles and Kagart exchanged brief, knowing glances.

The warrior groaned and his sister quickly wiped her eyes. In a flash, Kagart was rushing through the still open door after Adek.

"They are not prepared," Cylles whispered to her mother. "But when they see father, they will understand."

Kagart caught up with Adek.

"I am tired of this foolishness, Kagart. Rajel will tell us the facts." Adek's voice was hard as he fought the rising panic in his twin hearts. "I am sure it is serious, but we will help father through it – even if it takes the best Healers of the empire."

They entered their father's bedroom.

Each froze and gazed in shock at the sight before them.

Floating rigid in the middle of the room was the body of their father draped in linen and surrounded by a dozen humming machines.

The haggard face was pale – etched with a frozen expression of deep sleep. All along his exposed body numerous wires disappeared into his skin, connecting him to the machines. Inserted into each nostril was a slender tube, but what drew Adek's eyes was the clear pipe that ran into his mouth and deep inside the throat.

The unconscious Krangok floated with his arms outstretched in the grip of the Medi-Unit and its anti-gravity field, the palms of his large hands turned upward with his fingers curled.

On one side a Healer and nurse continuously monitored the dials and glowing displays.

Rajel stood with bowed head on the other side, gently holding three of his father's fingers. The sight struck Adek as odd – a warrior holding the hand of another warrior.

A sense of dread gripped his being.

His father was so still – only the mechanical rise of his chest betraying any evidence of life. The numbers on the life support displays varied only slightly with each *precise* breath.

Adek could not take his eyes away from the still form of his father. He felt a crushing emotional anguish, and this inner distress grew until it threatened to suffocate him. Adek's mind raced in a sudden flurry of confusing thoughts.

Finally, one thought grew into focus.

Something was wrong...

The overwhelming feeling now squeezed his twin hearts until his vision blurred. Adek hurriedly wiped his eyes to clear his vision. He focused again as his father's chest rose methodically – right on cue.

He gasped with realization.

"The machine is breathing for him!" Adek shouted.

"And it takes the place of his failed hearts," Rajel said with great sadness.

Adek stared at the machines. "The Healers can replace his hearts."

"But they cannot replace his damaged brain," Rajel whispered hoarsely.

Adek reached clumsily for his short sword and stepped towards the hated wires and pipes. His father would not want it to end this way – not like this. He would cut the wires and tubes and allow his father to die with honor.

From all directions hands grabbed and pulled at him. He winced as a strong blow flung the sword from his grasp. There were shouts and angry yells all around and then he felt himself thrown to the floor. Adek kicked and swung his fists, and he came free momentarily, but more arms quickly pinned him down.

He screamed his rage.

***

Adek awoke later, the passage of time blurred as he wiped his eyes to push the drug-induced fog out of his mind.

He rolled out of bed, sudden remembrance of where he was jolting him to action. He quickly clothed himself and walked out of the darkened room.

Adek found them all in the library.

His mother was sitting, staring at him somberly while he entered. Cylles was still by her side, one arm across her shoulder.

Cylles's eyes narrowed, watching Adek's every move.

Kagart was talking in a hushed voice with Rajel in one corner, both keeping a careful eye on him as well.

Adek looked around at the other figure.

Jenser, the fifth-born son, was here now. Jenser, the great Trader, the great businessman. Along with Cylles and Rajel, they managed his father's vast business interests across many sectors of space.

Rajel, the second-born son, helped them direct the Trade fleet from here on Rath, but his primary oversight was for the factories that provided for all who lived on their worlds.

But it was really Cylles, with her fastidious efficiency, who kept it all organized and profitable.

Adek growled under his breath.

Those three along with his father had made the House of Anka the richest of all the Krangok.

Adek would have nothing to do with it. He did not need a female telling him what to do.

He and Kagart were the warriors of the family – honored warriors. As had been Sagat, the fourth-born son – now dead.

Adek felt the pain of his brother's death stab his hearts again.

But at least Sagat's death had been one of honor.

It had been at the Battle of the Blood Nebula, the decisive battle of the War of Stam.

Once again, his mind's eye watched his brother's warship crumple and explode. And once again, Adek screamed.

Without a thought for himself or his ship, Adek charged the battleship with his cruiser. At point-blank range he fired every weapon while his own ship rocked under direct hits.

But he destroyed the enemy warship with a final spread of torpedoes.

The battle cry of his father echoed over the comm system of every ship while he led the Anka squadrons against the heart of the enemy fleet. And once again, he felt his hearts pounding with pride as he pulled his cruiser alongside that of his father while they took on the core of the Stam fleet. They exchanged broadside after broadside, black space laced with the crossing lances of death until the battle had been won.

Kagart had been patrolling the Nasardian sector during that famous battle. Even now, he rued how he had missed the battle which was now sung in celebration alongside the greatest battles of Krangok legend.

Adek smiled – for a moment. The sickening memory of his father pushed every other thought out of his mind. He leaned forward to speak, but Rajel spoke first.

"Wenger's ship draws near," Rajel said matter of fact.

Everyone was coming home – now the sixth son.

"Where was he trading?" Adek said. His voice was a hushed semblance of its normal tone.

"With the Tagon, he was negotiating a new trade agreement for us." Jenser answered instead of Rajel. The younger Krangok drew closer to his eldest brother. "He was given priority passage through their space. His corvette arrived at our Sector border two hours ago, three hyperspace jumps from us. He will be here anytime."

Adek grunted acknowledgement. He looked over to where his mother sat with Cylles.

His mother's eyes were far-off, but at least she was no longer crying. Cylles gently caressed their mother's hair.

He turned back to Rajel and Kagart. Both their faces were drawn and haggard as if they had been fighting a long battle with the enemy. They gazed back at him, their faces empty of all emotion.

Adek felt he must look the same way. Suddenly he had no energy, no fight left.

This must be the way an ancient Krangok feels, the way he feels when his body fails him at last – like his father.

"What happened to our father?" Adek sighed.

Rajel bowed his head. Taking a slow breath, he spoke. "One of his hearts burst. The other took over, but the pressure grew too great, and it began beating irregularly." Rajel looked away. "It was all so sudden, if we'd have gotten a Healer to him right away…"

"It still wouldn't have been enough," Cylles said, interrupting him.

Adek turned to her.

She grasped her mother tighter around the shoulders while she spoke. "It burst the main artery in his brain stem. His brain was flooded with blood as the pressure grew out of control – too much was damaged."

Rajel's eyes became far off.

"Before he lost consciousness, he called for P'tar," Rajel said in a low voice.

"What!" Adek shouted as he stared in disbelief at him. "Is that why you keep him chained to the godless machines?"

Kagart drew back in surprise, staring at Rajel like Adek.

"And what good will the Final Rite do for him," Adek growled with contempt.

"He knew it was hopeless," Cylles said emphatically. "And when the machines are turned off – when his last moment of life comes – he will share his final, precious thoughts with us, mind to mind."

Adek spit onto the hardwood floor and ground the sole of his boot into it. He marched hurriedly to the far wall while his thoughts raced at light speed.

The room grew deathly silent.

In spite of his bitterness, he knew it was his father's right to ask for P'tar. Adek realized he was not angry with any of his siblings, and he wasn't angry because his father had asked for P'tar, although he personally did not want to participate in sharing minds with his family.

He was angry because the father he loved was about to die.

Adek turned to the others. "What of the seventh son? He should be here before we initiate P'tar." Adek had not wanted to mention the last son, even though he was Randurn's favorite. He could never understand the boy's devotion to exploration at the expense of both Trade and the Fleet.

"Cagar's exploration ship is far past the N'Dik systems inside unexplored space. We have received the first answer from him just this hour. He is searching for a wormhole he suspects exists and which he hopes connects back to the Zadek Sector – still a full Quadrant away from Rath," Rajel said. "Even then, he may not make it in time for P'tar." Rajel pursed his lips. "We may have to do it without him."

348

Adek slowly looked around at each of them. "What will it matter to us if we *feel* and *see* father's last thoughts?"

"He loved his family."

Every eye turned to their mother.

"He loved his children." She whispered so low they almost could not hear her words. "He wants to share with you, communicate with you, one last time."

"He will already be remembered as a great warrior. He is already praised as our greatest Trader. We do not need P'tar." Adek looked around at the strained eyes staring back at him. "I do not need to be connected to his dying mind to feel his last thought."

"It will be hard," Cylles agreed.

"No!" Adek snapped. "That does not matter to a warrior."

"Then what?" she asked.

He placed his hands on his hips. But he could not put what he was feeling into words.

"Well, he will soon dwell in Ely'yar with all others who have passed before." Kagart placed his hand on Adek's shoulder. "Perhaps Adek is right. For me, knowing that is enough – that he will soon enter eternal Ely'yar."

"Blasphemy!" Rajel shouted.

Kagart and Rajel locked eyes.

"It is written that the dead sleep awaiting the great Reanimation." Rajel's breathing increased with his rising anger. "Even though our bodies return to the ground, the Giver will…"

"Infidel!" Kagart shouted back with burning eyes.

"Apostate!" Rajel drew out his long sword. In his left hand, he wielded a dagger.

"Shall we fight over religion here in our father's house?" Kagart shouted in challenge, drawing his own weapons.

"What better place?" Rajel sneered.

Adek stepped back after their blades clanged together with metallic fury.

The others also backed off while the two brothers brought their swords to bear. Grunts and growls mixed with curses when blades bit into skin, only to be parried before they dug too deep. Around and around the two circled, sword and dagger pointed at the other, while they waited for the next opening.

Suddenly the base of Kagart's sword slammed into Rajel's head, sending him hard to the ground. Kagart stood above his brother with his arms at his sides, holding his weapons at the ready. He snarled and started to raise his sword.

Adek came unseen from behind and pinned Kagart's arms within his mighty grasp. He brought his mouth close to his brother's ear.

"*It is enough,*" Adek whispered angrily. "Be assured that just because you have bested your brother in battle, it does not mean you are right."

Kagart sneered while he struggled vainly to free himself from Adek's grip.

"It only means your swordplay is better – nothing more," Adek growled.

The soft sound of crying drew their attention as Rajel rose from the floor.

"Stop it, please," their mother begged between sobs. "Isn't the death of your father enough, without another of my sons dying." Her legs suddenly collapsed, and she started to fall to the ground. Cylles quickly grabbed her and Jenser rushed over and held her from the other side.

At just that moment, one of the common soldiers marched inside. He paused wide-eyed, looking around the room.

"Speak quickly," Adek commanded. "And then leave even faster."

"Sir," he bowed. "I bring word that your brother, Wenger, that his ship has landed."

The family looked around at each other, each suddenly remembering the terrible deed before them.

Still holding Kagart fast, Adek walked him farther away from Rajel who was now returning his own weapons to their scabbards.

"No more," Adek whispered firmly.

His younger brother nodded.

Adek freed Kagart and walked toward the large window that looked out upon the garden his mother tended. He shook his head with a warm feeling, remembering all the times he had seen his parents walking among the paths between the flowers and exotic plants.

Suddenly, he was a boy again – old memories flashed in his mind for the first time in a hundred years. He remembered fondly all the good food and the games his family had played when they were children so long ago. He remembered the vacations together to far-off planets, especially to the island world of Angor. There had been so many wonderful vacations spent at that beautiful place.

Adek turned and looked at his brothers and Cylles. He looked not simply at their faces, his gaze searched past the fine wrinkles and the patches of gray in their hair. He looked deep into their eyes, and he could still see the children they had all once been.

And now together, they would bury their father after P'tar, the Final Rite.

***

The next day dawned warm and cloudy. Adek looked out the window at the shadows of the huge clouds slicing across the landscape when he realized someone was talking.

"Bakaball."

"What?" Adek turned.

"The grandchildren are playing Bakaball," Rajel repeated to Adek. Rajel and Adek's other brothers joined them at the window.

And so did Cylles...

"Father was so proud of us when we won at Bakaball." Kagart smiled with remembrance.

"He was prouder that he had fathered enough sons to field an entire team!" Rajel laughed.

Even Adek smiled as he remembered how his father used to direct them and their roaming defense. He could see him now, smiling confidently as he gave the signs to the two outfielders and the three infielders. Yes, he well remembered all the secret signs his father had them memorize so the other team wouldn't know which defense they were putting into motion just before the pitch to the batter.

Wenger had always been the catcher. He enjoyed the strategy of calling each pitch along with the pitcher. But sometimes with an especially tough batter, father would send signs to Wenger on which pitch to send in on a particular count.

Adek had always been the pitcher. He was the strongest and most accurate pitcher of all Randurn's sons.

He remembered with pride those wonderful games and how he had struck out many of the best batters of his age. Of course, a pitcher's role was not simply to pitch. As soon as he had hurled the ball to the batter, he had to prepare himself at the spot on either side of the mound that his father had signaled for their defense. A good pitcher could influence which side of the field the batter would hit towards if he made contact – unless he was an exceptional batter.

Adek's eyes narrowed with another memory.

No, Cylles had pitched too. In fact, Cylles had relieved him in the final inning of the Rath Trophy game and gotten the final outs. His arm had failed him that last inning and his father had taken him out. That had been their first major victory as a family team.

Adek grimaced with the bittersweet memory.

"It's good for them." Rajel nodded. "They will not dwell on what is to come."

"I wonder what father's last thought will be?" Wenger asked out loud.

The five sons looked at each other.

"It will be his greatest feat," Adek said with complete confidence. "It will be his victory at the Blood Nebula."

"No, dear brother, I completely disagree." Rajel rose slowly, looking at the others for their reaction. He smiled. "The House of Anka is the richest and most powerful of all the Krangok. This accomplishment will be his last, most cherished thought."

"Money is only a necessary evil, brother," Adek countered. "Victory against a deadly enemy who would take everything from us, that will be his cherished thought as he leaves this life."

"And I will argue even against that, eldest brother." Jenser stood with open arms. "It is *war* that is the necessary evil. But business, especially the Trade fleet he built, that takes a special and creative force." He tapped his forefinger against his head. "His last thought will be on the greatest Trade fleet that sails the galaxy."

"Here, here!" Echoed a chorus of agreement from two other brothers.

"But actually, you can even leave business out." Wenger said, surprising the others.

"He valued his name above all – he valued his honor most of all. His reputation will be his last and most cherished thought he shares with us." Cylles stepped beside Jenser and Wenger. She looked from one to the other.

"I agree with Wenger," Kagart said. "He valued integrity and our family's position among the other

354

houses – his last thought will be sitting in honor on the Throne of Anka with his family around him."

They all nodded silent agreement.

"He valued his honor above all," Adek agreed grudgingly.

"We will soon know his last thought." Cylles said with a solemn tone.

"Is the seventh son close?" Wenger asked.

"His ship will land tonight," Cylles answered.

"Then we should attach the nodes that will connect us to father's mind for P'tar." Adek rose to go and accomplish this part of the Final Rite.

"It is already done." Cylles watched her brother closely.

Adek felt his anger growing. "I am the eldest son! Randurn will have specified in his Death Orders that I would execute his last wishes."

"You were never around, Adek. He entrusted this honored duty to me." Cylles looked around at her other brothers, who nodded silently in agreement with her. "I am assigned as Executrix by his Death Orders." She gazed steadily at Adek. "I am the eldest child; it is acceptable by Krangok law."

Adek felt his hearts grow sad once again. It seemed that this feeling would stay with him forever.

He wondered deep inside how he had failed his father, why he had chosen Cylles instead of him. He felt ashamed somehow.

Inside his twin hearts, he knew Cylles was right. He had not even had time for a wife, much less being with his father here on the home world.

He did not deserve to execute his father's last Orders.

"When the youngest arrives, we will all gather around father. I will then whisper to him that we are disconnecting the machines." Cylles's eyes moistened with tears. She paused, her lips trembling with the thoughts of tomorrow. Clearing her throat, she steadied herself. "We will all be connected prior to the termination of the machines, all holding hands in a circle around his bed. Only then will I enable P'tar so we can listen to his mind."

"It is an intrusion," Adek said angrily. "We have no right to invade the mind of another being, much less our own father."

"P'tar devices are closely regulated," Rajel said. "They are used primarily for this Rite."

"And sometimes for secret interrogations," Kagart added. He pursed his mouth with thought. "Unethical, yes. But it is quite effective."

"And sometimes a husband and wife will share everything – each wearing a Master P'tar cap." Cylles smiled.

Rajel laughed out loud. "But that is rare, indeed. What couple would share their innermost thoughts and secrets with each other! And could their marriage stand up to such total honesty."

"You might be surprised," Cylles smirked. "After all, father has been happy with one wife all these years – unlike some others."

Rajel and Kagart looked around the room uncomfortably.

Adek smiled to himself. He knew both had taken multiple wives, and both had discovered the pleasure and pain of such unions the hard way. Still, at least they had families where he had none.

Adek looked down at the floor.

"The P'tar is tested," Cylles said while the silence continued.

Every eye fixed on her.

"It is the Way – all must be ready for the final moment."

The brothers stared at her, willing her to finish.

"He thinks of mother mostly. I shared his thoughts for but a moment."

Everyone nodded in agreement.

"Adek."

Adek looked up; surprised Cylles had spoken his name.

"One of father's last Orders is for you to assume headship of the House of Anka."

Surprise etched his face – and disbelief. "I cannot do this thing. My place is with the Fleet." Adek stared at his sister. "It is my duty."

"Nevertheless, it is father's order for you. You will need to make your home here. You will give up direct command of your ships and squadron, but you will maintain overall command from here as did father." Cylles turned to her other brothers. "Adek will also assume father's role over all business interests. However, I am designated to directly manage all business matters and trading contracts. I will be Adek's first officer of our House."

Rajel started to object.

"You have specific orders as well," Cylles added quickly. "Father directed that Rajel is to provide Adek with the necessary training before he takes over. Afterward, you will travel to the capital world of all the Krangok – Kahkalla – to live with the royals representing our House."

Rajel nodded slowly.

With a twinkling in his eyes, he smiled at Adek.

"You will lead our family, Adek. I will assist you as directed."

In his hearts, Adek felt fear and resentment. As the oldest son, his primary duty had been the protection of the realm. He had served well. But the ways of war were all that he knew.

"I cannot," Adek said with heavy voice. With pleading eyes, he looked at his sister and then at each of his brothers. "I am a warrior. My life has been among the stars." He stood, pacing the room with sudden energy. "I know nothing of business – or of trading. And I certainly know nothing about running a House, running a family. I would make a better *explorer*."

Cylles reached for Adek.

"I cannot do this thing!" Adek pushed Cylles's arm away. "I defer to Rajel as second-born son."

"We will let this decision wait until after P'tar," Rajel said after a moment of reflection.

All in the room nodded.

But Adek again stared off into the garden outside the great window.

Into this somber atmosphere their mother entered. She walked as though she entered a grand ballroom. With the greatest elegance, she walked up to each of her children and squeezed their arm or their shoulder – never saying a word but only gazing into their eyes.

Each child saw the deep sadness that haunted her brown eyes.

She did not need to say a word.

"I would show you something." She walked slowly over to the room console and typed a command.

Across the wall-screen an image suddenly appeared. The girlish face laughed back at them, or really at the camera.

And the youthful Krangok female was very pregnant.

"You look too young to be with child," Cylles laughed.

The mother of Randurn's children smiled proudly.

"Which of my siblings do you carry?" Adek asked.

He gazed at his mother's youthful image and wondered what it must have been like to have known her back then – she looked so happy.

"I carry my oldest son."

Adek looked again, now with surprise.

"I had thought this long lost, but I was going through the old databases and found it had been misplaced." She smiled at Adek. "Now, look at these."

The close-up of a boy in grade school with his classmates and teacher came into focus.

"It is Adek!" Rajel and Kagart said together with mirth.

"Were you ever that young... and cute?" Cylles laughed.

"No, that is a picture of your father," Mother said.

"Really." Several said together with surprise.

More images flashed by on the screen, each of them now discernible as their father, but each one showing him a little older. But always he smiled. And his smiles increased with the wedding pictures, and then of him cradling his children one by one as the years melted away before their eyes.

"I would have some of these for my library," Rajel smiled.

"Yes, mother. You must make us all copies. I have not seen these for a very long time," Cylles said wistfully.

An hour went by in relative silence, punctuated from time to time with joyful laughter as the images of young children flashed quickly by.

And the adults they had become laughed with those children of yesteryear.

Adek enjoyed the pictures more than he realized. As he lay in bed that night, many of the images of his youthful father and mother kept appearing in his mind. They looked so happy with each other and their little children.

As the midnight hour passed and the early hours arrived, Adek found he was still restless. He finally gave up on sleep. He walked the darkened hallways until the growing light of the dawn reminded him that the final day of his father's life had arrived.

In the deep shadows his lips trembled, and his first tear fell. Suddenly there came a sound he had not heard since his early childhood so long ago– the sound of his own broken-hearted whimpers.

Adek cried for his father.

***

The seventh son waved at them.

Cagar was a youthful version, almost a twin, of both Adek and Randurn.

The family was gathered and ready for P'tar.

They made their way one by one to their father's bedroom where his body floated inside the anti-gravity field and still connected to the life-support machines. In silence they gathered around him, each casting brief glances at the still form.

Cylles stood on her father's left side next to his face – a face composed in the deepest semblance of sleep. Randurn's wife stood on the right side opposite Cylles.

Adek took his mother's hand and stood in his place while each son took their own position around their father's body according to their rank by age. As they held hands, the Healer came behind each one, beginning with their mother, and placed the meshed fiber cap upon their heads.

Within seconds, they felt the briefest sting that signaled the device had inserted its tiny probes into their scalp.

Adek pressed his mother's hand momentarily as he saw her eyes press shut with pain. She opened her eyes and smiled back sadly.

In the grasp of his right hand, he felt the large hand of Rajel. He turned and their eyes locked.

Adek was surprised to see Rajel's eyes already moist as if he would begin crying here before all the others.

Rajel noted Adek's disapproving expression.

"It is acceptable to mourn in front of the family," Rajel said with a rasping voice.

"Adek never cries," Cylles said. "I never remember seeing him cry, except as a young child."

"True," Kagart agreed readily. "He will be strong for all of us."

Adek saw all the others watching him. He grunted but did not answer. His throat was full of the same sad emotions burning inside him.

But he would not cry in front of them. He would be strong.

The Healer placed the P'tar cap on the seventh son and then whispered to Cylles. A look of panic flashed across her face. But her eyes locked with Adek's firm gaze.

Adek nodded to her.

She took a wavering breath. Cylles leaned close to the ear of Randurn as he floated unmoving, the mechanical rise of his chest the sole evidence he was still alive.

The dying man had been fixed with the P'tar cap yesterday, but the mesh was more tightly woven so that it seemed like a black spider's web pressed against his head. This Master P'tar cap would translate the synaptic pulses of his mind and then amplify and transmit them to the others connected in their miniature network.

In contrast, all the other P'tar caps were designed for reception. However, their caps would transmit enough in order that each could be identified – the dying Krangok would realize they were connected although he would not receive their specific thoughts and feelings.

The two caps were designed differently, specifically for this use – for good reason.

Cylles's lips trembled next to her father's ear.

"P'tar will begin father. We bid you good-bye now." She choked and pressed her eyes shut, fighting her tears. Seconds went by as she tried to regain control. She freed her hand from Cagar and wiped her tears away. Finally, she spoke again.

"We wait for your final sharing, father."

Several groans emanated from around the circle as the Healer flicked the master switch to the *off* position.

Adek's twin hearts filled with sadness. And he suddenly realized what he hoped his father would share with him – he wanted his father to remember him, to remember *their* times together...

The Healer reached over and enabled the P'tar.

Suddenly Adek felt dizzy, he felt his body begin to sway and float. It was like he was in two places at once.

"Close your eyes!" Cylles called out urgently, realizing that some had forgotten.

Adek quickly closed his eyes.

He was somewhere else. He was with a young, beautiful female – Randurn's wife-to-be.

And for the very first time, Adek felt and knew what love was.

Adek choked back his tears. In the distance, he heard sobs and whimpers, but he could not tell where from where they came.

He concentrated again.

Adek felt his hearts beating irregularly.

Or was that his father's hearts beating irregularly?

He realized he was holding his breath.

No, he couldn't breathe any more. He had forgotten how to breathe!

He knew he was dying...

An overwhelming dread filled him.

In that instant, he felt the presence of those connected to him – he felt his wife and children and knew they were with him.

A feeling of inner peace flowed throughout the circle of minds.

Still, he knew he was dying.

Suddenly, there was the happy sound of cheering and the voices of young children…. The sounds of Bakaball.

There they were...

Adek was on the mound staring intently at the batter. And there was Wenger wearing his facemask behind the batter and giving Adek the signs for the next pitch.

Rajel and little Cagar were moving in the outfield as if they were going to defend right center field and left center field and leave the edges of the outfield open.

But it was a feint.

Randurn had signaled them already. Adek would be throwing high heat over the inside part of the plate, corresponding to the coming defensive move.

Cylles was beside him holding a datapad. Her bright, innocent eyes gleamed like miniature suns.

The field of seven boys suddenly came back into view.

The boy on the mound came set. Young Kagart moved away from first base and moved toward second base to defend a spot between those bases while Rajel sprinted toward deep shortstop to get into his position. He back-stepped quickly into the grass of the outfield to play deep.

And there was Sagat backing up to defend the line behind third base.

Randurn's famous 'counter roaming defense' was being played to perfection as now the outfielders reversed their motions and began to run back to defend straight-away center and left field.

The lanky form of young Adek reared back on the mound and threw with all his might. And with all his hearts…

But there was something more.

Inside his twin hearts, which Adek felt beating once again, he was filled with a warm, wonderful, and *living* feeling. This emotion suddenly filled his entire being with such gladness that it made him feel as if he could fly without the need of any starship. It made him powerful. And yet, he could not discern what this emotion was that filled his essence to the brim!

Was it love? Was it passion?

And then he knew – absolutely.

Adek was filled with an incredible sense of caring.

This magical feeling made him feel that he was in the middle of a dream – dreaming and yet aware he was dreaming.

And the dream was so wonderful that Adek never wanted it to end.

Rajel's hand left his grasp.

Adek opened his eyes.

He looked around at his brothers. Each one was crying, most were sobbing. They looked at him, their faces filled with grief.

Adek shifted his gaze to his sister. She had lowered her head into her hands, sobbing uncontrollably.

He turned to his mother.

She smiled back at him, tears running down her eyes.

"It was so beautiful," she whispered to him alone. "I felt, I almost felt like I was back there with him again." She reached out and hugged Adek tightly, putting her head on his chest.

Adek held his mother a few moments.

"He loved his children so much," she whispered.

Adek began to cough, pushing the burning sorrow back inside. He took his free hand and pressed his eyes to prevent the tears from falling. But they fell anyway. He wavered, but felt his mother grasp his arm more tightly.

"We must go," Adek commanded in a deep voice. "P'tar is finished."

***

The three days of mourning finally passed. The family prepared to go back to their normal responsibilities.

Cylles stepped beside Adek, who stood by the great window that looked out on the garden their mother tended. They stood silent a few moments, each enjoying the rainbow of colors the myriad of flowers presented their senses.

"It almost seemed that father was sending me a message personally," Adek whispered.

Cylles bit her lip. "We all felt that. He could sense us as well, each of us. We all helped him, and he helped us."

"I was surprised to see Kagart break down and sob like that." Adek shook his head.

"It was the hardest thing I've ever done." Cylles looked away nervously.

Adek felt she might begin crying again, but she held her composure.

"It was comforting to see your reaction, Adek. You seemed almost, well, your expression was almost like you'd had some kind of revelation!"

"It was so... personal," Adek groaned. He let out a soft sigh, he gazed intently upward as if he were studying something far above.

Cylles looked up at her brother. She studied his face intently a moment. "Kagart has returned to your starship. And I was just informed he has requested permission to disembark."

"Yes, I have given Kagart command of all my squadron in addition to his own. He returns to lead them."

Cylles smiled. "Does that mean you will heed father's last orders and take command of the House of Anka?"

"And the family," Adek added. "Yes, I will take command."

Cylles slipped her arm around Adek and hugged him tightly. "What made you change your mind?"

"Some children playing Bakaball with their father."

Cylles nodded.

"Do you realize why that specific game was his final thought?" She asked.

"I am unsure. It wasn't the game where we won the championship. It wasn't even a game where we beat one of the rival houses." Adek shook his head.

"That was the last game all his children played together as a team. And that specific pitch, that was last time we ran his famous defense. You left for training the next week. And soon after, Kagart left. More games were played, but some of his sons were missing." She squeezed Adek's arm.

Adek paused, trying to gather his thoughts and feelings. "I realize now that family, that family is the most important duty. But it will be hard for me. I have never been in one place for very long." Adek's eyes became far off. "Except here, when I was young."

"I will help, I am your right hand now. And so will Rajel and the others as they report to you. You will learn quickly, and you will learn to enjoy this new life."

Adek chuckled. "Will I find a wife and have children of my own one day?"

"I hope so." Cylles smiled. "Do not let your new duties take up all your energy. Then you will indeed have time."

"Yes," Adek said. "Father showed me that no matter what great deeds he accomplished in war and business, it was all for his family. Family was the most cherished thing to him. He showed me that in P'tar."

Cylles's smile widened. "Family and friends."

"We must always make sure of the more important things – simple as they may seem." Adek paused in thought.

"It's all in how we live… and how we die."

The Fighting Fish of Paramelee

"Something fishy is going on around here."

I waited for a response from the alien in front of me.

"Hmph, that's why we're here! To catch fish!" The muscular, red-skinned alien replied with a smile.

He was bigger than the average alien and he looked nothing like a human. He had a great, big square head with no hair, and the red skin across the top of his head glowed when he spoke. This of course was quite distracting; talking to an alien while his head glowed different shades in rhythm with his speech. His thick neck was the same width as his square head, except it was round in shape.

His unbuttoned shirt revealed the deep, red skin was taut across his broad chest. Six thick arms bulging with muscles extended at forty-five degree angles from his shoulders and gave him a fearsome appearance. He stood on four short but stout legs and he had a short, thick tail.

But he did have two eyes, a nose and a mouth filled with pearly white teeth.

Other than that, he looked nothing like a human.

Yep, this guy was a big, red alien. And in that first instant, I could tell he wasn't your average one either. I immediately hoped I wouldn't be paired with him when we were assigned boats.

And even stranger than all that, he was carrying eighteen rods and reels – two in each hand and six strapped across his back – I know, I counted them.

What did this guy think he was going to do with all those fishing rigs?

"No, I don't mean that in a good way. I mean something fishy is going on around here, like something ain't right." I rolled my eyes and gripped my rig tighter. "Hey, you don't mind if I ask you a personal question, do you?"

He turned and glared down at me with two, large green eyes. "Try me."

"Why in the world are you bringing eighteen fishing rigs with you when we're only going out fishing a few hours today?"

"A great fisher must be ready for any eventuality, puny human. We could run up on some huge game fish that require the stoutest rigs, or we might come upon a bunch of smaller fish where we need finesse and a lightweight rig. I am prepared for any kind of fish! *I am a real fisher*!"

I snorted and laughed at the same time. "Why don't you simply carry one rig and program it for the fish you want to catch?"

"I like to fish the old-fashioned way. Pick the correct rig for the fish I'm after. The only thing I program is the lure – to simulate the image and movement to attract the right fish." His pearly white teeth gleamed from his red face.

"I prefer a fully programmable rig myself – keeps things simple". I smiled back.

"Captain Byl is my name, I'm from the planet Waacdelrrearraifladfeewxixfdyys."

"What a name! Bet you can't say that three times real fast!"

"Byl, Byl, Byl." Captain Byl promptly replied.

"No, no, I mean the name of your world!" I laughed.

"Waacdelrrearraifladfeewxixfdyys, Waacdelrrearraifladfeewxixfdyys, Waacdelrrearraifladfeewxixfdyys!"

"Easy for you to say!" I laughed even louder. "My name is James J. Jones, and I'm from Earth, the greatest fishing planet this side of the galactic center."

"Hmph," Captain Byl said with a dubious tone. "The fishing on my world is second to none, not even your Earth can compare!"

"Actually, you're both wrong." The alien behind us chuckled. "Or why would the three of us be here on Paramelee?"

Captain Byl slapped his right foreleg and laughed out loud. Of course, he dropped three of his fishing rigs. He quickly picked them up and looked them over carefully for any nicks or scratches.

"My name is Kweel. I'm from Yeek."

Kweel, in complete contrast to Byl, was almost human in appearance – two arms and two legs – with the exception that he was covered by orange, iridescent scales and he had a long muscular tail. Two pairs of black, beady eyes stared at us from his glowing orange face. He was short for an alien, standing only about four feet tall at the most and a pungent aroma emanated from his orange body that reminded me of four day old road kill.

Other than that, he was pretty close to looking like a human.

"Paramelee is known as the Fishing Paradise!" Kweel added.

Each of us standing in line raised our rigs – one, two, three or eighteen – in salute to the promise of a great fishing trip. We had paid a pretty penny to travel here for the weekend. I know I had. Not to mention the thirteen jumps through hyperspace just to get to this out of the way world. I mean, it had taken me *almost* forty-eight hours to get here from Earth!

I was more than ready from some good fishing.

Kweel leaned up to me. "What did you mean by, *something fishy is going on here*?"

On this side of the large room standing in line along with us, were aliens just arriving on Paramelee. We did look a motley crew, I'm sure. The only things we had in common was that each of us carried a fishing rig or two – or eighteen – and we each thought we were greatest fisher in the universe.

However, the aliens on the other side of the room were leaving Paramelee. And they looked much different.

True, they each carried a fishing rig like we did. But most of the rods were warped, twisted or broken. And even more strange, almost every single alien limped or hobbled, while the many had an upper appendage in a sling or else were heavily bandaged.

Those of us in the arriving line now gazed over at the walking wounded in the exit line with an air of the slightest suspicion about what we were getting ourselves into.

One of the wounded fishers stumbled, drop his crutch and fell to the floor with a huge thud. The others around him quickly helped their fellow back to his three feet while others shook their heads in empathetic concern.

An alien saw me staring at them. He suddenly burst toward us shouting, "Don't do it! Turn around and leave! Don't even think of fishing here!"

I paused, a certain feeling of impending dread struck me as I gazed over at those poor souls.

The robots of Paramelee quickly surrounded the alien who had shouted to us. They wrapped a few more bandages around his head, completely covering his mouth while doing it, and then hurried him along to the exit at the far end of the room.

"I wonder why they did that?" I asked out loud.

"Tooth ache," Kweel suggested.

"Cold sore, perhaps," Byl added.

Finally, the robots assisting us hurried us through until we finally made it to the long rows of computer terminals so we could obtain our fishing permits. I sat down at one with Byl on one side and Kweel on the side.

"Welcome, James J. Jones of Earth." The artificial voice emanated from a speaker next to the terminal. "Please state the reason for your trip."

"I want to fish!" I answered enthusiastically.

"What is your current status?"

"Hmmm, not sure if I understand the question." I cast a puzzled expression at the video feed.

"What level of fisher are you? Professional fisher? Amateur Fisher? A proficient fisher? A weekend fisher. Or just a good liar?"

"Why, I'm none of those!" I replied in shock. I crossed my arms and grimaced at this ungracious insult.

"We are sorry. Perhaps you are that rare kind of fisher from your world?"

"You're getting warm," I said.

"Ah yes, so you are the *greatest* fisher from your world."

I tenderly caressed my fishing rig with innate pride. "You got it robot, I'm an expert angler!!"

"This is good, since we only allow the best of the best to fish here on Paramelee. After all, it wouldn't be much fun for either you or the fish if it was any other way!"

"Fun for the fish?" I asked suspiciously. I remembered the line of wounded and limping fishers exiting Paramelee. "What's going on here?"

"Nothing! Our fishing tournament is one-of-a-kind. *We promise it will be an experience you will never forget!*"

"That sounds better."

Suddenly, sirens blared and red lights flashed throughout the entire room. The robots started running around waving their arms with their electric eyes flashing in unison to the red lights on the ceiling.

"Is this some kind of red alert?" Captain Byl asked, leaning closer to the microphone.

"Even worse," replied the artificial voice. "We have detected that some or all of you are lying!"

"Of course someone's lying, we're a bunch of fishers," Kweel said.

"Every one of you have answered that you are the *best on your world*!" This time, the artificial voice emanated from every speaker on every terminal. "We do not believe this can be possible. And most important, we must match your fishing skills to the comparable fighting fish. If we do not do this correctly, it is possible that you could be injured. Or worse..."

That line of wounded fishers flashed back to my mind.

"Okay," I said. "I'm not the greatest fisher on Earth. But, I am an expert." I smiled sincerely.

The red lights and sirens slowly began to fade.

"Good," the artificial said over every speaker. "Now we show that only fifty percent are the greatest and the other fifty percent are merely expert fishers."

"Now for the most crucial questions, each of you must answer honestly and sincerely. And most important, please do not exaggerate."

"No problem," I replied. "I never exaggerate."

Everyone in the room holding a fishing rig grinned and nodded agreement.

"Excellent, now for the first question." The artificial voice paused. "Each of you must answer by speaking into the microphone on your collar."

I sat my rig down and stared at the speaker sitting on the desk before me. And through every speaker, the same words were uttered.

"Why do you like to fish?"

I must confess, the question caught me totally by surprise. I thought they were going to ask something deep. Instead, this simple query to a bunch experienced anglers?

I leaned forward and replied very sincerely, "I love the battle, feeling the fish bend my rod almost in half, jumping clear out of the water as he fights me every inch of my sonic line. That's why I like to fish."

I nearly jumped out of my chair the next instant.

Sirens wailed and lights flashed red. And now the lights in the room dimmed. It sounded like a full scale invasion had started. I looked around and noticed all the others had also stood up and were looking around with puzzled expressions.

"Yes, great fishers of your worlds, that's why we like it too! Fish versus fisher! One on one, strength against strength. And here on Paramelee – *the fish fight back!"*

Captain Byl raised his arms and rammed the butt of his rigs on the floor and exclaimed, "Too much talking, let's start fishing!"

The sirens wailed louder.

"Please note, it's always catch-and-release here on Paramelee. You don't eat the fish, and the fish don't eat you. But there is an extra prize in our Tournament today. For the fisher who lands the biggest fish and gets his or her picture taken with it, and then releases it back to the ocean, you'll win 100,000 Galactic Credits!"

My mind focused on only one part – *the fish don't eat you...*

I glanced around and many of my fishing brethren had the same expression of deep concern that I had. That line of wounded fishers leaving the planet began to gnaw at me.

"Do you agree to this Tournament rule fishers?" The loud robot voice roared.

"Catch-and-release it is." I agreed. The others added their agreement.

"The next most important rule of fishing on Paramelee – no metallic hooks allowed!" The artificial voice stated in a serious tone.

"That means you can only use a Force Hoop on your lures," the voice added.

"Doh, you mean no real hooks?" Kweel complained loudly.

"Nothing so primitive and especially nothing that can injure the fish. The authorities' primary function here on Paramelee is to protect the fish first, then provide a fishing experience for all to enjoy. And third, protect the fishers themselves."

"Hmmm, not sure I like your priorities." Byl shook his head.

"Never mind, get on with it,' Kweel said.

"What is a Force Hoop?" A small alien fisher asked.

"Personally, I like Force Hoops. I smiled at the artificial voice. "They're clean and efficient and can be used on any size fish."

"Go on," the little alien said.

I reached inside my shirt pocket and pulled one out. I held the small spherical device up for all to see. The lights glinted off its multi-faceted sides as I rolled it between my fingers and my thumb.

"The electronics inside it create a tiny tractor beam when activated. After your rig's computer determines the color, size, and movement of the bait fish, a tiny holographic projector envelopes the device and it *becomes* the bait – the lure."

"What happens when the fish take it?" Captain Byl asked.

No fish can break that bond of the tiny tractor beam of a Force Hoop. And if you've programed your rod and sonic line correctly for the specific fish you're after, you've got him!"

"How is that safer than a hook?" The small alien asked.

"The tractor beam will not cover the fish's gills. It can still breathe. And the mouth is not affected either, the Fish Hoop holds the fish's entire head in place. There's no way the fish can escape."

Byl snorted. "I like to set mine to a timer setting. It's more sporting that way."

"True," I agreed. "Most tournaments require it. If you cannot land the fish within the pre-set time limit, the Fish Hoop releases the fish."

"All fishers on Paramelee will use a setting of fifteen minutes," the artificial voice chimed on cue. "If you haven't had your picture taken with fish fifteen minutes after first contact, you and the fish are released."

"I and the fish are released…" I murmured with confusion.

"I wish they'd let us use a 'Fish Caller.'" Captain Byl said with a deadly serious tone.

"What?" I shouted incredulously. "A Fish Caller? There's no such thing! Everybody knows that!"

Captain Byl rose with an angry expression. He growled and flexed the biceps on each of his six arms so tight it seemed it would rip apart his shirt sleeves. He towered over me and glared even harder.

"Are you insulting me, puny human?"

"Well, I don't think so."

"But you don't believe there is a Fish Caller, when I state I have seen it with my own eyes."

"And where did you see this contraption?"

"It was advertised on the Holo-TV, of course. *And certified by one of the most distinguished starship racers in the entire galaxy.*"

"How much does it cost?" I asked.

"Nineteen Credits and ninety-nine cents. And you get free delivery if you order one before the commercial is over." Captain Byl nodded confidently.

He then growled menacingly as I fought to keep from laughing out loud. But this was just too good to let it go that easily.

"I guess this Fish Caller is really a tiny Hula Girl who wiggles her grass skirt enticingly and then winks at the first fish that comes near?"

Kweel slapped his tail against the desk and roared with laughter. In fact, everyone in the entire room began laughing hysterically. Even the artificial voice began to laugh in its weird kind of electronic way.

They all laughed even harder when Byl picked me up and put a massive hand around my throat.

380

Byl pulled my face right up in front of his face until our very noses touched. Man did his breath stink!

"I am going to beat you so badly that even a medical scanner won't be able to tell what you are when I'm finished! And then..."

"Okay, okay. I believe there is such a thing as a Fish Caller. Would you mind putting me down now, before I pass out."

Byl turned his square head to one side, which was kind of cool, and looked at me a moment from that angle to see if I was serious. He nodded and sat me back down.

"How about you show it to me," I suggested. "Maybe it does work."

"Hmmm, well..." Byl hem-hawed.

"What!" I shouted. "You don't have one? I thought you bought it off the Holo-TV."

"No, I only said I saw one advertised."

"But, you said it works."

"That is what Big Daddy Statsmos said on the commercial."

"And you believed that!"

"Hey, I like Big Daddy Statsmos. He's a great racer. He has the fastest starship in this quadrant, puny human!"

Somehow, the red alien's logic defied reason. Or his reasoning was defying logic. Or he was just plain incredulous. Or maybe all three.

"Does Big Daddy fish?" I asked.

"No, but he said it works!"

"Why didn't you buy one and try it?"

"I wanted to talk to someone who used one first."

I rolled my eyes and snorted. "So, it could be a tiny Hula Girl for all you know. Did they show you one on the commercial?"

"Well, no. But they showed Big Daddy with some great big fish he'd caught with it."

I put both my hands on my waist and began swiveling my hips. I then slowly turned around in my best imitation of a life-sized Fish Caller.

The room erupted in laughter again.

"Enough! We need to finish." The artificial voice growled.

We were asked more questions about our fishing prowess and then we reviewed the habits and lures used on the best game fish on Paramelee. And then using some mysterious algorithms, the artificial life form matched each of us up to the right fish. Basically, we were put into the same boat and advised to go after the fish that matched our skill set.

It all seemed a bit odd. But then again, the entire thing seemed a bit odd.

In the final analysis, Captain Byl, Kweel, myself and an alien named Doriwan were assigned the same boat. And the fish we were out to catch were the Sailfin Corvettes, Tigerbiter Fighters and Purple Zephyrs – those were their common names translated into our respective languages.

They sounded fun to me.

Of course, we were warned for the umpteenth time – never be lured into trying to catch a Thumper, a Sawfin Lionfish or a Thousand-toothed Jawfish. And unless we were just plain stupid, never ever go after the dreaded Ironhead – even if they came to us and begged to be caught.

At last, it was time to fish.

We raced out toward the horizon where the sky met the sea. Within an hour we were out of sight of land and our robot guide slowed the boat to a complete stop. The robot quickly deployed a 'hover platform' and Captain Byl stepped out on it carrying his eighteen fishing rigs and three boxes of artificial lures along with a lunch box and two large jugs of water.

I wasn't sure how he was able to carry all that equipment with just six hands.

The robot drove the boat about two miles away and in quick succession Kweel and then later Doriwan were left alone each on their own 'hover platform.'

After the robot deployed the platform from which I would be fishing, I gathered my own gear and prepared to step over the side. I carried my two rigs, one box of lures and my lunch box and a bottle of water, balancing them carefully while I stepped onto my platform.

I had never fished from a hover platform before, but it seemed stable. A small anti-gravity engine kept it level about three feet above the waves. It was twelve feet by twelve feet, so I had plenty of room to fish.

I sat everything down and quickly added a Force Hoop to my lure and programmed it as the preferred bait to attract the Sailfin Corvettes. I also added a micro-camera about a foot above on the sonic line. I held the rod steady and turned on my E-5000 reel.

I programmed my rod's tensile strength to match a big Sailfin Corvette and automatically the sonic line's strength was also set.

A glowing holo-screen appeared in the air while my reel loaded all its software. In less than a minute, the world below became visible. Several large schools of fish swam about a hundred yards east of my position. I noticed several larger fish following one of the closer schools and soon my E-5000 identified the lurking predators as juvenile Thumpers. The fish inside the schools were simply bait fish, so I used my forefinger and searched under the sea toward the south.

There were fewer fish in this direction, so I punched on the holo-screen to determine what the bottom looked like. To my surprise, a strange fuzzy blackness grew visible about two hundred feet down. I'd never seen anything like that before.

I slowly turned around while my E-5000 searched for the bottom in every direction. But everywhere the blackness prevented my rig from sensing anything below that same depth.

Strange!

But by my slowly scanning in a circle, a red dot began blinking on the holo-screen. I spoke some quick commands and the glowing screen focused in on the target. Yes, it was a nice Sailfin Corvette, just what I had programmed it to find. It was over ten feet in length and about eight hundred pounds of pure fighting fish.

"Target acquisition!" I commanded to the E-5000 and in less than two seconds it had calculated the range.

I pointed the end of the rod and aligned it to a target floating in the distance that my E-5000 had generated. I pressed the trigger and 'whoosh', my lure sailed through the air in a smooth arc right through the target and splashed into the water about two hundred yards from the platform. I punched another command and the small motor on the lure fired up and it quickly raced in the direction of the big fish.

I felt my heart pounding with excitement.

In the next moment, I punched a command to enable the underwater camera. A stunning view of the murky depths came into focus on my holo-screen.

Myriads of tiny plankton parted in waves before the camera until the ocean view cleared. The water was crystal clear now while the lure and Force Hoop dove deeper on a collision course with the unsuspecting game fish.

I glanced to the upper left and noticed the dot that represented my position and then the red blinking icon that represented the Sailfin. In between, a yellow blinking dot was rapidly closing the gap with the Sailfin – that was my lure!

I found it difficult to breathe while I watched the lure getting closer and closer. I sent another command and the lure slowed and then it began to swim in a dancing motion, imitating a hurt prey fish that the Sailfin especially enjoyed eating – per the data fed to my E-5000 by the authorities of Paramelee.

I actually jumped up six or seven inches off the platform when I noticed the red icon lunge forward at my lure icon.

It was all too easy. How in the world did anyone catch fish before there was an E-5000?

Suddenly, a huge mouth appeared in the middle of picture from my camera.

In the next instant, my sonic line zipped out of my reel so fast the red warning light flashed ominously.

'That wasn't right?' I thought. 'Even the biggest Sailfin shouldn't push my E-5000 to the red zone on the first lunge.'

I hit the brake and felt the sudden weight of the big fish. My shoulder's strained against the terrific pull of the fish. I glanced up at the holo-screen and saw the green light that meant the Force-Hoop had successfully enveloped the prey.

I laughed out loud and hit a button to reel in fifty feet of line.

And then the fish really took off!

My rod began to bend double and the motor on my E-5000 groaned while the Sailfin Corvette fought back. After the reel finished bringing in the line, I hit another button and let the fish run it back out. I'd tire it down before I reeled it in all the way.

The line began to sing while the fish raced away. Once again, the warning light on my reel flashed red. This fish was stronger than what I had programmed my E-5000. For the first time, I felt the fish might overpower my settings and get away.

I hit the command to slow the fish gradually.

For about one second, everything was fine.

I entered the command to reel in one hundred feet of line when the Sailfin leaped out of the water in the distance.

"What the?!" I shouted.

It wasn't a Sailfin Corvette! The fish that cleared the water displayed the hyper muscular body of the dreaded Thumper!

It was at least 6 feet long.

The fish began to pull harder. In fact, the entire hover-platform began to move. I looked around with growing concern, but we continued to pick up speed as the fish fought against the reel. In another moment, the motor on my E-5000 began to scream in complaint.

Suddenly, the fish hit another gear.

I glanced up and saw that the platform was moving almost twenty clicks per hour.

I quickly typed some commands on the holo-screen and then my reel went into overdrive. Now the E-5000 really screamed as the fish fought. But the line was slowly being reeled back. And even better, it seemed the fish was tiring. I noticed that the platform was only moving ten clicks per hour now.

And then the fish turned.

I saw the red icon closing with my platform's icon at an incredible speed!

My fingers danced on the controls and the line zipped back inside the reel like lightning. I kept glancing at the screen and then back out to sea while the red icon closed. I knew the fish was coming to me now. And it was coming to the surface while it closed.

My heart was racing like a jackhammer.

I checked the screen and realized I only had about three hundred feet of line still out. That crazy fish was closing faster than my reel could wind it up!

And then the craziest thing happened – I saw the fish.

My heart pounded after I caught sight of its huge back cutting through the water heading straight for me. It seemed like it was a missile bearing down on its target.

I hit the command to break the sonic line.

But the fish continued to close at an unbelievable speed.

At the last second, that fish leapt out of the water and soared through the air. And just as it was eyelevel with me, that fish winked at me.

I gasped.

The huge fish landed on the hover platform and began thrashing violently.

In an instant, I realized if I could grab the fish and get my picture taken, I might win the Tournament prize.

I jumped on the fish to try and hold it still.

In the next instant, I was flying through the air.

I turned and saw that the fish was thrashing so hard it generated momentum toward me.

I grabbed at the huge head.

The fish twisted in my grasp and whirled and the huge tail came around and smashed into my body so hard it sent me flying toward the water. I landed just on the edge of the platform.

I heard thrashing and glanced around in time to see the fish twisting his muscular body to strike me with its tail for the final blow.

I rolled toward it and put my arms around it in a vain attempt to hold it still.

It was like a wild bucking horse now. Its body banged me down hard and then I was flying through the air in the other direction.

I sat up in a daze.

As if in a dream, the huge fish thrashed and jumped toward me to strike again.

The mighty tail smacked me again and I saw stars, and then I swear that fish balanced itself on its head and smacked me several times in a row and with a final effort struck me so hard I almost blacked out.

As I lay there, I felt the fish pushing me toward the water.

But I had no fight left in me.

Suddenly a siren rang out.

"Fifteen minutes is over – no winner this time."

Laying on my side, the fish winked at me again and thrashed its way back into the water.

"Yeah, something was really fishy about this Tournament." I thought.

I lay there for a long time. I couldn't believe how badly my arms and legs were aching. I felt like I had been beaten up. And I had!

I reached for my poor E-5000, I could smell the tiny bearings inside it smoldering from the feat it had just performed. Finally, I sat up.

I just sat there a long time, simply shaking my head.

We were all equipped with communication devices. I had the earpiece in my ear and a tiny microphone extended down my cheek. I hadn't heard from any of the others since we dropped them off. I had decided to call Kweel when a sound came through the earphones that chilled my very soul.

The hairs on my arms stood up and shivers went up and down my spine like lightning bolts. At first, I couldn't figure out what it was, I only knew that it was something frightening, something horrendous, something so unspeakably terrifying that it made me want to cry out too.

It was a single, ear-splitting shriek of pure unadulterated terror.

Finally, I realized what it was.

Captain Byl was screaming like a girl.

The platforms did have a small anti-grave motor so we could move to different fishing spots. After I realized that Captain Byl was screaming at something threatening his very life, I did what any decent, honest-hearted person would do – I drove the platform in the opposite direction.

But Byl's screams increased. And now I could hear a barrage of splashing noises mixing in with his pitiful cries.

I decided to turn around and see if I could help the poor alien.

For some reason, my E-5000 couldn't pinpoint Byl's fishing platform. But the sensors did indicate the sound was growing louder so I knew we were getting closer. My stomach began doing backflips when I saw something new appear on the holo-screen.

The water was getting shallow. It was only fifty feet deep here. Dozens and dozens of fish icons now appeared.

Red warning lights flashed over every one of them. A bunch of the dreaded Ironheads were swimming right in the direction of Byl's screams.

I commanded the anti-grav engines to stop. I got out my e-binoculars and scanned the sea ahead. I knew it would be too dangerous to get any closer with Ironheads. I wondered how in the world Byl had gotten in the middle of them.

Out of nowhere, a small island appeared.

My mouth dropped open.

A few dozen swimsuit-clad babes were running nimbly along the beach. I noticed a banner and realized these young bathing beauties were part of the famous sports photo-shoot for the upcoming calendar. I had found their secret location here – one planet out of the entire universe! What a coincidence!

And then my heart skipped a beat.

On the beach, I saw a dozen smoking grills brimming with food and so many coolers of beer that they couldn't be counted. I had found paradise!

Captain Byl screamed again in my earphone. My E-5000 finally pinpointed the big alien farther to the left of the wonderful, beautiful island filled with girls and beers.

Byl's screams were growing fainter by the second.

I did what any red-blooded man from Earth would do – I headed for the island.

The anti-grav motor screamed at full speed. But somehow, the island never seemed to come any closer. I opened a panel and started punching at buttons, trying to urge more speed out of the craft. And yet, the island always stayed just out of reach... like a bad dream.

Suddenly, the warning sirens from my E-5000 got my attention. I looked up at the holo-screen.

I was surrounded by Ironheads.

Slowly, I turned the platform away from that tempting paradise island. I held my breath. Something in the water caught my eye.

The Ironhead is built like a bulked up super-barricuda shot up on steroids. The exception was that instead of a pointed snout full of vicious teeth, the Ironhead's snout was thick and round like a cannonball.

For the second time in my life, and I hope the last, a fish winked at me.

All at once, Ironheads of every size were swimming lazily around the platform, like they didn't even care. I could see their muscles rippling under their scales and I knew at once this was a game fish that I didn't want to mess with.

But no! They were a fish! And I was a fisher.

Forget about the warning!

I stopped the platform and quickly fixed my line and rigged it with a new Force Hoop and a lure I knew these fish couldn't resist. I studied the Holo-screen a moment until I found a fish that wasn't the biggest, but it wasn't the smallest either. I targeted it and hit the trigger, my line sailed out in an arc and soon the special lure was speeding right for the fish.

The Force Hoop set.

All at once, Ironheads were leaping out of the water from every direction. They came right at me. I leapt to the right and rolled across the platform – all the while never dropping my fishing rig and keeping the line taut.

I avoided the first wave unscathed.

But seconds later, more erupted out of the water.

After that, I don't really remember much.

I do seem to recall my screaming – like in some surreal dream (nightmare) – and trying in vain to dodge all those fish flying at me like living missiles of death. In my dreamlike memory, I again feel the overwhelming realization that they are trying to knock me into the water with them. But I can't let that happen! What would happen then? Would they eat me alive?

All I remember is running and dodging and ducking and dancing – but there was no place to run and no place to hide. I am helpless in the midst of that rain of Ironheads flying out of the water at me.

I do remember quite vividly when my E-5000 squealed its last and my rod broke in two. And I remember waving my arms trying to push those nightmare creatures away while their iron snouts pummeled me again and again.

Then one particularly large Ironhead hit me dead center in my chest.

In my nightmare, *I am falling... falling... slowly falling into the water seething with deadly Ironheads.*

Thankfully, I don't remember anything after that, almost like my mind blocked out what happened next because it was so horrible.

Three days later, I woke up in a hospital bed.

I wound up with my right arm broken in two places, my left ankle sprained, five broken ribs, and a concussion. And my butt was bruised so badly that I had to wear a specially padded diaper for an entire month.

My only comfort was that I didn't seem to be hurt as badly as Captain Byl and Kweel.

Kweel's tail had been broken in four places, which I understand is very painful for them. I also learned they used their tail to fend off attacks, and I can only imagine the poor alien lashing his tail in defense against that wall of incoming fish. He had also broken both his arms and lost half his teeth, though I was told he would grow them back eventually.

Byl was even worse – all three left arms broken, two of his four legs had torn ligaments, and the bruises up and down his broad back had changed his red skin to deep purple. The poor alien couldn't talk either; all he did was lay there mumbling the same words over and over – another Ironhead... another... another....

And about once an hour, he'd suddenly sit straight up in bed and scream like a girl.

The doctors mentioned he was suffering from some kind of Paramelee fishing post-traumatic syndrome – I never could make out the medical term. I only hoped Byl would snap out of it before he got home and his wife found out what happened.

I knew I was never going to tell my wife what really happened.

After a few days, we were all released.

Captain Byl, Kweel and myself were led to the debriefing room before we could be granted our exit status. The room was a smaller version of the bigger room where our entrance interview took place – there were only five stations in total. We each sat down at a terminal and waited for the artificial voice.

"We trust you enjoyed your fishing here on Paramelee?" the voice state with electronic precision.

Captain Byl's head twitched violently, and he moved his body as if to duck an invisible Ironhead. He did that quite often now.

Kweel brought his heavily bandaged tail around and he held hit like a newborn baby in his arms. He grimaced at his own nightmarish memory the voice had triggered.

I simply groaned.

"The authorities here on Paramelee wanted to congratulate you on a fantastic fishing experience and offer you a "free pass" to return and fish again. This is a great honor; we only offer this opportunity to fewer than five percent of all fishers who come here."

My entire body convulsed in horror at the mere mention of another fishing trip on Paramelee.

"No!" Kweel squealed. He coughed and when he spoke his voice had returned to his normal male tone. "No, we just want our exit approved so we can leave."

Captain Byl and I nodded our approval.

"But, there is one thing I'd like to know." I paused thoughtfully. "How was it that I saw all of those earth women in bikinis participating in a photo shoot for next year's special calendar edition. I mean, now that I think about it, it seems too much of a coincidence. And they had case after case of my favorite beer too."

"It was a lure." The artificial voice replied.

"A lure?" We all said together.

"Yes, here on Paramelee, the fish are all sentient. You noticed that your scanning devices were blocked at a depth of just over two hundred feet. Below that depth is where the fish cities exist."

The three of us looked at each other dumbfounded.

"Captain Byl was shown a holographic image on the island that corresponded to his greatest desire, as was Kweel. The Ironhead programmers displayed something from your world in order to lure you into their favorite fishing waters. And once you were there, then the real fun began."

"What?" we all three shouted.

"The Sailfin Corvettes, Thumpers and Ironheads had a great time fishing for you, we do hope you'll change your mind and come back."

Even as the artificial voice spoke those words, I could imagine those fish smiling and laughing somewhere.

"Nope, I'm out of here."

"We have one last item to present you, per the contract you signed. For a preview of your fishing pictures, please turn to the large screens on the wall."

We all turned.

My eyes focused on the middle screen, where my visage was displayed.

I cringed.

There on the huge screen I saw a picture of myself. I was underwater and upside down, holding my breath and pushing my arms out frantically. There were bruises on my arms and my expression was one of sheer panic. But that wasn't the worst part.

All around me, Ironheads posed with big smiles on their fish faces while they pointed at me with their fins in triumph.

"Does this mean what I think it means?" I asked with rising embarrassment.

"Yes, your photographs are now proudly displayed as trophies by the fighting fish of Paramelee."

This story is for Captain Joe Leier and David Brown
And everyone who had the pleasure to fish with them.

Xenocracy

Sometimes I look up at the stars and wonder,
Is there intelligent life out there?
Or are they just like us...
-- Anonymous

A huge snowflake glowed electric blue in the center of the screen.

But it wasn't a snowflake, and it wasn't complete.

The live feed from the drone flying high above began to zoom closer onto the alien's amazing creation. This alien snowflake stretched its hundreds of angular tendrils out over a mile from the glowing central section. Across North America, 23 just like it had also appeared in the last 24 hours, each in various stages of completion.

In all the other continents, except for Antarctica, other snowflake complexes materialized and grew and pulsated with life shortly after each alien starship landed. In China alone, 44 snowflakes grew more tendrils with each hour that passed.

The tendrils of the 'snowflake' grew out of the center where the alien starship rested on the ground. As people streamed toward a starship, they entered the bluish tunnels and were guided to a section where cables and wires moved magically around each person and quickly attached themselves. Small holo-screens appeared on the bluish walls and glowed bright with unreadable ciphers and letters.

If all the sections were currently full and a new group arrived, new extensions of the tunnel materialized out of thin air.

The people called it magic.

Our best guess was nanotechnology on a scale never dreamed by humanity.

Hundreds of people continued to arrive every few minutes. Hover platforms arrived to meet them and carry those too sick to enter on their own.

Tens of thousands who had traveled far and wide were currently inside the massive complex of tendrils. And every hour tens of thousands left happy and smiling.

Word spread quickly.

By the third day the alien snowflakes numbered 144, each located at various remote sites around the globe. The young and the old, the rich and the poor, the sick and dying, they all came for a single purpose – to be healed.

Despite the unbelievably large crowds that drew closer with each moment, they moved forward in a calm and organized manner. Many whispered excitedly with those nearest them as they walked toward the nearest tendril of the massive snowflake. One thing was the same about everyone, their eyes beamed with burning expectation despite their gaunt, sick condition. And even those being carried upon stretchers smiled.

The aliens had brought more than their starships with them. They had brought hope for the critically sick, the crippled and even the dying.

In contrast to the wide-open countryside, this moving mass of humanity also seemed odd for what was missing - the Raxth would not allow automobiles anywhere near where they landed. The aliens had quickly informed the inhabitants of earth that *cars were poison,* one of their rare messages in those first few days after their starships began to orbit Earth.

The other message was even more simple - *if you were sick, if you were dying – come to us.*

Hundreds of thousands abandoned their cars, trucks and buses and walked the last few miles toward each of the large alien complexes.

The aliens cured those whose bodies were wracked by Leukemia, Parkinson's Disease, MS and every disease known to man – they even cured those suffering stage four of any type of cancer. The odd-looking aliens first performed a scan of the person after the hover cables and wires connected to the person. Next, their computers analyzed the person and the disease from which they suffered. Within a few minutes, an alien doctor would enter the room. After briefly reviewing the glowing lines on their display screens, they cured the sick with a simple wave of their twinkling instruments over the patient's body.

And everyone walked away completely cured.

It was surreal, bizarre, and miraculous all at the same time.

Countless times, those that had just been healed hugged and even cried while they laid their heads on the shoulders of the strange, alien bodies of the Raxth. The aliens remained strangely aloof, briefly returning the appreciative embraces, and then silently urging the cured to leave with a wave of their thin, fragile arms to cure the new people arriving every minute.

Happy beyond belief, they walked away to begin their trip back home.

The people of earth were quickly mesmerized by the technological magic and miracles of the Raxth. On social media, on the news feeds, everywhere across the Internet, they couldn't read enough about the aliens. Sickness, disease, and pollution proved no match for the alien technology.

In the middle of the Pacific Ocean, the island of floating trash and plastic three times the size of the state of Texas was 'removed' in less than a day. And yet, plastic and trash existed in smaller islands across every ocean.

The massive clouds of smog choking the cities of Los Angeles, Lahore, Delhi, Beijing, Mexico City and a dozen others were cleared in mere hours after the Raxth ships moved over them and applied their technology. Sadly, the sickening pall of pollution returned a few days later after the ships returned to orbit.

Yet we understood - the aliens were demonstrating that they could help us conquer pollution everywhere.

The Raxth were givers, that fact quickly became obvious. And more, everyone around the world soon realized that mankind was on the verge of something truly incredible, something unimaginably wonderful – an event that would prove to be the most significant in all human history – first contact.

For the Raxth, despite uttering very few words in the first days after they arrived, revealed by their actions an infinite wisdom and a gracious benevolence unheard of in the entire history of humankind. Despite the lack of verbal communication, the Raxth demonstrated the one thing humans could understand - *love*.

And on the 40th day, the aliens called a press conference.

***

The Prime Minister of France looked tired, mused President Williamson of the United States. But no world leader had really had much rest these last few weeks since the alien's arrival, even though there had been no overt threats to humankind. Still, it was unnerving the things these super-beings could do.

"They're coming." The Presidential aide pointed at the door.

"Well, I guess we'll learn what their agenda is at last," President Williamson said to President Mugana of Kenya.

"Let us hope so." Mugana sighed.

President Williamson nodded, rubbing his hands together with his mounting nervous energy.

"We asked them some questions last week after they opened up - sort of a test." Williamson reflected out loud. "A group of our eggheads from MIT, Stanford and other universities compiled a list for them. You know, the great questions of our age... if there really is a Universal Theory to unify Quantum Mechanics and Einstein's Theory of Relativity. We asked them about the existence of tachyons and dark matter and the feasibility of faster-than-light travel... oh, I don't remember the rest. They gave us the answers... in the same hour we asked each question."

Mugana gazed at him with keen interest.

Williamson smiled. "And there they were - our most brilliant scientists and researchers, poring over this mountain of data and mathematical formulae thousands of screens long." President Williamson began to chuckle, shaking his head thoughtfully. "And our best minds were stumped after the first few screens, it was all so far above their heads. They were still sitting there mumbling to each other and scratching their butts when I left."

"But the important thing is that the Raxth freely provided us the answers to our scientific questions," Prime Minister Hancock of Australia added, standing beside the two world leaders.

"How do we know that?" Williamson's eyes narrowed. "Our greatest minds can't even fathom a fraction of it so far. If they're that much more advanced than us, they could be putting one over on us."

"That," Mugana began, "is frightening."

The doors opened, and three of the Raxth entered. All eyes fixed on them as the room became ghostly silent.

The Raxth were extraordinarily slim with three sided bodies. Three slender arms moved with their careful gait down the hallway filled with world leaders. Their heads appeared misshapen compared to the rest of their fragile-looking bodies - their huge, oblong heads seemed unsteady sitting upon their tiny necks. Forty-seven small, black eyes were scattered across each alien head and made it seem like the aliens could see everything in all directions.

Two of the aliens stopped while the other stepped forward and began to speak.

"I am Trith of the Raxth. My people bring you the greetings from the rest of the known galaxy. We are happy to help mankind in its terrible plight, and to help you to become one with the rest of us."

A wave of murmuring swept the room. Trith held up one of his hands.

"We will guide you, as is our way when a... shall we say a young, unlearned sentient race is encountered. As a parent cares for and helps its offspring reach adulthood, so we shall do for you. And the rewards that await you - to travel the galaxy with us, to explore, to live a normal lifespan! But humankind has much to learn first. Do you wish this grand opportunity to advance yourselves eons in a single generation? We offer you Xenocracy. And to live Concordia and allow it precepts and principles to guide your life as it does for all in the universe."

"He's telling us we're backwards and stupid," Prime Minister Dubovich of Russia whispered amid the enthusiastic applause that erupted.

"Intergalactic country bumpkins," Hancock chimed.

"And it's true," Mugana added while he clapped enthusiastically. "Compared to them."

More murmuring swept the room as all but one of the aliens left. Williamson made his way to it.

"May I ask," President Williamson said in a strong voice so all in the room could hear. "What do we need to learn, in order to come up to your level."

Trith looked silently around the room a moment at the expectant faces of humanity. When he finally spoke, he spoke with a gentle sadness.

"First... you must learn to stop killing yourselves with your technology. And second, you must stop destroying this beautiful planet."

***

"You still practice war!?" Trith said in utter disbelief. "And you are a Level VII Pre-Concordia society?"

President Williamson felt a hot flush of embarrassment. "I thought you knew that from the comment you made last week at your official welcoming! You know, your press conference.'"

Trith shook his head. "No, I meant the way you were poisoning yourselves, the waste you are wallowing in from your technology, especially from your automobiles. Our initial studies indicated that you must have advanced so quickly that prudent analysis of some of the long-term negative impacts had been overlooked. That can be understood in the excitement of advancement for a such a young race. But you must learn from those terrible mistakes and not repeat them." Trith's forty-seven eyes widened. "But war! That is unimaginable for a sentient species at this level."

405

"Well, yes, we still wage war." President Williamson began. "Sometimes...um... it's the only way to settle a conflict between nations. That is why we keep a standing army, a navy, and missiles."

Trith's forty-seven eyes blinked in unison. "Our initial studies of your scientific and cultural achievements indicated that your civilization should be long past war. That is for primitives!" Trith scratched the hairless skin of his oblong head. "You must have developed some horrific weapons with your present state of technological advancement."

President Williamson felt like a child being scolded. "In our society, war is… common." He looked down. "And yes, some of our weapons are horrific."

"Then one of the first edicts of Xenocracy for Earth will be to outlaw war - all human divisions must denounce it." Trith paused in thought. "It will not be acceptable conduct war any longer."

Williamson chuckled at the outrageous thought.

Trith eyed him with concern. "What is humorous?"

The President shrugged. "I guess the thought of no more war. It's been a part of our history, all through it – every nation, every empire." He looked questioningly at the alien. "Are there not conflicts, or wars, between the different races of the..." He paused, searching for the word.

"Concordia - the Galactic Society of the accepted sentient races." A troubled look covered Trith's features while he paused in deep thought. With a nod, he continued. "There is no war, none for times

406

untold, my human friend. We have differences, but these are dealt with in a civilized way. You will learn of it in the Teachings – the principles of Concordia."

"Sounds too good to be true."

"Why say this, human?" Trith asked in puzzlement.

"Well, it sounds great, but... I mean, humans have always wanted to end war, but we've never been able to do it. No war, it's just a little inconceivable."

"Humans seem to feel a need to hate something, for something to be their enemy. It seems to be as much a part of your mental and philosophical makeup as love and justice. And yet, there is no Evil Empire in the known galaxy, there is no all-powerful evil that needs to be conquered." Trith's black eyes sparkled with intelligence. "There is nothing for you to fight."

President Williamson whistled with a puzzled expression on his face. "But there is evil. We must fight it every day here…"

"Why?" Trith shook his sadly. "Why do you fight wars? Why do you kill?"

"Well, other nations try to take what is ours…"

Trith's arms waved in the air. "What do you mean by those terms – *take what is ours*?"

President Williamson shrugged. "I mean, another nation may try to occupy land we own."

"What?" Trith gasped. "You own land?"

"Why, yes. Each nation owns a section of land. Even individuals own a small section of land and the houses they live inside. They own goods inside their houses - possessions."

"Ownership!" Trith shouted. "I begin to understand now this system you call economics and this strange concept of money. We still don't fully understand how humans assign value to this term – your money is ludicrous to us."

"Don't the sentient races of the universe operate in some kind of economy? I mean, how do you buy and sell?"

"No one can own the land," Trith said simply. "Just as no one can own the water or the air. We do not buy and we do not sell across all the worlds of the universe. We do not have possessions."

"What?" President Williamson shouted. He stared a moment in disbelief at Trith. "What do you do when you want something? Or when you need something, like food or shelter?"

Trith paused a moment. He turned and began operating the controls on one of the devices that communicated with his orbiting starship. The alien peered intently at the screen.

"I am searching for a term you can understand since you have not yet studied the precepts of Concordia," Trith paused a long moment in silence. Suddenly, he smiled. "Ah, yes. I think you will understand this."

President Williamson waited expectantly.

"We share."

"*You share?*"

"Do you not understand that term? I thought it was simple yet broad enough to explain how the different races of Concordia exchange goods. It is the equivalent of your concept of economy that we operate for Concordia."

"You share?" He said a second time with more emphasis. "I mean, I understand how children share toys. But we're talking about entire populations of worlds. Here men and women, corporations... even farmers and the food industry– they produce goods to buy and sell. Our goal is to make a profit. How do you manufacture goods for others – like food to eat, clothes to wear, items for entertainment and equipment for transportation needs."

"We share."

"But how do your manufacturers obtain the raw materials to produce an item?"

"We call them Producers in Concordia. If raw materials are needed, the producing organization will ask Harvesters to share raw materials with them. If an individual needs food, a Grower will share some of his harvest. If an individual needs clothing, a Producer will share some of his clothes. We share."

"Doesn't someone get ripped off that way?"

Trith paused, a puzzled expression on his oblong face. "Oh, you mean the concept of not obtaining a fair exchange?"

"Yes, like in trading. It sounds like Concordia is based on principles of trading for something of equal value."

"You are wrong, we do not trade. We share. It works out fine for everyone. After all, one person shares with others, but many more share with him. It is the same with major Producers – they share their output to any who ask. And many Harvesters of raw material will share what is asked of them. We simply share – there is no thought of assigning value in any of our dealings. And there is certainly no money or profit. You see, your inherent fallacy of placing a fictitious value on items or goods has warped your thinking so much that you find it hard to fathom *reality*."

President Williamson sat down in his chair with a glazed expression.

"You share," he whispered.

"The basic principle of Sharing is stated as – *"What you want or need for yourself, give the same to others..."*

The President's eyes narrowed with emotion. "We had an ancient prophet say something very similar..."

"Proceed."

"Whatever you want others to do to you, you must likewise do to them." President Williamson shook his head

"A very wise statement." Trith's many eyes peered at him. "And do you follow this precept?"

President Williamson sighed. "Some try..."

"You are a great leader on this world. We realize that for many centuries you have lived with this concept of money, commerce, and profit. You accept it as reality because it is the only reality you have known." Trith paused, carefully observing the president's expression.

"But it is in fact not." Trith crossed his three arms. "You must open your mind to the precepts and principles we will teach you – beginning with sharing. This is most imperative since you are a leader. You must be willing to accept the true reality practiced by the rest of the universe."

President Williamson rubbed his chin with a confused expression.

Trith looked upon the human and smiled sadly. "Perhaps you should meditate a while on what I have shared with you today. Hopefully, the full import of it will become evident to you. After all, it is a relatively simple concept to grasp. You said even your children know how to share."

President Williamson stared at Trith with total disbelief.

"Do you have any more questions for me?" Trith smiled.

"Let's get back to war; maybe I can grasp that concept better. After all, we humans have always wanted to eliminate war. We've all strived for world peace for centuries. We've tried many times." He stood up and crossed his arms.

"It is most surprising that with this great desire to end war and with your level of intelligence that you have yet to eliminate it!" Trith paused.

The tall alien stood completely still, deep in contemplative thought. The strained silence grew with each painful second.

"Don't you have rogue individuals who want more than what is shared with them so that they feel the need to take it? President Williamson blurted out. "Or the need to kill in order to take it?"

"Absolutely not!" Trith gasped in shock. "If anyone needs something badly, others will share with him until he has so much, he will notify them

411

to stop sharing. No one in Concordia, no one in the entire universe, goes to sleep in want of anything!"

It was Williamson's turn to gasp.

"Why do you fight wars?" Trith asked after another long silence.

"We fight our enemies. There are those who hate us."

"Not outside of your world. The concept of Good versus Evil and the need to fight, to make war, to hate... is something *peculiar* to humans." Trith shook his head. "Millions of different alien cultures live together in peace throughout the universe – each different, and yet each is the same – *the same inside*. We coexist in total harmony." Trith smiled openly. "Hatred and prejudice are learned concepts. War is also a learned concept."

Trith leaned forward. "They can be *unlearned*, by taking in knowledge and practicing the principles of Concordia."

"It's impossible for me to comprehend such a thing – a universe without war? Or ownership? Or business?" Williamson shook his head in disbelief.

"Let us hope that humans can comprehend. Because if not..." Trith added cryptically.

***

Trith met with Angth and Paeth of the Triad later that evening to review the latest research - more surprises awaited.

"Humans are actually starving to death and dying from diseases they already have the technology to cure," Angth said with a profound sadness.

"How can that be? The humans here in the northern hemisphere seem to have a problem with overeating. There is enough food produced on this planet to support a population several times larger than present." Trith shook his head. "Your finding must be flawed; their technology in food production is adequate.

"The reports are true; our very own Healing ships have come across this... paradox. In the southern hemisphere a large percentage of the sick that are brought to be cured are suffering from extreme malnutrition. And some have even died in our hands, too far gone!" Angth's eyes glistened with tears. "They told us they could *not afford* to purchase food."

Trith's slender body trembled with anxiety.

"Deeper research into human nature and their habits show some are actually suicidal! They purposely inhale or ingest toxins into their bodies that slowly destroy their bodies! And worse, these poisons are produced for their enjoyment." Angth's body shuddered with repulsion.

Trith's slender mouth dropped open in shock.

"One of the mass-produced poisons is named cigarettes. There are many others. We must reevaluate this species, Trith." Angth crossed his three arms.

"There must be an explanation, Angth. They have produced much good. In their arts, in their music, great beauty that all species can appreciate." Trith's voice trembled.

"And I have news even stranger," Paeth said with great solemnness. "I have studied in more detail the process humans call Economy. It forms the basis for their global culture. And it too, is most disturbing."

Trith waited with mounting concern.

"The leading industry of humanity, that which makes the most profit...is the sale of weapons - implements of war."

Both Trith and Angth gasped.

Soon the silence grew like a living thing. But deep inside, Trith began to understand the monstrous cycles humanity had cursed itself with throughout its marred history. He understood even better why they could not move beyond practicing war – they were trapped in so many different ways by their warped, incorrect thinking.

"Even more perverted," Paeth continued, "the second most profitable business is the sale of mind-altering drugs - supposedly illegal in all their sub-cultures. And yet it thrives in all cultures!"

An expression of great sadness crept over Trith's pebbled face.

"We could be wrong about them," Angth added with finality.

Trith nodded sadly. "And yet Concordia states they must be given an opportunity to succeed. We must continue the process." Trith's small black eyes became distant. "I believe they can be taught."

"But if not, there must be EXcalga." Angth said with a tone of finality.

Paeth nodded slowly in agreement.

Trith did not reply.

***

A few weeks later, Xenocracy began as the people of Earth, given the freedom of choice by the Raxth, cast their votes to join the rest of the known galaxy in Concordia. Concordia promised to rid mankind of all its diseases. Concordia would eradicate crime and violence and end war. Concordia would usher in a new system where all people and aliens would truly be equal, and all would benefit.

It had been a landslide victory.

Concordia promised even more…

There would be vast advances in science, medicine, and technology – all would be shared with humans. It was even guaranteed that the human life span, incredibly short by their standards, would be lengthened to well over five hundred years with only the first application of their medico-technology – a more *normal* lifespan would be possible later.

And after the technological miracles they were still performing every day, there was no reason to doubt the rest. A new dawn had arrived for the human race - a new universe revealed itself almost as in a dream.

Xenocracy.

But not all agreed.

***

"First they want to outlaw our cars. Then they want to do away with money, they say Concordia doesn't operate like that. But now! Now, they want to end war. What are these aliens doing to us? Pretty soon, we won't even be men anymore!"

The small crowd murmured its agreement. From somewhere in the back shouting began to grow. The speaker motioned for silence.

"Sure, they can cure disease. They say we can even live ten times longer than we do now. But what's life gonna' be like? I'll tell ya' - we'll be like *them*!"

Angry shouts of agreement erupted while the speaker smiled at them. Finally, the crowd was ready for more.

"And just think of this, if everyone is practicing this Concordia, if everyone is doin' it... you couldn't get a *decent war* off the ground if you wanted to!"

The crowd roared its agreement. Hundreds now raised their clenched fists and shook them angrily in the air.

The Pro-Humanity movement began. Within a matter of weeks, their ideology spread like a virus over the internet until it boasted members in every part of the world.

***

"We'll leverage the fanatical movements for our own ends," Col. Young said to his aide. "It's time for Operation Recovery - time for the military to straighten things out."

The aide looked puzzled.

"That operation is for retaking control of our government in the event of a hostile takeover?" He said with surprise.

"And something far worse has happened. Not just our government has been taken over, the entire Earth has been taken... by them!"

"But Xenocracy was voted into power! Can we speak for the entire human race?"

Col. Young remained silent a moment in thought. "True. We will contact our counterparts from selected former human governments. This has to be an international mission." Col. Young smiled strangely. "We'll show these pacifist aliens that man is still in control of his own destiny - our destiny." His eyes burned with fierceness.

"The world will be right once again, just as it was before they came." He added ominously.

***

The Concordia centers were built in a matter of hours.

In every major city around the world, the alien pyramids grew out of the ground as if by magic. The small glowing tubes and tendrils were created using nanotechnology. Individual molecules were programmed by the alien ship's powerful onboard computers and then reproduced, the shimmering threads intertwined and grew more numerous every second until they eventually became a round pyramid-shaped building. In addition, the nanotechnology created everything else inside - the alien furniture, the lighting, the computers, and the environmental systems.

In a single day, thousands fully functioning buildings as tall as the Burj Khalifa building were

417

erected around the Earth. The huge structures glowed an electric blue with an iridescent sheen that made them seem alive standing next to the simple glass and concrete towers of mankind.

And the masses began to come, to learn the ways of Concordia - to become a part of the civilized galaxy.

Micah Jenkins, Network Engineer, was one of millions who joined the Concordia classes to learn about the great cycles of the universe, to learn the principles of life, to learn Concordia.

***

"Tell me, please," Micah looked up at the dark eyes of the alien. "How can anyone travel beyond the speed of light? Our science says that this is impossible. But you do it with ease in your starships."

Trith smiled knowingly. He spread his three thin arms wide and spoke. "All is exactly as it was at the universe's beginning. Each planet, each galaxy, still resides in the exact place it was formed. It is only space that has grown with time – nothing else."

The alien's forty-seven eyes grew thoughtful. "Space and time, forever intertwined," he whispered earnestly.

Micah's mind raced in circles.

"Understand this first, and then you can begin to understand how we travel among the stars so easily." Trith's benevolent expression turned to puzzlement.

"Now I would ask a question, so I can better understand humans and their ways. I especially want your personal viewpoint." Trith eyed him carefully. "Do humans understand they are killing the most crucial life form necessary in sustaining the life cycles of this planet? Without them, the cycles will all ultimately fail! Do you know which it is? And why it is so important?"

Micah paused, trying to guess which one it was among all the life on Earth.

Trith's eyes narrowed.

"Trees!" Trith finally said, with obvious frustration. "Do humans not realize even this most basic fact, the importance of trees to your planet's cycles?"

Micah cleared his throat nervously.

"And what is one of the primary reasons that man kills trees?" Trith raised his three arms.

"Books? Houses? Furniture?" Micah asked hopefully.

"Toilet paper! And you possess the knowledge to produce an artificial equivalent that is biodegradable, more efficient, and much softer too." Trith shook his head with disdain.

Micah rubbed his chin in thought.

Trith continued.

"Your wonderful planet too, we thought at first that you did not comprehend how you were destroying it. But now, it seems you do this knowingly. And for what - the imaginary accumulation of riches."

Trith leaned closer. "The very water you drink and air you breathe - the wholesale destruction of

419

animal and plant life – allowed to happen in order to further your economy?"

Micah cleared his throat nervously.

"Do you want to see your world ruined by pollution? Do you support these tragic consequences? Or do you fight to right these wrongs?"

Micah looked away.

"How do you feel about a system that causes such tragic consequences? Does it need to be changed?" Trith's voice, mercifully, grew silent.

"I-I don't like the way things are. But what can one person do about it? Could we redesign cars so they don't pollute? I've heard rumors it is possible."

"Your system gives evidence that money and life-style are more important than the health of individuals and the health of your planet." Trith looked hard at Micah. "Humans could have redesigned cars long ago with pollution-free engines. And not only pollution free engines, but engines that work in harmony with the environment. Man possessed such technological knowledge decades ago."

Micah kept his eyes averted, unable to look the alien in its 47 eyes now.

Trith's expression softened. Slowly, he smiled.

"Deep inside your hearts, what do humans really desire, please tell me?"

"We want a better life. We want a safe world for our children to grow up. We want a world where there is peace and security for all."

"Well said!" Trith said enthusiastically. "Yes, those are wise and noble desires!"

Trith and Micah smiled at each other.

"And yet, those same things have been the desire of many generations of humans. Why hasn't mankind achieved them?"

Micah's face burned with embarrassment and shame.

"Now, now, young student of Concordia, I have questioned you enough. Your heart is in the right place, we just need to help you to benefit yourselves, and help you to achieve harmony with the rest of the sentient races of the galaxy."

Micah smiled.

"Now, Micah. Do you have any more questions for me before we end this personal class today?"

Micah looked up at the blue sky. "Will we go to the stars with you?"

Trith sighed deeply while his many eyes followed his student's longing gaze upward. "Humans are... the great pretenders. You have always dreamed of traveling out among the stars and living with other sentient races. And yet, you have never learned how to live with your own kind on this single world."

***

Weeks passed and millions flocked every day to the blue pyramid-shaped buildings. They came to take the classes of Concordia. They marveled at the computer hookups that allowed communication to alien teachers hundreds of light years away. The alien teachers spoke with the students and answered their questions in real time without any perceptible delay, despite the vast distances. But the students especially loved the video feeds that provided them with their first glimpse of life on other planets - the myriad planets of Concordia spread across the universe.

Trith, along with Angth and Paeth of the Triad, continued their evaluation of the human species. And the more they looked, the more they found that puzzled them about the human race. They soon uncovered knowledge about the massive extinctions of Earth's flora and fauna – many simply due to the destructive greed of mankind. Most of the diseases plaguing man were due to his own negligence, or his pursuit of pleasure. And the chief causes of war – religion, ethnic hatred, or lust for power - made absolutely no sense to the Raxth.

Trith wondered what it was that humans really wanted despite his words of hope and peace and harmony.

But then he focused on the things that humans treasured above all else - the artifacts and writings that were preserved for future generations, to inspire and guide them. Trith found hope at last.

He eagerly called the next meeting of the Triad.

"Are they ready? Can they learn?" Paeth asked with obvious doubt.

"A better question is, are they capable of learning. Ever? Or are their *self-destructive tendencies so ingrained that they can never be taught?*" Angth looked around at the others with a solemn expression.

Trith looked at Angth - straight into his many eyes.

"They can be taught."

"How can you say this? Look at the evidence - they kill each other simply because their skin is a different shade or because they live in a different geographical section of the planet. And look at their home planet! They spill refuse and toxic chemicals into its air and waters and soil. It has become so polluted that they ingest lethal chemicals with every breath of air, every drink of water, and every bite of food. The natural cycles have been damaged. And due to the complex toxic mixture and longevity of the pollution, even our technology has not been able to discover a way to fully reverse it!" Angth paused to catch his breath.

"It is a great sorrow about this beautiful planet. I pity them." Trith nodded.

"They are indeed pitiable. These humans believe this life they've created, these artificial systems that warp and control their thinking, is the only way to live," Paeth said sadly.

"Humans cannot even perceive that they're trapped by them," Angth added.

"The precepts of Concordia will need to root out centuries of falsehood and fantasy that has blinded this poor people. But I repeat; I have discovered that they can be taught."

"Tell us," Paeth pleaded.

"I have found their innermost desires among the treasures they store in special buildings called museums. There they preserve writings secular and sacred - poetry, songs and prose that inspire and are inspired. Their heartfelt dreams are also in the artwork, when they dream of a better world, a better life. Across all ethnic lines and nationalities, these writings and artwork reveal that mankind's deepest, most ardent desire is peace and love and harmony. They all wish it, deep inside."

Angth and Paeth remained silent.

Trith continued.

"Their poets and philosophers, authors and songwriters, have called it many things: Utopia, P'eng-lai, Elysium, Swarga, Nirvana, Paradise, and Heaven. Humans yearn for a better world – a world with no sickness, no pain, and no tears. A world with no war, no poverty, and no injustice. Their innermost desire is to live in that better world."

"If it is true that they *all want peace*, why is it they have not achieved it yet?" Angth asked impatiently. "They still practice war! Acts of violence fill every culture. They even *entertain themselves* with violence! How are they ever going to learn to hate it?"

"They have tried, all through the centuries. They move a little closer with each generation." Trith sighed.

"But never close enough, and not fast enough for a species this technologically advanced. What is wrong with them? Why can't they achieve harmony and peace?" Paeth shook his head with doubt.

"Their aberrant behavior is so deeply ingrained within their psyche; they do not even *realize* they have a problem. They believe that war and hatred is normal. They believe that they must have bad and evil in order to enjoy good and peace."

Trith paused and took a deep breath.

"That is why they cannot comprehend our way of life in this universe."

The Triad remained silent, digesting the truth of mankind's warped mental condition.

"They must be given a chance to learn," Trith said.

Angth and Paeth closed their eyes simultaneously. Trith realized they were meditating on what he had shared, and he too closed his eyes and waited. For long seconds, the three aliens mediated on Trith's words, analyzing the history of mankind in the light of this revelation.

"It is possible." Angth and Paeth whispered together.

"The human race must be shown they have a problem. And once they realize they have this aberrant, deep-seated problem as a species, they can finally work to overcome it - with our help." Trith paused, holding up his arms. "They will even learn to hate these deviant desires that have haunted their minds and emotions all throughout their history... and reach a harmonious existence at last."

Trith smiled and added.

"It is their deepest desire to live in peace and harmony with all."

The Triad talked long into the night and next day. It was decided that mankind had potential. Mankind could learn and overcome their condition and then become a species both tolerant and kind -

one that could live harmoniously along with the vast variety of alien sentients of Concordia.

And at last, join the rest of the universe.

***

The automatic weapons smelled heavily of oil and death. The boxes of ammo were stacked high in piles next to the doorway.

Col. Young stood among the soldiers.

"You men are the best – carefully trained by each of your former governments to become part of this Special Force." He smiled savagely.

"As you know, the destiny of mankind has been taken out of its own hands. In a flurry of emotion after first contact, the majority of the planet voted for Xenocracy. They thought they were voting for better health, for the cleansing of pollution, for ending war and prejudice, and to travel out to the stars."

The room grew silent.

"What they didn't know, was that we would have to forfeit who we are – to stop being men and women! Worse, we would have to become like them! Well, that is going to stop today."

The metallic sound of an ammo clip being slapped into position punctuated the silence.

"There will be another protest by the Pro-Humanity movement tomorrow. We will be there too. The ruling Triad will make one of their little speeches about peace and Concordia." His dangerous smile widened. "And we will let our weapons speak! We will show them that we are still men!"

The shouts and war whoops filled the windowless room. They died away when a soldier stepped beside the leader.

"What about civilians? There will be women and children in the crowd."

"Collateral damage."

Col. Young's eyes narrowed while he paused.

"Our mission is to kill the leaders of Xenocracy, the Triad, *no matter the casualties*. We'll send a message to the entire universe they'll never forget."

***

Micah heard the shouting outside and felt his nervousness grow. He remembered his wife's words that morning just before he left for the Concordia Centers.

"Are you going there again? Don't you want to be with your own family anymore? *Don't you want to be with your own kind*!"

Micah pulled at his collar as if it were suddenly too tight.

And then the tall, lanky form of Trith was beside him - the alien he called friend.

"How are you today, human friend?" Trith asked in greeting.

Micah smiled sheepishly, the angry shouting outside the walls still rising to a crescendo in anticipation of Trith's speech. Micah searched for something to say - something to get his mind off what waited outside.

"Trith... how old are you? I've always wanted to ask. I mean, with no disease to cut your life short, you must live a long time, right?" Micah raised his eyebrows questioningly.

Trith smiled. "I am in your time keeping over 32,000 years old."

Micah's mouth fell open in amazement. "That's ancient!"

Trith suddenly straightened, unsure of this human expression or the import of those words. Then he smiled. "I am still quite young, not even in my middle epoch yet."

"Wow," Micah laughed. "I can't even imagine living a thousand years."

"Yes, I get to accomplish much. Life is the most important thing in the universe, friend Micah. You must always remember that. Without life, there is nothing. Hold life precious – value all life."

"Yes, I will." Micah looked up at the benevolent alien with a warm glow.

"And one day, your species will be able to do what you have always desired." Trith patted Micah's shoulder lovingly.

The human and alien smiled at each other.

"Well, it is time for our talk today. The Triad has decided to base the subject of our discourse upon Love. Love..." Trith paused and smiled. "Let us go."

Paeth and Angth joined them at the main door that led to the outdoor amphitheater. Both Paeth and Angth wore expressions of concern. Angth opened the door and the angry voices outside rose to a new crescendo.

"Is it wise to mix with the humans in the crowd with *this* going on?" Paeth paused, searching for the correct human term. He nodded. "With this demonstration going on outside. It seems tense outside. Should we wait for another time?"

"It is time. Many months have gone by; humans have shown they can live with those different than themselves. They have the right to peacefully demonstrate various viewpoints." Trith prepared to step outside.

"They are not dangerous," he added.

They all stepped outside and suddenly the shouting faded.

Micah was surprised at first. He knew that the Pro-Humanity movement had targeted this speech to protest directly before the Triad, but he had expected the worst. This respectful silence surprised him.

On seeing Micah and Trith enter the stage together a single person in the crowd shouted vehemently. He shouted two simple words. But he uttered them as the ugliest of obscenities.

And he pointed directly at Micah while he shouted.

"*Alien lover!*"

The very air became electrified with those two words. Micah, for the first time in a very long time, felt ashamed of being seen in the presence of Trith here at this moment. He cringed while all the cameras focused on him and realized people all around the world were looking right at him. He stopped while Trith continued across the stage.

The vast crowd now began chanting the vulgar slogan in a rhythmic unison.

"*Alien lover - Alien lover - Alien lover – "*

Over and over, louder and louder, with more burning emotion with each repetition, the words continued to be repeated. Still, almost an equal part of the throng remained silent, not agreeing with the sentiment of the others, for they had come to learn.

The electric atmosphere continued to grow until it became unbearable.

Trith paused beside Paeth and Angth in the center of the stage.

"Their words are of love – alien lovers. But the tone seems to represent a negative emotion?" Paeth blinked his eyes questioningly at the other two.

"Oh, the paradox of humans. Can we really teach them?" Angth lamented again.

Trith raised his three arms for silence, never noticing the strategically placed men and women moving rapidly forward among the large crowd.

"I will demonstrate to you and them. Humans really do want love," Trith said, standing before the microphones. The alien smiled out at the crowd.

And through his embarrassment, Micah saw the flash of gun metal in the crowd. With a sickening dread, he knew exactly what was about to happen – right before his eyes.

As if in a movie, Micah saw Trith raise his hands. He suddenly felt the overwhelming helplessness of one being swept along by a raging flood – trying in vain to swim against the irresistible flow. Everything seemed to slow into a surreal slow motion while his mind tried to fathom the heartless atrocity about to take place before his disbelieving eyes.

And that single instant seemed to freeze into eternity.

Micah rushed forward while several automatic weapons were uncovered and pointed at the stage.

Screams erupted from the crowd.

People began shoving and turning away after they saw the guns and realized how close death was - that they would see blood running in the streets in the next moment.

A little girl cried out in fear right in front of the stage.

The gut-wrenching staccato of machine gun fire ripped the air, drowning the growing screams. The chanting immediately stopped. People now began running, trampling others in their panic to escape.

More gunfire ripped through the air.

In the crowded throngs the bullets killed and maimed, not caring if the being had two eyes or forty-seven.

Tears streamed down Micah's cheeks as one of the alien forms on-stage crumpled into a heap and dark blood spurted in every direction.

Micah's feet suddenly felt like lead. The tragedy continued to unfold in a surreal slow motion while he ran toward Trith.

More weapons' fire roared out, this time the sound so close it chilled his soul. And then the air was alive as bullets began ripping into the stage all around him. The whizzing bullets flying past his head made him duck instinctively.

But still he ran toward Trith, who simply stood there as if frozen in place.

Men and women fell in bloody pools all around the base of the stage while their pitiful groans filled the air.

Micah leapt forward.

In the face of chaos, Trith looked out upon his assassins in silence - uncomprehending silence – watching while dozens were murdered right before his eyes.

"Get down!" Micah shouted to Trith, suddenly finding his voice. "Get down! They'll kill you!"

Col. Young forced his way closer to the stage. Now he pulled his military issue pistol from its holster. He stepped between the dead and dying people with his gun aimed at the alien's head. The stupid alien just stood there, like he was asking for it.

"Die, you potato headed monster!" Col. Young shouted angrily.

The pistol belched.

But right at that moment, Micah leaped across the still frozen form of Trith. Micah felt the searing impact of the forty-five-caliber slug tearing into his flesh and ripping through his organs.

He screamed.

The impact of the weapon at point blank range threw him back into Trith, knocking him over.

Trith began to shake uncontrollably.

But even with his mind frozen with shock at the horrendous, unimaginable things happening all around him, Trith wrapped his arms around the dying human's body.

Micah's body shuddered while blood steamed out of his chest. Trith held him closer. And tears began to stream from the alien's eyes.

With crimson blood rapidly spreading across his chest, Micah looked up at his friend and took a final breath.

A shimmering light filled the air around Trith and the still form he held - in the next instant, they disappeared.

***

Up in the alien starship orbiting the Earth, all the crew suddenly moved at a frenzied pace. Dozens of Raxth rushed to the transporter room and the forms lying all over the floor. One of them slipped and fell on the growing pool of crimson blood covering the white floor.

The thick stench of blood and fear filled the air.

Tiny tears streamed down Trith's forty-seven eyes while he held the unmoving form of Micah. He looked from the breathless form he held to that of Paeth stretched beside him. The black blood had all rushed out of his body and Trith knew that it was too late for him.

And for the first time in his life, Trith did not understand.

"Why?" He whispered through his tears. "Why?"

Two Raxth raced to Trith and the human he held.

"Please, Triad Trith. We must use our instruments on this human. It may not too late for him."

433

Trith began sobbing while they pried his weak arms away. He sat there crying uncontrollably, his body shuddering with each painful sob.

Slowly, he stood.

He began walking, stumbling among the dead and wounded all around.

"How many?" Trith asked numbly to one of the Medico-healers.

"Thirty-three humans are dead. Twenty-four Raxth dead." The Healer bowed his head sadly before he continued. "Angth is badly wounded. And Paeth is... dead."

Trith swayed and moaned.

"Come... here." The weak voice of Angth pleaded from where he lay stricken.

Trith looked down upon his friend, wracked by the pain of twelve bullets inside his body.

"There must be... EXcalga." Angth coughed on the black blood that streamed out the corner of his mouth.

The tears now flowed freely from Trith.

He nodded in agreement.

He stood up and looked around at the men, women and children, along with the wounded Raxth. His eyes paused on a child lying motionless on the floor. The little girl looked to be no more than six years old.

"Yes." Trith whispered with finality. *"There will be EXcalga."*

***

The Raxth shuttles all returned to the orbiting starships within an hour of the massacre. World leaders communicated their sorrow and their sadness to the aliens – but silence was the only answer in return. A day passed, then a second day. And the eerie silence sent shock waves across planet Earth and its citizens.

In the news and across the internet, the headlines were about Armageddon come true - the wrath of the godlike aliens in retaliation of this heartless, unprovoked attack. As the days of silence from the powerful ships orbiting above continued, the terrible sense of foreboding increased.

Throughout every sector of humanity, a certain fearful anticipation grew. After all, these advanced creatures could retaliate with weapons of unimaginable power and Earth would be helpless to stop such an attack.

The former human leaders petitioned for mercy. The perpetrators had been quickly arrested and imprisoned. Surprisingly, these murderers had turned out to be men and women trained in combat by their own former governments, from before Xenocracy.

It was communicated to the Raxth that these perpetrators would be severely punished.

Still, silence was the only reply.

Former President Williamson and the former leaders personally pleaded to the Raxth in a single broadcast together. Their message was simple and sincere - let not the aliens vent their wrath on helpless humankind for the deeds of a few.

Finally, after seven long days, the Raxth responded. They scheduled a final press conference.

All around the Earth at the scheduled time, TV displays, tablets and laptop screens came alive with the same picture - a single, forlorn alien face.

Trith smiled sadly back at mankind.

"I come to you with great pain in my heart for what must now be..."

All around the Earth, everyone stared at their screens in rising fear.

"We came in peace, to bring you Concordia - to welcome you to the stars. We brought our medical technology, to heal you. We brought our science, to enlighten you. We gave all freely, out of the love that all sentient races of the known universe have for each other." Trith sighed, slowly shaking his head. "The love you should have..."

Trith's head shuddered ever so slightly.

"I have loved you, mankind. As a parent teaches beloved children, so I tried to teach you."

The world waited, hanging on Trith's every word.

"And so, the most historic occasion in the history of mankind draws to a close." Trith shook his oblong head. "The judgment of Concordia upon the human race."

The human race held its collective breath.

"You have been evaluated, humans... and found deficient. You will be abandoned - ostracized by the rest of the universe. We shall erect a barrier around your solar system to prevent you from infecting the rest of the universe."

On every screen around the world, the alien visage disappeared.

"What... what does it mean?" The aide stammered.

Former President Williamson turned to the aide beside him.

Williamson sighed.

"It means – we have been rejected. And like a leper colony, we are to be isolated by this barrier. In effect, we've been expelled by the rest of the universe."

Former President Williamson stared off into the distance. Slowly, his expression changed to sadness.

"We failed..."

***

"You must account for the possibility of deception." Angth lay in his bed still convalescing. Two of his arms were heavily bandaged and his face was deathly pale.

Trith's eyes narrowed.

"Never have we seen this level of duplicity across a planet's population. Their flawed society has produced this terrible trait and encouraged it." Angth sighed.

"We have added programming to identify this trait and prevent inaccurate results." Trith replied.

"We can never allow this polluted society to corrupt the peace of Concordia." Angth said with a sober tone.

Trith nodded agreement.

He walked slowly to the transporter room where the last of the human wounded were being readied to return. As he entered, one familiar face smiled at him.

Trith reached with his three arms toward Micah. They embraced warmly, gently, for Micah was still sore from the procedure that had replaced his heart and one lung with molecularly regenerated equivalents.

"I can't believe you're leaving. I can't believe it." Micah said through his tears.

"I wanted to take you with me, friend Micah." Trith paused to wipe Micah's tears with his third hand. "I wanted to take my favorite student with me to the stars."

The alien and human cried in their mutual embrace. For a long, heartfelt moment, they comforted each other.

"What will we do now?" Micah finally asked.

Trith stood back, still holding Micah with two of his arms.

"The human race has been sentenced; human civilization has failed. But there is one last hope we leave you as *individuals*."

Micah looked eagerly into Trith's forty-seven eyes.

"We are leaving the Concordia Centers active. If any so desire, they may continue with the programs. There will be no direct communication, but the computers will be active to teach those who desire to be taught, who desire to live Concordia. We will be recording your activity."

"Why?" Micah asked.

"You proved by saving my life that there is something noble in the human heart. Your almost fatal sacrifice is what allowed me to keep the Centers open, with the permission of the rest of the sentient races of Concordia," Trith said happily.

Micah grasped Trith's hand and squeezed it gently.

"You understand how precious life is – it is the greatest gift. And yet, you were willing to give your life for mine. For an alien at that." Trith smiled proudly. "And why?"

Micah felt something grow inside his heart, a feeling of triumph.

"Because I cared." Micah smiled weakly.

"Because of love." Trith nodded.

They embraced again.

"I believe there is good in humans as individuals. They must learn to let it guide their lives." Trith smiled down at him.

"Most of all, I believe in love." Trith added.

"So do I," Micah whispered.

"Yes, I suspect that some... that many humans do. And if this is true, they will seek out Concordia – seek it and find it. *And prepare themselves*," Trith said a mystical tone.

"How will we know how to prepare ourselves?" Micah asked hesitantly.

Trith smiled one last time into the human face he loved – the human who had saved him from certain death.

"You will know, friend Micah. And one day, we will return."

Micah and the other humans standing beside him became very still. They gazed at the alien Teacher with expectant expressions.

"I will bring my starships with me, to take any who are prepared - prepared to live Concordia."

Micah felt his new heart skip a beat.

"I will take you to live among the stars. If that is what you really want..."

Other novels by Tony Chandler

Mothership
Winner 2002 EPIC Award – Best in Science Fiction

In the midst of Galactic War a new life-form is born--an AI starship. But with all its weapons and sophisticated programming, the sentient starship is not equipped for its greatest challenge--that of becoming the mother to the last three children of humanity.

The deadly T'kaan soon begin the hunt again after they discover that the human race is not quite extinct. As Mother faces these impossible odds, she discovers that deep inside her massive memory systems she holds another treasure--a knowledgebase that contains all the science, lore, wisdom and art of the human race since the beginning of time. Now Mother must fight not only to save humanity from extinction, but also from being forgotten by the rest of the universe...

Borne on Wings of Steel
The sequel to Mothership

Mother, along with their newfound friends, continue their search for other survivors of the human race who may have escaped the T'kaan genocide. They travel to the farthest known worlds of the universe, but fail to discover the first solid clue that anyone else survived. After many long months of fruitless searching, their hopes again begin to fade.

But there is conflict even within Mother's family. The torment and loneliness among the final three survivors of the human race create division where there should be love.

Minstrel leads them to a planet famous for its vast collection of data gathered from every corner of the known universe. Perhaps here among the greatest single store of data ever gathered by any alien race, they might discover if other humans survived the T'kaan genocide

THE SONG OF LIFE TRILOGY
Bluesky and Sunshine
Volume I

In the tradition of the classic animal fantasy novels of yesteryear comes a new novel... a tale about a young mockingbird and his family and their struggles against prejudice and hate. At its heart, it is a story about the power of love and friendship -- and how a hero is born.

Sunshine and her mate are devastated when one of their babies is born with a life-threatening birth defect. They do their best to nurture the disadvantaged baby, whom they name Bluesky. But their fears increase as they watch the tiny baby struggle to get his share of food in competition with his siblings.

Soon, all the mockingbird clans ostracize Bluesky and his entire family out of fear. Other youngsters refuse to play with him simply because he is different. Sunshine does her best to keep her family together, but the loneliness and rejection grow each day.

When Bluesky realizes that he and his birth defect are the real reason for all the hatred aimed at his family, the little mockingbird decides to make the ultimate sacrifice in order to protect his family from the terrible injustice that is tearing them all apart.

The Journey
Volume II

In the tradition of the classic animal fantasy novels of yesteryear comes a new novel... a tale about a young mockingbird and his family and their struggles against prejudice and hate. At its heart, it is a story about the power of love and friendship -- and how a hero is born.

Sunshine and her mate are devastated when one of their babies is born with a life-threatening birth defect. They do their best to nurture the disadvantaged baby, whom they name Bluesky. But their fears increase as they watch the tiny baby struggle to get his share of food in competition with his siblings.

Soon, all the mockingbird clans ostracize Bluesky and his entire family out of fear. Other youngsters refuse to play with him simply because he is different. Sunshine does her best to keep her family together, but the loneliness and rejection grow each day.

When Bluesky realizes that he and his birth defect are the real reason for all the hatred aimed at his family, the little mockingbird decides to make the ultimate sacrifice in order to protect his family from the terrible injustice that is tearing them all apart.

The Singer
Volume III

The epic conclusion to the trilogy 'The Song of Life.'

The Last Dragon of the North
Tony Chandler and Virginia Chandler
"A hard hitting adventure. One rousing dragon-fighting story, with a thin slice of romance along the way." -- Piers Anthony

Owain Armstrong has been hired to hunt down a red dragon that is killing livestock across Wiltshire . The only evidence is a bloody patch on the ground and the head of the dead animal. Owain begins to track this nocturnal predator when news of another dragon comes – a much bigger dragon.

During his journey, Owain meets up with the famous dragonslayers of the Northern

Band: Katja, a beautiful blonde deadly accurate with a crossbow; Erik, a massive man short of temper and always eager to fight; Lars, a man as cunning as he is strong; and finally Edlund, their dynamic leader.

When meeting Owain, the band of weary slayers long had been on a quest to kill the last dragon of the north. But they soon hear strange tales– tales of the Green Dragon Inn and the monster that lives inside the mountain.

And for a price, anything is possible...